DELIGHTED

BERTRICE SMALL
SUSAN JOHNSON

DELIGHTED

NIKKI DONOVAN
LIZ MADISON

BRAVA

KENSINGTON PUBLISHING CORP.

BRAVA BOOKS are published by

Kensington Publishing Corp.
850 Third Avenue
New York, NY 10022

ISBN 0-7394-2529-3

Printed in the United States of America

Contents

THE AWAKENING

Bertrice Small

Prologue

Paris—October 1793

His eager passage impeded, the governor of the Île de Cité prison said, "You did not tell me you were a virgin, Citizeness de Thierry." There was a pleased smile upon his face.

"I feared you would not want me inexperienced," the girl half whispered. It was difficult to speak bent over the table as she was, her nose just touching its rough top. "I do want to please you, monsieur, and you did promise me a favor for a favor. Would your pleasure have been as great had this road been frequently traveled?" *Sacrebleu!* She had never realized that a man's penis would feel as if she were being skewered like a piece of meat.

"You honor me, Citizeness de Thierry," the governor said, complimenting her as if he had been raised at court. "I assure you I am not in the least displeased. Continue to please me, and you shall certainly have your favor." Then drawing himself back just slightly, he thrust hard into the girl.

Renée de Thierry cried out, unable to help herself. The old whore in their cell had told her that the deflowering would hurt, but then the pain would go quickly.

"If you would please the citizen governor, citizeness," the toothless crone had said, "wiggle your hips, and make sounds of enjoyment. Even if a man gives no pleasure, you must pretend that he does."

Renée sighed, moaning low, thrusting her hips back into the governor's fat belly. "Oh! Oh!" she cried out. *"Ohhhh!"*

The governor laughed, delighted. "By God, my pretty citizeness, I believe that you are a born whore, but then I have been told so many of you aristos are. We'll have a great deal of joy from one another, I promise you." He pushed himself forward again, and again, and yet again into her, his breath coming now in short, excited pants. "You shall not be mistreated, *ma petite,*" he groaned, pleasure washing over him as his hard cock probed her hot, tight depths.

His weight pressed her full breasts flat against the tabletop. The pain, as the old whore had promised, was almost immediately gone. This wasn't really as bad as she had anticipated, Renée thought. If she could not save Jules, and Marie-Agnes, at least she would save their child. "*Yes!*" she hissed. "*Oh, yesss!*" She could sense the arousal in his very movements, yet she seemed to have detached herself entirely from what was happening to her.

"You like it, do you, Citizeness de Thierry?" the governor chuckled, even more pleased now than he had been before. "You like having my love lance filling your tight little hole? Well, my fine aristo wench, I'll be happy to oblige you. If I hadn't popped your cherry myself a moment ago, I should not have believed such enthusiasm could be engendered by a virgin. Virgins are supposed to be retiring." He grunted low as his climax approached. Then he exploded his juices into the girl, half collapsing atop her.

"*Mon Dieu! Mon Dieu!*" Renée cried, genuinely surprised as she felt the hot spurts of his lust filling her, and overflowing down the insides of her milky, trembling thighs.

"*Mon Dieu* indeed, citizeness," the governor replied heartily. He drew his shrunken, and flaccid, member out of her juicy nest. Pulling her up, he turned her about to face him, thinking as he did that she was a pretty creature despite her dirty face, marked with the evidence of her tears. Almost tenderly the governor ran his finger down the wet runnel on her face. "Very well, citizeness, you have been honest with me. Now, what do you want? Do not ask for your brother, or his wife. I cannot give you their lives."

"Their baby," Renée said softly. "It is only three months old, monsieur, and surely no threat to the revolution. It is a little girl, born on the fourteenth day of July, *monsieur!* Is that not fortuitous? Born on the same day the revolution was born. *Please, monsieur!*" Renée de Thierry's cornflower blue eyes now overflowed with the tears she had tried so heroically to hold back. *"Please!* I will do whatever you want, *monsieur!"*

"If I spare the child, citizeness, must I also spare you revolutionary justice?" the governor asked, wondering if the girl was really worth the difficulties he would incur if he was found out.

"Send my niece to the convent of St. Anne, which is near the Cathedral of Notre Dame, *monsieur,"* Renée answered him calmly. "I will go to my death gladly knowing that our little Marguerite has been saved!"

She had given him her virginity, a most precious gift indeed, in her effort to save the infant. And now she was willing to die for the child as well. François de la Pont found that he was genuinely moved. They lived in a cruel world where few were willing to sacrifice themselves for another life. Yet this girl, a hated aristocrat, was willing to give all she had left for an innocent. No one would miss a baby, the governor decided to himself. The de Thierry family were hardly notables. He pulled the girl against him roughly. "Very well, *ma petite,"* he told her.

Renée, to her deep mortification, burst into fulsome tears, quite soaking the governor's shirt as she clung to him. "Oh, thank you, *monsieur!"* she wept.

He stroked her hair. "And no one will miss you either," he said. "I will see that your name is kept off of the execution lists. I will repay my debt to you in full." In all of this madness, François de la Pont, a fishmonger's son, educated by some miracle, and a soldier, remembered that he was an honorable man.

Renée looked up at him. *"Debt?"* Her young voice was confused. "You owe me no debt, *monsieur;* rather it is I who owe you."

"You gave me your virtue, citeness. In return I shall give you your life. As for the infant, they are too difficult to guillotine." He did not bother to tell her that infants were usually bashed against the guillotine posts while their horrified relations looked on in agony, prior to going to their own deaths. "Go back to your cell, and return with the child. Then I shall have it sent to St. Anne's. If you are to spend your time pleasing me, you will have no time to expend in the care of your niece." He smiled down at her, and Renée de Thierry, because she knew it was expected of her, smiled back shyly.

"*Merci, monsieur,*" she replied once again.

"*Merci,* citizen," he gently corrected her, untangling her from the embrace.

Renée caught her lower lip with her top teeth in a charming gesture of contriteness. "*Merci,* citizen," she said softly, and she curtsied to him prettily.

"I cannot wait to see you naked," he said boldly as he caught a glimpse of her pretty breasts. "Tonight, little one, I shall begin to teach you all the things you will need to know about pleasing me, or any other man." Turning her about, he smacked her bottom, chuckling once more as she squealed with surprise.

Renée de Thierry followed the guard from the governor's apartment, back through the dank prison corridors to the half-lit cell where her brother and his wife, and a dozen others, were incarcerated. Along the way the guard stopped, pushing her up against the stone walls of the prison, fumbling for his male member as he tried to raise her skirts.

Renée slapped him hard. "Are you a fool that you would touch me knowing what you know?" she demanded. "I belong to Governor de la Pont now."

"You won't always belong to the old goat," the guard muttered, disappointed, jamming his hand down her bodice and squeezing her breast.

"No, I won't," Renée agreed, pulling his rough hand away. "When I do not, we will discuss this matter again. For now I shall not tell the governor that you tried to assault me." It was at that moment she decided if she must whore to survive, she would do so only for the high and mighty of this new order. Never for lowlifes like this creature!

"All right," the guard grumbled. "But you don't know what you're missing, wench. I'm much more lively than your ancient lover." He led her out of the alcove where he had pushed her and back to her cell, shoving her inside. "You have five minutes. Then I'll be back for you, citizeness."

"Give me Marguerite," Renée said immediately to her sister-in-law.

"*What have you done, Renée?*" her brother demanded angrily.

"I have saved your daughter's life," Renée answered him fiercely. Jules could be such a pompous fool sometimes, even if he was her brother. "She will be taken to safety to be raised by the nuns at St. Anne's near the cathedral. I would have bargained for your life, and Marie-Agnes, but he told me not to even consider it. *What have I done?* I have done what I had to do, Jules!"

"Who is *he?*" her brother wanted to know.

"Governor de la Pont," Renée answered him.

"That traitor?"

"I do not care what he is, Jules. I only care that Marguerite is saved from this horror. She is an innocent."

"But you no longer are," her brother snarled, and then he slapped her across her defiant face. "*Whore!* You have given yourself away. Now no decent man will have you!"

Renée de Thierry burst out laughing, the sound echoing eerily in the dim light of the cell. "All those men you deem decent, brother, have been murdered by this revolution, or they have fled France. Our world has been turned upside down, and you still cannot face it! I have done what I had to do to save your child. I ask no thanks of you. Sooner than later I, too, shall go to visit Madame la Guillotine, but for now I amuse Citizen de la Pont, and my niece will be saved."

"My father always said you were too willful, Renée," was the cold reply. "My daughter will remain with her parents. You have squandered your virtue for naught."

"Jules!" Marie-Agnes's voice was pleading and strained. She understood far better than her spouse the sacrifice her young sister-in-law had made to save Marguerite.

"My sister has behaved like a whore, wife. She has become a stranger to us. De Thierrys do not accept favors from strangers," the comte said stonily, his handsome face set, his blue eyes cold.

"You would allow your child to die a needless death?" Renée demanded furiously of her brother, not quite able to believe what she was hearing.

"Our family descends from the lords of the Gauls, and the Roman conquerors," the comte began loftily. "Better our line ends here and now, rather than accept disgrace, and defeat."

The cell door was opened again; Renée's guard was there in the light of his flickering lantern. "Your time is up, citizeness," he said.

"Give me Marguerite," Renée said quietly.

"*No,*" her brother replied implacably.

But then Marie-Agnes, Comtesse de Thierry, quickly thrust her daughter into the arms of her sister-in-law. "Keep her safe! Tell her of us if you survive," she said. "God bless you, Renée, for what you have done!" Unashamed tears ran down her pale, thin face.

Clutching the baby, Renée turned swiftly before her brother might stop her and snatch the infant back. She hurried from the cell, never once turning. She heard the door clang shut behind her with the finality of death.

"*Whore!*" her brother shouted after her. "God damn you for the disgrace you have brought upon our name. *Whore!*"

Tears running down her cheeks, Renée ran from the sound of his angry voice. She would never forget this moment even if she lived to be an old woman, which seemed unlikely.

"Come on," the guard said. "The governor said we're to take the brat to the nuns. Then you are to be brought back here. The old goat is practically chomping at the bit to get you into his bed again, citizeness." He laughed rudely.

Renée heard her brother's curse. Her heart was heavy despite her victory in saving her niece. She stepped out into the Paris streets for the first time in six weeks, blinking in the afternoon sunlight. It was autumn. The air was cleaner than any she had smelled in days. Marguerite stirred in her arms, whimpering softly. Renée looked down at the infant. "Your papa is a fool, *mignon,*" she told the baby, "but I am not. We will survive, you and I. *We will survive!*"

Chapter One

Paris—1821

"You will leave this house immediately, *madame,* taking nothing with you but the clothes on your back," Lord William Abbott said to his stepmother. "After all, you brought nothing to my father but your insatiable greed for his possessions, you damnable French whore!"

Lady Marguerite Abbott stared shocked at the man before her. Finally she spoke. "You are wrong, William, and you know you are wrong. Your father and I loved one another. We sought to make you a part of our family, but you would not have it."

"You made my father leave me. *Leave England,*" Lord Abbott accused her.

"Your father brought me home to France because he believed your jealousy of our children could only be relieved if we were not living at Abbottsford. If we left it to you, even before it was legally yours, Charles felt that perhaps you would feel more secure as his heir. Our children could not change that. After what happened to Henry . . ." Her voice trailed off.

"Too bad you couldn't prove that I killed the little brat," William Abbott mocked her. "But you couldn't, could you?" He laughed meanly. "Don't you ever wonder how I did it?"

Lady Abbott grew pale. She knew that if there'd been a weapon at hand—*any weapon*—she would have used it on him. He had killed her infant son. She knew it. Charles had known it, but there had been no way to prove the heinous crime. After that, she had been frightened living at Abbottsford, especially when she became *enceinte* with Emilie. "This is my house," she said, attempting to turn the subject away from her murdered infant son.

"No, it isn't," Lord Abbott replied. "When my father died, everything he possessed came to me under the law, *madame.*"

"Your father had a will," Marguerite said.

Reaching into his coat's inside pocket, Lord Abbott drew out a thin document. "Do you mean *this*, madame?" He smiled nastily as he unfolded the parchment. "Let me see now, what it says. Ahh, yes. Here is the part that will be of interest to you. *I bequeath my home in the village of Vertterre to my beloved wife, Marguerite Abbott, née de Thierry; and order that my estate pay her a stipend of two thousand pounds annually for her support, and that of our daughter, Emilie. To my daughter, Emilie, I leave a dowry of one thousand pounds.*" Lord Abbott tore the document into several pieces, slowly, and quite deliberately fed them to the fire in the hearth. "I expect this is the only copy," he noted. "Now, it would appear that under the laws of both France and England I am my father's only legitimate heir, *madame*."

Marguerite Abbott was no fool. "There is always the widow's mite under the law, William," she told him.

"But by the time you have found the means to obtain and pay for a lawyer, *madame*, I shall be safely back in England. Whatever my dear sire has possessed here in France will belong to other owners, *or* I will have taken with me. You will have a very difficult time unraveling the muddle I make. How will you support yourself and your brat while you do?" He laughed. "Of course I can take Emilie off of your hands, if you wish, *madame*. I know an Arab prince in London who is quite fond of small girls. He would pay a fortune for a little blue-eyed blond maid. It might even reimburse me for the monies my father expended on you, *madame*. How old is my half-sister now? Six? Such a delicious age, is it not? The prince will see that Emilie lacks for nothing, in exchange, of course, for certain liberties." He laughed.

"You are vile!" Lady Abbott said angrily. "That you would even suggest such a thing but bespeaks your monstrous nature, William! Do you not feel the least modicum of guilt in falsely disinheriting your sister and me? I was your father's wife for ten years. Your own mother, God bless her, was not married to Charles for so long."

"Why should I feel guilt?" he demanded of her. "My father was much too old to remarry when you enticed him, and then seduced him into marrying you. He was forty-four to your seventeen! I was a year your senior! Do you know how foolish you made him look? An old man panting, and drooling after a chit, just out of the schoolroom, damnit!"

Marguerite shook her head sadly. "You never understood, did you, William? You father and I loved one another. The years between us meant nothing. They were meaningless. Please, I beg you, if you choose not to honor your father's wishes, keep your monies, but do not take my home from me. Emilie and I must have a place to live. All of our memories are here. Your father is even buried in the village churchyard, William. Take whatever else you wish, but leave us this house," she pleaded with him.

"The house is sold," he told her coldly. "The new owners will arrive tomorrow to take possession of it."

"But my things!" she cried.

"You have nothing, *madame,*" he insisted. "The house was sold furnished. I have turned the servants off. The new owners may want to hire some of them back, but I do not intend paying further wages."

"Your father—" she began.

Lord William Abbott slammed his fist onto a table by his side. "*My father!* I am sick unto death of hearing your praises for and laments about my father, *madame!* What did he have that I do not, pray? I have been told my entire life that I am his mirror image, yet you never noticed me that season in London. *No!* You only noticed Charles Abbott, but not William. *Why?* I will tell you why. It is the plain truth that he had the money, and I did not. You never saw either of us. You only saw what my father could give you. You did not see that I wanted you. You only saw my father's wealth." William Abbott's face was beet red with his anger, and his frustration.

"That isn't so, and you are horrible to say so!" Lady Abbott cried, astounded by his revelation. "Loving your father had nothing to do with his wealth, or his features, William. I loved him because he was loving, and kind, and gentle, and amusing; but how could you understand that? Your whole life has been driven by your self-interest!"

"Was he a good lover, *madame?* Was my father able to make you scream with pleasure? Or did you please him with the whore's tricks you learned from your aunt?"

"You are disgusting," she returned coldly.

"He must have stuck it to you at least twice for you bore him two brats. Or did you have a lover? Or perhaps a series of lovers to sate your appetites?"

"I do not have to stand here and listen to your revolting speeches," Marguerite Abbott said, the tears beginning to come. "I loved your father, and I was faithful to him always, William. Let any say it otherwise, and they will lie!" She turned from him to go.

"*Bitch!*" he snarled, and reaching for her, he yanked her back against him. "Before we are through, *madame,* and I throw you back into the gutter from where you came, you will give me what you gave my father! I will fuck you until you beg for mercy, whore! You will come to know what a real man is!" His hand ripped at her bodice. There was spittle on his lips, and his eyes were wild with his lust for her.

Marguerite struggled within his grip. An anger such as she had never before felt rose up in her breast. *This man!* This evil creature who looked so like her beloved Charles would not have her. She felt a strength such as she had never known pour into her. With a shriek she clawed at his face, her nails raking down his cheeks, drawing blood. Her knee came up as hard as she could bring it into his privates, and his ensuing howl brought a satisfied smile to her face, especially as his grip upon her loosened and she was able to pull away.

"*Cochon!* You are a pig, William, and you will never have me! *Ever!*" Then she laughed bitterly. "You are surprised that I know how to defend my honor, eh? Well, the nuns who raised me taught me, you monster! Even at my English school we were taught such little tricks." There was no pity in her eyes as she looked at her tormentor, now bent over with his pain. "You have taken everything from me that you could, William. But you will have neither my honor, my child, nor my memories. Those belong to me, and they are worth far more than any of the monies you have stolen." She turned and left him, still writhing with his pain, in the lovely salon she had decorated so beautifully when she had first come to Vertterre.

In the foyer of the house her maid, Clarice, and Clarice's husband, the undercoachman, were waiting for her. Wordlessly

Clarice wrapped a cloak about her mistress, tsking at the torn bodice. She shepherded Marguerite out the door of the house, helping her into a small coach.

"He will not miss it," Clarice said matter-of-factly. "It was in the back of the barn, and he probably never even saw it." She climbed in behind her mistress, and pulled the door shut.

"The horses," Lady Abbott said.

"If he wants 'em, he can come after them, but he won't. He will not want to appear publicly to be a bully. He had done his worst. Now he will scurry back to his England," Clarice said sensibly as the coach drew away from the house.

Marguerite looked sadly at what had been her happy home for the last six years, and the tears slipped down her cheeks. There was nothing to be done. Now she had to decide how she was going to survive, as well as protect her small daughter, Emilie, at school in Paris. "Where are we going?" she asked her maid.

"Why, to Madame Renée's, of course," Clarice answered her mistress.

Of course, Marguerite thought. Where else would she go at a time like this but to her aunt's establishment in Paris? She sat back and closed her eyes. Renée had always said that when one door closed, another opened. Her aunt was a pragmatist. She always had been. But it was this very quality that had saved both of their lives during the Terror. Naturally Marguerite didn't remember the Revolution, having been an infant, but Renée had told her everything. She had been very frank about how she had whored for the prison governor in order to save their lives, although she could not save the lives of Marguerite's parents. She had whored when she had finally been released from the Île de Cité prison in order to pay off her niece's fees at the convent of St. Anne. But, Renée pointed out, she had never walked the streets seeking clients.

Governor de la Pont had been generous to his young mistress. Renée had carefully hoarded his largesse to her. She had gained the freedom of the old whore who had shared her imprisonment, and learned all she could from the woman about her trade. Celine had served Renée faithfully until her death. When she had left prison, Renée had enough monies to purchase a small house in the Île de Cité district. There were two rooms upstairs and two rooms downstairs. Together she and Celine had cleaned it and found furnishings for it. And then Renée had gone into business, entertaining her former lover and the gentlemen he brought to her home. She was an elegant and cultured hostess with a quick wit and a generous nature.

Renée de Thierry's reputation began to spread. Soon the second bedchamber in her house had a resident, a young intelligent country girl to whom Renée taught manners, skills in music, how to make small talk, and how to always please a gentleman. *Chez Renée* began to host important and famous gentlemen. Renée bought a larger house, this one overlooking the River Seine. It was rumored that the Emperor Napoleon came to visit Madame Renée regularly.

Chez Renée did not accept callers in the month of August, or on Christmas Day or Easter. In August, Madame disappeared from Paris, but no one knew where she went except Marguerite, who was with her aunt then. While Marguerite had lived in France as a child, they had gone to a seaside village in Brittany where her aunt watched the little girl as she played on the sand by the sea; and where they walked together down verdant country lanes in early evening before the peach-gold light faded. At the end of the summer that Marguerite turned six, she did not go back to Paris with her aunt. Instead her aunt took her aboard a sailing yacht owned by one of Renée's old friends, an English duke. There the child bid her aunt farewell, and was taken to school in England.

In England, Marguerite spent her holidays with the duke and his large family. He would be her legal guardian, it was explained, as long as she was in England. The following August her Aunt Renée arrived from France to take her to Cornwall. It was there they vacationed each summer after that until Marguerite was married in a seaside village quite similar to the one in Brittany. And as much as Renée wanted her niece to regain the social position that the revolution in France had cost their family, she would not give her permission for Marguerite's marriage to Lord Abbott until he had been made fully aware of the entire truth of their situation.

Lord Abbott had nodded gravely when Renée de Thierry had

finished her recital. Then he said, "You say that Marguerite is legally born. She is the daughter of Jules and Marie-Agnes, Comte and Comtesse de Thierry. That she was ensconced within the Convent of St. Anne in Paris at the age of three months when her parents were executed; that she visited your house in Paris two days each year until she was six, when you sent her to England. Here she has been in school, her guardians being the Duke and Duchess of Sedgwick, under whom she made her debut. That while she is aware of your, um, enterprise, she has never had any part in it. Is that correct, *madame?*" Lord Abbott had eyes the color of sherry, and a quiet way about him. He never raised his voice.

"That is correct, my lord," Renée had answered him. "When she lived in France, my niece was too young to understand my pursuits. She visited my home on Christmas and Easter. There were never any negotiations conducted on those days, and no gentlemen were permitted in my house then. There was a time, sir, when the de Thierrys held great places of honor in France. The house in which my brother and I were raised contained armor that our ancestors had worn into battle. The hall was hung with banners brought from the crusades, and the wars we fought for king and country. The revolution changed all of that. My brother chose to sacrifice himself for a France that is gone, that had become an anachronism. I chose to survive. Jules and his wife martyred themselves, but I would not allow them to martyr Marguerite. She was three months old when they perished. So," and here Renée paused with a wry smile, "I seduced the governor of the Île de Cité prison."

"How old were you?" Lord Abbott inquired, for he was indeed curious. Renée de Thierry might be a courtesan, but she was still every inch an aristocrat.

"Sixteen, a virgin, and frightened to death," Renée told him frankly. "Fortunately François was both kind to me, touched by the sacrifice I was making, and a practical man. He saved my life, keeping my name from the lists of those to be guillotined. That first day he allowed me to take Marguerite to the convent outside the prison walls, and leave her with the nuns. After that I lived in his rooms and became his mistress. When the Terror was over, he freed me to do as I pleased for marriage to a man of his station was not an option. I fear I am a snob despite the fact my world was gone. It was necessary that I support my niece. However, I never wanted her to follow in my footsteps, my lord. I wanted her back in the world from which we had both come, but any man who seeks to marry Marguerite must understand both her history, and mine. If you still wish to wed my niece knowing what you do, then you will have my blessing. While I should like to see Marguerite wed, I will, once she has, absent myself from her life to save your family an embarrassment. But, sir, if you decide to cry off, I will certainly understand."

"Perhaps you would," Lord Abbott had replied, "but I do not think our Marguerite would. You are a brave woman, madame. I salute you." And Lord Abbott had kissed her hand.

Marguerite de Thierry Abbott found her mouth turning up in a smile as she remembered the tale her aunt had repeated to her when Renée had told her that Lord Abbott, knowing their past, still sought to have Marguerite as his wife. And her life with Charles had been a blissful idyll but for the death of their infant son. Now what was she to do? She had, like the women in her family before her, been educated to be a wife and a mother. It was all she knew. As a widow without means or a home of her own, and a daughter to raise, what future did she have?

"We are here," Clarice said, breaking into her mistress's thoughts as the carriage drew up before the elegant discreet house in the Rue de la Victoire.

A footman ran out to open the coach door, surprised when a lady, garbed in the black of a widow, stepped out. "*Madame,*" he said. "This cannot be the house you seek. You have made an error. Allow me to help you back into your vehicle." He bowed.

"I am Lady Abbott," Marguerite said. "Madame Renée is my aunt." She moved past the footman and through the open door of the house, past a second footman into the black and white foyer.

"*Madame,* are you all right? Let me take you to your aunt at once." François de la Pont came forward. He was no longer a young man, and Napoleon's campaigns had aged him further. Retired from the military and the government, now he served as Madame Renée's majordomo. He took her cape from her shoulders, saying to Clarice as he did, "You know where it goes."

Then he lowered his voice as Marguerite hurried off to seek her aunt. "Is she staying?"

"Of course she is staying," Clarice said. "The new milord has sold her home out from under her, and sent her penniless into the streets. Where else could she come?"

François de la Pont nodded. "Tell Louis to put your horses in the stables and bring her baggage inside. I will go and see where Madame wishes to put her." He shook his head. "She should not be here, of course, but you are right, Clarice. Where else could she go?"

Marguerite had found her aunt in the house's main salon, a beautiful room whose walls were covered in pale gold moiré silk which were hung with paintings of naked gods and goddesses, and all manner of fabled creatures. *"Tante!"*

"*Chérie!* Why on earth have you come here?" Madame Renée arose, embracing her niece and kissing her on both of her cheeks.

"William Abbott has sold the house and thrown me into the streets. He even threatened to take Emilie and sell her to some Arab prince friend of his in London. Thank God he doesn't know where she is, *tante!*" Then Marguerite burst into tears.

"Oh la la la la!" Renée said. "What of Charles's will, *ma petite?* Surely he had a will? You are entitled to at least something, as is our little Emilie. I cannot believe that, knowing his son the way he did, Charles did not make some provision for his wife, and daughter." She drew the sobbing younger woman to a settee, and they sat together.

"William had Charles's will. I do not know where he got it from, *tante.* Probably from that poor old *avocat* in the village that Charles had draw up the document. He came to the house after the funeral, before William arrived, and left an envelope he said was to go to my stepson. What a fool I have been, *tante!* I never realized that the packet contained the will. Charles left me the house, and an income, and a dowry for Emilie. William read it to me. Then he tore the parchment up, and burned it in the fire. I am sure there is no other copy. He is Charles's only male heir, and the bulk of my husband's estate is in England. Charles was not a rich man, but two thousand a year for me, and a dower of a thousand pounds for Emilie would have not beggared William in the least. How could he be so cruel?"

"He was an unpleasant young man, as I recall the Duke of Sedgwick saying," Renée replied. "Well, *ma petite,* do not fret. We will engage an *avocat* for you. I have friends, Marguerite, as you know."

"*Tante,* William will be gone by tomorrow. With no proof of what my husband wanted for me and my daughter, I have no case. Besides, you could not fight for my widow's mite here in France. We would have to go to England. I cannot take the chance that Emilie's reputation be damaged in a court case, *tante.* He has beaten me."

Renée de Thierry rose from the settee, and going over to an inlaid table, she poured them both a small flute of champagne from the open bottle on the silver tray. Handing one of the crystal flutes to her niece, she sat back down. "I must think on it, *chérie,* but you are right. Little Emilie must be protected at all costs. Still, there must be a way to have our revenge on this Englishman."

"I must stay with you, *tante,* and beg shelter for Clarice and Louis. We have nowhere else to go, and no funds even if we could find a place. William sent me from the house with naught but the clothes on my back, I fear."

"Clarice will have seen to your possessions, *ma petite,*" her aunt said. "She is a clever wench, and she will have spied the lay of the land before William told you. The servants always know everything."

"William turned out my servants," Marguerite told Renée.

"They won't have gone far. Louis can go back to Vertterre tomorrow, and tell them to come here to you for references," Renée told her niece. "Ohhh, I wish I could get my hands on that devil who has turned your life and Emilie's upside down! When I think of what he did murdering your son!"

"It couldn't be proved, tante," Marguerite said, tears beginning to prick behind her eyelids again. She was suddenly so tired.

"He smothered the child!" Renée accused. "He seduced the nursemaid, and while she slept, he murdered his baby brother. I do not forget that the girl awoke, and saw him lift the pillow from the child."

"I know," Marguerite replied. "Charles and I both believed Mary, but Charles also loved his son. Besides, the girl's word would not have been believed in a court of law, *tante.* It would have been said she was a loose woman, who seduced the master's son, and neglected her duties towards her charge. We both realized there was nothing we could do. Charles hoped for another son, but Emilie was born to us instead. And then he became ill, and we both knew there would be no other sons for Charles Abbott." She sighed. *"Mon pauvre Charles."*

"Have you eaten?" her aunt asked. *"Non?* Then you will eat with me, *chérie.* We do not receive callers until after ten o'clock in the evening. By then you will be safely tucked away in your bed, away from my little enterprise, and my clients. We must keep your visit discreet, Marguerite. I have struggled your whole life to retain your respectability even if I couldn't retain mine. If we are to find you a new husband, you must not be tainted by me."

"Tante, be sensible," Marguerite said. "I have nothing. No house. No jewels. No monies. I am a penniless widow with a child. Who in his right mind would want me?" She chuckled almost to herself. "I shall have to learn a trade, *tante.* Do you think I would make a good seamstress, or hat maker? I cannot be a governess, for then I could not be with my little Emilie at all, and I will not have that."

"We will think on it tomorrow," her aunt said. "For now, let us repair to my *salle à manger,* and have something to eat. I will introduce you to the two young ladies who reside currently with me."

Madame Renée led her niece into her private dining room, where two attractive young women were already waiting. They each wore a simple, loose-fitting house gown of a single color. "This is my niece, Lady Abbott," Renée said to them. "Marguerite, this is Josephine, whom we call Josie, and Leonie. Sit down, everyone." She turned to the maid. "You may serve us now, Lisbet."

The wine was poured into crystal goblets, and a rich cream soup was ladled out into the handled bowls. This was followed by a dish of oysters and prawns served on individual plates decorated with watercress and sliced lemons. After that, a platter with leg of lamb was offered, the meat surrounded by roasted potatoes, onions, and carrots. There were also small stuffed quail on a platter decorated with grapes. Under the shocked eyes of Josie and Leonie, and the amused glance of her aunt, Marguerite ate heartily.

"*Madame,* she will get fat!" the blond Leonie whispered to her sponsor.

"*Non,* she will not. My Marguerite has always enjoyed her food, but she never gains an ounce," was the reply.

"Is she really your niece?" red-haired Josie asked.

"Yes, she is," Madame Renée said quietly.

"Is she joining us?" Josie inquired.

"*No!*" Renée spoke almost sharply.

"Why not?" Leonie demanded.

"Yes, *tante,* why not?" Marguerite said suddenly, surprising them all, as she wiped her mouth with her linen napkin.

"*Marguerite!* It is unthinkable!" Madame Renée cried. "Everything I have done I have done so you might retain your station, the station in life to which you were born."

"As that time came to an end for you, *tante,* it has now come to an end for me. As you had my fate to consider, I have Emilie's. I cannot support my daughter making flowers, or making bonnets or gowns. I only have one thing to sell. Myself. I am not as young as these two ladies with us at table, but I am not too old either." Marguerite reached out, and patted her aunt's hand reassuringly. "I am not a virgin, nor have any reputation left to protect. What does it matter that I am the only child of the late Comte and Comtesse de Thierry, or the honored widow of the late Lord Charles Abbott, if I cannot pay my child's school fees, and she will starve in the streets?"

"I will find a little house for you by the seaside where you may live in respectability. I will pay Emilie's school fees," Renée said desperately.

"*Tante,* I am twenty-eight, I have been a wife, and I am a mother," Marguerite responded. "I cannot continue to take from you. The time has come for me to earn my own way. This is how you can help me."

"Was it nice being a wife?" Josie asked Marguerite. "Yet it must have been very dull too having only one man to fuck you. I like having a variety of lovers in my bed."

"Ohh, yes!" Leonie agreed. "It is true that variety is the spice of life, and oh la la, I do like my spice!" She grinned mischievously.

"My husband was ill the last two years of our marriage," Marguerite told them. "I have not had conjugal relations in all that time."

"Ohh, you poor thing!" Loenie replied. "Not to be stuffed daily with a stiff cock? How terrible for you!"

"We have more than enough gentlemen to go around, *madame,* don't we? Another girl would take nothing from either of us, and would certainly add to the reputation of your establishment," Josie said.

"*Oui! Oui!*" Leonie agreed. "She is very beautiful, madame, with her pale skin and her dark hair. Together the three of us make a truly striking trio! Please say she can join us!"

"If you do not, *tante,*" Marguerite threatened, "I shall be forced to find another sponsor in another establishment. I am certain that someone would be pleased to have the famed Madame Renée's niece whoring for them." She cocked her head to one side as her eyes met those of her aunt's.

"There is a difference between entertaining a lover, and giving your husband his marital rights," Madame Renée said. "Because you are my niece does not mean you can succeed as I have succeeded."

"We will not know unless you let me try," Marguerite said.

Renée de Thierry shook her elegant head. "That we should have come to this point after all my sacrifice. Very well, Marguerite. Over the next few days we shall ascertain if you are able to make the transition between respectable matron, and respectable whore, but understand that while I will endeavor to help you, I am not happy that you have decided to follow in my footsteps."

"Yes, *tante,*" came the meek reply, and their two companions giggled mischievously.

"And if I feel you cannot do this thing, then you will allow me to purchase a cottage in Brittany for you, and pay for Emilie's school fees," Renée said.

"I can do it," Marguerite said stubbornly.

"That is what I fear," her aunt returned.

"Did you not give up everything for me?" Marguerite said softly.

"I did it so you wouldn't have to, *ma petite,*" Renée sighed.

"Bravo!" Josie cried.

"Can she join us tonight?" Leonie asked.

"Certainly not!" Madame told them. "Tonight Marguerite will go quietly to bed, and rest after her terrible ordeal."

A sweet dessert wine was poured as the table was cleared of the dinner plates. Poached pears and tiny meringues were served to conclude the meal. Then both Josie and Leonie hugged Marguerite, kissing her on both cheeks before they left the dining room to go and dress for the evening. Each expressed her delight that Marguerite would be joining them shortly, and promised to share their secrets for success with the gentlemen with her. Madame and her niece returned to Renée's private salon.

"Why do you have them dress to receive their callers when they are only going to undress?" Marguerite asked her aunt.

"What a man cannot easily see is far more intriguing than what he can see," Renée replied. "Also, the gentlemen who come here are not ravening monsters whose only concern is to get their cocks into a hot cunt, *ma petite*. Passion should be cultivated as elegantly as possible. Both Josie and Leonie can discuss the latest politics, and are well read, I assure you. Having been given another road to travel, both would have been considered ladies. It is an illusion men enjoy. As they enjoy seducing my girls. Slowly, and pleasurably. Removing a woman's clothing adds to that, as does the removal of a gentleman's garb. How one treats a lover is far different than how one treats a husband. I would imagine Charles was very polite in his approach to you. And you, *chérie,* I taught to be obedient after I explained the necessary facts. But did you ever know passion with him?"

"I loved my husband," Marguerite said.

"I know you did, *ma petite,* but did you know passion in his arms? Passion is quite different from love."

"I do not understand, *tante,* what it is you mean."

"No, I did not think you did, Marguerite. Let me see if I can put it another way. Did your husband's desire for you ever make you swoon with pleasure? Did his glance arouse in you a lust to be possessed by him? Did you soar into the skies with the culmination of your love making?"

The younger woman burst out laughing. "Why, *tante,* what delicious and girlish imagery you pose. I don't believe I have ever soared, or swooned, in my whole life. Charles had my entire devotion as was proper and suitable. I had his devotion. Marriage is for the purpose of children, *tante.* The nuns at St. Anne's taught me that as a little girl. How does one soar without wings?" she giggled.

"You have never known passion?" Renée de Thierry was shocked by her niece's revelation. How like her father she is, the older woman thought. Jules was as cold as ice, but I will not allow my darling child to go through her life without knowing passion. *"Ma chérie,"* she said quietly, "there is much you need to know before you become a proper courtesan. Having had a husband is simply not enough. For now, however, you need to rest yourself. You have had a terribly trying day with that wretched stepson of yours. I will send François to the convent to tell the Reverend Mother Othalie that Lord William Abbott is not to be allowed access to his half-sister, if indeed he discovers where she is." Renée arose from the settee where they had been sitting together. "Come, *ma petite,* and I will show you to your room. It is at the top of the house, and no one will disturb you there. My clients never venture above the third floor, nor are you to leave the top floor once you have retired in the evening, Marguerite."

"Will I always live there, *tante?*"

"*Non.* Once I think you are ready to join us in our enterprise, you will be assigned your own bedchamber on the third floor with Josie and Leonie. And Marguerite, perhaps for Emilie's sake it would be wise that from now on you be introduced as my niece, Mademoiselle de Thierry, and not Madame Abbott. *N'est-ce pas?*"

Marguerite nodded. "I agree," she said.

Renée led the younger woman upstairs to the top floor of her Paris house saying, "The entire floor is yours, and your servants'. My own servants sleep below stairs, or above the stables. The women who do the heavy cleaning live elsewhere, and come in daily. You will be private and safe here, *ma chérie.*" She opened a door, ushering Marguerite into a charming but simple bedroom beneath the eaves, where Clarice was waiting for her mistress. "*Bonsoir,* Clarice," Madame said as the maid curtsied. Then Renée turned to her niece. "I leave you in good hands, *ma petite.* I usually do not arise until noon, but Cook is in the kitchens before six." She kissed Marguerite on both of her cheeks. "Sleep well, *chérie.*" Then she turned again, and was quickly gone down the narrow staircase.

"She said me and Louis could have a room here too," Clarice told her mistress. "I thought this was a bawdy house, my lady."

"Indeed it is," Marguerite replied, laughing, "but it is an elegant bawdy house. My aunt entertains in a very *recherché* manner. There are but two young ladies. Gentlemen of means, and of breeding, come to call. They drink, they gamble, and they amuse themselves with Josie and Leonie. Sometimes if a gentleman takes my aunt's fancy, she honors him with her company. I understand there are men who come just in hopes of catching Madame Renée's fancy. Soon I will be joining them."

"*Madame!*" Clarice's large brown eyes were wide with surprise.

"What else am I to do, Clarice?" Marguerite asked.

"Couldn't your aunt . . ." Clarice began.

"*No,*" Marguerite said firmly to her maid. Clarice had been with her ever since she married Charles. She had had a French father and an English mother, and was bilingual. And she had been trained by the Duchess of Sedgwick's own maid. When Lord and Lady Abbott had removed themselves to France, she had come with them, and it was there she had met Louis, who had been hired to drive Lord Abbott's coaches. They had married, and were completely loyal to Marguerite.

"What about little Miss Emilie?" Clarice asked.

"I shall be able to pay her school fees myself. As I shall use the name I was born with, and not the Abbott name. She will not be tainted by my behavior."

"As long as no one figures out that Lady Abbott is Mademoiselle de Thierry," Clarice said sharply.

"You know I would do nothing to harm my daughter. I should send her to England to the duke and his family, but I fear William

Abbott," Marguerite told her maid. "For now, Emilie is safer at St. Anne's."

"Perhaps you're right, my lady, but when I think of you, such a proper lady being brought so low," Clarice sniffled.

"I shall remain a proper lady," her mistress assured her. "I shall just take lovers in order to earn my living now. I no longer have a husband to look after me, Clarice, and no hope of one in my pitiful and poverty-stricken state."

"You got your jewels, my lady. I saw to that when I packed your things. We knew what Lord William was up to, for he could not resist trumpeting what he was going to do to gain his revenge on his father for marrying you all them years ago," Clarice said.

"Ohh, Clarice, you did not take the Abbott family jewels with us, did you? They rightfully belong to the new Lord Abbott. He will have the law on us, and this is the first place he will look!" Marguerite had gone pale as her maid had proudly given her recitation.

"*The Abbott jewels? Non, non,* my lady. I did not take *them*. I only took the pretties that your husband had made especially for you. That wicked villain who disinherited you would know nothing of them, nor has he a right to them. I thought you would want them for Mademoiselle Emilie one day," Clarice explained.

Marguerite heaved a deep sigh of relief. "Oh, yes, Clarice! How thoughtful you are, and far more sensible than I was in this situation."

"You were gently raised, *madame,* and you are not used to such wickedness. For the master's son to have done what he did and left you without a *sou,* when the master meant for you to remain in your home and raise your daughter comfortably. Well, I ain't got the proper word for it in either English or French," Clarice said firmly.

"Oh, Clarice, I certainly could not do without either you or Louis. You shall not want, I promise you."

"We are with you, *madame,* warm, fed, and dry. We was paid our wages Michaelmas last for the year. You owe us nothing. And even if you did, we would stay by your side," Clarice said loyally.

"Bless you both," Marguerite told her servant.

"I should get you ready for bed now, *madame.* We have both had more than enough today," the maid declared.

"Yes," her mistress agreed. "We certainly have."

There was a basin with warm fragrant water for washing. Marguerite bathed her face, hands, and neck as Clarice put her garments away. She brushed her teeth with the silver-handled bristle brush Renée had given her. Clarice wrapped her in a warm night garment, and tied her nightcap beneath her chin with its pink ribbons. Marguerite climbed into bed, sighing gustily as she sank into the featherbed and drew up the satin down quilt. "Ahhh," she murmured, realizing her eyes felt heavy. "I did not know how tired I was until this very minute."

Clarice smiled, and snuffed the candles. *"Bonsoir, madame,"* she said as she slipped from the room, closing the door behind her.

"Bonso . . ." And Marguerite was asleep.

Chapter Two

Renée de Thierry looked about her gold and white salon and smiled with pleasure. The coming of spring always brought out so many of her clients. As much as she disliked the thought of Marguerite joining their little group, she had to admit that she needed another girl. Unlike other brothel owners, Madame Renée did not call attention to her enterprise with a dozen half-naked young women sitting in open windows, boldly importuning gentlemen passers-by to stop. She was discreet, and the young women in her employ were more than just whores, as she had explained to her niece earlier. Often gentlemen visited her home just for an evening of discussion, music, and camaraderie. She allowed them to play cards, provided the stakes were not outrageous and there were no disputes. They drank her most excellent wines and champagnes. And when moved to do so, they went upstairs with Josie or Leonie to exercise their baser natures. Sometimes a gentleman was even allowed the privilege of remaining overnight. However, only the most favored of Madame's clients were accorded that prerogative.

And there were rules that had to be followed when treating with her girls. Madame made certain that new arrivals understood that, and that her longtime patrons remembered she would allow no brutality or cruelty toward her girls in a gentleman's pursuit of Eros. She was not against the use of the delightful variety of toys kept in the bedrooms that could but encourage pleasure, or add to it. In fact, her girls were frequently the instigators of the use of such games that could but prolong a gentleman's enjoyment, and bring him back for more.

"Madame." César d'Aubert, the Duc de Caraville, bowed over her hand, kissing it.

"César! How nice to see you again," she told him. "Have you been in the country, *monseigneur?*" He was an outrageously handsome man with black hair and bright blue eyes.

"Worse," the duke replied with some humor. "I have been at the king's beck and call for most of the winter, *chérie.* I realize that as one of the nobility, I am supposed to rejoice in the restoration, but between us I was quite happy under the republic. King Louis sends his regards, Renée. He says he hopes to visit your home again soon."

"He is a kind man, César," she replied, smiling. "And very intelligent too."

"Except in the matter of managing France," the duke responded, lowering his voice as he said it. Then he smiled. "Allow me to introduce my American cousin, Beauford d'Aubert. He prefers to be called Beau."

Madame Renée held out her hand to the slightly younger man. "You are most welcome to Chez Renée, monsieur. Has your cousin explained my rules to you?"

"He has, *madame,* and I vow I shall keep each and every one of them," Beau answered her.

Renée laughed, but then she said, "See that you do, *mon brave.*"

"I understand there is a new girl with you," the duke began.

"Not yet, *monseigneur,*" Renée replied quietly.

"You know I always enjoy the first taste, Renée," the duke said as quietly. "Where did you find her?"

"She is my niece, César, and until today, quite respectable as I once was. You know of our family's history."

"Of course! The infant you saved during the Terror, eh?"

"The same. She has been recently widowed, and her English stepson had cheated her out of everything. I will not bore you with the sad tale. She has a child to support, and no other means of earning her bread. I am not happy with this turn of events, but I can, unfortunately, see no alternative for her. I would gladly support her and her little girl, but she is proud like all de Thierrys, and today I realized how much like her papa she is. She will take nothing more from me, and has chosen this path herself."

"Why is she not here then tonight?" the duke asked.

"Because she is woefully ignorant of sexual matters except as a wife," Renée responded. "She will need some tutoring before I can introduce her into our midst. She is very beautiful, and will be quite desired, I assure you."

"I shall look forward to the day," he said. Then he added, "Do not wait too long, Renée, for her unskilled ways may very well prove an aphrodisiac to some of us."

"You are always so greedy for a new experience," Madame chided the Duc de Caraville, tapping his arm with her fan. "Remember, passion is best cultivated slowly, my dear César. Now run along, and show your handsome young cousin about. I see Josie already has her eye on him. She might forgo your company for that of your cousin's."

"Or perhaps she will entertain us both," the duke said with a wicked smile.

Renée laughed, and then turned to greet some of her other guests. Tonight she had a full dozen of them. There was Count Marco Cirello, who usually made his home in Rome. Married, the father of seven, and well known at the Vatican, he came to Paris for his pleasures and his privacy. The twin Persian brothers, Prince Kansbar and Prince Kurush, identical in every way, were already playing cards with the Irish horse breeder, Lord Kieran Darby, and the great Bavarian landowner, Baron Ernst Amalhardt. Leonie had seated herself at the pianoforte, and began to play. She was immediately joined by one of Napoleon's retired generals, Vachel Egide, and Michel Georges, a wealthy merchant from Nantes. Fabian de Eustache, a well-known banker, had now engaged the young American in eager conversation, Renée noted. He was always looking for a new and profitable business opportunity. The duke had joined Josie and Prince Dmitri Romanov on a striped sofa.

Looking about, Renée could see it was going to be a quiet evening. She smiled as Josie arose from the settee and, taking Prince Dmitri by the hand, departed the room. Then she frowned. With so many gentlemen tonight, and only one young lady currently available—*sacrebleu!* What was the matter with her that she hadn't realized before now that she really did need another girl. Possibly even more than one.

"Where is your niece?" César d'Aubert asked as he came to her side.

"Asleep by now, I suspect," she answered him.

"I want to see her," the duke said.

"César! I have said she is not ready by any means to greet visitors. I am not being coy. She nursed her husband devotedly in his last years, and then to have her home and small inheritance snatched by her stepson has been a terrible shock. The dastard even threatened his little half-sister, and then attempted to rape Marguerite," Madame Renée explained.

"I only want to see her," the duke replied. "Come with me, Renée, and show me. If she is sleeping, she will never know I spied on her. If she is awake, I will not enter her chamber. Is that not a fair agreement?" He smiled winningly at his hostess.

"Ohh, César, I never could resist you," Renée finally agreed. "Come along, *but only you*. Your American must remain here."

"Beau is deep in conversation with Monsieur de Eustache," the duke noted. "Two men of business in a courtesan's home discussing banking, slaves, and crop yields," he chuckled. "I despair of my cousin, chérie. These Americans are as bad as the English."

She laughed as she led him up two flights of stairs to the fourth floor, and down the corridor to Marguerite's bedroom. In her hand she carried a taperstick that lit their way in the dark hall. She put a finger to her lips, and then she slowly opened the chamber door. As they softly stepped inside, they could hear the sounds of the young woman's breathing.

"Hold the candle up," the duke whispered low.

Renée raised the light to shine over her face.

Marguerite lay upon her back, one arm across her torso, the other sprawled above her head. Her dark curls tumbled from beneath her dainty nightcap. Her pale skin was almost translucent in the candlelight. Her closed eyelids were shadowed in violet, her thick eyelashes spread across her pale cheeks like open-winged moths. Beneath her modest night attire her bosom rose and fell rhythmically.

César d'Aubert leaned down, drew the quilt aside, and gently pulled the ribbons holding Marguerite's garment closed. They unfastened easily. Reaching out, he drew the halves of the fabric aside, baring her breasts to his gaze. They were full, and round like the ripest peaches.

"Exquisite," he murmured. Then he turned abruptly, and left the bedchamber.

Renée quickly drew the coverlet up, not bothering to attempt to retie the pink ribbons on her niece's nightgown. Then she hurried from the room, and downstairs. On the landing below the fourth floor she found the duke awaiting her.

"*How soon?*" he demanded.

"I must have time," she began, but he waved her excuse aside.

"A week, *madame*. You have one week to prepare her for me. I will wait no longer." He took Renée's hand and led her back down to her salon. After he had seated her, César d'Aubert said, "Tell me about her."

"I sent her to school in England when she was six," Renée began. "Her guardians were the Duke and Duchess of Sedgwick."

"How did you know an English milord?" He was curious.

"The duke and his friends amused themselves during the revolution rescuing aristocrats, and others unfairly singled out for a visit with Madame la Guillotine. I helped them. Remember, César, not every noble family was as foresighted as was your papa, removing his family out of France before the Terror. When

I needed to get Marguerite to England, he arranged it. He and his wife treated her as one of their own daughters. They gave her a season in London just before she was seventeen. It was there she met Charles Abbott. He was a widower, many years her senior. He fell in love with her, and sought my permission to marry her. I was honest with him, but it made no difference. It was a happy marriage but for the son of his first union, who hated Marguerite. That is why they came back to France to live. She may tell you about it if you become friends.

"But she was a wife, César. You know what that means. She yielded dutifully to her husband's wishes, but never allowed herself to feel desire, having been taught it was not ladylike. For her, the only purpose of copulation is to produce children. My niece, while beautiful and desirable, has never felt passion. She admits to it. She has never been awakened, César. Now she thinks to follow in my footsteps, not knowing what is involved. She must have some small knowledge before I allow you or anyone else to have her. She is likely to be quite shocked to discover how powerful an emotion lust is."

"Do not overburden her with facts, dear Renée," the duke said. "I can think of no more delightful a task than bestirring and arousing the beautiful Marguerite to know her own passions. Promise me you will not let any of the others have her until I have had my appetites sated."

"But of course, César. You are certainly my choice for breaking her in, but please, I beg you, be kind to her. She has never had a lover but for Lord Abbott. He adored her, but was not from what can I gather in my talks with my niece, a thrilling lover. He took his quick pleasure, and was kind to her, but no more."

"I cannot wait to see the look in her eyes when I bring her to the point of *la petite morte*," the duke said excitedly.

"César, César!" Renée mocked him gently. "You are always so eager for new experiences. Of all the men I have ever met, you are certainly the most experienced."

"From you, *ma chérie*, that is a great compliment," the duke replied. "Will you honor me?" he asked her.

"What of your handsome American cousin?" She smiled up at him.

The Duc de Caraville's glance swept the room, and then he chuckled. "Beau is still in deep conversation with Monsieur de Eustache. *Le bon Dieu,* I despair of him."

"Let me see to my guests first," she told him. The two princes were still deep in play at the card table with the baron and Lord Darby. Leonie was gone from the room as was Count Cirello. Josie was listening intently now to General Egide's stories, while Prince Romanov had seated himself at the pianoforte and was singing a rather bawdy song about the English regent while Count St. Denis played the instrument. Monsieur Georges was drinking wine, apparently quite content when Renée stopped by his chair.

"May I get you something, *monsieur?*" she asked him. "It is so nice to see you up from Nantes again. Business is good?"

"Excellent, *madame,* never better," Monsieur Georges replied. "And as always the hospitality you offer is the finest. Do not fret yourself about me. Mademoiselle Josie has said she will entertain me when the general tires of his memories. She is a kind young woman, *n'est-ce pas,* Madame Renée?"

Renée bent and kissed the gentleman on his cheek. "She is very kind, *oui.* Now tell me, will you be long in Paris this trip?"

"Just the usual few days, but I shall be back in two months, for there is nothing finer than springtime in Paris," he responded.

"And when you return, I shall probably have three, if not four, young ladies to entertain my guests, *monsieur.* My niece, a widow, is joining my household, and if I can find another suitable girl, well then, will that not be nice?" She smiled at him.

"I may have a young lady for you," Monsieur Georges surprised her. "Beautiful, but a trifle rough about the edges. She is too delicious a piece to roam the streets, which she will shortly be driven to if I cannot find a place for her. She is the daughter of one of my silk weavers. He is ill, and will soon die. I have been kind to her."

"Is she a virgin?" Renée wanted to know.

"No, I have seen to that," Monsieur Georges said with a small smile. "Nor is she diseased. I have also seen to that, *madame.* I know the kind of young lady you prefer, for have I not been coming here for over ten years. Michelle needs refining, but she is most enthusiastic."

"If she is willing to come, bring her to me when her papa is gone, but not before. And see that she learns to read and write. If she is suitable, I will reimburse you any expense involved."

"Excellent, *madame,*" Monsieur Georges replied. "You are a most excellent business woman." He arose and, bowing, kissed her hand.

Her guests would be fine without her for an hour or so, Renée knew. Returning to the duke's side, she took his arm, and they left the salon. Renée's bedchamber was not on the floor above with the girls, but rather toward the rear of the house on the same floor where the salons were located. The duke knew the way, having been there many times before. No sooner had they entered than he pushed her against the closed door and kissed her hard. His lips moved from her lips to her neck and bared shoulders. His mouth was hot on her flesh.

"Take off your damned clothes, Renée," the duke said impatiently.

She laughed. "So eager, *mon brave.* I hope you will not act this way with my niece. You will terrify her."

"I want to fuck *you,*" he answered her bluntly, pulling off his own garments. "Having seen the exquisite Marguerite, I am suddenly very hot to fuck, *chérie.*"

"As Chez Renée strives to please its guests, *monseigneur,* how can I not comply with such an easy request. I shall be happy to stand in for my niece tonight." Renée quickly stripped off her bodice, skirts, undergarments, and shoes.

"Damn, *madame,* but for a woman of any age you are in incredible form," the duke said, smacking his lips. "I believe your niece has inherited those fine round breasts of yours." His gaze moved appreciatively over her lush form. She had a very narrow waist, but her full hips certainly matched her full bosom. He pulled her against him, his swollen cock rubbing against her dark bush. "On your back, wench!" he growled in her ear as they fell to the bed.

Renée wrapped her legs about her lover, sighing with pleasure as he slid into her. "You need a young wife, César," she told him. "I shall soon no longer be able to keep up with you."

"I know," he agreed, "but the thought of impregnating some pale virgin just for the sake of an heir revolts me. I may let my younger brother and his brats inherit from me. Then I can continue to do as I please. Ahhhh, bitch, you are hot for me too, *n'est-ce pas?*" He thrust deeply into her again and again until both were weak, and most replete with the pleasure their bodies had given to each other.

Afterward they drank champagne, lying naked, until finally Madame Renée arose and, after bathing her private parts, dressed once more. "You may remain the night if it pleases you, César," she told him with a small smile, preparing to leave the room.

He stretched his long frame lazily. "*Non, merci,* but I must be home early for a meeting with the king. It would not do for me to appear in the same clothing I wore today, would it?" He chuckled. "Poor old Louis, but then I forget, you like him."

"He is a decent, if old-fashioned man," she responded. "He comes to talk with me, nothing more, for he is not able as you know, poor soul. But I often wonder if any man would have been able with that ugly princess he married, even given his difficulty. He was always astounded that the revolution had the courage, as he puts it, to execute his brother and his brother's family."

"What do you talk about with him?" The Duc de Caraville was curious. King Louis XVIII was indeed intelligent, but he was also a man with a great sense of his own importance, and not a great deal of common sense.

Renée laughed softly. "We speak on literature, and poetry," she said. "And he loves gossip, what little I may give him without breaking any confidences. He has great charm, but surely you recall that he had a very unfortunate marriage with his Savoyard princess. He has a rare physical deformity. The marriage was never consummated. Perhaps if it had, they both would have been happier."

"There are other ways . . ." the duke began.

"His difficulty leaves him unable to enjoy even the most innocent of carnal pleasures," Renée replied. Then she shook a warning finger at the duke. "But you did not hear that from me, chérie."

The duke grinned. "Eh, what?" he replied, putting his hand to his ear in a gesture of attempting to hear better.

"*Bonsoir,* César," she told him. "I will see you again soon."

"Tomorrow night, Renée, and have the luscious Marguerite available for me to meet then. I promise to give you your week, but I do think the little beauty should be familiar with the man who will awaken her senses."

"You are very wicked," she chuckled, waggling a finger at him again. Then she closed the door, and hurried off down the corridor to the salon to see how her other guests were enjoying themselves.

At noon the following day Marguerite joined her aunt in Renée's bedchamber, bringing with her a tray of delicacies. Setting the tray on the nearby table, she poured her aunt a porcelain cup of strong Turkish coffee, mixing the appropriate amount of sugar into the cup first. Handing it to Renée, she put a hot flaky croissant on a plate with some sweet butter and strawberry preserves. Taking the plate, Renée gobbled the croissant and demanded another. "Passion increases the appetite," she said.

"And the waistline," Marguerite teased her relation.

"I am no bigger than I was as a girl," Renée said, but then she amended, "well, perhaps a trifle more ample in certain areas."

"Your bosom?" Marguerite said innocently.

"You are a wicked child," Renée replied, laughing. "*Mais oui.* My breasts, and my hips, and perhaps my waist, but only a little. A man likes a woman with a bit of flesh on her bones."

"Will they like me?" Marguerite wondered aloud.

"Oh, yes, chérie, they will *all* like you. Are you certain that this is the life you want, *ma petite?* Take my generosity. Let me send you and Emilie to Brittany. This life does not have to be for you."

Marguerite laughed. "*Non, tante.* I must learn to be independent like you have been. In that way I shall never again be at anyone's mercy. If I had been stronger, wiser, I would have seen that Charles gave me a copy of his will. I would have seen that the *avocat* read that will publicly before my stepson arrived from England. There was time, *tante,* but I was foolish. And because I was, William Abbott rendered me helpless, or so he thought. Had he not threatened my daughter with his vileness, *his own baby half-sister,* I could not have come to my decision. So, *tante,* I will follow in your footsteps. If I am good at my profession, perhaps one day you will allow me to manage this enterprise of yours. I hope I can be worthy."

"And Emilie?" Renée asked.

"Emilie will remain at St. Anne's for the interim, *tante*. Until I am certain she is safe in England, I dare not send her there. She is young. She will not understand what I do any more than I understood until you told me," Marguerite said.

Renée nodded. *"Non,* you are right, *ma petite.* Now I must ask you a question. Will you join us tonight in the salon? You need do nothing more than converse with my guests. They are all gentlemen."

"I had not thought you would want me in your salon so soon," Marguerite said hesitantly.

"I think it is better that you see what is involved, *ma petite,* sooner than later. I shall also take you to observe one of the girls with a lover. Perhaps then you will decide this life is not for you," Renée told her niece. "I will have a gown sent to your room, *chérie,* for you will not have anything suitable among your wardrobe, I fear."

"But, *tante,* I am in mourning," Marguerite said.

"Not in this house, *chérie.* In your heart you may continue to mourn your Charles, but in my salon you must be charming and tempting," Renée replied quietly. "You are fortunate to be so fair. You will be ravishing in almost any color. Now run along, *ma petite.* I must nap for a while before arising."

"But, *tante,* you have only awakened an hour ago," Marguerite said. "Do you always rest so much?"

"Of course, *chérie.* When I rest I neither frown nor smile, both of which lead to premature wrinkles. A lady cannot be too careful of her appearance when she reaches that certain age," Renée noted.

"And have you reached that certain age, *tante?*" Marguerite's light blue eyes were twinkling with mischief.

"Not quite," Renée admitted, "but I am, I fear, very near." She waved the younger woman away. "Go along now. Josie and Leonie will tell you all about the gentlemen who come here. You are less likely to be frightened of them if you know something about them. Remember they will know nothing about you other than you are my widowed niece." Renée closed her eyes, and drew her black satin sleep mask down over her eyes again. "Go away, *chérie.*"

Marguerite tiptoed from her aunt's bedchamber and hurried down the corridor to a small blue and white salon, where the other two young women were now seated in loose house robes, and sipping cups of green tea while they nibbled on miniature meat pasties.

"Madame says you will join us tonight, but only to be social, not to fuck. *Sacrebleu!* I cannot wait until you are ready to fuck. Last night there were a dozen men here and but the two of us, although Madame took the duke off to amuse herself. Leonie and I were up all night satisfying the others."

"You see more than one gentleman a night?" Marguerite asked.

"Usually," Josie said, tossing her tangled red curls. "And each one is different. I always thought a cock was just a cock, but Madame Renée showed me otherwise."

"They will certainly enjoy fucking you," Leonie said, licking a crumb from the corner of her mouth. "You are beautiful, of course, but not having known a man's passion in several years, you will be very tight, almost a virgin again," she giggled.

"*Mon Dieu,* I hope not to suffer like a virgin as I did on my wedding night," Marguerite told them.

"*Non! Non!*" Leonie reassured her. "The virgin shield does not grow back, *chérie.* Your love sheath will just be very tight, and how the gentlemen love a tight sheath. Josie and I douche with a mixture of alum and warm water, as Madame taught us, to retain the tightness. We'll show you how to do it too."

Marguerite nodded, then she said, "Tell me about who comes."

"They all *come* when we have them," Josie giggled wickedly.

"*Non! Non!* I meant . . ." Marguerite blushed.

"She knows what you meant," Leonie laughed. "I see it is up to me to be serious. Well, *chérie,* there is the Duc de Caraville. Tall, dark, and dangerous. And, mon Dieu! What an insatiable lover! General Egide. He is older, and content to have a simple fuck. He was one of Napoleon's generals. Occasionally Monsieur Georges comes to visit from Nantes, where he is a wealthy silk merchant. Sometimes he brings us beautiful bolts of material. He can be most generous. Count Cirello comes from Rome because he is so respected there, but because his brother is a cardinal, he dare not misbehave. He comes to Paris several times a year, and is *very* naughty here."

"How is he naughty?" Marguerite asked.

"He likes to bottom-fuck," Josie explained. "Ever been bottom-fucked? Try it once, but if you don't like it, stay away from the count! Tell her about the Persians, Leonie."

"They are princes. Identical twins and ambassadors to the court from their own king. They like to have a woman together, and they always come at the exact same time. It's amazing! And then there's Lord Darby. He raises horses for racing at Ascot, and Prince Dmitri Romanov, a cousin of the czar. He comes from St. Petersburg twice a year. He is a famous gambler, and very lucky too."

"The others aren't as interesting. Count St. Denis, Monsieur de Eustache, who is a banker, Baron Amalhardt. Now the baron likes to spank us before he fucks us," Josie explained.

"I thought my aunt allowed no brutality," Marguerite said nervously.

"He doesn't hurt you. Just gives your buttocks a good warming, which seems to make his cock hard as a rock. He can ream a girl for half an hour before coming, *chérie*, and you will come a dozen times before he does. He's really quite wonderful," Josie sighed.

"*Oui!*" Leonie agreed. "He is a true artiste with his love lance. He has a wife in Bavaria. They have been wed for twelve years, and they have eleven children. That is why he comes to Paris so often. The baroness is always breeding, poor woman."

"If that is so," Marguerite fretted, "can we not become with child? Has it ever happened to either of you?"

"Madame sees we are given a little potion that prevents any unfortunate *accidents*. It is put in the food we eat, or perhaps the wine, but Madame Renée protects us. She has always protected her girls."

"Oh," Marguerite said. Then, "Are those all the gentlemen?"

"The regulars, *oui*. The duke did bring us his American cousin last night," Leonie said. "He is as handsome as the duke, but"—

she giggled—"his accent is so funny despite his French heritage. He is, however, as enthusiastic and charming a lover as his cousin," she concluded.

"*Mais oui!*" Josie seconded.

"He had you *both?*" Marguerite's voice was very shocked.

"Oh la la, *chérie,* he had us both *twice!*" Josie said, laughing.

"Oh, my," Marguerite said nervously.

Blond Leonie put an arm about the beautiful widow. "Do not let us frighten you, *chérie.* Once you have been fucked a few times by a few of the gentlemen, you will no longer consider that it is anything special. In fact, you will have to work hard to prevent yourself from being bored. That is why we know all manner of little tricks that keep us, and our guest, interested and interesting. And the men who come to Chez Renée come only by recommendation and invitation. Madame carefully screens them so there is little likelihood of troublemakers or dueling."

"What about the authorities?" Marguerite asked.

"Madame always has friends in high places. Sometimes King Louis comes to call," Josie said. "He likes Madame Renée. She speaks to him of the old days, of the *ancien régime* before the revolution. He is comfortable with her, and she understands him."

"I never knew," Marguerite said slowly.

"Why would you, *chérie.* You were a respectable married lady with problems of your own to manage. Tell me, how old is your little girl? Does she look like you?"

"Emilie is almost seven," Marguerite answered, "and Charles always said she looked like me. I wish I could send her to school in England, but her half-brother is an evil man. He has threatened my child."

"She will be safer here in Paris, where you have friends," Josie said firmly. "Now, what will you wear this evening?"

"I do not know," Marguerite said. "Tante Renée says she will have a gown for me. My wardrobe was not large, and with Charles ill these past few years, we did not entertain, so my clothing is simple."

"For a woman with a child, you have such an air of innocence about you," Leonie noted, almost enviously. "The men will be attracted to you like flies to a honey pot. They love seducing virtue."

"Her beauty complements ours," Josie remarked. "A redhead, a blond, and a brunette. Oh la la! *Quelle trio!*"

The others laughed. Leonie gave Marguerite a cup of the fragrant green tea, and she nibbled on a pastry of minced quail. It was, she thought, like being back at school again in England. Then the door opened, and Clarice entered the room.

"*Madame,* your aunt has sent up a gown for you. Come, and let me make certain it fits, but if not, I will need time to alter it. Her maid tells me you are to come to the salon tonight." Clarice's tone was disapproving.

"This is my faithful serving woman, Clarice," Marguerite said. "Clarice, Mademoiselle Leonie and Mademoiselle Josephine."

"Is that burly serving man with the twinkling eyes yours too?" Josie asked Marguerite.

"You keep your hands and your bold looks from my Louis, Mademoiselle Brazen!" Clarice snapped angrily. "We are a respectable married couple."

"Oh, dear," Leonie said, struggling not to giggle.

"It isn't my fault, *chérie,*" Josie replied pertly, "if a man looks at me and winks."

"Impudent baggage!" Clarice responded. "I'll scratch your eyes out if you toy with my man."

"I haven't time to trifle with a servant, *chérie,*" Josie answered her. "Not when there are so many rich gentlemen to entertain me and give me presents."

"Come, Clarice," her mistress said quickly, standing up. "I want to see the gown *Tante* has sent me to wear tonight. What color is it? Is it pretty?" She hurried her servant out the salon door.

"We shouldn't be here, my lady," Clarice said.

"Where else are we to go?" Marguerite asked quietly.

Clarice was silent.

"Tell me about the gown," Marguerite repeated.

"Lavender silk with a neckline that is, I think, far too low to be decent, but then I suppose that isn't its purpose, *madame,*" Clarice replied, her voice deprecating.

"No, you are right," Marguerite agreed as they climbed the stairs to her room. "The gown will have been made so I may show my wares to my aunt's visitors. I know little about shop-keeping, but I do know to sell an item one must display the goods prettily, Clarice."

"My lady! My lady!" Clarice almost moaned. "I do not know how you can do this!"

"I don't know either," Marguerite said, "but I know that I must." She opened the door to her room and stepped inside. "Let us look at this situation in a logical fashion, Clarice. If you remove morality from the equation, what is left? I have known a man. Now I will know a variety of men."

"But you loved his lordship, and you were his wife," Clarice protested. "You will not love these men."

"No, I will not," Marguerite replied, "and isn't that better? A workman has his tools. My tool is my body. I hope to use it well enough to earn my living with it. One day Tante Renée may choose to retire from the hurly-burly of Paris. When she does, if I have done well in my apprenticeship, I will take over her little enterprise. I shall never again be at the mercy of any man, Clarice. I know Charles did not mean to leave Emilie and me helpless, but he did. I cannot ever permit that to happen to us again. I have no parents or relations other than Tante Renée who can help me. Without her I would have died or starved, or worse. She gave up everything for me. Now I will do the same for my darling child. I realize that you do not approve of my decision, Clarice. I want you to stay with me, but if you feel you cannot, I will give you a reference now so you and Louis may seek employment elsewhere. Perhaps the new owners of my home might desire your services."

"As if we would leave you, my lady!" Clarice huffed.

"Then perhaps we should look at the gown now," her mistress suggested gently. This was difficult enough for her without her servant carping and fussing at her over her decisions. Did Clarice really think given another choice she would have taken this path? And now tonight she would be put on display to tempt the carnal appetites of strangers. Gentlemen who would be willing to pay her aunt good coin to use her body for their temporal pleasures.

She swallowed back a cry of despair. Yet her aunt was not forcing her to this. Indeed Renée was more than willing to support her without this sacrifice, but Marguerite knew she couldn't allow it. At sixteen her aunt, daughter of an aristocratic and noble family, had given up her virtue to save Marguerite from certain death. And for all of Marguerite's twenty-eight years Renée had labored as a courtesan, guaranteeing that her niece lived the life to which she had been born. Now Marguerite felt she had no choice but to do the same in order to protect her own daughter.

Clarice helped her into the gown Renée had chosen. It was very beautiful, but as Clarice had noted, the neckline was shockingly low, particularly given the fact that her little corset pushed her breasts up so high they were practically tumbling from the bodice.

"Oh, my," Marguerite said softly.

Clarice wisely held her tongue, but shook her head with open disdain.

Marguerite gazed at herself in the long mirror that was in a corner of her bedchamber. Her dress was of lavender watered silk with delicate black lace roses decorating the full skirt, and a matching black lace falling tucker that fell over the fitted bodice with its narrow waist. The sleeves were small and puffed, leaving her arms bare. Her breasts, despite the modest deception of the falling tucker, swelled over the top of the neckline. There were kid gloves to her elbow, dyed to match the gown, and fastened with a long row of tiny pearl buttons. And there was a black lace fan. On her feet she would wear black silk slippers. While she was not used to such elegance, Marguerite knew her gown had been designed in the latest fashion. There was nothing vulgar about it. Although the neckline was suggestive, wasn't that the idea? She sighed. "It's beautiful," she said.

"Needs a bit of a nip in the waist," Clarice remarked dryly. "Your aunt ain't the slip of a girl she once was."

Marguerite giggled. "Don't tell her that, I beg you," she pleaded with her servant.

"Can't fault a woman who houses me and Louis without a word of complaint," Clarice remarked. "She don't keep many servants, you know. Cook in the kitchen with a helper, a housemaid, two footmen, a wench to serve them two mademoiselles of hers, her own Bertilde, and Monsieur François. There's a mother and daughter who comes in daily to do the heavy cleaning. They're all well paid, fed, and housed to keep their mouths shut regarding the nature of this house, of course, and the two dailies don't know what goes on here, not that they would complain."

"You've obtained a great deal of information in just a day," Marguerite noted, unbuttoning her gloves and stripping them off as Clarice unfastened the gown.

"Best to know the lay of the land in a new situation," Clarice said tartly. "I'm happy to say that everyone is pleasant to deal with here, my lady. If here is where we're going to be for the rest of our lives, it's better to be friends with everyone."

"Yes, it is," Marguerite assented. "While they are different from the women I have known, I must admit that Leonie and Josie are really very nice, Clarice. They have promised to educate me with regard to, as they so delicately put it, their *little tricks*. After all, if I must be a whore, I should be a good one, eh?"

"Courtesan, *ma petite*," her aunt said, entering the room. "Whores are those poor souls walking the streets who can only fuck a man, but know nothing of how to entertain him elegantly, with charm and grace. Now, let me see the gown before Clarice takes it off of you."

Lady Abbott's maidservant rolled her eyes at Madame Renée's fine distinction, but she dutifully did up the gown's bodice again.

"It is a beautiful garment, *tante*," Marguerite said.

"*Mais oui, chérie,* and it certainly suits you," her aunt agreed. "The color is perfect, and in deference to your mourning, I have chosen a less potent color trimmed with black. It gives you a fragile look." Her blue eyes narrowed speculatively. "Men will, I think, want to protect you, *chérie*. A little training, and you will be a sensation." Then she continued in a brisk, no-nonsense voice. "Tonight you will come to the gold and white salon just before ten o'clock. You will seat yourself at the pianoforte and play. If I choose to introduce you to any gentleman, I will. Each will be advised before entering the salon that you are not for their amusement at this time. You are to be decorative, no more. And, *chérie*, only one man will really approach you tonight. That is the Duc de Caraville, César d'Aubert. I have chosen him to be your tutor, Marguerite. He will force you to nothing, so you need not be afraid of him, or any of the others for that matter. I do not allow ruffians in my house."

"Is he your lover, *tante?*" Marguerite asked, curious.

"On occasion, *oui,* he is," Renée responded frankly. "And you may believe me, *ma petite,* when I tell you that he is a marvelous and very skilled lover. He will awaken your senses, *chérie,* and give you a great deal of pleasure when and as he does. He is a most charming man as well."

"You like him then," Marguerite said.

"Yes, I do," her aunt answered.

"Is there a Duchess de Caraville, *tante?*"

"*Non.* César is too much of a sybarite to take a wife. He will probably always be. His brother has sons so the title will not go to waste."

"His family survived then," Marguerite said inquisitively.

"César's father saw the handwriting on the wall. He got his family, his servants, and his wealth out of France before the Terror," Renée replied. "He had a younger brother who had already gone to the Louisiana territories, somewhere near New Orleans." Renée turned to Clarice. "Alter the waist," she said. Then she advised her niece, "Get some rest, Marguerite. Tonight will be a very exciting evening for you, I promise."

The younger woman bit her lip briefly, and then she asked, "Am I to . . . I mean tonight . . . if he asks . . . with him?"

"Only if you want to, *chérie,*" Renée said with a smile, "but you really need only be decorative. César will not force the issue. But if not tonight, then one night very soon he will persuade you on your back, Marguerite. I promise you, *chérie,* after the first two or three men, it is very easy."

"I hope so," Marguerite said softly, but Renée was already gone out the door, her little heels clicking down the stairs.

Chapter Three

Marguerite sat at the walnut pianoforte in the gold and white salon, her slender fingers, sheathed in the lavender kid of her gloves, slipping easily across the black ebony and white ivory keys of the instrument. She played softly, her cornflower blue eyes every now and then looking up to sweep about the room. The gentlemen there tonight all wore the formal black evening attire made popular several years before by the Prince Regent of England. She could see that they were curious. Some nodded imperceptibly in her direction, and one or two of them sent a small smile her way. Marguerite didn't know if she should smile back, or even acknowledge them. *Sit and play,* her aunt had instructed her, and she did, her beautiful face an imperious mask to the men who studied it for a hint of just what kind of woman she was.

And nothing was as she had imagined it. She might have been in any aristocratic salon in Paris, or London for that matter. The voices in the room were low, and well modulated. Some gentlemen played whist at a beautiful little mahogany card table that had been brought out for them by a footman. Others sat with the three women, laughing and chatting. Marguerite played on. Now and again Josie or Leonie would depart the salon with a gentleman. And when they eventually reentered the chamber once again, it was discreetly, without fuss. If she had not known what the women were doing when they left, it would have all been quite ordinary.

But she did know what they were doing. Her aunt had been quite frank in disparaging her conjugal life with Charles. Renée had inferred that Marguerite had no idea what was really involved in making love with a man. Well, what else could there be but lying on her back with her eyes closed while her breasts were fumbled, and then to be penetrated by a cock? Seeing all this elegance and exaggerated refinement, Marguerite began to believe that her aunt was just painting a picture for her clients of something that did not really exist.

"*Bonsoir,* Mademoiselle Marguerite," a deep voice said, jerking her from her thoughts. "I am César d'Aubert." He leaned against the pianoforte lazily, his dark eyes plunging impudently into her shadowed cleavage.

Marguerite looked up, her cheeks burning to her mortification, but her voice was strong. "*Bonsoir, Monsieur le Duc,*" she replied.

"May I sit next to you, *mademoiselle?*" he asked politely.

"What if I said *non, Monsieur le Duc?*" she responded pertly, although she hardly felt bold.

"Then I should not sit," he murmured suavely. "If you prefer to inhabit the bench by yourself, *mademoiselle,* I am content to stand here admiring your beautiful breasts. I saw them last night while you slept. They are even lovelier than your aunt's bosom."

"*Monsieur le Duc!*" Marguerite didn't know whether to be angry or not. Despite appearances, this was not a respectable house.

"Eventually, my dear, I am going to fuck you," he told her frankly. "Tonight, and tomorrow, and perhaps even the evening after that we shall get to know one another better. You are very beautiful, *mademoiselle.* Look about you. All the gentlemen are eager to fuck you, but your aunt has said I shall be the first." He smiled at her winningly. "Now, *mademoiselle,* bring your pretty tune to an end. We are going to walk together, you and I, and I am going to see how well you can kiss."

"*Monsieur le Duc,*" Marguerite protested faintly, "my aunt has said that—"

"I know what Renée has promised you, my dear. I have promised her in turn that I will not force you to my will, and I will not. You have chosen a courtesan's life, *mademoiselle,* and it is advisable that sooner than later you spread your thighs to accept a sturdy cock. The longer you wait, the more your respectable nature will battle with the magnificent demimonde you are going to become," the duke said.

"I don't know . . ." she tried again to speak.

"I know you don't," he replied with a small chuckle, "but I promise you are going to learn, *mademoiselle,* and you are going to be very surprised by what you learn. Or are you really a little coward, and are going to allow Renée to continue to support you?"

"I am not a coward!" Marguerite replied indignantly, bringing her tune to a noisy end and standing up. "Lead on, *Monsieur le Duc!* I will follow, and I believe I kiss very well."

"We shall see," he responded, laughing, as he led her over into a secluded corner of the salon where they might sit upon a pale rose satin loveseat together. He put his arm about her waist in order to draw her closer.

Marguerite felt her heart begin to hammer erratically, particularly when he bent his head to kiss the tops of her breasts. *"Ohh!"* she exclaimed.

"Do not tell me no one has ever kissed your bosom before?" the duke said, surprised by her reaction.

"My husband. Sometimes. But certainly not when I was fully clothed, or in a public salon," Marguerite told him.

"My dear beautiful *mademoiselle,* I am astounded," the duke told her. "You are a most exquisite creature, and to realize that no one has ever appreciated your deliciousness is very amazing," the duke told her. "I shall worship each and every inch of you when the moment comes."

"Monsieur le Duc, I do not know what to say to such an extravagant bouquet of compliments," Marguerite said, her pale cheeks pink once more. "Do you always speak to women in such a fashion?"

"Non," he admitted, "but you bring out the poet in me, my lovely *mademoiselle."* Then he kissed her.

She had not seen it coming, although she realized that she should have. Did he not say he was going to kiss her? His lips were warm and firm against hers. For a moment she wasn't certain what to do, for no one other than Charles had ever kissed her. She felt guilty.

"You are holding back," he murmured against her mouth. "Are you feeling sinful, *ma petite courtesan?* Do not. Yield yourself to me, Marguerite. *Now!"*

His lips closed back over hers again, and to her surprise she felt a distinct thrill race down her backbone. *Charles was dead.* She was free to enjoy the addresses of this man, or any man who desired her for that matter. She let herself relax, and her lips softened against his, even as his fingers caressed the curve of her jaw and slid down the silky column of her throat.

"Much better," he approved, tipping her heart-shaped face up to meet his gaze. "Next, *ma petite,* you will give me your tongue."

"*What?*" What on earth did he want with her tongue?

César d'Aubert laughed, genuinely amused. It was practically like instructing a virgin, which he had done once or twice in his life. "I want you to put your tongue in my mouth, and I shall put mine in yours," he explained. "You will find it exciting. Later on I shall show you the many other things a tongue can do to amuse lovers." He drew her close again, his lips meeting hers, his tongue swiftly darting past her teeth and into the warm cavity of her mouth to meet her tongue.

The touch of it made her weak with excitement, Marguerite thought dizzily. Her darling Charles had certainly never done this amatory thing. Indeed Charles's kisses had been most chaste in comparison with the duke's hot embraces. And very much to her surprise, Marguerite was discovering that she liked this virtual stranger's advances. Daringly she plunged her own tongue into his mouth to play with his. The two fleshy organs writhed and twisted about each other in a heightening frenzy of excitement.

The duke felt his male member growing harder and harder within the confines of his trousers. He was very surprised that his partner was able to accomplish this feat under the circumstances. He drew away slightly, enchanted by the bemused look in her cornflower blue eyes. Then taking her little gloved hand, he placed it squarely upon the bulge in his trousers, saying as he did so, "You must always accept the responsibility, *ma petite,* for your deliciously naughty actions." Then he began to kiss her again with slow, burning kisses that quite left her weak and feeling very helpless.

Marguerite yielded easily now to his passion, only crying out slightly when his hand thrust past the silk and lace of her bodice to fondle her breast. "Ahhh," she murmured as his thumb and forefinger began to roll a nipple between them. Her bosom felt suddenly swollen, and her bodice tight. She could actually feel moisture between her thighs. Her cheeks were hot and flushed.

She knew if she could not draw a deep breath, she was going to swoon in his arms. She pulled her head away from his. *"Monsieur le Duc,* you are overwhelming me!" she told him prettily. "You must stop now!"

His dark eyes met her lighter ones. "I do not want to wait, Mademoiselle Marguerite. I want to take you upstairs *now!"* he groaned.

"Non! Non! I could not. Not *now.* I am practically fainting with your attentions. I have never been approached so audaciously. I know what I am becoming, but we have just met tonight. I am sure I am not ready yet to be intimate. Remember what you promised my aunt, *Monsieur le Duc.* You are an honorable man, I know." She gently, but firmly, removed his hand from her bodice.

"Remain by my side," he commanded her, "while I regain my composure. *Sacrebleu, ma petite!* I have never been aroused so quickly by any woman as I have been by you."

"You flatter me, *monsieur,"* Marguerite told him. He had never been so aroused? To tell the truth, neither had she! Were all other men like César d'Aubert? She suspected not from what Josie and Leonie had said to her previously. Suddenly she realized that it could be very interesting finding out. She looked quickly about the room. The twin princes were eyeing her speculatively. What was it like to be taken by two men at one time, she wondered? And how was such a thing accomplished? She would have a lot of questions for her two companions. As much as she loved and trusted her aunt, she was not quite comfortable asking such intimate questions of Renée, who had after all been like her mother.

The lady in question now joined them, seating herself to the duke's right, her black silk skirts falling across his dark trousered leg. "I see," she noted, archly eyeing the still stiff protuberance in his crotch, "that my niece has pleased you, César." She patted the bulge mischievously.

"I would go upstairs with her now, but for my promise to you both," the duke said.

"I have not yet chosen a bedroom for her there," Renée told him calmly. "A perfect jewel must have her own perfect setting, eh?"

"I would take her here, on this settee," the duke growled.

"Now, César, you know we do not use my salon for lustful pursuits except on St. Valentine's Day, but of course, that will happen next month."

"You do it here?" Marguerite said, shocked.

"It is a custom of this house that on St. Valentine's Day the gentlemen who come pick one of the girls, and then they all pleasure themselves with her here in the salon. It is our tribute to Eros himself, *ma petite*. I think you and the duke had best chart your path soon for I suspect you, being our new treasure, will be chosen this year to offer such sacrifices to the god and goddess of love."

Marguerite swallowed hard. *"All the gentlemen?"*

"Those who are here tonight," her aunt replied calmly.

"I don't think I could—" Marguerite began.

"Of course you can." Renée waved her protest aside. "By the time the evening is over, you will have been well fucked in every way imaginable, *ma petite*. So, you had best begin learning your lessons from César very soon, *chérie*."

Able to stand now, the duke arose, and kissed first Marguerite's hand then Renée's. "Until tomorrow, *mademoiselle*," he told the younger woman, his glance burning. Then he walked away to engage the redheaded Josie in brief conversation, and shortly thereafter led her upstairs.

"She will pay, my poor Josie, for your refusal," Renée laughed softly. "How nice you were able to rouse him so well. I knew he would be the right tutor for you, *ma petite*. Now go upstairs to your chaste bed, *chérie*. I will have to decide tomorrow which bedchamber is to be yours. César will not wait longer than that, I can see."

"Charles never kissed me like the duke did," Marguerite said.

"Husbands never kiss their wives like they kiss their other women," Renée replied. "I will never understand why a man thinks the woman he has chosen to wed, and bear his children, couldn't possibly be interested in lustful pursuits with him. But I should have little business if that were not so, ma petite. Women like to fuck every bit as much as men do, but wives, it seems, are taught not to admit to such a thing. A man wants to see a bit of enthusiasm when he sports himself, yet let a poor wife show any emotion, and her master begins to wonder if she is respectable, or what she has been up to with another man while he was at his club. Faagh! Men can be such fools."

"Charles was always faithful to me," Marguerite said softly.

"I am glad," Renée answered her niece, knowing better but keeping silent. There was no need to spoil Marguerite's pure memories, for Lord Abbott had indeed loved his young wife. "I hope you will not feel guilty now that you have chosen to follow in my footsteps, *ma petite*. You were a good wife to your husband, but he is dead now. There is no law that says a widow must shut herself away for the remainder of her life. Particularly a young and beautiful widow."

"I liked the duke's kisses," Marguerite admitted, "and I will not feel sinful because of what I am doing."

"Good!" her aunt approved, and she stood up. "Go upstairs now, *chérie*. You have done very well. The gentlemen are all agog with your presence. They eagerly await their chance with you, but you do need to learn a few little tricks first." Renée kissed her niece on both cheeks as she drew the younger woman up from the settee. *"Bonsoir, ma petite."*

"Bonsoir, tante," Marguerite responded, and she hurried from the salon and up the stairs. As she reached the next landing, Josie popped from her chamber and called to her.

"Marguerite, come a moment." Then she disappeared back into her room.

The inside of Josie's bedroom was the color of a seashell, all peachy pink with white and gold furnishings. And on the far wall of the room was an enormous bed, its headboard painted with all manner of nymphs and satyrs cavorting about, and its draperies of velvet, held with heavy gold cord. In the center of the bed the duke lay sprawled, quite naked. Josie was attired in little more than a diaphanous gauze robe. The air in the room was fragrant with lilies. A fire blazed in the fireplace, the flickering candles giving the chamber a soft golden glow. Marguerite stood frozen momentarily, like a deer caught by hunters. Her startled gaze was held by the duke's dark eyes.

"I want you to join us," he said quietly.

"I . . . *cannot,*" she half whispered.

"Of course you can," Josie said, slipping an arm about

Marguerite's waist, her other hand stroking her friend's cheek soothingly. "It will be very nice, I promise you."

"I think I am afraid," Marguerite confessed, feeling her cheeks begin to burn. The duke's organ was . . . was . . . much larger than Charles's had been. Was he deformed? Or had her husband's member been small?

"You don't have to be fearful, *chérie,*" Josie answered her. "César really wants to fuck you. I thought that if you did it with a friend encouraging you this first time, it would be easier for you. After all, you've never whored before, and the first time is always the hardest. You don't have to if you really don't want to, but waiting for just the right moment seems rather foolish." Josie's hand rubbed the back of Marguerite's neck in a calming fashion.

"Would my *tante* object? Does she not want me to wait?" *Sacrebleu!* She couldn't take her eyes off the duke's cock. She was mesmerized by it.

"Madame is just being kind because she knows what a hard decision this has been for you, but she will not be angry if you leap boldly into these uncharted waters. Especially with César, and with me," Josie purred. "I can see that you are curious." Her fingers began to unfasten the little pearl buttons at the back of Marguerite's bodice. Drawing the garment quickly off, she lay it aside. Then she undid Marguerite's skirts, and they fell to the carpet with a soft whoosh. Smiling into her friend's eyes, Josie turned her head and kissed Marguerite's lips lightly. Then she took the other woman's hands and encouraged her to step from the puddle of fabric, but not before she had undone the tapes holding Marguerite's petticoats to her corset.

"*Mon Dieu!*" Marguerite cried softly, realizing she was now wearing only her little brocaded corsets, stockings, garters, and slippers.

The duke arose from the bed, coming over to kiss the startled young woman softly. "You may go if you choose," he murmured in her ear. "Rape does not entice me, *mademoiselle.*" Reaching down, he fondled her bare buttocks.

Marguerite swallowed hard. "But seduction is an entirely different thing, eh, *monseigneur?*" she returned. His big hand was warm against her skin.

He laughed softly. *"Mais oui,"* he agreed, his dark eyes meeting her blue ones.

"Don't you want to be fucked?" Josie asked. "You may take my word for it that César is very good at it. I will be here to comfort and aid you, *chérie."* Meeting no resistance, she began to unlace Marguerite's corset. When she had finished, she drew it off, crying out as she did, "Ohh, what pretty bubbies you have! Are they not quite the loveliest you have ever seen, César? They are so perfectly round, and will fit into your palms quite nicely." She took Marguerite's hand in hers. "Come along," Josie encouraged. "The bed is more than big enough for the three of us."

Marguerite's eyes went to the bed. She swallowed hard again. She knew that if she decided at this very moment to leave Josie's room, the duke would not protest her going. He would bide his time, and Renée would be patient with her. Yet what was to be gained by waiting? She was either going to follow in her aunt's footsteps, or she was going to let Renée purchase that damned cottage in Brittany. And what would be there for her in Brittany? A respectable marriage? With whom? Some local landowner who needed an unpaid servant to raise his children? A retired officer with a pension barely enough to cover his own needs, let alone a wife? Or would she remain here in Paris and become a courtesan?

"Do you know how exciting you are standing there in your little slippers and black stockings?" the duke asked her. He knelt and, unfastening her garters, rolled the stockings off her legs and over each foot. Then his hands closed about her buttocks, and he buried his face in her thick, dark bush.

Marguerite's eyes widened in surprise. A small noise, not quite a gasp and not quite a cry, escaped her.

"I would tell him to behave himself," Josie chuckled, "but alas, Marguerite, he doesn't know how. Let us get on the bed now, or he will kneel there all night with his head in your pussy." She drew her companion over to the bed and, climbing onto it, pulled Marguerite with her.

Stay or go? the voice in her head asked. But it was too late now to go, she decided. Josie had settled herself with several large pillows behind her back. She had drawn Marguerite up between her plump thighs and was starting to fondle her breasts while she murmured endearments to her friend. "You've never been touched by a woman, have you, *chérie?* But it is nice, isn't it? We are not rough with each other. Ahh, *chérie,* what soft skin you have!" The duke joined them, almost crawling up from the foot of the bed and kneeling before the two women, enchanted by the tableau they offered.

"Spread your legs for him, *chérie,*" Josie said low in Marguerite's ear. "If you do, he will do something very nice to you, I promise." She kissed her friend's ear, her tongue teasing it for a brief moment.

Fascinated, Marguerite complied with the request. It was all so very strange, but Josie's gentle voice and hands were mesmerizing. She was beginning to feel quite languorous. Why wasn't she embarrassed? Or at least ashamed? But she wasn't. Josie continued to play with her breasts, and her voice was somehow reassuring. Marguerite watched the duke, who sat back on his heels, staring at the space between her open legs for what seemed to be a very long moment. Then he spoke.

"Show me your treasures, *chérie,*" he said. "Take your fingers, and draw your nether lips apart for me. Yes. That is it. Now keep them just as you are doing. Do not move unless I tell you. You have no idea how beautiful you are there. I have never seen such perfection." He moved himself forward, and she suddenly felt him stroking her with something.

"*Mon Dieu!*" she cried out, realizing he was licking at her with his tongue. "*What are you doing!*" She tried to struggle, but his hands gripped her hips tightly.

"*Stay still!*" he growled at her.

"It's all right, *chérie,*" Josie assured her. "Do not be afraid. Close your eyes, and feel how nice it is. A man with a facile tongue is truly a blessing, and César is quite expert at what he does."

Ignoring every instinct she had, Marguerite forced her eyes to close, and tried to relax once more. There were so many sensations. Josie's hands were lovely as they fondled and played with her flesh. The duke's tongue was indeed skilled at sending thrills throughout her entire body. It was all so very wicked. Yet she could not help herself. She was actually beginning to enjoy these carnal attentions, she realized. Then his tongue found her love button. Once Charles had touched her there. It had been heavenly, but Charles had said afterward that a good woman should not react in such an enthusiastic fashion as she had. He had never again touched her there. She knew now, however, that showing unbridled excitement for her two companions would please them greatly.

"*Mon Dieu!*" she moaned as his wicked tongue flicked relentlessly back and forth over her sentient flesh. This was divine! This was what she had always wanted. And then she was overwhelmed with a wave of delight that filled her from her toes to the top of her head. "*Mais oui! Mais oui!*" she cried excitedly.

"Ohh, *chérie,* that is so good, isn't it? I can see you are quite ready. Tell him you want to be fucked, Marguerite! Tell him!"

"He knows!" she heard herself cry out. She opened her eyes and smiled boldly at César d'Aubert.

Immediately the duke mounted her, his member penetrating her enthusiastically as Josie continued to hold her against her ample breasts. His big cock filled her, and sent her senses reeling. It was wonderful, and she couldn't get enough of him. Within moments she was coming, her juices flowing, her body quivering, but the duke was not yet satisfied. He gently pushed her aside, pistoning Josie until the fiery-headed girl was crying with her own pleasure and the duke was momentarily satisfied. They lay together in a tangle of arms and legs as at last their breathing quieted. And then there was silence.

Finally Josie jumped up from the bed, walking saucily across her bedchamber, her cone-shaped breasts bouncing. "We need some wine," she said. She poured two goblets, took a sip from one, and then brought them over to the bed where the duke and Marguerite still lay. "I must bathe quickly and get back to the salon, *chéries.* We have a full house tonight. It will not do for me to leave Leonie with all the gentlemen." She hurried over to a basin, poured water into it, and taking up a soft cloth, began to wash herself. "Always after a bout of Eros, *chérie,*" she instructed Marguerite. "After all, you have to remember that you'll be entertaining more than one gentleman of an evening, and they all love a pretty pussy. You don't want to leave any reminders of a past liaison, *ma petite.*"

Marguerite gazed at her wide-eyed as Josie nattered on. She watched as the duke casually got up from the bed to help Josie with her laces and her buttons. Then as she was leaving her bedroom, Josie gave her friend a wink.

"Take her upstairs, César. I'll need my bed again soon enough," and she was gone out the door humming.

Finishing her wine, Marguerite arose from the bed. "The maid will straighten the bed," she said.

"Of course. I will have her bring your garments upstairs." He pulled her into his embrace. "You were quite delicious, *ma petite*. Almost uninhibited, I think. I am going to teach you a great deal, and I shall enjoy doing it. Now run along, and get some rest. I shall tell Madame that we have made a nice beginning. Next time, however, I want the entire night, and I want you all to myself. Do you understand, *chérie?*"

"Give me my petticoat, *Monsieur le Duc*. I cannot walk naked through the corridor," she said.

"Why not?" he demanded, leering just slightly.

"Because my maid and her husband share the top floor with me, and I would not embarrass Louis by appearing *au natural.*"

"You are such a lady, Marguerite, I wonder if we will ever make a good whore of you," the duke noted as he handed her her garment.

"You claim to be an excellent teacher, *monsieur*. Let us see what you can do with me. I am now curious to try the other gentlemen, you see, so you cannot take forever."

He grinned at her. "Perhaps you do have possibilities, *mademoiselle*. We shall see."

"*Bonsoir, monsieur,*" she told him, and then hurried from Josie's bedchamber upstairs to her own room.

There she found Clarice awaiting her, asleep in her chair. She awoke her maidservant, instructing her, "Find Louis, and have him fetch me water for a bath."

Clarice nodded, but said nothing. Her disapproving glare was more than enough for Marguerite. I will be damned if I am going to argue with her, Marguerite thought. She knows our situation. Did she really expect me to change my mind, and continue to live off my aunt's generosity? I am no longer a child! She climbed into her bed while Clarice set up the porcelain hipbath.

Hearing Louis with the two footmen in the corridor outside, Clarice snapped at her mistress, "Pull up those covers, my lady.

You don't need to go showing your wares like them two others downstairs! After all, these ain't paying customers."

Marguerite almost laughed aloud, but she restrained herself and meekly drew the coverlet up to her chin.

The three men staggered into the little bedroom, and emptied their buckets into the bath.

"Another trip will do it," Louis said to his wife.

"No need," Clarice replied sharply. "My mistress can wash in what you've brought. Now get out, all of you!" She hustled them to the door and, closing it behind them, bolted it tightly. "Don't trust those two scurvy footmen," she said irritably. "Come along now, madame, and let us get the stink of that duke off you."

"How do you know it was the duke?" Marguerite asked as she climbed from her bed and into the little tub.

"He made it quite plain that he would be the first," Clarice said. "Ohh, the shame of it! That the daughter of the noble Comte and Comtesse de Thierry should fall so low! There might have been a time when he offered for you, my lady."

"Never!" Marguerite told her servant. "The de Thierrys were noble, but the duke has royalty in his ancestry. Besides, I am not even certain that I like him. Now give me the soap, Clarice, and see that my night garment is warm."

Afterward as she lay in her bed, clean, dry, and warm, Marguerite realized that she had come closer to the truth than she had expected. Of course she didn't really know César d'Aubert, but she had already decided that while his manners were flawless, and while he was certainly handsome, he was also arrogant. His only interest in Marguerite was in being the first to possess the body of a respectable widow brought low. He wanted nothing more of her than that. For a moment she felt a curl of anger, and then she laughed to herself in the darkness. A woman in her position didn't fuck a man for love. She did it for money. And sometimes perhaps for her own pleasure. Only now, at this moment, did she fully comprehend the sacrifice Renée had made for her.

She would make that same sacrifice for her daughter, and pray to God that Emilie would never be put in their position. She was wide awake, her thoughts tumbling about her head. She finally understood how she was going to bear this. The men who would use her body didn't matter. She would care nothing for any of them. Whores, and her mind recoiled from the harsh word, *courtesans,* she superseded the former colloquialism with the more elegant word, courtesans did not have emotions. Giving herself to a variety of gentlemen was merely a professional duty. And until she became bored like Leonie and Josie, and even her dear Tante Renée, she would enjoy what she was doing when she could. And her elegant breeding and background would but add a piquancy to her actions.

To her surprise, when she finally slept she awoke late, and it was her aunt who aroused her. *"Bonjour, ma petite,"* Renée greeted her as she sat herself upon the edge of the bed. "What a naughty minx you were, or so both Josie and the duke say. What made you change your mind?"

"Josie suggested it would be easier the first time if I was with a friend. She was right, *tante.* It was. And since this is the life I have chosen, it seemed foolish to further delay my debut."

Renée nodded. "Very wise, *chérie.* The duke says you show great promise. He will arrive tonight, and has requested that you keep him company for the entire evening. What do you think?"

Marguerite nodded. "Tonight, yes, *tante,* but after that I wish to join you and the others in the salon. I have no desire to become the exclusive possession of the Duc de Caraville. While I may lack experience, common sense would tell me that there is only so much he may teach me. I am curious to experience the others."

"Yet if César wanted to take you for his mistress, *chérie,"* Renée mused, "would that not be better for you? You could maintain your dignity as his mistress."

"I should rather follow in your footsteps, *tante,* than ever again be at the mercy of one man. I know Charles loved me, and that he thought he was protecting us, but he wasn't. And then I foolishly trusted the village *avocat,* and then my stepson. Now I will trust no one but myself, *tante.* Last night I lay in the arms of a courtesan while I allowed a man, not my husband, to make love to me. There is no going back for me now. I have set my course, and I will follow it."

"Very well," Renée said. "Now, *ma petite,* I have chosen a bedroom for you on the floor below. When I have gotten you up, I will show you. Come! Come!" She took her niece's hand and pulled her from the bed.

Laughing, Marguerite slipped her feet into her slippers and followed Renée downstairs. The room her aunt had chosen for her was at the corner of the house, and overlooked the gardens. The wooden floor was covered in a floral Aubusson carpet in shades of cream and gold. The painted panels on the walnut walls showed scenes of erotic play that featured ancient gods and goddesses sporting with their nymph and satyr companions, as well as exotic birds and beasts. The moldings about the panels were painted gold. The warm walnut furniture was decorated in cream and gold leaf. The centerpiece of the room—a great bed with a padded headboard of cream and gold striped silk that matched the bed's draperies—immediately caught Marguerite's eye.

"Lie on the bed a moment," Renée said to her niece.

Marguerite complied, and looking up, she saw the wooden canopy was painted with a wickedly sensual scene. Across a turquoise ocean with its cream and gold tipped waves, Neptune, the god of the sea, rode a great silver porpoise while a golden-haired mortal female in his grip sat facing him while being vigorously used by the god, even as he bent forward to suckle upon the girl's plump rosy breasts. Mermaids and their mermen swam about them, encouraging their master in his love play. "It's beautiful," Marguerite said, "and very suggestive, *tante,* as it is undoubtedly supposed to be." She sat up. "I think black satin upon the bed. It will accentuate my fair skin, don't you think?"

Renée nodded slowly and then she said, "What has happened to you, *ma petite?* You are suddenly almost callous."

"How should I be, *tante?* Did you really enjoy all the men that you have ever had over the years?"

"No, of course not," Renée replied, "but I assure you that each one believed he was the best lover I ever knew, Marguerite. You may play the cold-hearted madame in the salon, but in this room you must be all fire and excitement so that each man who makes love to you believes that he, and he alone, was able to breach your defenses to reach your heart," the older woman advised. "And there will be times when a man amuses you, or gives you real pleasure. You will be grateful for those times. You must never, however, feel guilty, *chérie.* Now, tell me, how did you like the duke?"

"In comparison with Charles, more vigorous, and I was indeed surprised by the emotions he aroused in me. Or perhaps it was Josie's gentle seduction. I do not know. However, whether I like him or dislike him, I cannot be certain," Marguerite admitted frankly.

"You need do neither, *ma petite,*" her aunt said. "Trust me when I tell you he is an expert lover, *and* he will never be cruel. Some men you will find care only for their own pleasure, but César gains equal pleasure from giving pleasure to the woman he is with. You could not have a better tutor. Now, I am starving! You are to remain here. I will have Clarice and Louis bring your possessions downstairs. They may continue to live where they now are. I shall have a *petit déjeuner* sent up to you immediately. You are much too thin, *ma petite,* and a gentleman likes a woman with a little meat on her bones."

"When will I be able to see Emilie?" Marguerite asked her aunt.

"On Sunday, *chérie.* We will both go to visit the convent. On Sunday we do not, as you may recall, receive visitors," Renée replied. Then she hurried from the room.

Marguerite now began a thorough inspection of her new bedroom. There were marvelous draperies of gold velvet at the windows. There was a huge armoire and a bureau to match the bed. There was a loveseat in cream satin sprigged with gold fleur de lis, several tables, and side chairs. The lamps were crystal, Irish, she thought. Curious, she opened the armoire, and discovered to her surprise that there were several beautiful gowns in it, including the gown she had worn the previous evening. There were matching slippers as well set neatly beneath the skirts. Investigating her surroundings further, she pulled the drawers of the bureau open to find exquisite silk corsets, drawers of both silk and fine lawn, house robes folded neatly, beautiful stockings, and a whole array of garters.

Clarice entered carrying a tray, Louis in her wake with his mistress's small trunk, which he placed by an elegant dressing table. Then bowing, he backed from the room.

"Come and eat your breakfast, although this is an odd time for a breakfast," Clarice said. "Louis and me ate hours ago."

"We will keep odd hours now, I fear. Where are the rest of my things?" Marguerite asked her maid.

"Madame instructed us to bring only the very personal items, my lady. She said you had all the clothing you would need here. I packed everything away in case we should need it someday. I brought your jewelry, Mademoiselle Emilie's miniature, your combs, brushes, and the like." She curtsied.

"Thank you, Clarice." Marguerite sat down at a small table and, lifting the napkin on the tray, suddenly realized she was very hungry. The tray held two perfectly poached eggs in a sauce flavored with dill, several flaky croissants, a little crock of sweet butter, and another of raspberry jam. And there was her aunt's favorite Turkish coffee. Marguerite smiled. She had never really been able to get used to the India tea her husband so loved. She set about to eat her meal with enthusiasm.

"Glad to see your appetite's back," Clarice noted approvingly. "You've been real peckish since his lordship died, and come to think of it, you didn't eat a great deal at all in his last months. I may not approve of what you're doing, my lady, but being with your aunt again is good for you."

"She says gentlemen like a woman with meat on their bones," Marguerite giggled.

"Well, if anyone would know what a man likes, it would be Madame Renée," Clarice agreed. "She's certainly made a success of knowing what a gentleman wants."

Marguerite finished her meal, and decided to nap. The house was very quiet, and they would not all meet until early next evening. And at ten o'clock the guests would begin arriving. The duke would expect his latest plaything to be ready, and waiting. Tomorrow she would join the others in the salon, she had told her aunt. She hoped that she would be ready for such an adventure. She must learn all she could tonight from César d'Aubert.

Chapter Four

Opening the door to Marguerite's bedchamber, the Duc de Caraville stared appreciatively at the tableau that greeted his dark eyes. The budding courtesan lay sprawled and naked upon her bed; her milky white skin in sharp contrast to the black satin covering beneath her. Her black hair tumbled about her shoulders. An equally thick thatch of dark curls adorned the mont between her shapely thighs. About her slender throat was a narrow band of blood red velvet. The entire room was bathed in a golden glow from the many candles that burned. More candles than he had ever before seen. The air was heavy with the scent of summer lilies.

César d'Aubert closed the door behind him. A slow smile lit his handsome face. He nodded his approval as for the first time he got a really good look at Marguerite. She was absolutely exquisite, and it seemed a shame to him that a woman of noble breeding should have come to this. She was not tall, and she was very daintily made, but she had wonderful breasts as he had previously noted; generous, though not overgenerous hips; a neat little waistline; and slim feet. She was, he thought, as perfect as any woman could be.

"So this is why you did not come to the salon," he remarked, walking over to the bed and seating himself next to her.

"I thought it unnecessary to be there tonight," she replied in cool measured tones. "After all, everyone knows of your arrangement with Tante Renée, monseigneur, and I wanted to prepare a little surprise for you alone, *my first lover*. Are you pleased?"

"The effect is quite satisfying," he told her. "Now, *chérie*, spread yourself open for me, using the third and fourth fingers of each hand. Then with a single second finger you will play with your little love button while I undress. We have a long night ahead of us." He stood up and began to disrobe. First he removed his black evening tailcoat and set it aside, loosening his white cravat to lay it atop the coat. "You are not playing with yourself, *chérie*," he scolded, his voice slightly disapproving. He unbuttoned his black and white brocaded waistcoat.

"I have never done it before," Marguerite slowly answered him.

"There is a first time for everything as you will soon learn, *ma petite*. Now, obey me!"

"And if I do not?" she demanded of him, her look both curious and defiant.

The duke lay the waistcoat on the chair with his other garments. "Marguerite, this is not a battle of wills between us. You wish to become a courtesan, and so it is your duty to please me in any way that I request. Now take your finger, and begin. You will not be ready for the next step until you do."

Hesitantly she touched herself, never imagining that she could actually do such a thing, but she did.

"Don't watch yourself," he instructed her. "Watch me, and let your little finger have its way." He undid his pleated-front white shirt, putting it with his other things. Then he sat down to remove his shoes and stockings.

She watched him, both fascinated and repelled. A tiny tingle of excitement was beginning to arise from deep within her. The duke stood up and undid his trousers. He had a broad smooth chest and a narrow waist. Beneath the black trousers he wore white silk drawers, which he also removed. His buttocks were firm, and when he turned about, she saw again his male member. Even at rest it was large, and long. *No.* Charles had not been either as large, or as lengthy.

Bracing himself, one arm on either side of her, the duke leaned down and found Marguerite's mouth. He kissed her slowly and deliberately. She could feel the heat from his big body as his tongue began to play with hers. She suddenly realized that her fingers were wet with her own arousal. It was at that moment he thrust two fingers inside her, murmuring against her mouth as he did, "Do not stop playing with yourself while I frig you a bit, *chérie*."

Marguerite felt his fingers thrusting within her even as her own fingers teased at her excited flesh. A low moan escaped her.

She moved her hips in order to facilitate his actions and her own enjoyment more. His lips moved to her ear, and he murmured to her, "Little whore! How you are relishing this, aren't you?"

"*Yes!*" she admitted, and then protested as he removed his fingers and, pushing her hands aside, pinched her love button sharply.

"You do not come, *chérie*, unless I allow you to come," he said in a stern voice. Then sucking suggestively on his fingers a moment, he rolled over onto his back saying, "You must learn to pleasure me in a similar fashion, Marguerite. Put yourself between my legs now. I shall teach you to lick my balls and suck on my cock. Your aunt is quite skilled at that pursuit. I hope you will be too. Come, *ma petite,* and if you do well, I shall give you your first fucking of the evening, although it shall by no means be the last."

She did as he had asked her, getting between his long legs, but she looked at him for further instructions.

"Kneel forward," he said to her. "Lift my cock with one hand to hold it out of the way, and use your tongue on me. Ahh, yes, *chérie,* that is nice. *Very nice!* How warm your little tongue is."

He was faintly hairy there, but the task was not entirely unpleasant, Marguerite decided. In fact it was rather exciting to be using her tongue on such an intimate male part. Daringly she opened her mouth, and took his pouch in between her lips. Her tongue flicked relentlessly about the flesh, feeling most distinctly the round twin spheres contained therein. She could feel his male member within her hand growing larger and throbbing between her fingers. He groaned but the sound was one of distinct pleasure.

"*Mon Dieu,* you little bitch! Who taught you so well? Let me free before I waste my cream," the duke ordered her, gasping to restrain himself from exploding with excitement. "I thought you had never done this before."

"I haven't," Marguerite said, and unable to help herself, she swept her tongue up his now rock-hard love lance.

César d'Aubert shuddered, yet he somehow managed to hold on to his vaunted control. "You have, it would seem, a predilection for this sort of amusement, *chérie,*" he said through gritted teeth. "I shall tell your aunt. *Mon Dieu!* Cease this moment! I cannot wait, and I must fuck you now!" He pushed Marguerite onto her back, and was upon her in an instant, entering her body in a single smooth move. *"Ahhh!"* he groaned, and he began to piston her enthusiastically.

Marguerite wrapped her arms and legs about the duke, closing her eyes as she did so. My God, she thought, I am already bored with him. Is this how it is to be with all men now? I suppose it must, for I feel no love in my heart any longer, and I never again will, but he must be more than satisfied if I am to be a success. She moaned convincingly, crying out his name, *"César!"* Could she come? Yes, she could, and that made it all the more convincing. He had engaged her body nicely, and Marguerite shuddered with pleasure as he poured his juices into her, gasping with his own pleasure.

Rolling off her, the duke closed his eyes, and within a minute he was asleep, exhausted from their efforts. A lover, obviously, was not much different from a husband, Marguerite thought. Of course, in the duke's case he would awaken and want more. Josie and Leonie were right. There was very little to this profession she had chosen, but her aunt was right too. What would set her aside from the others would be her breeding and her charm, which she was certain the duke would share with the other gentlemen. She closed her eyes, but she did not sleep. Remembering Josie's advice of the previous evening, Marguerite arose and, finding the basin and pitcher, bathed herself so that she would be fresh and ready for the duke when he awoke.

Hearing a faint tap at the door, she went over and opened it. Both Josie and Leonie were outside. They put a finger to their lips and beckoned her. Not considering her nakedness, she followed them down the hall to Josie's bedchamber. Inside she found both the count and the baron.

"Marco and Ernst have to leave Paris tomorrow," Leonie explained.

"And they wanted a little taste before they departed," Josie continued. "It will be months before they come back, Marguerite."

"But the duke has arranged with my *tante,*" Marguerite began.

"He always sleeps for two hours afterwards," Leonie said.

"There is time, and he needn't know, nor Madame either, unless you wish to tell her tomorrow." She smiled her pretty smile.

"Will we get in trouble with my *tante?*" Marguerite asked.

"Non, non," Josie said, and then she explained, "The baron and the count pay Madame a yearly fee, like all of the gentlemen who come here do. It is like a club, and as no money exchanges hands on a daily basis, Madame cannot be accused technically of running a brothel. It also allows Madame to pay her bribes promptly, which keep the authorities from our door."

"What of guests like the duke's cousin, the American?" Marguerite asked.

"Guests are rarely allowed, and must be preapproved by Madame. She insists on meeting them for luncheon in the Bois, and then always asks when they arrive if the rules have been carefully explained, and if they will abide by them," Leonie elucidated.

"A paid member of Chez Renée can visit as often as he chooses," Josie said. "Now, will you honor Marco and Ernst? Oh, do not say you will refuse them," she pleaded prettily.

"I am still very new at this, *messieurs,*" Marguerite said, but she was eyeing both men speculatively. Each had a little quirk, if Josie and Leonie were to be believed, but if they stayed with her, she wouldn't be fearful. "You will remain?" she asked.

"Of course," Josie said. "We don't want Madame to know that we've been naughty until after the fact."

"Were you naughty with the Duc de Caraville, *mademoiselle?*" the baron questioned her. He was an attractive man of medium height, blond, blue-eyed, and stocky.

"He seemed to think so," Marguerite answered, lowering her gaze.

"Tell me," the baron purred, slipping an arm about her and drawing her close by his side. "Whisper in my ear." A hand fondled her breast.

Marguerite leaned over and murmured softly in Baron Amalhardt's ear. When she had finished, she licked the ear provocatively.

The baron smiled a slow smile. *"Ach du lieber, fraulein,* you have been very naughty indeed. I regret that you must be spanked." He removed his coat.

"Oh, baron, must I?" Marguerite said, pretending to be afraid.

Josie and Leonie looked at each other delightedly. Marguerite was behaving exactly as the baron would wish, as they had carefully explained to her this afternoon.

The baron sat down on Josie's bed, dragging the seemingly reluctant Marguerite with him. "Over my knee with you, *fraulein!*" he said briskly, and then his big hand descended onto her bottom with a loud smack. *"Gott in himmil,"* the baron cried in delight. "This is a *derrière* worthy of me!" He smacked her again, and yet again.

Marguerite wiggled her hips and cried convincingly, but her companions had not lied when they said it really didn't hurt, but her flesh was certainly being well warmed by the baron's hard hand. As he spanked her, Marguerite could see from her slight vantage that Leonie had undone the count's trousers and was kneeling before him. His cock between her rosy lips, she suckled upon him.

And then the baron was standing up and pulling Marguerite with him across the room to bend her forward over a round marble-topped table. "Spread your legs, *fraulein,*" he growled in her ear, and when she had, he entered her love sheath from behind, and began to pestle her with his thick, hard member, while his hand fondled her two breasts. She came three times in quick succession, but then the baron withdrew from her. His place was taken by the count. In that brief moment Marguerite remembered that the Italian nobleman preferred Sodom's portal to Venus's.

She turned her head and gasped to him, "You will be the first there, *monsieur*. Be gentle, I beg you!"

He nodded, understanding, and she felt him rubbing her rosy fundament with oil. His hands pulled her buttocks apart as Josie brought his lance to the ready. The count pressed forward.

"Ohhh," Marguerite squealed. He gained a slight entry, and it felt very, very big in that place she had never considered a woman would entertain a manly cock. *"Ohhhh!"* He carefully pushed further, and his hands suddenly clamped about her hips to steady them.

"Arch your back," he told her.

Marguerite complied, gasping as the count sank his love lance to the hilt within her tight rear passage. She wasn't certain she could breathe, but then with slow and majestic strokes of his weapon he began to move upon her, sliding almost out, and then grinding his way back to her again. He was careful, but it was nonetheless uncomfortable. She didn't really like it at all. Finally with a groan he stiffened, and she felt him spurting his juices within her. The count finally withdrew from her with a satisfied sigh.

"You are delicious, *mademoiselle*," he complimented her. "I shall look forward to my return from Roma in a few months' time."

Arising from her bowed position, she turned to face him. "I will be pleased to receive you, Count," Marguerite said, remembering her aunt's admonition that every man should be made to believe he was the one who gave her the greatest pleasure. She kissed Count Cirello upon his fleshy lips, smiling as he patted her bottom.

"Now I had best return to the duke, *messieurs*," Marguerite told them. "I hope I have pleased you both. God speed you both in your travels." She hurried from Josie's room and back to her own, where she quickly washed again, lying down next to the duke, relieved to have a moment to herself. Then it dawned upon her that she had entertained three randy cocks this evening within the space of two hours. And the night was yet young! Just barely midnight. There absolutely could be no more going back now for her. Like her aunt, she had become a courtesan.

The duke awoke and availed himself of her body twice more before he departed her bedroom. Marguerite did not awaken until almost noon of the following day. She was sore, and her head hurt from all the wine she had consumed the previous evening. Indeed the carafe on the table was empty. She suspected that her aunt had put something in the wine to encourage and sustain passion. She would get used to it as one could get used to anything.

That evening she joined her aunt and the others in the salon. Her gown of rose brocade with its silver bows was exquisite, and flattered her fair coloring. She was still tired, but Josie and Leonie were full of energy. The redhead was wearing a bright green gown, but Leonie was more sedately garbed in cream and sky blue, which favored her blond coloring. Renée, as always, wore black.

"You are still fatigued, I can see," Renée fretted. "The duke obviously was at his best."

Josie giggled, and Leonie bit her lip to restrain her laughter.

"*What?*" demanded Renée. "What have you two wicked creatures done? Tell me at once!"

"While the duke was sleeping, you know Madame that he always sleeps afterwards to restore his stamina, so while he slept we brought Marguerite in with us for a short time."

"And who was with you then? *Mon Dieu,* do not tell me! The baron and the count?" Renée was almost scandalized. "*Ma petite.*" She turned to her niece. "Are you all right?"

"It was interesting, *tante,*" Marguerite said. "I do not enjoy the count's perversion, and will not do it again, if given the choice; but the baron is rather amusing, and his spankings did not harm me. Rather I found it was arousing. But then the duke awoke less than an hour after I had returned, full of life and eager to fuck, which he did several more times before he departed my bed. I suppose after a time my endurance and tolerance for such active evenings will increase."

The two young courtesans burst out laughing, but Renée was not amused, scolding them roundly. "Shame on the pair of you! Such a night was much too much for my niece her first time. If you ever do anything like that again, I will put you both out on the street!"

"*Tante, tante,*" Marguerite interceded for the pair, "they did not force me. They asked me, and I agreed, for I am eager to learn whatever I must as quickly as I can. It will but add luster to your already peerless reputation. Please do not be angry. I am tired. Nothing more. And with each passing night I shall be less tired as my strength builds." She kissed Renée on both of her cheeks. "Now say you forgive Josie and Leonie. They have been very helpful to me."

But Renée was not to be easily placated. She fixed her blue eyes on the two miscreants, and said, "*You have been warned.*"

At that moment the guests began to arrive. Marguerite seated herself at the pianoforte and began to play. The count and the baron were missing, as was Monsieur Georges, who had returned to Nantes. Several of the gentlemen were, as usual, playing cards; the duke and his cousin were nowhere in evidence, having obviously not arrived. The two princes came and sat on either side of Marguerite. They pressed against her, smiling. They were both very handsome, and to her surprise, their eyes were gray. She would have thought the twins had dark eyes, given their exotic origins.

"How does one tell you apart?" she questioned.

"Most don't," Prince Kansbar answered.

"When you have finished your charming tune," Prince Kurush said, "will you come upstairs with us, *mademoiselle?*"

"Of course, *monseigneurs,*" she agreed. "I hope I can please you, but you must remember this is but my second night."

"We will broaden your education, *mademoiselle,*" the prince to her left replied with another smile.

Again her room glowed with candles, and the scent of summer lilies. Helping each other, the trio quickly disrobed and adjourned to the big bed, where the two men began to kiss and caress Marguerite. She found their attentions extremely exciting, and while her mind remained detached, her body responded enthusiastically, which but aroused them to great heights of passion. The twins almost came to blows over who should have her first, but Marguerite calmed them.

"I am told you enjoy taking a woman together. One of you may fill my love sheath, and the other my mouth. And then, *chéris,* you will reverse yourselves. Is that not fair?" She spread herself open, and the prince who had been licking her thighs immediately covered her fair body with his own body, while his brother positioned himself above her so that he might put his distended cock between her lips.

It was an interesting situation, Marguerite considered as she matched the rhythm of her lips and tongue to the rhythm of the lover who rode between her legs. And as she had been assured, the twins came together, their love juices overflowing on one end and almost choking her on the other. Both were delighted and satisfied with Marguerite's solution for them. They cuddled her between them afterward, praising her skills. Then she brought them wine to drink, and bathed their private parts tenderly as well as her own. After a while they began a second bout of passion, this time changing positions so that the first prince now filled her mouth and the second fucked her enthusiastically.

Afterward the princes took Madame Renée aside downstairs in the salon and engaged her in conversation, both men speaking excitedly, their hands moving as if to punctuate the points they wished to convey. But Renée shook her head, gently at first and then more strongly. A look of identical disappointment suffused the faces of the two princes, but Marguerite could see Renée had finally somehow placated them. They kissed her hands, and joined Count St. Denis and Monsieur Eustache at a card table.

Madame Renée walked across the salon to join her niece. Linking her arm in Marguerite's, she said, "They wanted to buy you from me, and were very disappointed that I refused them, but I explained that I had promised your husband I would always take care of you, and swore a blood oath to him on his deathbed. That was the only way I could prevent them from making off with you, *ma petite*. Gracious! You have pleased all the gentlemen who have visited your bed so far. The duke is filled with praises for you, and I had notes from both the baron and the count before they departed Paris. This was not the life I wished for you, Marguerite, but you certainly seem to have become quickly skilled at it in a very short time. Perhaps I misjudged Charles's prowess."

"Non, *tante,* you did not. Charles was a pedestrian lover, but it would seem that I have a talent for being a whore," Marguerite said to the older woman. "I enjoy most of it, and I seem able to do so without thinking too greatly on it."

"Thank God for that, *chérie,*" her aunt remarked. "Guilt has no place in our lives. We must truly be daughters of joy for the men who come to us. Ahh, here is César and his American."

The two gentlemen immediately greeted Madame Renée, and then she introduced Marguerite to the duke's cousin. He bowed over her hand.

"Will you be in Paris long, *monsieur?*" Marguerite asked him.

"Until the spring," he answered her.

"I hope that you are enjoying your visit with your cousin."

"César and I are very different," Beaufort d'Aubert replied. "His life is spent in the pursuit of pleasure, having learned absolutely nothing from his revolution. I, on the other hand, am a man of business. I own a large plantation on the Mississippi River about twenty miles north of New Orleans."

"Are there red Indians there?" Marguerite asked him.

"Yes, but many of them are being driven further west with the expansion of our country," he explained.

"What do you grow?" she inquired.

"Sugar, mostly, some indigo, and whatever we need to survive. We are very self-sufficient, *mademoiselle.*"

"You are married?"

"My wife is dead," he said. "In childbirth last year, but she left me a son."

"I, too, am widowed," she told him. "I have a little daughter at the convent school of St. Anne here in Paris."

"Why do you do this, *mademoiselle?*" he queried her. "You do not seem like the others. You are finer."

"*Merci,* Monsieur d'Aubert. You are kind, but I do *this* because I have no other means of supporting my child. My husband was an English nobleman, who like yourself was widowed. I married him when I was seventeen, having met him in London during my season. My parents were the Comte and Comtesse de Thierry. They were murdered in the time of the Terror. Madame Renée is my aunt. Her sacrifice saved me, although being an infant I remember nothing of it. She sent me to school in England when I was six. The Duke of Sedgwick was my guardian there. My husband was some years my senior. His son was not much older than I, and bitterly resented his father's remarriage. That is why we came to France to live. After Charles died, his son destroyed the will providing for his half-sister and for me. He sold our home, and left us penniless and helpless. Please, *monsieur,* do not presume to judge me."

"Could not your aunt take care of you?" he asked her.

"She saved my life, and saw that I was raised as my parents would have wanted me raised, but how can I ask any more of her? This life is my choice, *monsieur,* not hers," Marguerite said, irritated.

"May I take you upstairs?" he requested of her.

"Of course, *monsieur.* I hope your cousin, the duke, has spoken well of me," Marguerite said, taking his hand and leading him from the salon up the stairs to her room. Once inside she turned and, slipping her arms about his neck, kissed him.

Beaufort d'Aubert untangled her from the embrace. "Let us sit down and talk, *mademoiselle.*"

"You do not want to fuck me?" She was surprised. Both Josie and Leonie had said he was a vigorous lover.

"Perhaps, eventually, but for now I would prefer just to talk with you. Will you bring me some wine?" He smiled a quick smile at her, and Marguerite thought how unlike the duke he was. Where César d'Aubert was extremely handsome, his cousin was not. The American had a rather plain face, but his eyes, which were green she noted, were kind. She poured a crystal goblet of wine and brought it over to him. He had seated himself on her settee, and now patted the cushion next to him. "My Christian name is Beaufort, but I am called Beau by my friends, *mademoiselle.* Shall we begin as friends?"

"If it pleases you, of course. I am called Marguerite," she replied. "Tell me, Beau, do you always come to a brothel to make friends?" Her blue eyes were questioning. No, he was not quite plain, yet in comparison to the duke . . . but she must not compare this man to his cousin, she decided. "Were you born in the Americas?"

"No. I was born here in France, but we left for the Louisiana territories when I was six. My grandfather had just died. He, my father, and my uncle, César's papa, anticipated, though not entirely, what was to come. My father and uncle attended the Estates-General in May of that year, 1789. They saw that the king was reluctant, no matter his fine speeches, to cooperate with the reformers. He was distracted by the fact the dauphin was ill. The nobility wanted nothing to change. The church wanted nothing to change, although they were sympathetic to the Third Estate. The Third Estate was suspicious of the king, the nobility, and the church. My family could see there was going to be violence. César's father took his family and servants to Rome to wait out the storm. My mother's godfather had left her lands in the Louisiana territories, and so my papa decided that was where we would go. A month after we departed—we were at sea, in fact, when it happened—rioters seized the Bastille, killing its governor and several others. By the time we reached our destination, the Assembly had voted to abolish all privileges and feudal rights belonging to the nobility. We did not learn of that for months afterwards, but such things are not important in the Americas."

"In the Terror," Marguerite told him, "my father, my mother, and Tante Renée were arrested for no other reason than they were nobility. There was, my aunt tells me, no hope when that happened. You went to tea with Madame la Guillotine just for the accident of your birth. But she was just sixteen, and didn't want to die. My family was in a cell with all manner of people, and there was an old whore. When her brother wasn't looking, my aunt spoke with this woman. Then she boldly demanded one day to see the governor of the prison. When he learned that this sixteen-year-old daughter of the nobility sought an audience, he was curious. She seduced him. In return he allowed her to save my life. I was put into the same convent where my own daughter goes to school today. My aunt became the governor's mistress."

"But your parents were killed," Beau said.

"They could not be saved. François would tell you that himself. He is Tante Renée's majordomo here. She took him in when Napoleon fell and he left the army. Of course, it has been years since they were lovers. He protected her during the worst, and freed her to go her own way afterwards. She gives him a home in his old age. I think he would have married her, but that he felt she was above him socially, which of course, she was. Would you like more wine, Beau?"

"Did you love your husband?" he asked her.

"Yes, very much. Did you love your wife?" she countered.

"Yes. Elisa, however, was too young to be married. In retrospect I am not certain she would have ever been mature enough to be a wife. She was beautiful and loved her pleasures, but she was not happy to learn she was with child. It meant she could no longer ride, or go to balls, or even appear in public in New Orleans. She sulked for months."

"Perhaps," Marguerite suggested, "she had a premonition that her confinement would end unhappily."

"My beautiful Elisa only thought of her own pleasures, Marguerite," he said. "A premonition would have been too deep a consideration for her. While I loved her, I quickly realized I had made a great mistake in marrying her."

"What of your son? *Pauvre petit sans sa mama,*" Marguerite sympathized. "He will never know his mother. At least my Emilie will always remember her English papa."

"My son is safe on my plantation, watched over by my sister, who has come from her Convent of the Sacred Heart in New Orleans while I am away." He tipped her face up. "You have a kind heart," he told her. Then his lips gently touched hers. "You should not be here," he said quietly.

"I arrived less than a week ago," Marguerite said softly. "In that time I have been used several times by your cousin and the other men who call Chez Renée their *club.* I am long past the pale, Beau."

"Take your hair down for me," he said in reply.

Reaching up, Marguerite pulled the pins from her hair and lay them aside. Her tresses poured over her shoulders, and down the back of her gown. "Does it please you, Beau?"

The dark green eyes looked deeply into her cornflower blue ones. His hand gently reached up to caress her face. "You are so very beautiful," he told her. He caught a curl between his fingers and kissed it almost reverently.

To both her shock and horror, Marguerite felt herself reacting to Beau d'Aubert in a way she had not reacted to any of the other men in her aunt's house. She blushed, and suddenly found herself at a loss for words with this man.

"Tomorrow is Sunday," he said. "I am told that your aunt does not receive visitors on Sunday. May I call on you, Marguerite?"

"Call on me?" *Mon Dieu!* You would have thought he was courting her by his elegant behavior.

"I thought perhaps we might have a picnic," he explained.

"A picnic?" *Sacrebleu!* She was starting to sound like a perfect fool. She pulled herself together. "I am sorry, Beau, but on Sunday I visit my daughter at her convent."

"I will escort you there, wait, and then escort you home," he replied.

"Impossible!" Marguerite cried. "I am taking Emilie to the

Bois. It would confuse her if I arrived with a gentleman escort so soon after her papa's death."

"She will never see me," he said. "I will bring you to her convent, and return afterwards to walk you back to Chez Renée."

"If you do not want to fuck me, I must go back downstairs," Marguerite said, standing up abruptly. This man was treating her with respect, and he was confusing her.

"Oh I do want to fuck you, Marguerite, but not tonight. However, you need not return downstairs. It is almost midnight, and Madame's guests are required to depart at midnight on Saturday, my cousin tells me. We are not allowed to return until Monday evening. Your aunt, César says, is very strict about it. It is, he says, one of her rules." He drew her back down to the settee. "I am going to kiss you," he said, and then he did. This time, however, his mouth displayed far more experience, pressing firmly upon hers as he pushed her back against the arm of the settee.

Marguerite's heart began to hammer wildly. What was happening to her? Her lips softened beneath his, and she kissed him back with genuine feeling. *But she shouldn't!* A good courtesan never involved her emotions, never entangled them with her enterprise. The kiss was warm, demanding of her, yet tender. *Oh, so sweetly tender.* His mouth moved from hers to kiss her closed eyelids, her face. Kisses trailed down her throat, finally reaching her chest, where he inhaled the fragrance from between her shadowed breasts, kissing the tops of them, as she half swooned in his embrace. *This was magic! It was heaven!* And then the porcelain clock on the mantle began to strike midnight.

With a final kiss on her lips, Beau d'Aubert arose and bowed to her. "What time shall I come tomorrow?" he asked her.

"At noon," she said weakly.

"*Bonsoir,* Marguerite."

"*Bonsoir,* Beau," she responded.

With another small bow he turned and left her seated, closing her bedroom door behind him as he went.

Marguerite sat silently. The only sound in the room came from the crackling fireplace, and from the mantle clock, ticking. Then she heard the gentlemen in the street below going off in their carriages. She heard François locking the entry to the passageway leading to the street that lay below one of her windows. And then the question arose in her mind. What did Beau d'Aubert want of her? He hadn't been like the other gentlemen. He had treated her like the widowed Lady Abbott, not Marguerite, the newly fledged courtesan at Chez Renée. It had been a totally unnerving experience. She had to speak with her *tante*. Getting up, she hurried downstairs to Renée's bedchamber, knocking before she entered. One never knew with Renée. Renée was alone except for her elderly maid, Bertilde, who was putting away her jewelry.

"Ahh, *ma petite*," she said. "Did you enjoy the young *American*?"

"He did not treat me like the others," Marguerite replied, seating herself upon a small, velvet chair.

"What did he do?" her aunt asked. "He was not bestial, brutal, or cruel, was he? I shall have him banned from my house if he was!" She peered closely at her niece. Marguerite didn't look as if she had been abused. In fact, she looked distinctly bewildered. "What is it, *chérie*? Bertilde!" She turned to the servant. "Go and find us something to eat. Bread. Cheese. Fruit. Do not stand there listening to us! Meddlesome old creature," she grumbled fondly as Bertilde shuffled out the door.

"We did not . . ." Marguerite began, then stopped. "He did not . . ." She thought a moment. "He behaved, *tante,* as if I were who I used to be instead of who I am. We kissed, nothing more. He wishes to escort me to St. Anne's tomorrow. He will not take no for an answer."

"Indeed," Renée said thoughtfully. "He is widowed, César says. You made it clear that you have known other men since you came here to my home? He understood?"

"Yes, *tante*, I made it very clear. He says he wants me, but we will first get to know one another."

"Interesting," her aunt noted. "Do you know how the wife died, *ma petite*?"

"Childbirth," Marguerite said.

"So it is unlikely he is a man who loves men," Renée mused. "*Chérie,* I do not know what to say. The men who visit here are usually direct in their desires, but some men prefer to play a game of courtship. Monsieur d'Aubert will be here the entire winter. Perhaps this is what he wishes to do. If he continues to evince interest in you, Marguerite, I shall allow him to have your exclusive company as long as it pleases him. I shall ask him tomorrow when he comes to escort you to St. Anne's."

"Are you not coming with me?" Marguerite asked her aunt.

"Do you wish me to come, *chérie?*"

"But of course, *tante.* Emilie adores you. You are like her *grandmère.* She would be very disappointed if you did not come. Besides, Monsieur d'Aubert is only going to escort me to the convent. I would not allow him to be with Emilie under my current circumstances."

"You are right," her aunt agreed. *"Très bien!* I shall go with you, *chérie.* Now, tell me what else it is that is troubling you."

"When he kissed me, my emotions became involved. They have not with the others. With them I am able to divorce my body's pleasure from my thoughts. But not when the *Americain* kissed me, *tante."*

"Sometimes it happens," Renée shrugged fatalistically. "You are not, after all, made of stone. Once in a while a man will attract you more than you want him to do. But, *chérie,* it is nothing, and you must not distress yourself over it."

"This is all so different, and so new for me. I never really understood, *tante,"* Marguerite admitted.

"The men and their attentions? They are pleasant for you?" Renée wondered.

"I never knew that men could be so different, and yet all the same," Marguerite said with a small laugh.

"You have pleased every man who has had you, *ma petite.* I believe that despite my reservations you may have a bright future. Both the duke and the two princes praise the skill of your lips and tongue. Where on earth did you ever learn? Certainly not from Charles!"

"It seems to be a natural talent, *tante,"* Marguerite said, blushing. "When the duke told me what to do, I did it, and gracious, it did seem to please him. Then the twins wanted me together, and as I do not like being taken via Sodom's entrance, I used my mouth. They seemed quite pleased."

"Indeed, *my petite,* they were. I will have to be careful that they do not try and kidnap you from me," she said with a chuckle. "Ahh, here is Bertilde with a little nibble for us. Come, *chérie,* and pour us some wine. You have done very well in your first week with me, and I am indeed pleased with you."

Marguerite stood up, and going over to the table, she poured them the wine. Turning, she handed her aunt a crystal goblet. "It is certainly a different life from anything I ever imagined," she said.

"And you are not unhappy?" Renée inquired.

"Non, *tante,* I am not unhappy," Marguerite said.

"But neither are you happy," Renée observed.

"One cannot have everything," Marguerite said.

"And why not?" Renée replied. "I do, and I want it for you as well, *ma petite.*"

"*Non, tante.* I do not believe I shall ever really be happy again now that my husband is gone. My only concern is for Emilie. I do not want her becoming what you and I have become. But how can I assure she remain respectable without becoming a victim to her husband one day? Emilie must be both proper and independent. It will not be easy."

Chapter Five

Beau d'Aubert had spent thirty-two of his thirty-eight years in the New World. While he was French by birth and spoke the language, he considered himself an American, particularly since when he was twenty, the United States had purchased the Louisiana territories from the French government. As he had told Marguerite, he was as different from his cousin, César, as night was from day. The *ancien régime* into which he and César had been born was long gone, swept away by the winds of war and the shifting times. However, with a restored Bourbon king on France's throne, César did not accept these changes, but Beau, from his American perspective, did.

He had not been back to France since his childhood. Much had changed, and yet nothing had changed. The nobility who had survived peopled the royal court, along with the new nobility who had been created in Napoleon's time. It was all very interesting, but Beau knew he did not belong among them; that once he returned to his plantation, he would not come back to France again. With his wife dead, he had taken the opportunity to revisit the land of his birth, where he hoped to find a new wife to go back with him.

As the first cousin of the Duc de Caraville, he was welcomed in all the best salons. He met any number of eligible young women, but they were all too much like Elisa. Spoiled, charming, and much too soft for a life three thousand miles from Paris and twenty miles upriver from New Orleans. Eighteen- to twenty-year-olds who were world-weary, and oversophisticated. He sighed. And there was no one at home either. But then he had seen Marguerite in her aunt's salon. The drawing room of a brothel, and César had imparted her history, relishing the fact that he would be the first to debauch her.

It was indeed sad, his older cousin admitted, that a young woman of such respectable lineage should be brought so low, but the poor creature had no other choice. So why should the duke not take advantage of the situation? And afterward when he had had her, César had bragged that he had brought the beautiful Marguerite to *la petite morte* not once, but several times. *And,* the duke noted, she sucked cock better than any woman he had ever known. "You must have her too, cousin," the duke had enthused.

So Beau had taken Marguerite upstairs to her bedroom, but as much as he desired to make love to her, he needed to get to know her first. Unlike César, who frequented several fine brothels, taking his lovers easily and without a care for any of them, Beau d'Aubert had never made love to any woman with whom he was not involved on another level. And there was something about Marguerite that made him want to protect her. He had seen the blankness in her beautiful cornflower blue eyes when she had offered herself to him. She did what she had to, and it almost broke his heart, especially as he now saw the reason why she had joined her aunt.

He had arrived at Chez Renée at noon. Marguerite and her aunt had been awaiting him, but he was not even allowed past their front door. They came out to him, and together they walked to the Convent of St. Anne. Marguerite looked particularly beautiful, he thought, in her crimson velvet pelisse with its beaver collar and matching beaver Valois hat atop her head. Renée wore a dark blue velvet greatcoat and a blue satin Bourbon hat with pearl fleur de lis trim. Marguerite was quiet, but Renée chatted easily with him.

"How handsome you look, *mon brave*. Do not tell me an American tailored your clothes, for I shall not believe it," she teased.

"No, Madame Renée, like César, I have a French tailor," he admitted. "But his shop is in New Orleans, not Paris."

"This New Orleans, is it as beautiful as Paris?" she demanded.

"There is no place as beautiful as Paris, but New Orleans is very lovely," he told her.

"I live here year after year but for my Augusts in Brittany," Renée said. "When Marguerite was little, we went there each summer. In the years she was in England, we went to Cornwall. They are quite similar."

"You speak English then?" He was surprised.

"Of course," she said. "I was sixteen when the revolution changed my life, but before that I was a well-educated, and well-brought-up little aristo like so many others. Marguerite's guardian in England, a duke, and his friends made several trips to France to rescue innocents. I helped them. I did not waste my time as the mistress of a prison governor, nor did I entirely betray my class. But neither did I, like my overproud and foolish brother, Marguerite's father, martyr myself to a dead past. Now, what is it exactly that you want of my niece?"

The suddenness and the directness of her question surprised him, but then he laughed. "Her exclusive company for as long as I am in Paris, Madame Renée. I don't want her being offered to any other man. I realize I have come into your house as my cousin's guest, but since I will be here for several months, I should like to pay a year's worth of dues to Chez Renée in exchange for the privilege of your niece's company. I hope I have not put it badly. I mean no offense."

"I shall be delighted to take your money, Monsieur d'Aubert. You have not offended me in the slightest. As for Marguerite, you must ask her if she is willing to give you her exclusive company. I am content to abide by her decision," Madame Renée said. "Wait, however, until you escort us home later."

"And if she agrees?" he asked.

"Then you may come on Monday evening, and we will discuss your fees, eh?" Renée smiled pleasantly at him.

"*Merci, madame,*" he responded.

"Ahh," the older woman said, "here we are at St. Anne's." She patted his arm. "Return for us in four hours, *monsieur.*" Then with Marguerite she turned away from him.

He bowed to both women politely, and continued on down the street until he thought it safe to turn about again. They had disappeared, and so he took up a position in a doorway to watch and to wait. He was rewarded several long minutes later when Marguerite, her aunt, and a little girl exited through the doors in the convent walls. They started down the street to the park near the river. Beau d'Aubert followed them at a discreet distance.

It was a bright winter's day. There was no wind, and the February sun shone down on the raked gravel paths of the park with its leafless trees. There was an old chestnut vendor hawking his wares, and the women stopped to purchase a paper cone of the hot nuts. After they had walked a short distance, they sat down upon a marble bench, sharing the nuts with the little girl who accompanied them. And when the treats were all gone, Marguerite arose, and together she and her daughter tossed a brightly colored ball back and forth.

The child was charming, Beau thought. Her hair was a mass of ringlets, its darkness being broken by a bright yellow silk ribbon. And she was very fair like her mother. She wore a rather severe little greatcoat of an indeterminate gloomy color, but when she ran and her dun-colored skirts blew, he could see her dainty white pantalets. She was like a wild creature let out of its cage, dashing about, chasing her ball, her cheeks growing bright red with her exertions. There was not, he suspected, a great deal of activity other than one's studies in her convent school. That she adored both her mother and her great-aunt was obvious. The afternoon began to wane when suddenly the little girl fell, crying out sharply. Almost at once Renée and Marguerite were at her side. *And so was Beau.*

Marguerite's startled eyes met his. Then she turned her full attention to her daughter. "What has happened, Emilie?"

"I have twisted my ankle, *Maman,*" the child replied.

"Let us get you up," Madame Renée said briskly, but no sooner had Emilie attempted to put weight upon her foot than she cried out again, collapsing onto the grass, sobbing.

"I will carry her," Beau said quietly. "Neither of you ladies is strong enough, and it is a distance back to Mademoiselle's school." He bent, and said to the child, "Now put your arms about my neck, Emilie."

"How do you know my name?" the little girl said as she slipped her arms about him.

"I heard your maman call you by that name. Is your name Emilie? Or is it perhaps Cinderella?" He lifted the little girl up easily.

Emilie giggled. "I am Emilie," she said. "You are funny like my papa used to be. My papa is dead, you know."

"I am sorry, Mademoiselle Emilie, to learn that," Beau told the child, "but he is certainly in heaven with the angels, and watching down over you."

"That is what Soeur Marie Regina says when she wants me to be good," Emilie confided. "I am not always good, but I do try."

"I am certain that you do," Beau answered her gravely as he carried her from the little park and down the street leading to St. Anne's.

Watching him chat so easily with the little girl, Madame Renée had a sudden blinding thought. The American was a widower. Her niece was a widow. True, Marguerite's behavior of the last few days would be considered completely unforgivable by polite society. *But only if polite society knew about it.* And Monsieur d'Aubert did not intend remaining in Paris, or in France. He had come to find a new wife, but obviously no one in the elegant salons of Paris had caught his eye. *But Marguerite had caught his eye.* The duke? Could he be silenced if his cousin chose to make

Marguerite his wife? The others did not worry her. They were of no importance. *But the duke!*

Mon Dieu, mon Dieu, but she was getting ahead of herself. There was a chance, just the barest chance, that Marguerite could escape this life she had never been meant to lead. When the American came to see her on Monday, Renée decided, she would not accept his money. She would wave it away, and tell him that it was not necessary, that Marguerite was his for as long as it pleased him. Then she would light a thousand candles to St. Jude if the American fell in love with Marguerite. And if he fell in love with her niece, he would certainly want to marry her. *Dare I hope?* Madame Renée asked herself silently.

Marguerite walked by Beau d'Aubert's side, murmuring encouragement to her daughter. He had obviously followed them to the park, but why? Yet thank goodness that he had been there. And he was being so kind to Emilie, and Emilie obviously liked him. He didn't have to be kind to her child, Marguerite considered, to gain her favor. She would do whatever he wanted, whenever he wanted, and any way he wanted it because she was a courtesan, and he was paying for her favors. His cousin, the duke, she knew, would not have been as kind to her. *Had not been.* César d'Aubert was interested only in exerting his power over her, and exhibiting his sexual prowess as a lover.

They reached the school, and Marguerite tugged on the bell outside the doors, which opened almost immediately.

"*Sacrebleu!*" said the ageless-faced nun who had opened the portal. "What has happened?"

"I fell and twisted my ankle, Soeur Anne Marie," Emilie volunteered. "This gentleman, he is an American, sister, carried me all the way from the park."

"I will take her, *monsieur,*" the nun said, reaching out for Emilie.

Beau transferred his burden to the religious women, then bowing to them, he departed down the street.

"She will be all right, Lady Abbott," Soeur Anne Marie said reassuringly. "May we expect you next Sunday?"

"*Mais oui,*" Marguerite answered. She reached out and brushed a tangled curl from her daughter's cheek. "Next time do not run so fast," she said softly, a small smile touching her lips.

"*Non, Maman,* I won't," Emilie replied.

"Say *bonsoir* now to your *maman,* and your *grand-tante,*" the nun instructed the little girl.

"*Bonsoir, Maman. Bonsoir, Grand-tante Renée.* The chestnuts were very good. *Merci,*" Emilie said sweetly.

"*Bonsoir, chérie,*" Madame Renée told the child, and she kissed her forehead. "I shall come next Sunday with your mama."

"*Bonsoir, ma petite,*" Marguerite said, and she, too, kissed Emilie. Then with a deep sigh she turned away with her aunt, and together the two women began their return to Chez Renée.

As they reached the corner and turned into the next street, Beau d'Aubert joined them. "She will be all right, the little one?"

"Yes," Renée said quickly before her niece might answer. "Just a childhood mishap. You should not have followed us, *monsieur,*" she scolded him gently, "but thank heavens that you were there for us."

"Yes," Marguerite agreed, taking her cue from her aunt.

"She is going to be as lovely as you one day, Mademoiselle Marguerite," Beau told her.

"Pray God she is not like me," Marguerite said, tears springing to her eyes. "My aunt knows I mean her no disrespect, but I do not want my child ending up a courtesan as I have." Then she quickened her gait, almost running up the street away from them.

Renée put her hand upon Beau d'Aubert's arm. "She was not meant for this life, *monsieur.* You understand?"

He nodded. "I do," he said.

"Come on Monday, *monsieur,* but I will not take your money. My niece will favor you for my sake, and I will keep her for her sake from the other gentlemen who visit my house. *Do you understand?* And you will not hurt her? She is not as determined or as strong as she thinks she is in this matter."

"How many others besides my cousin?" he asked her.

"The two princes," Renée answered, conveniently forgetting the baron and the count. "Once. Marguerite has only been with me a few days." Then she looked directly at the American. "What will your cousin think of your little arrangement, *monsieur?*"

"I do not care," Beau responded. "I have not been back to

France in over thirty years, *madame*. My cousin and I have only renewed our kinship for my convenience sake. We Americans are different."

"Reputation, *monsieur*, is the same the world over, I assure you," Renée advised him. "Marguerite de Thierry has no reputation in Paris for she is still a virtual unknown. That cannot last as long as she makes her home with me. Lady Marguerite Abbott, however, has an excellent reputation as a good wife and mother. You understand me, I know, but let us see what happens."

They had reached the door of Chez Renée. Marguerite was nowhere to be seen. Beau d'Aubert bowed over Madame Renée's hand. "I concur, *madame*," he said smoothly, and then he turned, departing off down the street.

She watched him go, her face impassive. She had not mistaken his interest in Marguerite, which transcended his interest in Marguerite as a courtesan. He was intelligent. He had certainly not mistaken her meaning with regard to her niece. Renée entered her house and, seeing her majordomo, said, "Fetch the girls to me in the salon right now, François. I must speak with them."

"You have *that* look in your eye, Renée," he said, smiling.

"You come too," she told him.

This would be important, he thought, as he hurried off to find Josie, Leonie, and Marguerite. What had happened? Well, they would all know soon enough. "Madame wants us in the salon," he said to each of them as he came upon them.

Several minutes later they all gathered in Madame Renée's private salon, and the lady in question wasted no time in coming to the point. "There is a chance, the tiniest chance, that the American is interested in Marguerite as a wife."

"*Tante!*" Marguerite flushed nervously. "Why would you say such a thing? I am no longer fit to be anyone's wife."

"*Yes, you are!*" her aunt declared. "And I will smack anyone who says otherwise. Do you *all* understand me?"

"Ohh, Marguerite," Leonie said, "wouldn't that be wonderful?"

"Yes," Josie agreed. "Certainly your curiosity is now satisfied regarding men and lovemaking. If you have an opportunity to go back to the life that you were meant for, you must take it, *chérie!*"

"I am glad that you all feel that way," Madame Renée told them. "The little incident regarding the count and the baron never took place now, did it?"

"*Non, Madame Renée,*" Josie and Leonie chorused.

"My niece has made love with the duke and the princes. No others," Renée said. "Certainly she is no worse than any respectable, and noble young widow, freed of her marital obligations, and curious prior to making another match."

"*Of course, Madame Renée,*" Josie and Leonie agreed.

"In future Marguerite will not join us in the gold salon. She will entertain Monsieur d'Aubert exclusively for the time being," Renée said. "Is that understood? And there will be no gossip regarding my niece. I know we need another girl. Monsieur Georges has offered me a candidate from Nantes. I was going to wait until his next visit, but I shall write him tonight asking him to send her up to Paris."

"*Tante,* this is madness," Marguerite said.

"*Chérie,* I do not mistake the signs. I am too old a fox, and too knowledgeable in the ways of the world. You have an opportunity to escape this life. You must take it! I should never forgive myself if I didn't encourage you in this, Marguerite. You have dabbled now in my profession, and I know that you do not like it. You will do it for Emilie's sake, *but you do not like it.* The American seeks a wife. No one has attracted him until he met you. If we fail, then we fail. But you must try!"

"How?" she asked her aunt.

"By being yourself, and not a courtesan. He has treated you like the lady you are, Marguerite. Now encourage him to seduce you, and when he does, bind him to you, *ma petite,* as only a woman can bind a man. You are no longer the innocent virgin who married Charles Abbott. You are a woman, full-blown. Do you want this life I have lived all these years, or do you want to be what you once were? The choice is yours, Marguerite. Choose wisely."

"What of the duke? Is he not the head of his family? Will he allow his cousin to marry a woman to whom he has made love? A woman his cousin found in the most elegant brothel in Paris?" Marguerite questioned her aunt. "Am I not already tarnished? Was I not the moment I stepped across your threshold, *tante?*"

"In Paris, in France, perhaps," Renée responded. "But the American means to take his wife home to this Louisiana. It is unlikely he will ever return to France. You have no reputation here yet, *chérie*. Lady Abbott, on the other hand, is well thought of in society. The American will have wed the widow of Lord Charles Abbott, not a girl from a brothel. And what man who has met you here will ever go to the Americas? Not even the duke would leave his comfortable life in Paris. You must take this chance, Marguerite!" She smiled at her niece. "As for César d'Aubert, I will manage him, you may be certain. Do you think I will allow him to ruin your opportunity? Faugh! *Never!*"

"And we will help you," Josie said as Leonie nodded enthusiastically.

"You will do no such thing!" Madame Renée said. "The last time you helped her, well, we know what happened then. Praise God that the duke never found out! Let the American introduce her to the pleasures he wants. My niece still maintains a certain innocence about her that is most pleasing. If she behaves with too much skill, he will not want her for a wife, but rather a mistress. I do not want that. If she is going to be a mistress, she can just as well remain in France and be one. I am not allowing my darling Marguerite to go across an ocean without the protection of a husband's name. Now, if it is settled, you may all return to your rooms to enjoy the remainder of your day."

The three young women departed, leaving Madame Renée with her old mentor. "Do you think you can pull it off?" he asked her.

She shook her head. "I do not know, François, but it would be the solution I pray for, and the fate I know my niece would prefer."

"How will you handle César d'Aubert?" he questioned her.

Renée smiled. "Let us say I know his secrets, François. Secrets he would rather the rest of the world not know. If the American falls in love with Marguerite, and she with him, *they will marry*. And the duke will give them his blessing, or I will reveal to everyone that which he has kept hidden all these years. César d'Aubert is a snob of the first rank, François. He will not want to be held up to ridicule."

Yes, she knew the duke's darkest secret. As a boy in Rome he had defied his father and married an older woman of less than stellar reputation, whose only interest in him was his inheritance and his title. His father had assured him the marriage was a sham and insisted that César wed his choice, the virgin daughter of a wealthy Florentine merchant. The marriage was celebrated. Only afterward was it discovered that César d'Aubert's first wife was indeed his legal wife. The Florentine merchant's daughter, already pregnant with César's child, went mad. She was confined within the walls of a convent, where she bore her child, a son. César d'Aubert's wife was yet alive in Rome, but was paid to remain there in obscurity. The merchant's daughter continued to live in her total madness behind the walls of the Florentine convent. The duke's bastard was raised by his maternal grandparents, who had taught him to hate not just the French but the d'Aubert family in particular.

Renée had learned this not from César d'Aubert, but from a wealthy Florentine who had visited her years ago on several occasions. Seeing the duke at Chez Renée, he had told his hostess the story, curious that no one in Paris knew it. And while the duke pretended to prefer his pleasures over marrying and having a legitimate heir, Renée knew the truth. She had never expected she might have to use her knowledge, but she had no intention of the duke spoiling Marguerite's chances with the American. Still, it was not a certainty yet.

Monday evening came, and her salon was strangely empty. There were a few gentlemen, but Leonie and Josie were more than up to the challenge. She had written Monsieur Georges in Nantes, sending her missive off by private messenger earlier in the day. The duke and his cousin arrived. Renée made it her mission to personally entertain César d'Aubert while Beau hurried upstairs to Marguerite.

Stepping into her bedroom, he saw she was awaiting him in a simple house gown that matched her eyes. Marguerite smiled tremulously.

"I didn't know what I should wear," she explained. "My aunt says you have requested my company exclusively, and that she has approved such an arrangement. I thought it rather foolish to dress as if I were going into the salon. May I offer you some wine?"

"*Merci, mademoiselle,*" he replied.

She poured the ruby red liquid into a delicate Venetian wine goblet and handed it to him. Then she poured herself some wine.

"May I toast the most beautiful woman in Paris?" he asked her.

Marguerite blushed prettily. "You flatter me, *monsieur,*" she replied.

"I could spend my life flattering you, Marguerite," he told her, setting his goblet down, his arm slipping about her waist. "I find it charming that you can blush," he said, looking down at her. "Do you always blush when you are complimented?"

"Charles used to say so," she admitted softly.

"An observant man," Beau d'Aubert murmured, his lips brushing her lips. He took her goblet from her, and set it down upon a small table with his own crystal. "I want to make love to you, Marguerite." His voice was husky with his emotion. "But I will only make love to you with your permission. You are in this house by an accident of fate, *cherie,* but I shall not take advantage of you because of it."

Marguerite looked up shyly into his face. His look was questioning. He was treating her as if he had come to court her. *Was it really possible?* Was Renée correct in her observations and conclusions? "You are kind, *monsieur,*" she said low, her heart skipping several beats.

His big hand caressed her heart-shaped face, the knuckles grazing along her jaw line. "How can I not be kind to you?" he questioned her. "You arouse my senses, you confuse me, you fill me with desire, my beautiful Marguerite. *Let me make love to you!*"

"I am not like the others," she told him. "They say you are a wonderful and tireless lover, but they know how to engage your interest. I have not the experience, although your cousin may say otherwise," she finished, flushing.

"I pay little attention to César for he is wont to brag on his women and his prowess," Beau told Marguerite. "It is difficult to know where the truth begins and where it ends with César. Let us put my cousin and the two princes from our minds. What happens in this lovely room is between you and me. What has gone before doesn't really matter to me. You aren't a virgin. You are the widow of a respected man. Do you understand?"

She began to weep softly. *"You are kind!"* she insisted to him.

He stroked her dark hair gently, murmuring to her, "How can I not be kind to you, Marguerite?" Then he tilted her face up, and his mouth descended upon her mouth in a tender, yet burning kiss.

He held her against him with a single arm. His lips on hers were wonderful. There seemed to be nothing dark in his desire for her. She let her lips soften beneath his, hesitantly opening her mouth to his tongue, shivering as the two fleshy organs made contact. They stood there kissing and kissing until her legs gave way beneath her. With a soft laugh he picked her up in his arms and sat down, cradling her, upon the ivory and gold settee by one of the windows. Opening her eyes, she looked up at him, and blushed again for his gaze was a burning one. "You will incinerate me if you keep looking at me like that," she said.

"Like what?" he gently teased her.

"Like you would enjoy eating me up like a meringue, *monsieur,*" Marguerite told him.

"No more *monsieur,* Marguerite," he said to her. "I want to hear my name on your adorable lips."

"Beau," she whispered, tasting the word. *"Beau!"*

"Marguerite! *Ma belle* Marguerite," he groaned. *"Je t'adore!"* Then he began covering her face with kisses, his lips moving swiftly over her cheeks, her forehead, her closed eyelids. *"Je t'adore!"* he repeated, his hand brushing over her bosom with a light touch.

Her heart was hammering wildly. His touch caused her to murmur softly, and with pleasure. This was so very different from any of the others, even from her beloved Charles. He was gentle, and while she realized that he was filled with his desire for her, he was not hurrying her along the road to passion. Indeed he seemed to be leading her, and she found that she was very eager to follow him. Was this what it was like when a passionate man cared for you? Her husband had loved her, she knew, but his love had been so restrained, and she had never known until she had come into her aunt's house that a man could be wild and fierce in his loving of a woman.

The hand skimming across her gently pushed aside the front of her gown to touch her bare flesh. He tenderly cupped a single breast, his palm cuddling it, feeling its warmth, its sensual weight. Raising his head, he stared down at her closed, trembling eyelids. A faint smile touched his lips, and he shook his head in wonderment. This was no courtesan. And whatever part of her his cousin and the two princes had had, it wasn't this. It wasn't what she was shyly giving to him as he held her in his arms. His dark head dipped to kiss her breast. A faint aroma of lilies rose up to greet him.

"*Mon Dieu,* Marguerite, you are so damned beautiful," he groaned.

"I am afraid," she whispered to him.

"Do not be!" he pleaded with her.

"But I am, Beau," she insisted.

"No! No!" he told her. "Ohh, God, darling, don't you see that I'm falling in love with you?" He had spoken the words in English.

"How can you love me?" she replied in the same tongue. "Not after what I have become. I am surely no better than Josie and Leonie."

"*No!*" He shook his head at her. "You are the most respected widow of Lord Charles Abbott, Marguerite. It doesn't matter to me what has happened to you this past week. It is no worse than any other widow's behavior. I vow it is expected that a widow taste forbidden fruits before she marries again. It stems her curiosity, and certainly guarantees her fidelity to her new husband. Besides we are not going to live here in France, or in England. We are going to live on my plantation, The Arbor, in Louisiana. You, and Emilie, and the children we will have together, my naughty little love."

"*Are you asking me to marry you?*" Marguerite said, incredulous. Oh, Tante Renée had said she suspected this was his intent, but for him to voice it now, so soon, surprised her. She hadn't even been certain that her aunt knew what she was talking about. She half believed Renée was more hopeful than anything else.

"Yes," he said, "I am."

"What if we are not suited?" Marguerite demanded.

Beau burst out laughing and, tipping her from his lap, stood up, unbuttoning his trousers to unleash his cock. "I think," he told her with great understatement, his hand wrapped about the long, thick pestle of flesh, "that we are."

She stared, fascinated. Not even the duke possessed so magnificent an instrument of love. Shrugging off her robe, she fell to her knees and took him in her mouth. She simply could not help herself. For a moment she suckled upon him, but then taking him in her small hand, she began to lick his length slowly and with relish. She did not see him smiling down on her, pleased.

Beau d'Aubert began to quickly divest himself of his clothing as she pleasured them both. His black evening coat, the cream and black brocade waistcoat, his silk cravat. His fingers flew down the line of studs holding his shirt together, and he shrugged it off. Her hot little tongue was driving him wild with its delicious caresses. He groaned as she lifted his cock up, and began to run her tongue about his pouch. When she bent low and took him into her mouth, he almost howled with the bursts of pure pleasure that exploded within him. He could barely concentrate on undoing his trousers.

Then Marguerite looked up at him, her mouth wet, her eyes glazed with her own desire. Reaching up, she pulled his trousers and drawers down even as he pulled her up to stand before him.

"I . . . I . . . I couldn't help myself," she admitted to him, even now as her eyes stared at the rock-hard length of him.

"I don't ever want you to *help* yourself," he told her. Then he laughed weakly. "I find myself at a disadvantage." His trousers and drawers were bunched awkwardly about his ankles.

"Come," she said, leading him carefully across the room to her bed. He sat down, and kneeling, she quickly drew off his black evening slippers and his white silk stockings.

He did not wait for her to yank his trousers off, but kicked them away himself as he pulled her atop his body. "Now, Lady Abbott, you will pay for your very naughty ways, which I pray you will never outgrow. And in answer to your question, yes, I am asking you to marry me. What is your answer?" He swiftly rolled her onto her back.

"If you would truly have me, Beau, then, yes, I will marry you," Marguerite said, and then she gasped as he began to push himself into her waiting body. He was so big. And she wanted him so very much! His probing love lance slowly, slowly propelled itself forward, opening her with little effort, only to be imprisoned by the hot tight walls of her sheath. She murmured, and her eyes closed with the sheer pleasure of it all. She instinctively wrapped her legs about him to allow him even deeper access.

He moaned appreciatively, shoving himself as deep as he could go, his groin grinding into her furred mont, and then he rested a brief moment. When he could no longer bear the sweetness of being within her, he began to move energetically, his big cock flashing back and forth within her.

Marguerite almost screamed with the waves of delight that began to wash over her. Her nails raked down his long back. Her little white teeth sank into the fleshy part of his shoulder in an effort to stifle her cries, but she was unsuccessful. *"Ohhhh! Ohhhhh!"* She thrust herself up at him, catching his rhythm and eagerly imitating it. "Oh, Beau! Do not stop!" she pleaded with him. *"Do not stop!"* She soared! She flew! She was finally flung down into a warm and whirling darkness that tenderly enfolded her.

When she finally bestirred from her swoon, she was shocked to find him still buried within her, still as hard as an iron rod, and still eager to fuck. He moved teasingly upon her, smiling as her eyes widened. "I have never known a man like you," she whispered.

"No, my darling, you haven't," he agreed. "Your English husband, may God have mercy on his soul, was not passionate, was he?"

"No, but he loved me," Marguerite loyally defended Charles, "and I loved him."

"You will love me more," he promised her with a wicked grin. "Now as for the rest of your not particularly vast experience, Lady Abbott," and he began to thrust himself slowly in and out of her. "César, I know enjoys his *mastery* of his partner. I suspect he is a boring lover, *n'est-ce pas?*"

"Yes," she agreed, "he is." But of course, the duke had certainly opened her eyes to the delicious adventures of lustful play, Marguerite considered silently to herself.

"Tell me about the princes," he said, his hands moving beneath her buttocks to raise her up more to his salacious advances.

"They come together," she murmured. "Ohh, God, Beau, this is unbearably heavenly! Please, please, don't stop. *Ohhh,* yes!" His hands were fondling her bottom, the strong fingers kneading her flesh provocatively.

"*Together?* You had them both at the same time?" How very interesting, he thought. "Sharing a woman with another man can be exciting," he noted.

She nodded. "One in my cunt, and one in my mouth," she told him.

"Not your bottom?"

Marguerite shuddered. "Gracious, no! How unspeakable!" She remembered the count, but her aunt was correct. Beau should never know about the count.

"It is not a perversion I fancy," he admitted to her, "especially when my lover has such a delectably tight little sheath." He began to pestle her once more in earnest. This time they reached passion's peak together, both crying out as one, with their great pleasure.

Afterward Marguerite lay happily within his strong embrace, her dark head upon his broad, smooth chest. Beneath her ear his heart beat quietly. Had he meant the proposal he had made her? Really? And she had said yes. But what did she truly know about Beau d'Aubert? He was obviously wealthy, and owned land across the ocean in the Americas. He was a widower with a son as Charles had been, but at least this son would grow up knowing only her as his mother. He would not be like Charles's dreadful son. Marguerite wondered to herself if she could marry a man she didn't love. Yet this was an opportunity such as she was unlikely to ever again receive, especially in her straitened circumstances. Beau was kind. He wanted her. *And* he was an incredible lover. She would be a fool to refuse him. She could easily learn to love him, and she would.

But, the little voice in her head said, what about your decision to never again be victimized by a man? And what of your desire to become a woman of independent means like your aunt? Will you not once again be at the mercy of a husband, of a man, if you accept Beau d'Aubert's proposal of marriage? If indeed he actually wants to marry you, and was not just amusing himself at your expense. He is, after all, César d'Aubert's cousin.

"What are you thinking about?" she heard Beau ask. "I can hear the little cogs and wheels turning in your head, Lady Abbott. Should you not be thinking only of me, and how wonderful it is that we have found one another?"

"Did you really mean to ask me to be your wife?" Marguerite said seriously. "Or was it just a part of your passion?" Boldly she raised herself up from his chest and looked down into his face.

"The first night I came to Chez Renée," Beau answered her, "I looked across the salon, and there you were at the pianoforte. You looked so fragile, so delicate in your lilac gown, and so unlike the others. I fell in love with you in that same moment, Marguerite. I did not believe such a phenomenon as love at first sight could really happen. Is that not for unfledged girls still in the schoolroom? But when César demanded first rights of you from your aunt, I wanted to kill him. And afterwards when he bragged on his conquest of you, I wanted to kill him even more. You are a lady, my darling. Your blood is noble, as is ours. Yet my cousin could only think of satisfying his lust on your fair body."

"Ohh, Beau," she said to him, "how can you love me then knowing that I have lain with the duke and with the two princes?"

"How can I not love you, my darling? You are so brave and so honorable. I know that had it not been for little Emilie, you would have sooner starved in a corner somewhere than taken up your Tante Renée's enterprise. You have sacrificed yourself even as she sacrificed herself for you, but you do not have to do it, Marguerite. I love you. I will protect you. I will protect Emilie."

"If I do not learn to love you, Beau d'Aubert," Marguerite answered him, "then I am a bigger fool than even I have imagined." She bent down to kiss him, and sighed happily as his arms closed about her once again. But one thought nagged her. She couldn't be left helpless should the unthinkable happen, and she be widowed again. Still, Renée would know what to do. Her aunt always had the right answer.

"When shall we marry, *chérie?*" he asked, returning to the French tongue he had earlier spoken.

"I think as soon as possible, Beau. My reputation must not be allowed to cast a stain upon your good name, which, it could if I remain here with Tante Renée."

"I am in agreement," he concurred. "In the morning we shall speak with your aunt, and then with my cousin. For now, however, I want more of you."

"I am in agreement with you now, *monsieur*," Marguerite said with a twinkle in her cornflower blue eyes. Then she began to kiss him again.

Chapter Six

"I thought you more sophisticated, cousin," the Duc de Caraville said coolly. "A gentleman does not marry a whore."

"Lady Marguerite Abbott is the widow of an English gentleman, the only child of the late Comte de Thierry, César, and I am indeed going to marry her," Beauford d'Aubert replied in an even voice.

"She is a whore, an elegant one, I will grant you, but a whore nonetheless. I have had her. The two princes have had her, and God knows how many others in this house have had her besides us," the duke snapped.

"In a week's time?" Beau responded dryly. "No, cousin, you, and the princes only."

"Yet you would still give her our name?" The duke was incredulous.

"What of the beautiful widowed Madame de Cannes?" Beau demanded. "You introduced her to me at court, and considered her an excellent candidate for my wife."

"I still do," the duke replied. "Fleur de Cannes is an exquisite woman, and would do our name proud."

"You have been fucking her for two years now, cousin, even before her husband died. Explain to me the difference between Madame de Cannes and Lady Abbott. Both are widows of good family who have embarked on little adventures of the flesh, although I would consider your Madame de Cannes far less desirable because she cuckolded her poor husband, while my Marguerite nursed her husband devotedly until his death. Damnit, César, you know what happened, and when she came to her aunt for protection, you took advantage of her!"

"Is that what the little whore told you?" The duke's handsome face darkened with his anger.

"She told me nothing, César. Indeed she is amazed that I would make her an offer of marriage because of the life she has lived this last week."

"Then she is far wiser than you, cousin," the duke told Beau scathingly. "I cannot blame her for accepting even though she surely must know better. I shall go to Madame Renée myself, and say you were drunk with wine and lust when you spoke. I will withdraw the offer. Madame will certainly understand, and so should the beauteous Marguerite. Renée has always been a practical woman."

"You will do no such thing, and if you attempt to do so, César, it shall be my great pleasure to kill you," Beau told the duke.

"Mon Dieu, you can't possibly love her! You barely know her. Granted she sucks cock like no other woman I have ever had, but she is really quite boring on her back. *Ouch!*" César d'Aubert fell back into a chair, his hand going to his newly bruised chin. "You have hit me, cousin!" he cried, astounded.

"If you find her boring, cousin, perhaps it is because your only interest in her was for your own pleasure, and not hers," Beau said.

"I brought her to *la petite morte*," the duke answered loftily.

"But with me she gained *la grande morte*," Beau returned with a smile. "And, César, I do love her, odd as that may seem to you on so short an acquaintance. She is not meant for the life her aunt leads. You know it as well as I do. Marguerite is delicate and fragile. She is meant to be a wife. Her blood is respectable, her first husband eminently so. She has not been at her aunt's long enough for her true identity to be made known. And as we will not be living in France, but in Louisiana, there is little likelihood of any gossip tarnishing the reputation of Madame d'Aubert of The Arbor Plantation. She has an adorable little girl to whom she is an excellent mother. She will be an equally good mother to my baby son. Now wish me well, César, and stop being a pompous fool."

"How will you explain how you met? And where she was living when you did?" the duke wanted to know.

"We will say we met in the park near the convent school of St. Anne that her daughter attends. Her aunt has already taken a small apartment near the convent for Marguerite and her two servants. The proprietor of the building is an old friend of Madame Renée's. Marguerite moved in this morning. We shall court publicly and properly for the remainder of the winter, and be married in April before we leave for Louisiana. I have already booked us passage. I would wed her tomorrow, but Madame Renée thought it better this way," Beau concluded.

"Yes," the duke agreed. "Renée has always been most discreet. She may be the finest courtesan in Paris, cousin, but she has never once forgotten she is a lady of the ancien régime. The king is quite fond of her, you know."

"Then you will give us your blessing," Beau said quietly.

"We will see," the duke replied. There was obviously no arguing with his American cousin, who had lost all sense of who he was, who their family were. I shall need time, César d'Aubert thought to himself, to consider how I may foil this misalliance, but stop it I will.

Renée, of course, was pleased, almost smug in her triumph, the duke thought that night as he visited her home. "This is madness," he told her angrily as they lay in her big bed.

"Non," she said firmly. "It is a perfect solution for both Beau and Marguerite. My niece could never be happy living the life that I do, monseigneur. She was brought up as her parents would have brought her up had they survived the Terror. You know that to be the truth. Marguerite is an excellent match for your cousin. They will, I firmly believe, live happily ever after."

"He will always remember that I had her first," the duke replied meanly, but Renée laughed.

"In the beginning the thought may possibly creep into his head now and again when they quarrel, but eventually his love and his passion for her will erase all those memories. He will recall only the times they have had together, César. And being an ocean away from Paris in his Louisiana with Marguerite will help. You will never leave France, César. You rarely leave Paris except for the races at Deauville in the summer." Renée smiled down into his handsome face. "Let it be, *mon brave,* and give them your blessing. You know how rare it is to find true love and real happiness in this world today. Be glad that they did. But for the last week in my house, my niece's life has been exemplary. The few men she has known here make her no worse than any other merry widow."

"Perhaps you are right, *chérie,*" the duke said convincingly, but his mind was even yet considering how he would prevent his cousin from marrying Marguerite. There had to be a way, but first he must learn where she was now living. "My cousin says you have taken quarters for your niece near her daughter's convent," he said. "You were very wise, Renée, to remove her from your house as quickly as possible. Your regular clients can, of course, be managed. Other than myself and the princes, none have had Marguerite, eh?"

"No others," Renée lied facilely. By the time the baron and the count returned, Marguerite would be long gone, and she could obtain their silence without difficulty.

"She has servants to look after her?" he probed gently.

"Of course. Her Clarice and Louis. They are a married couple, and have been with her for years." Renée chuckled mischievously. "Clarice was quite disapproving of Marguerite's residence here, and made no secret of it. As for poor Louis, he didn't know which way to look that his wife wasn't scolding him. They are both mightily relieved to be in other quarters, and overjoyed that their mistress will be remarrying such a fine gentleman. Beau has asked them to come to Louisiana, and they have agreed."

"And the building is respectable?" the duke asked.

"Of course," Renée replied, almost irritated with him for such a foolish question. "It is a lovely apartment with windows that overlook the river. The owner is Monsieur George's brother-in-law, Monsieur Dupuis. He and his wife live in the building along with six tenants. I was very fortunate that it was available, but there was a death," Renée explained.

"You have thought of everything, *chérie,*" the duke said smoothly. He was, however, already formulating a plan. His

American cousin was too stubborn to change his mind. Beau fancied himself in love. And so it must be Marguerite who changed her mind. The only way to bring her to that decision would be to debauch her so entirely that her honor, and he knew she was honorable, would not permit her to marry Beau. He smiled to himself. It really was the perfect plan, and it would permit him to enjoy her favors once more. And he would bring the princes with him too. They had very much enjoyed Marguerite, to the point of even attempting to purchase her from her aunt.

He must act quickly to end this tragedy in the making. But first he would discover the exact location of Marguerite's new abode. He suspected that both Josie and Leonie would know. And then he must learn the daily routine of her day. Of course, his cousin and the servants would have to be temporarily disposed of so he could have access to his lovely and unsuspecting victim. César d'Aubert felt a thrill of excitement race through him. For once he was not being bored. Indeed this was going to be a delicious adventure.

He learned that Marguerite's little pied-à-terre was located on the first floor of the building. Its bedroom and salon windows faced out on a tiny garden terrace overlooking the River Seine. It would be simple to gain entry from there, the duke decided. He followed Beau one afternoon to learn the location of the building itself.

Renée, however, was not as trusting of César d'Aubert as he believed her to be. He had not yet given his blessing to the young lovers. His interest in Marguerite's abode was too keen. And then the two Persian princes let slip to Josie that they had been approached by the duke to partake in a carnal adventure. The princes were sybarites, but they were intelligent. They suspected that the duke meant some mischief. While they were disappointed to have lost the beautiful Marguerite's company, they did not wish to lose their privileges at Chez Renée. They were more than aware that the king was Madame's friend. If they harmed her, or those she considered her own, they could easily find themselves sent home in disgrace. They both far preferred Paris to any place else on the earth including the shah's stifling court. So on Madame Renée's advice, they enthusiastically pretended to go along with the duke's plan, lulling him into complacency.

Marguerite and Beau were completely unaware of the plot and counterplot around them. They had eyes only for each other. Each morning the American would arrive to join his beloved in a *petit déjeuner*. He was perfectly dressed and coifed. No one seeing him strolling down the street would have known that he had spent the entire night in Marguerite's bed, slipping out through her garden each morning before the dawn to return to the duke's house, where he changed his clothes. His valet, a young freed black named Pierre, kept his master's secret, pleased to see Beau happy again.

One afternoon as the lovers walked with Madame Renée in the little park on the river, she finally told them of the duke's duplicity. Marguerite was astounded, but Beau was very angry. Renée put a restraining hand on his arm. "There will be no violence, *mon brave*," she told the young man. "Sadly your cousin does not see that France has changed. He is, alas, a snob. I have spoken with Father Joseph, the priest who ministers to the nuns at St. Anne's. He will marry you this Sunday in the convent church. Only those who love you and wish you no ill will be there. Afterwards you will have a private wedding supper in your little abode. On Monday we shall present the duke with a fait accompli."

"And if he still objects, and threatens to blacken Marguerite's name publicly?" Beau demanded.

"Your cousin has a rather terrible secret he would prefer not to have revealed. The papers documenting his sins are with Monsieur Paul Kira's banking establishment in the Rue de la Paix. As you are my sole heir, Marguerite, should anything happen to me, these papers will be turned over to you. However, you may rest assured that nothing is going to happen to me," she concluded with a smile. "It will take but a word in César's ear to disarm him."

"Tante, my poor Charles has only been gone four months," Marguerite said. "I feel guilty remarrying so quickly."

"Charles would want it under the circumstances," Renée declared. "Besides, who can say that you and Beau would not have met even if you didn't come to Paris? And if you had, he would have loved you, and you would have had to accept his proposal, *chérie*, because he is determined to return to his Louisiana."

They both laughed, and Marguerite said, *"Tante,* you are, despite your rather unorthodox life, a romantic at heart."

"I fear, *ma petite,* that you are right," Renée admitted. "Now, what shall you wear on your wedding?"

"We should tell Emilie first," Marguerite said. "I hope she will not be too upset. She loved her papa very much."

"But she has also come to love Beau," Renée observed. "Have you not seen it, *chérie?* Emilie will be happy for you, and happier that you are taking her from St. Anne's to Louisiana."

"And she will be tutored at home by a governess," Beau promised. "I will not let you and your daughter be separated again, Marguerite."

His words caused her heart to swell momentarily. In the past weeks she had come to love him. She could not remember ever being so wonderfully happy, even with her beloved Charles. "Let us go this afternoon and tell Emilie. The three of us!"

Emilie was, as Renée had predicted, overwhelmed with her delight that Beau d'Aubert was to be her stepfather. "And the wedding will be here? This Sunday, *maman?* And shall I be your attendant?"

"Mais oui," her mother proclaimed.

"And what shall I wear? Ohh, I cannot wait to tell the girls that I am leaving St. Anne's!" Emilie said excitedly.

"Have you been so unhappy then?" Marguerite looked stricken.

"Oh, *non, maman,* I love it here, but I would far rather be with you. Will I have to go to a new school in Louisiana?"

"You will be taught at home, *ma petite,"* Beau said. "I have a little son from my first marriage, and he will be your baby brother. We will need you with us to help take care of Michel."

"And will there be more babies, Papa Beau?" Emilie asked innocently.

"I hope so," Beau told her, casting a burning glance toward Marguerite. "I want you and Michel to have several brothers and sisters, Emilie."

"Très bon!" Emilie declared enthusiastically.

The wedding was celebrated in late afternoon that Sunday. The guest list was small. Renée, François, Josie, Leonie, Clarice,

Louis, and Beau's valet, Pierre. Little Emilie attended her mama, dressed in a gown of pink and white striped silk, her pantalets edged in pink silk rosebuds, a wreath of silk flowers in her dark hair. The groom was garbed in a dark gray coat, a white ruffle-fronted shirt, a jonquil yellow brocade waistcoat, and cream-colored pantaloons. The bride's gown was pale blue with a pleated bodice, the hem decorated with a wide band of lace. The gown had long sleeves with a double lace cuff at the wrists, and puffs from the shoulder to midarm. There was a pink cameo pinned at her waist, pearl bobs in her ears, and about her slender throat was a gold and pearl chain from which dangled a matching cross.

The choir stalls were filled with the nuns from the convent. Many remembered the day when Renée had brought the infant Marguerite de Thierry from the Île de Cité prison, and into their care. They had not been at her first wedding, and so it pleased them to be at her second. She would, the Reverend Mother Othalie said, always be in the prayers of the sisters of St. Anne, even if she was an ocean away. Then the nuns in their black and white garb sang the mass, and Father Joseph, the convent confessor, performed the marriage service. Afterward they adjourned to the main salon of the convent, where a civil official awaited to perform the civil ceremony, necessary since the revolution. Wine was provided, the papers signed, and a toast to the newly married couple made.

"When are we going to Louisiana?" Emilie asked her parents.

"We sail from Calais on the tenth of April, *ma petite*," her stepfather told her.

"But that is two weeks away," Emilie said, dejected.

"You must finish out your school term," Beau told her, "and your mama and I should like our honeymoon."

"Thalia du Pont says honeymoons are naughty," Emilie replied primly.

"I certainly hope so," Beau murmured softly.

"Thalia is wrong," Marguerite said, blushing. "She is too young to know such things. I am surprised she would spread such misinformation based on her own ignorance."

"Quite right, Madame d'Aubert," Reverend Mother Othalie said. "Now, I believe you must leave us. Mademoiselle Emilie must return to her dormitory, eh?" She smiled at the adults and, to Marguerite's surprise, gave her a tiny wink.

They thanked the nuns for their kindness, and the newlyweds bid their few guests adieu, walking hand in hand down the street to their little apartment where Clarice, Louis, and Pierre would have now set out a small wedding feast for the bride and groom. Monsieur Claude had been notified that his tenant, Madame Abbott, married her suitor, Monsieur d'Aubert that afternoon. He and his wife were waiting to tender their felicitations as Marguerite and Beau returned from St. Anne's.

In the little salon a wedding supper had been laid out, but the three servants had discreetly disappeared to their own quarters in the attic. A linen cloth was spread on the table, a fire burned in the fireplace, and the candles in their silver candelabra flickered, casting a golden glow over all. Beau seated his wife, and she began lifting the covers from the dishes, serving him his supper as she did. There were oysters that had been baked in cream, dill, and white wine; a plump capon stuffed with dried fruit, chestnuts, and bread; a long silver dish of asparagus with a Hollandaise sauce; a plate of tiny lamb chops; potato puffs; delicate little haricots verts; fresh croissants; sweet butter; a small round of Brie cheese; and a bottle of champagne. On the sideboard was a Genoese cake, fresh fruit, and another bottle of champagne.

"How on earth did Clarice and Louis manage to obtain such a feast?" Beau wondered aloud, swallowing an oyster, a beatific smile lighting up his face.

"I am certain it is all my *tante's* doing," Marguerite decided. "You know what a romantic soul she is." She helped herself to several slices of capon and two tiny chops. "I am ravenous!" she admitted.

He watched her eat, amused by her great appetite, but then her appetite for other tastes was certainly as great. "Do you always eat like that?" he asked as she slid the remaining potato puffs onto her plate to be followed by the last two spears of asparagus.

"Are you afraid I'll get plump, Monsieur d'Aubert?" she countered, her tongue licking the Hollandaise from an asparagus tip. "I have always eaten like this. Charles used to say it was my healthy and most unfashionable appetite that first attracted him to me. All the other girls would go from the ballroom into the buffet and pick. I, however, ate with gusto. The ladies who counted, those doyennes of Almack's, were quick shocked, I am told." She picked up a potato puff, holding it between her thumb and forefinger, and fed it to him.

Catching her hand, he licked her fingers slowly, and most suggestively. "Delicious," he pronounced.

Marguerite smiled a slow smile at him. "Shall we have dessert, *monsieur?*" she said softly.

"What are you offering, Madame d'Aubert?" he asked her.

"There is fruit and Genoese cake," she replied innocently.

"Perhaps later," he said, standing up. "For now I can think of a sweeter treat, Marguerite." He moved around the small table to draw her into his arms.

"Can this all be true?" Marguerite said softly. "Am I really your wife, Beau? And will we leave France in just a few weeks?"

"*Oui, oui,* and *oui,*" he responded, kissing her brow.

"I love you," she told him simply.

"I know," he said quietly. "And I love you."

The tears began to slip slowly and quite suddenly down her cheeks. "Oh, Beau, that you should love me after what I have been," she murmured low. "That you could make me your wife. I shall never be able to love you enough, I fear." She slipped her arms about his neck, burying her head in his shoulder as if to hide from him.

Gently he raised her face up to him and began kissing her, tasting her lips on his as if it were the very first time. Shivers of excitement raced up and down her spine, and feeling it, his own arousal was fired. He increased the pressure on her luscious mouth until it opened, allowing his tongue to slip in and forage within the hot cavern, fencing with her tongue, which came forth to meet his. Their passions flared up conjointly. He tore his mouth away from her to kiss her closed eyes, her cheekbones, her stubborn little chin, the tip of her nose. And all the while Marguerite's hands were desperately pulling at his garments to loosen them.

His cravat hung limp. She pushed his coat from his big frame.

Her hands fumbled with the buttons on his shirt, opening them, and slipping beneath to touch his warm, bare flesh, for he had worn no undergarment. A wicked thought crept into her head, unbidden. If he wore no upper undergarment, did he wear one beneath his trousers? Her hands smoothed over his broad chest, but then, her curiosity rising, she moved from his chest to grapple with his trouser fastenings.

"I am not *wearing* drawers," he murmured softly in her ear, and Marguerite blushed to the roots of her dark hair with the awareness that he had read her thoughts, but then she murmured back, *"Neither am I, chérie."*

Beau laughed softly, then he turned Marguerite about, his big fingers nimbly undoing the dainty mother-of-pearl buttons that held her bodice closed. Slipping the garment off her delicate frame, he pushed the straps of her sleeveless chemisette from her shoulders, pulling the garment down to bare her breasts. His hand slipped beneath them to cradle them in his palm. Kissing her shoulder, he said to her, "You are a most tempting armful, Madame d'Aubert. You fill me to overflowing with lust." His teeth sank into her flesh, nipping at it playfully. "Tell me you want me too."

"Oh *mais oui*, Monsieur d'Aubert, I very much want you," she told him. Marguerite arched herself back against him, her round bottom grinding provocatively into his groin. "Very, very much," she repeated.

She was making him hard, but it was too soon. This was their wedding night, and while they knew each other very well by now, he still wanted it to be wonderful and memorable for them both. Removing his hands from her breast, he began to undo her skirts, both outer and under. The fabric puddled about her feet, and he lifted her free of the garments even as she drew the chemisette over her head and tossed it to the floor with the rest. She was now attired only in her cream and blue striped silk stockings, held up by garters of pink rosettes, and her heelless round-toed cream silk slippers with their seed pearl bows.

He stepped back from her, his look admiring. *"Mon Dieu, ma petite* Marguerite, you are utterly perfect. You are like a small marble Venus, *chérie."*

In reply she giggled at him. "And you, sir, are all awry with your garments askew while I stand as God fashioned me."

He grinned, and began to pull off his remaining garments. "I do not believe, *madame,* that *le bon Dieu* made you with silk stockings and such suggestive little garters. Do not remove them yet. They are very tempting and exciting." He sat down to yank off his ankle-high brown leather shoes with their low square heels and his stockings. Then looking up, he beckoned her. "Come, Madame d'Aubert, and sit upon my lap. It is time for you to be naughty, I believe." He waggled his thick dark eyebrows at her wickedly. "Eh?"

She stood facing him, an index finger in her mouth, which she then withdrew slowly. "How naughty, Monsieur d'Aubert?" Her little tongue flicked swiftly over her lips.

"Very naughty, *chérie,*" he told her, and held out his hand. *"Very, very, very naughty."*

Her cornflower blue eyes moved to the thatch of dark curls between his thighs, where his love lance now bobbed eagerly. "I do not know if you are ready to be *that* naughty with me, *mon mari.*"

"You are trying my patience, madame," he growled, and reaching out swiftly, he yanked her to him, pulling her over his lap. His big hand descended upon her bottom with a satisfying *smack,* and she squealed, more with surprise than any hurt. The big hand spanked her four more teasing blows. "Are you ready to be naughty now, *madame?*" he demanded with mock severity.

"No! No!" Marguerite cried, wiggling her now pink buttocks at him. "You daren't spank me again, *mon mari!*" Her agitated motion sent her shoes flying.

"What?" He pretended to be outraged, but the truth was he was enjoying this game every bit as much as she was. "You would defy your husband, *madame?*" Then he rained six more spanks upon her hapless bottom, his own excitement rising as she wriggled and wiggled against him.

"Oh! Oh! Do stop, Monsieur d'Aubert. I promise to be bad! I do! *I do!*"

He slid a hand beneath her, his fingers pushing through her nether lips, feeling the sticky wetness of her juicy cunt. "You are deliciously wicked, *madame,*" he said softly, "and may you always remain so because it is for me you will cry out with pleasure." Turning her over, he fastened his hands about her narrow waist and lifted her up, lowering her onto his raging cock with a deep groan.

"*Ahhh!*" Marguerite sighed as she sheathed his hardness, then she squeezed him as tightly as she could, and he cried out. Her arms rested lightly about his neck. She leaned forward to rub the tips of her breasts against his smooth broad chest even as she raised her slender legs encased in their silk stockings to wrap about his middle. Her silk-clad toes tickled his spine.

"Ah, vixen, you are indeed ready to be naughty," he approved. "Now, will you do as I say, or must I spank you again?"

"I will do as you say, *mon mari,*" she vowed.

"No, do not close your eyes, *chérie,*" he said. "I want to see the look in them when I make you come, and it will not be long now, for you are a greedy wench. I can only imagine what our hot Louisiana nights will do to you. Now ride me, as you would your mount in the Bois."

"You are my stallion," Marguerite agreed, and did as she was bid until they were both so filled with pleasure that they collapsed into each other's arms gasping with their exertions.

Finally Beau arose, still holding his bride, and carried her into their bedroom. He lay her down upon the bed, and Marguerite reached up to draw him down to her. He came willingly, his hands molding themselves down her torso, filling themselves with her hips, caressing her legs. He took each foot in its turn and kissed it ardently. Sliding up over the silk sheets, he took each garter of rosettes in his teeth and drew it off. Next came her stockings, which he tossed aside carelessly. "*Je t'aime, ma coeur,*" he said softly. "*Je t'adore!*"

He moved his big body again, this time so he might lower his dark head to her beautiful little breasts. His hot tongue began to encircle a nipple. Around, and around, and around yet again until she began to whimper. He then took the entire nipple into his mouth, sucking hard on it, sending a sharp burst of sensation through her that enveloped her whole body. He now turned his attentions to the other nipple, and soon Marguerite was moaning as the pulses of rapture raced through her. He only ceased the wonderful torture when she began to tremble against him.

He next began a detailed exploration of her body with his tongue. The warm, silken flesh moving slowly, carefully down her torso, tasting her, sending her pulses racing as a wave of heat swept over her. The wicked tongue didn't miss an inch of skin as he slid over her petite body. He turned her over and began to tongue her shoulders, her back, her deliciously rounded buttocks, still showing a faint flush from her earlier spanking. He even licked the soles of her narrow feet, his tongue pushing between each toe suggestively.

"*Mon Dieu,* Beau, stop! You are killing me!" Marguerite cried.

He turned her back again, his eyes burning with his hunger for her. "Then, my darling Madame d'Aubert, we shall die together," Beau declared, and he lowered his head to touch her in the most sensitive place she possessed.

"*Ohh, yes!*" Marguerite half sobbed, her body seeming to burst into flame as his relentless tongue drove her, as his mouth tasted her.

Beau felt as if he would burst with his ferocious desire for her. The sweetness of her filled his nostrils as his tongue savored her honeyed musk. His head was spinning, but he could no longer control himself. Pulling himself up, he drove deep into her burning sheath. With a wild cry, Marguerite wrapped herself about him, pushing her hips up at him to meet his frantic rhythm. Her soft little sobs told him that she was near her release. He ceased his motion, lying quietly atop her, his love lance throbbing within her burning body.

"*No!*" Marguerite cried. "Do not do this to me! I am so near, and it is so wonderful!"

"You are in too much of a hurry," he admonished her, kissing her forehead. "Pleasure between a husband and a wife should be relished, slowly, *ma chère* Marguerite."

"I hate you!" she sobbed.

"No. You want me every bit as much as I want you, but I would not have it over too soon. Patience is not a bad thing, and this is our wedding night. I want you to always remember it."

Then he drove back into her, his rock-hard love lance pushing deep, forcing her down into the mattress with each fierce stroke.

She had been clutching at him in her passion, but now she began to rake his back with her nails, half crying with her pleasure.

"*Petite* bitch," he growled, and then he kissed her savagely, drawing her tongue into his mouth, sucking upon it relentlessly and without cessation.

I am dying, Marguerite thought, but she didn't care. Suddenly her love juices were crowning the head of his hot, hard cock. And in the same instant he released his own boiling tribute into her, crying aloud as together they shuddered with their mutual release. They fell apart, half-conscious with release and weak with their shared relief. Still he managed to draw her back against his chest, his big hand stroking her dark hair gently.

"Perhaps," he whispered to her, "we have made a child."

"Ohh, I hope so," she murmured back. "I never thought I should love again, Beau. I resigned myself to a life of shame. While I admire and love my aunt, I am not really like her at all. But then, as in the children's fairy tales, you came and you rescued me."

"How could I not, Marguerite? I loved you from the first."

"Your cousin will be very angry," she said, daring finally to broach the uncomfortable subject. "He will say terrible things to you, Beau. I do not want you to regret what we have done. It would break my heart."

"There is nothing César can say to me, *chérie,* that he has not already said. We have saved ourselves a great deal of difficulty by marrying quietly this afternoon. We sail for Louisiana in a few days, Marguerite, and we shall never see my cousin again. You will love my home, and New Orleans, while not Paris, is still a most delightful city to visit. We will grow old together, Marguerite, surrounded by our children and our grandchildren. Is that not the way it is supposed to be, Madame d'Aubert?" Then his lips met hers, and Marguerite melted into his tender embrace. The nightmare of Charles's death and all that it had entailed was over. Thanks be to *le bon Dieu,* she had awakened not just to a happily-every-after, but to a love such as she had never expected to know. How many women could say that, she wondered. And then laying her head back on her husband's broad chest, she answered him, "It is exactly the way it should be, Beau."

Epilogue

King Louis XVIII was sprawled in a comfortable tapestried chair in Renée de Thierry's private salon, his stockinged feet turned to the fire as he toasted his toes. "This is the only place where I am truly comfortable," he said, smiling up at his hostess, who placed an elegant Venetian goblet of excellent wine in his hand.

"I am pleased to hear you say so, Your Majesty," Renée replied. "You honor my house when you come to visit me."

"Come and sit next to me while César and I have our little chess game," the king invited her, turning from the hearth to the game table.

"I will," Renée answered him, "but first I have a little surprise for you, Your Majesty." She went to the door of the salon, opened it, and said, "You may come in now, *mes enfants.*" Then turning back to the king, she began, "Your majesty, may I present my niece, the widow of Lord Charles Abbott, and now the bride of Monsieur Beaufort d'Aubert, of Louisiana."

Marguerite curtsied, her pale yellow skirts billowing about her like a daffodil. "I am honored, Your Majesty," she said softly.

The king kissed her hand, and raised her up so they might speak. "Your parents were the Comte and Comtesse de Thierry, were they not? You look just like your *maman, ma chère.* Do you remember them at all? Such a terrible wicked thing, the Terror!"

"I was only three months old when they were killed, Your

Majesty," Marguerite answered him. "It was my Tante Renée who saved me."

"It was a brave act," the king agreed, "and one that should be rewarded, even now." He turned briefly to Renée. "I am bestowing your family's title upon you, *chérie*. You will be known henceforth as Renée, Comtesse de Thierry. That should cause a few eyebrows to waggle," he chuckled, then he turned back to Marguerite. "Your first husband was English?"

"I lived at St. Anne's, near the cathedral, until I was six," Marguerite explained. "Then I was sent to school in England. The Duke and Duchess of Sedgwick were my guardians. I met my husband during my first season."

"Sedgwick? Ah, but of course! He and his friends rescued several people from Madame la Guillotine," the king recalled. "Now tell me how you met this fine young *Americain?*"

"The duke introduced us," Marguerite said wickedly.

"When were you married?" the king inquired.

"Sunday, at St. Anne's, and naturally in a civil ceremony as well," Marguerite responded.

"You have given them your blessing, of course, César," the king said.

"Indeed, Your Majesty," the duke said through gritted teeth, a forced smile upon his lips.

"Do you play chess, Madame d'Aubert?" the king wondered.

"I do, Your Majesty," Marguerite said with a smile.

"César, give your cousin's wife your seat. She will play a game with me while you watch," the king commanded.

The Duc de Caraville arose and seated Marguerite politely. "Come and stand by your wife," he said to his cousin. "I am going to help myself to some of Renée's fine wine." He walked across the room to the sideboard, where the decanters and goblets were laid out.

"Let me pour," Renée said to him.

"*Bitch!* How you managed this I do not know," he snarled softly at her. "You have made an enemy of me, Renée."

"Do not be a fool, César. You know that they are right for each other. I will not accept your anger, especially as I have something very special for you later."

"But I've *had* her. Those two damned princes too!"

"They will say nothing. They know I have the power to have them sent home to Persia, and they would do anything to avoid ending up in the shah's court. Marguerite wasn't in my house long enough for anyone to remember her, César. Be fair, *mon ami.*"

"Why should I?" he demanded petulantly.

"Because, César, I know your secrets, and I also know that you do not want all of Paris to know them," Renée told him.

"What secrets?" he probed.

"Rome and, of course, the *difficulties* in Florence," she answered.

He sighed. "I suppose you have it in writing, and well attested," he grumbled. "Damn you, Renée, you are far cleverer than I ever imagined."

"That is because you see women only in terms of pleasure, César, *mon brave.* I did not survive the revolution because I was stupid."

He laughed and raised his goblet to her. *"Pax,* Renée, Comtesse de Thierry," he said. "I will forgive you, and I will forgive them as well. When do they sail for Louisiana?"

"In a week," she told him.

He shrugged. "So be it. Now, what is this little surprise?"

"I have a new girl," she began. "From Nantes. Her name is Michelle. She is sixteen, and you will be her first gentleman, but for her previous master. She is blond and has nice big breasts."

"She is amenable?" he asked.

"Very amenable," Renée assured him.

"Then let us hope his majesty makes an early night of it, Renée, but no matter when he goes back to the palace, I want my consolation prize."

"And you shall have it, *mon brave,*" she promised him. "Have you ever not had a good time at Chez Renée?"

And thinking back on it, the Duc de Caraville had to admit he hadn't. He smiled down at his hostess. "You are quite wicked, *chérie.*"

And Renée, Comtesse de Thierry, smiled back. "I am," she agreed. "I certainly am."

OUT OF THE STORM

Susan Johnson

Chapter One

Buckinghamshire, April 1894

The storm broke with a sudden violence, and the air turned cool. Blue lightning streaked across the sky, illuminating the squall line of racing clouds, as thunder crashed in rolling waves. And then, as if sufficient warning had been given, the rain descended in torrents.

In seconds, Lulu was soaked to the skin.

Perfect.

As if her day hadn't been wretched enough already.

Peering through the sheets of lashing rain, she tried to distinguish some recognizable landmark. After the disastrous note from her aunt—her heart still lurched as she recalled its contents—she'd been walking for hours and now . . . while she wasn't precisely lost . . .

She squinted into the driving rain.

Was the darkness due to the storm or the time of day?

She turned around searching for a familiar sight, heard a brief snatch of high-pitched peeping between gusts of wind and recognized the sound of young grouse. One of her gamekeeper's huts must be near. Swiftly moving through the downpour, she made for the faint squawking chorus, hoping the sound was coming from the brood hut nearest her home.

It wasn't, she realized, as the building's form materialized from the haze and the small porch came into view. It was the one at the boundary of her estate. The one her gamekeeper stayed in occasionally when his work kept him too late to make the long journey home. Which meant she was about as distant from the house as her many acres allowed.

She grimaced.

Could anything else go wrong today?

As if in answer, the sky opened up and discharged a veritable flood tide.

She was literally sputtering when she reached the low-roofed porch, and resting under the eaves, she drew in great breaths of dry air. The baby grouse sheltered under a lean-to attached to the side wall sounded oddly comforting—as though she had company in the storm. They brought back memories of her childhood when she'd spent time with their old gamekeeper, peppering him with questions, helping him with the baby birds, absorbing his kindness like a sponge.

It seemed like a hundred years ago.

A hundred lifetimes ago.

Shaking away her melancholy, she reminded herself she was considerably more privileged than a vast portion of the world. She should be grateful, not distressed. She should be thankful, as her grandmother used to say, for life's bounty.

And for a fleeting moment she was.

Until she remembered the note, left scattered in pieces on the drawing room floor.

Feeling a sudden chill, she unclasped the simple wooden door latch, pushed the door open, and stepped into the small room.

A single window offered a minimum of light. Tools were hung neatly on one wall, sacks of grain stacked beneath them. Several buckets and feeding pans lined shelves beside the door. A small stove sat in one corner, the pipe stack rising through the roof, and blessedly, a neat pile of chopped wood lay nearby. If she was going to be prisoner to the storm, she didn't relish shivering to death.

The cold was beginning to seep into her bones.

Quickly taking action, she soon had a cozy fire burning in the stove. Rummaging through a wall cupboard next, she found tins of tea and sugar. Braving the cold outside, she held a small pot under the porch roof and in moments had enough water to brew her tea. While the water came to a boil, she shed her drenched frock and hung it on a wall peg to dry. After a brief moment of hesitation in which she debated propriety against the clinging dampness of her undergarments, comfort won the day. Divesting herself of her chemise, drawers, petticoats, and stockings, she hung them up as well.

Since the gamekeeper stayed at the hut occasionally when the birds were hatching, further searching revealed a pallet and blanket neatly rolled up and tied with twine. Unfurling them near the stove, she brewed the tea, spooned considerable sugar into a mug, and poured in the steaming liquid. Sitting down cross-legged on the rough bed, she warmed her hands on the mug, inhaled the sweet scent, and smiled.

It was her first smile since she'd opened her aunt's letter.

Sipping the tea, savoring the flavor as it slipped down her throat and warmed her body, she decided happiness at the moment was distilled to the most basic of human needs—food and warmth. She grinned. Perhaps she'd discovered the secret of contentment.

Or at least a fine, temporary substitute.

After finishing her tea, she set about to find some provisions for her supper. She was lifting a tin of biscuits from the cupboard when she heard the footfall.

Apprehension raced through her senses. She listened more intently. There it was—clear . . . clearer now—crashing footsteps, as though someone were running, coming her way, the snap of twigs audible even through the storm. Stories of vagabonds flashed into mind; all the tales from childhood of ruffians and traveling gypsies flared front and center into her consciousness.

She was reaching for her chemise when she heard the heavy-booted tread on the porch, and before she could lift the garment from the peg, the door opened.

A huge shadowed form filled the doorway.

She shrieked.

"Forgive me." The door slammed shut. "I'll wait until you dress." The man's deep voice through the door was well bred, his words mannered and polite, but he wasn't asking for permission to come in. Lulu briefly debated refusing him entry. As quickly, she realized he was as stranded and stricken as she. Her only decision remained—which portion of wet clothing could be most easily donned. Her spring frock was a light flowered muslin—it had been a warm afternoon when she'd left; her undergarments were equally flimsy. Neither alone would suffice. Nor did she relish having the clammy fabric next to her skin. The gamekeeper's wool blanket would have to do, and with dispatch, she twined it around her, tucked in one corner to hold it in place, and made herself presentable in a makeshift sarong.

As a precaution, she took a knife from the cupboard before dragging the pallet into the shadows. Sitting down on it, she tucked the knife under her leg. Only then did she call out, "Enter!"

The door opened slowly.

Perhaps her visitor was as apprehensive, she thought, suddenly feeling less afraid.

"My apologies again for intruding," the stranger said, dipping his head in order to clear the low doorway. "But it's very wet out there." Once inside, he stood upright, pushed the door closed, and smiled. "I smelled the smoke from your fire."

He *was* a gypsy, dark and swarthy, with Romany eyes, or he might have been if not for his fine tailoring. Perhaps he was a very rich gypsy, Lulu thought with the inordinate cheer that had overtaken her with her tea. Had she brewed magic tea? she fleetingly considered, in this tiny hut deep in the forest. "Are you a gypsy?" she asked, as she might have as a child—with unabashed candor.

"My mother was," the stranger answered.

And if not a shiver, an unqualified flutter tore up her spine. She must be dreaming, she decided, experiencing a strange flood of warmth. But it was a very lovely dream. This gypsy was handsome as a prince, dressed in country tweed and leather and not at all frightening. "Would you like some tea?"

"I would." He began taking off his sodden coat.

He seemed not to notice as she rose from the pallet and poured tea into a mug, and his casualness only added to the incredulity—as though they were part of some otherworldly Grimm brothers' tale and soon the witch or fairy godmother would appear.

He hung his coat on a peg beside her frock, took the mug she held out to him, and sipped the steaming tea, his gypsy eyes smiling at her over the rim of the cup. "How did you happen to be out in the storm?"

"I was walking." It no longer mattered why, and she took instant comfort in the fact. "And you?"

"My automobile broke down."

So much for gypsy princes and fairy tales. "Your automobile?" The vehicles were rare. The Prince of Wales had one, the Tsar, the Kaiser, Sir Ernst Cassels, who could buy his own country if he wished. And now apparently, this very rich man.

"I made the mistake of driving without my mechanic."

"Certainly a mistake in the country. You'll have to take it back to London for repairs."

"After the rain."

Her brows flew up.

"If you don't mind?" he tactfully added, "Miss—"

"No . . . no, of course not," she quickly replied, her hesitation minute before she added, "Sarah—ah—Reynolds."

He took note of the brief falter, of the flutter of her lashes as she spoke. He bowed gracefully. "William Fielding at your service . . . or more aptly in your debt for allowing me refuge from the storm. Would you mind if I took off my boots? They're about to swim away."

"Please do. They'll dry by the fire." He was soaked through as she'd been, his chamois breeches fitting him like a second skin, she noted, but it was impossible to tell him to disrobe. Since the divorce, she'd taken a more cautious view of men. Not that she wasn't grateful to be rid of her husband, but the changes in her life had brought with them a new outlook—or at least they had until today. The letter had rocked her hard-won serenity, flooding her with indecision. "You must be visiting in the area," she quickly said, wishing to disrupt the disquieting train of thought that had to do with her aunt's message.

"I was thinking of it." He looked up from pulling off his boot.

He had remarkable eyes, dark, soulful, fringed with the most beautiful lashes, poet's eyes. "And now you'll be delayed . . . with your repairs."

Her voice held a small tremulous heat at the last.

He immediately took note.

She did as well, with shock. "I meant . . . that is—since there aren't any mechanics . . . and with the storm and all—"

"I understand." He kept his voice moderate, his gaze shuttered. Her agitation was plain. She'd not meant to express herself so, although her unintentional seductiveness was damnably intriguing. As was her lush beauty. All of it, he thought, the image of her voluptuous, nude form etched in his memory. He almost looked at his watch, wondering how much time they had until morning, the impulse predicated by a lifetime of amorous adventure. But he didn't, because clearly she was uncomfortable and he wasn't in the habit of pressing women.

He'd never had to.

"Should I get more water for tea?" he asked, wishing to put her at ease. He set his boots by the stove.

"Yes, please." She took a small breath, ran a hand through her hair, and then silently chided herself for acting like an untried maid. When she never had been and certainly wasn't now. "I should apologize," she firmly said, meeting his gaze directly. "I'm not usually so awkward."

"I barged in on you. It was my fault entirely. You sit, I'll make the tea, and you can tell me about Buckinghamshire."

He was as adept at making tea as he was at putting her at ease, moving about the small room with a casual familiarity, asking her questions about the area, listening to her answers with interest. When the tea was ready, he brought over a pail, turned it over to make a table, and set their cups with the tin of biscuits on it. "Would you mind if I hung up my shirt and waistcoat to dry and you may say no, if you wish. I won't take offense."

"What would you do if I took offense?" A playful note infused her question; his charm was contagious.

His grin flashed white against his swarthy skin. "I'd leave them on, naturally."

"Are you always so chivalrous?"

"Absolutely." She apparently wasn't going to take offense, so he began to unbutton his waistcoat. "My gypsy mother taught me well."

"Was she really a gypsy?"

He nodded, stripped his waistcoat off, pulled his shirt over his head, and after hanging them to dry, sat down on the floor Turkish-style and reached for his cup. "My father's family was appalled."

"How very romantic." But she kept her voice temperate with effort. He was powerfully muscled, like a gladiator—or a warrior from the steppes with his silky black hair and swarthy skin, with the faint slant to his eyes.

"It was," he quietly said and then his voice took on a briskness. "Do you like the tea? I make it very strong and sweet."

He obviously didn't want to pursue the subject and she graciously took her cue. She also took care to avoid any further thoughts of warriors or gladiators. "My parents had the most ordinary marriage. Arranged and cordial, perhaps distant would better describe it. And I do like your tea," she added, preferring not to discuss her parents' marriage either. It had been as disastrous as hers. "Try the biscuits."

He did and, with her permission, ate most of them, at which point he glanced upward at the pounding rain on the roof, then at the wall cupboard. "I hope we have more than biscuits to eat. I don't think we'll be having our dinner tonight."

"In that case, I hope you can cook."

"I can manage, provided there's something in the larder." Draining his cup, he rose and rummaged through the cupboard, holding each useful item aloft as he found it, including a small jug of cider he immediately uncorked and tasted. "Someone's a good judge of cider," he said with a note of satisfaction. "Would you like an aperitif?"

The mugs served an additional purpose and Lulu sipped on Thomas's cider while her companion opened cans and proceeded to heat and serve a veritable smorgasbord of foodstuffs. There was even a canned plum pudding for dessert and a candle to give them light. The pail top wasn't sufficient to hold the array, so it was spread out on a towel between them. When all was prepared, he refilled their cups. "To our shelter from the storm," he proposed with a grin, "and good company and good food thanks to the well-stocked cupboard. Please"—he waved his cup—"serve yourself."

Perhaps it was the hard cider, or maybe he would have noticed anyway, but when she leaned forward to make her selections, her bosom swelled in delectable mounds over the wool blanket that swathed her. He glanced away the first time, but as their meal progressed, he found it more difficult to ignore her large, sumptuous breasts, their deep cleavage, the swirl of her auburn curls on her bare shoulders. Concentrating on their conversation with effort, he kept his gaze politely focused on her eyes. But the necessary tact and restraint strained every chivalrous impulse he possessed, and despite his best behavior, either his chamois trousers were finally drying or his arousal was making them increasingly tighter. "I think I'll get a breath of fresh air," he finally said, coming to his feet. And probably a cold shower too if he wanted to continue to act the gentleman.

She watched him walk the short distance to the door, the dim light and small room enhancing his size, casting his musculature into heightened relief. And she felt a flutter of arousal when she'd been celibate by choice for a very long time. When she didn't care to feel aroused. When it was impossible to allow herself to feel desire for a perfect stranger . . . a man she'd not even felt comfortable giving her name to.

It was impossible, she repeated. Unthinkable.

But he was incredibly handsome, a devilish voice reminded her, and incredibly charming—and he could cook. As if it mattered. As if any of it mattered, a more practical voice of caution warned. She nervously glanced around the small room because she'd not had sex for almost a year and suddenly she wanted to. Under the most improper circumstances.

Who would know, her mischievous voice challenged. Out here in the middle of the woods in the middle of a storm.

The door opened and her gypsy returned, his half-nude body wet, glistening, his bare feet leaving footprints on the floor. "Is anyone expecting you home tonight?" His voice was low, almost a whisper, and his dark eyes held a searing heat.

When she might have been afraid, she felt only relief. "You're wet." Her absurd observation was in lieu of saying something even more absurd.

He seemed not to notice. "I'm trying to cool off. Answer me— is anyone expecting you home tonight?"

"What if I said yes?"

"I'd say what are you doing tomorrow?"

"And what if I said I'm busy?" But her equivocation was evident even to herself.

"I'd ask you about the next day."

She smiled. "You're persistent."

He shook his head. "On the contrary, I've been trying to talk myself out of this particular insanity."

"Why?"

"Because I'm only passing through and you intrigue me. I'd prefer just passing through."

She shrugged as she had in the past, when she'd played amorous games, when being dégagé had been a familiar pose, when men who were intrigued were a constant in her life. But she found she couldn't so easily say what she'd intended to say about the merit in passing fancies. "You're right," she said instead.

"I'm not sure I am."

She smiled again. "Why don't I be sure for both of us?"

"If only you could."

Her brows rose in the faintest arch. "Is that a threat?"

He kept his distance; he was really trying. "No, of course not. I only meant you can't be sure for me." He shrugged. "It's impossible."

"We're strangers, though." She meant for it to sound daunting, a barricade to what they both might be feeling.

"We'd never see each other again."

"Don't say it like that." Velvety and low, his words had been disarming.

"I thought you meant to give license."

"I meant we *aren't* acquainted."

"Ah . . ."

His silken murmur caressed her, fluttered through her vagina in a strumming drift of longing, stirred her already overwrought senses. "We don't know anything about each other," she said, more softly than she'd intended.

He moved closer at the obliging sound, squatted down before her. "What do you want to know?"

"Do you do this often?"

His surprise showed. He'd expected any number of other questions about his background and antecedents. "I've never done this before," he quietly said.

"If I decide . . . to—I mean"—even in the candlelight her blush was unmistakable—"oh, God, I don't know what I mean." She looked away for a moment, and when her gaze returned to him, she said in a rush, "You promise we'll never see each other again?"

"Not if you don't wish it."

"I don't."

He nodded.

A dead silence fell, only their breathing and the crackle of the fire audible.

Her lashes lowered before his dark gaze. "I shouldn't," she whispered. "I don't know you."

"I could change that."

She shuddered at the delicious promise in his voice, at her quivering desire, blamed her year-long celibacy for her irrepressible need. And he was so close . . . so splendid . . . and *large*. Her gaze dropped to the bulge in his chamois breeches and she caught her breath. "One more thing," she said on a suffocated breath, knowing what she was going to do. "You can't come in me."

"I won't."

She inhaled, clenched her fists.

His gaze slid to her hands and then back again to her face. "If you'd rather not."

"No . . . it's just that's it's been"—she blew out a breath—"a very long time and I'm not entirely sure . . ."

"We'll go as slowly as you wish. You decide," he offered, hiding his relief. It had taken every ounce of willpower he possessed to offer her deliverance in his current state of arousal. Thankfully she wasn't opposed, only uncertain. "You tell me what you want, what you need. It's up to you."

Maybe this was a fairy tale after all. He was offering her anything she wanted. Her sudden smile was radiant. "Are you real?"

He grinned. "I'm anything you want me to be."

She leaned back on her hands and surveyed him. "Because you want sex."

"And you don't?"

"I'm trying to decide."

"You already have." Leaning forward, he brushed her toes with his fingertips. "I can feel the heat from here."

"It's the stove."

"Among other things," he said with a boyish smile. "How long has it been?"

She hesitated for a moment. "Long enough that I feel like a novice."

A sudden frown brought his brows together. "You're not a virgin, are you?"

"Would that be a problem?"

"That would be a problem."

"How much of a problem?"

"Don't play games, darling." His voice was gentle, but his eyes were edgy. "I'm not in the mood. Tell me."

"What if I don't want to?"

He sat back on his heels, his expression suddenly uncertain.

"How much do you want to have sex?" Her query was light, flirtatious, his uncertainty oddly satisfying.

"There aren't enough words," he said, not lightly at all.

"Then maybe you'll have to find out for yourself."

"Has anyone ever told you, it's not wise to tease?" An undercurrent of danger imbued his words.

Whether oblivious or audacious, she ignored it. "But if you don't ruin virgins, I'm not at risk whether I tease or not."

"If you're *not* a virgin though," he silkily murmured. "Have you thought of that?"

"Oops." She hid her giggle behind her fingers.

His gaze narrowed. "How much cider did you drink?"

She grinned. "Just enough to have lost all judgment, apparently. Now then," she went on, mischief glittering in her gaze, "would you care to inspect me and see if I pass the virginity test?"

"No, I would not." His voice was gruff.

"We're here all night with the storm and we'll never see each other again." She lifted her brows. "But if you want to stand on ceremony . . ."

He didn't want to do anything but tumble her back on the pallet and ram his cock into her. While she seemed intent on play. "Fucking little tart," he muttered. On the other hand, she was a damned glorious sight.

"That's for you to find out, isn't it?" she flirtatiously countered. "Although I don't know if I qualify. I haven't made love for a year."

His erection swelled at the lustful possibilities, but a streak of cynicism responded as well. "Why not?" he carefully inquired.

"My goodness, we're suspicious."

"Cautious."

She grinned. "Let's just say I found God."

"Novel. And now you've decided to discard him?"

"He's on vacation."

"How fortunate," William dryly observed, but his reserve was obvious.

"I don't have any diseases if that's what you're worried about."

"I'm relieved."

"You're also the politest man I've ever met or else you don't like me," she playfully added. "When we're all alone in the storm. Should I faint and then you'll have to come to my rescue?"

"That won't be necessary." His wariness assuaged on a number of issues, he lay down beside her, stretched out, and tucked his arms under his head. "Since I've had sex more recently than a year, yesterday as a matter of fact, maybe there's no need to rush into this until we're better acquainted." He shut his eyes.

"What do you think you're doing?" Surprise and resentment flared through her voice.

His eyes half opened. "Paying you back."

"I apologize."

"Too late. And what if you're a virgin?" he said, baiting her. "You weren't clear on that."

"I'm not!"

"I can't take a chance." He closed his eyes again.

"Am I going to have to show you?"

His eyes lids lifted slowly. "Please, no demonstrations."

"You're very annoying."

"You started it."

"Regardless, you're not very gallant."

"Are you looking for gallantry? I thought you had something else in mind."

"Very funny. Damn you—"

"William," he offered.

"Damn you, William. After waiting a year to feel this way, to actually want to make love again, I have the misfortune of running into *you* in this secluded hut."

"Or perhaps the good fortune," he calmly observed. "But you'll have to ask me nicely before you find out."

"I will not!"

"Fine. We'll sleep. I don't suppose you want to share that blanket."

Leaping up from the pallet, Lulu stomped away, although her dramatic retreat was aborted by the restricted space in which to stomp. She was forced to return after three paces.

"You should have been on the stage," he said, grinning.

"And you're sadly lacking in manners," she snapped.

"Because I won't make love to you?"

"Yes, because of that." She couldn't believe what she was saying, no more than she could believe how much she wanted to make love to this tall, beautiful, maddeningly uncooperative man. Was it because of the outlandish manner of their meeting that this rare lust permeated the air? Or was there a finite limit to celibacy and she'd reached it. Or perhaps his beautiful gypsy eyes had her in their spell. "Tell me what you want me to say," she said, thin-skinned, restless, annoyed at both herself and him, "and I'll say it."

"That you're not a virgin, that you want me to make love to you. That you're sorry for toying with my feelings." Each word was unruffled impudence.

"You rude, insolent, cheeky, son-of-a—"

"You don't know what I am yet," he lazily drawled, every lounging inch of his magnificent body adding potency to his reply.

"And don't tell me I hurt your feelings," she irritably said.

His grin was roguish. "Maybe just a little."

"Hmpf. Just as I thought."

A seriousness entered his gaze. "I *do* need to know, however, whether you're a virgin."

"I'm *not*, nor have I been since my fourteenth year. Satisfied?"

His relief was palpable.

"Good God, you actually were *worried!*"

"Why shouldn't I be?"

"Because most men aren't. Not that you're commonplace in any way," she added, thinking instead how splendidly uncommon he was. Thinking as well, how much she wished to put that splendid body to the test. "I suppose, seeing how I made love a year ago and you did last night, if I want sex . . . *soon,*" she emphasized, giving him a vexed glance, "I'm going to have to ask you in some incredibly servile, truckling way." She sighed. "Very well. I'm sorry. I'm very, *very* sorry. Will you make love to me now?"

He came to his feet in a swift, effortless ascent. "I don't want servility." His gaze was curiously benevolent, considering the degree of smoldering lust also vying for position. "I'd be honored to accommodate you this evening. Most humbly honored."

Her smile was sunshine bright. "You can be very charming after all."

He smiled back. "I'm pleased you approve."

"I'll let you know later whether I approve." Provocative and teasing, she winked at him.

"Keep it up, darling," he drawled, "and you may never find out."

Her gaze dropped to his erection stretching his chamois trousers from crotch to waistband. "Really." Reaching out, she brushed her fingertips up the rampant, pulsing length. "You can keep that under control?"

"I don't need *you* for satisfaction."

"It depends on what kind of satisfaction you want."

"Or what kind *you* want."

"I have this overwhelming urge to slap you," she muttered.

"Maybe it's something in the air because I feel the same way." Her eyes flared wide. "You wouldn't!"

"What if I did?"

"Then you're no gentleman."

"But you're not really looking for a gentleman tonight, are you?" Reaching out, he slipped his finger under the edge of the blanket that girdled her bosom.

She couldn't find breath to answer with his finger burning into her flesh. She shook her head.

"That's what I thought," he murmured, loosening the blanket.

Gently pushing her shoulder with his other hand, he slowly turned her, unwinding the soft crimson wool until she stood naked before him. His practiced gaze traveled slowly down her splendid form. She was all that he'd remembered—utter perfection—small in stature, large-breasted, voluptuous, her slender waist flaring into curvaceous hips that reminded him blatantly of women's function as the font of fertility. His gaze came to rest on the auburn curls gracing her mons and he drew in a steadying breath. "I'll be right back," he said in a small strangled sound, and quickly moving away, he spread the blanket over the pallet.

He was beautiful as sin, she thought, watching him, his dark looks exotic, almost unconscionably handsome, as if he were the masterpiece of natural selection. His tall, bronzed body was powerfully muscled, his arousal equally virile, his allure magnetic. And he'd appeared out of the storm like some lavish gift from the gods.

Suddenly he turned and smiled, and the warmth in his eyes was wholly human.

"Your bed awaits you, Princess."

Was this some dream? she wondered, moving toward the rustic bed. If it was, she dearly hoped she wouldn't wake too soon.

He'd begun unbuttoning his trousers and further speculation was irrelevant with lust burning through her blood. He was only steps away, readying himself for her, wanting what she wanted. His hands were large, his movements deft; two buttons were already open. She shivered, desire washing over her in waves, the throbbing between her legs accelerating with paradise almost within her grasp. Moving closer, she brushed his hands away. "Let me," she breathlessly said, pressing her hands over his upthrust erection, shameless in her need. She could feel herself opening in welcome with the huge, hard contour filling her palms, with the pulsing life force hot against her hands. It had been so long . . . and fainthearted, she wondered if she could take him all? The monstrous length stretched above and below her cupped hands, and a small shudder of apprehension coursed through her body.

He had no such reservations, save for timing, his intent clear. He was going to spread her legs and fuck her—and soon. Covering her hands with his, he drew them upward to the gleaming head of his penis looming above his partially loosened trousers and curled her fingers over the massive crest.

"Are you ready for this?" he whispered.

Yes, yes, she wished to scream, but he was huge, so terrifyingly huge, reason held sway. "I think so . . ."

"Should we find out?" He began unbuttoning the remaining buttons because she seemed transfixed.

As his trousers opened and his erection was revealed, she gazed in awe. And when it was fully exposed, upthrust and rampant, she attempted to circle the monstrous proportions with her fingers. They didn't meet and she unconsciously whimpered, "My God." Fearful, but more ravenous still, she stroked the engorged length from top to bottom, sliding her finger down the distended veins. "Will this hurt?" she breathed.

"I won't hurt you," he promised, sliding off his trousers.

Mesmerized, she touched the very tip, the gesture, however delicate, vibrating deep inside her dewy heat. She bent her head to taste him.

"Don't." His voice was a low rumble. He swiftly raised her head. "I'm too far gone for that."

They stood close together in the candlelight, the heat of desire radiating from their bodies, carnal urgency drumming through their brains.

He couldn't remember ever feeling as though he were about to step into the abyss. His breathing was labored, his cock so hard it was aching, the woman before him so small her head barely reached his shoulder. What if he hurt her despite his promise? The way he was feeling—out of control, like he hadn't fucked in a decade—would he be able to stop if he had to?

She was trembling, no longer sure what day it was, or where she was or if it mattered who took the initiative. She touched him again—lightly brushing her finger down his chest.

He dragged in a breath, tamping down his most aggressive tendencies.

"I don't think I can wait," she said, looking up what seemed a great distance, her voice a wisp of sound. "I really can't . . ." And then, ignoring propriety if it even existed in this bizarre engagement, she pressed her body into his, reached up to grab handfuls of his hair, and wrenched his head down so he could see the urgency in her eyes. "Hurry!"

"Yes, ma'am," he breathed, hauling her down on the blanket, quickly rolling over her, easing one knee between her thighs.

She instantly spread her legs, clutched at his shoulders with such force, her nails sank into his flesh.

He softly grunted.

"I'm sorry," she whispered, quickly lifting her hands, shamed by her rapaciousness.

"No one's going to be sorry tonight," he said, husky and low, the head of his erection already breeching her labia.

She heaved upward to draw him in more quickly, arching her back, lifting her hips off the blanket in her eagerness.

There was little need for caution. She was dripping wet, her flesh yielding if not easily—yielding, his cock slowly sinking into her succulent flesh with a minimum of resistance. But a fragment of courtesy still marginally operated in his brain, and when he was buried to the hilt, he said, nearly breathless, "Am I hurting you?"

"No, no, no, no, no."

In his current ramming speed mode, it was the nicest possible answer. He kissed her for it and then gave her something she wanted even more than kisses.

He drove in a fraction more, gently . . . gently . . . and inhaled her gasp, the taste of her sweet in his mouth, the feel of her tight cunt right up there with the seven wonders of the world.

He was so large, so terribly, beautifully large; she was stretched taut, every susceptible nerve vibrating against his enormous size, her pulsing tissue greedy for him, wanting more. Flame-hot desire bombarded her brain, tore through her senses, wild delirium trembled just beyond reach.

He began to withdraw.

"No!" she cried, clutching his shoulders.

His brows lifted the merest fraction at her imperious tone and then he considered the delight in a woman of such desperation and half smiled. "You want this back?" He moved forward the barest distance and she purred, sighed, whispered, "Thank you," with such feeling he almost turned around to see if his guardian spirit was in the room because someone was definitely looking out for him. Some benevolent god or goddess had brought down the storm and brought him here—right here—to this there's-a-god-in-heaven paradise. Flexing his hips and legs for more leverage, he drove deeper in search of nirvana.

It was enough or too much depending on your point of view because she screamed and suddenly climaxed in a fierce, violent orgasm that lasted so long even a man of his experience took notice.

When it was over, when her whimpers subsided and the last vaginal ripple faded away, she eased her grip on his shoulders, languorously lifted her lashes, and said in a lush, wispy murmur, "That was definitely worth a year's wait . . ."

His smile was very close. "And we still have the whole night before us."

"I'll never survive . . ."

"Sure you will."

"Ummm . . . a pleasant prospect."

He moved inside her, delicately, side to side, ever so slightly forward as though testing the waters. "And it gets better . . ."

"You're very good," she whispered, exquisite sensation shimmering through her sated tissue. Not many men were so exemplary in their tenderness, so agreeably deft.

"And you're the ultimate temptation. I've good reason to take care."

"For your own pleasure."

"For ours."

Her eyes met his affable gaze. "You're polite."

"Would you prefer something else?"

The way he said it gave her pause and she wondered if she'd made a mistake. "No," she quickly replied, pressing her palms against his chest, suddenly unsure of this stranger.

He didn't move.

Save for his erection swelling inside her.

She cried out, jolted by the blissful pressure, not sure a moment later whether her cry was one of fear or rapture.

He knew though. He also knew he couldn't let her go regardless of her qualms so he forced his voice to a calmness he wasn't feeling. "Don't be afraid. I'm harmless."

"Hardly." But her reply was breathy with need, her body gorged full, throbbing.

Well versed in female sexual response, he understood the beautiful woman impaled on his cock was in rut, regardless of her unease. "You'll feel better after you come a few more times," he murmured, moving faintly inside her. "A year without sex." He smiled. "That's a long time."

His boyish smile helped mitigate her nervousness, as did the delectable rhythm of his rock-hard erection sliding slowly in and out in a languorous arousal. "I don't suppose you wait that long."

"Not usually."

"I'm allowed to be more greedy, then."

"Be my guest." Rotating his hips in a smooth, rolling circuit, he delicately glided over every turgid, throbbing dip and hollow of her vagina.

When she could speak again, she said, half-breathless, "What if I want everything?"

"Then you'll have it."

"Such blatant temptation," she purred.

"I'm way ahead of you. I've been tempted from the moment I stepped through that door."

"This must be kismet."

He softly laughed. "Or damned good fucking at least."

She smiled. "That's what I meant."

"Ah." They were in agreement.

He'd maintained the slow rhythm of his lower body as they'd conversed and she was finding it increasingly difficult to concentrate. Her senses were focused on the riveting flux and flow, the smooth, silken friction, and suddenly she rose to meet his downthrust.

"Stay there," she whispered, eyes shut, breath held.

"Here?"

"Yes, yes, yes—right there. I'll pay you back later . . ." She moved her pelvis in a provocative undulation.

His soft groan caressed her cheek. "That's not a bad start," he breathed, lightly gripping her hips, needing a moment to steady his nerves. Lord, she was small. Adjusting her minutely beneath him, he slowly withdrew, gauging the most prudent degree of penetration.

Murmuring in displeasure, she tugged on his shoulders, pulling him back.

He obliged, intent on pleasing her. But he moved cautiously, aware of his need for restraint. As if understanding his dilemma, she wrapped her legs around his hips, helping to ease his entry, allowing him deeper access. Her vaginal muscles were intriguingly strong, offering an intense, gripping massage down the length of his penis. Then she flexed them and his breath caught in his throat.

Was she practiced or artless? Although it didn't really matter, he decided a second later as he felt another rapturous ripple engulf his erection with such subtlety, he was reminded of the fleshly delights of Hong Kong.

She was damned good.

Her gypsy was extremely talented, not to mention well endowed, Lulu blissfully reflected. What good fortune.

They fit spectacularly in a fevered, skittish way—she fiercely impatient, he zealously controlled, both touched to the quick, scorched, hypersensitive to every nuance of feeling. The air was no longer cool, but hot, their bodies on fire as they mated in the remote hut lashed by the storm. Sweat beaded on his forehead, she was aglow inside and out, the slippery, fevered flow of their bodies approaching a state of carnal hysteria.

"More," she cried, close . . . close—reaching for the ultimate sensation. "Please, please . . . more!"

Even a saint would have succumbed and he was far from a saint. He was, in fact, by that time, maddened with lust, provoked, tantalized and so near climax he wasn't sure he could wait much longer.

But he had to—at least for a few moments more and he began counting backward from a hundred, fighting his orgasmic urges.

At ninety-four, she sank her nails into his back, rose into his downstroke, went tense in his arms, and sobbing and gasping, came.

Even for a man of his discipline—not a second too soon.

Jerking out, he arched his back against the convulsive tumult, the first ejaculatory spasms shuddering downward.

Suddenly, water poured through the ceiling overhead.

Lulu squealed.

William ignored the deluge, orgasmic ecstasy overwhelming cognitive function as he came on her stomach, the riveting rush of seminal fluid nullifying mundane practicalities. Until, moments later, postcoital reason returned, he finally heard Lulu's screams, felt the cold rain on his back, and quickly pulled them aside. "Sorry," he muttered, coming to his feet, lifting Lulu up. "I should have noticed sooner." He bowed his head faintly. "I beg your pardon, of course. You must be chilled."

The light from the candle burnished her shapely form, water glistened on her skin, damp ringlets framed her face.

"Actually, I'm on fire," she replied, a tremor in her voice.

His grin was instant. "Give me a minute," he murmured, grabbing two loose feed sacks from the floor. Reaching up, he stuffed them into the leak. Placing a pail under his stop-gap repair, he quickly hung up the pallet and blanket and turned back to her. "Now then"—he gazed at the semen oozing down her stomach and thighs—"you need some tidying up."

"That's not all I need," she whispered, her fingers clenched.

"You don't know how glad I am to hear that."

"While *I'm* pleased you don't think me too demanding."

His gaze flicked to his erection. "Not likely."

His arousal was undiminished, his penis stretching upward, nearly waist high. "I'm very lucky tonight," she breathed.

He dipped his head. "I'm equally fortunate."

"Are you always so amenable?" A seductive warmth infused her voice.

He looked at her for a potent moment. "Let's just say I'm highly motivated."

"I'm in heat. Like that." She pointed at his towering penis engorged with blood.

"How convenient," he said with a smile, picking up the towel they'd used for their tablecloth. "This . . . ah—compatibility of ours." And he set about wiping her dry—an action undertaken with circumspect detachment because they had only one towel as far as he knew, his sperm was running down her legs, and he couldn't afford to be distracted despite her soft moans. He was more interested in sex than foreplay. Luckily, so was she, he thought, kneeling to mop her stomach.

She ran her palms over his powerful shoulders, his hard, solid warmth incarnate male, the feel of him exciting her already overexcited senses. "That's good enough," she murmured, predacious in her need.

He looked up and smiled. "Soon."

"This is unbelievable," she whispered. "I'm never so . . . so— frenzied."

"It's bloody heaven." But he understood, too, how extraordinary the circumstances. He was out-of-his-mind impatient, driven when he never was—when he normally only played the game. Her wanton eagerness was a factor, he supposed, or the fact that her hot little cunt was so close he could bend over and lick it. Maybe the local cider contained some powerful aphrodisiac. Whatever it was, he didn't want it to end just yet.

Wiping away the last of his come from her thigh, he quickly dried himself, tossed away the towel, and slid one finger down the dampness of her cleft as though she were his personal property to do with what he liked. Gently probing her pliant flesh, he stroked the sleek verges of her labia, glancing up for a brief moment to gauge the urgency of her small incoherent sounds. Judging he still had time, he eased his finger in, circled the silken heat of her interior with delicate strokes, until her moans took on a new insistence. "Are you ready for fucking again?" he murmured.

His blunt query incited senses already inflamed, and she wondered if perhaps her year-long celibacy was the cause of her outrageous lust. Although the spectacular man kneeling at her feet was more than reason enough. Covetous of such splendor, not to mention his sexual talents, she whispered, "I should keep you locked away somewhere . . ."

"Or I you." He slipped another finger up her wet passage. "And then I could suck on your clit every day," he whispered, bending his head, shifting forward, running his tongue over the highly erogenous bit of tissue. "I could have you for breakfast . . ."

Her knees went weak. She suddenly had actual need of his strong shoulders as he leaned into the upward pressure of his hand and his lips closed over the tender nub of her clitoris. The pressure of his mouth and tongue was masterful—gentle, but not too gentle, slow at first and then slower still, his fingers sliding upward, stroking higher and higher, until minutes later, she was running wet, begging to feel him inside her, trying to draw him to his feet.

He didn't rise, but lifted his head and looked at her from under his long lashes. "Come this way."

"I don't want to." Fretful, impatient, her mouth formed a moue. "Get up! I want *you*."

Withdrawing his fingers, he said, smooth as silk, "I don't take orders."

A woman of wealth and position, she ignored his absolutism. "Don't be difficult. I just don't want to wait." Grabbing his dark hair, she pulled upward.

Knocking her hands away, he rolled back on his heels. "That fucking hurt."

Her expression was sullen. "I'm sorry."

"You'd better be."

She sniffed. "I'm sorry I mussed your precious hair. Now, are we going to have sex or not?"

He didn't answer for a moment. "It depends," he replied coolly.

"On what? On my subservience?"

"I wouldn't use that word."

His cool equivocation suddenly brought all her husband's iniquities and misused authority to the fore and she was reminded of the reasons she didn't miss Charles. "Forget it. I don't need you after all," Lulu abruptly declared and, hot-tempered, reached out, plucked a small garden trowel from a hook on the wall, leaned over without a second's pause, and eased the smooth wooden handle between her legs.

Wrenching the tool from her hand, William surged to his feet. "Let's not play games."

"You're the one playing games," she snapped.

"Because I don't immediately submit to your orders?"

"Yet I should comply with yours?" Her spine was rigid.

He blew out a frustrated breath. "You were begging *me* if I recall."

"To no avail, as *I* recall. Look," she tartly said, "I've gone a year without a man. I'll survive another night."

"Bitch."

"But not *your* bitch." She began to move away.

Dropping the trowel, he grabbed her wrist.

She turned back, her brows lifted. "Is there something more?"

"You might say that." Capturing her other hand, he forced her back against the wall, and leaned into her. "I was thinking about ramming my cock up your cunt."

"How gallant." But it was difficult to voice sarcasm when his erection was hard against her stomach and her body was traitorously responding.

"But then gallantry won't make you come again, will it?" he murmured, sliding his hands around her waist, lifting her to accommodate his height.

She struggled against his hold. "Let me go."

"Afterward"—his eyes met hers for a taut moment as he held her prisoner—"after I've had you." And bending his knees, he slid inside her with finesse, as willful as she, much stronger, forcing her up on tiptoe, raising her off the floor as he thrust upward and buried himself in her.

"No!" But even as she cried out, rapture flooded her senses.

"Hypocrite," he whispered. "You're so fucking wet, I could slide clear up to your throat. You *like* being filled with cock," he softly added.

She shook her head, but the movement was minimal with every nerve in her body tensed against the blinding ecstasy.

He didn't notice. He was wrapping her legs around his waist so he could press deeper. "Tell me how much you like this," he breathed, forcing her legs wider, slipping his hands under her bottom, securing his hold.

"Damn you!" But she was already feeling the first quivering, orgasmic flutters.

"Tell me." Pressing her back against the wall, he ground his crotch against hers in a hard, exacting rhythm that put exquisite pressure on her mons and clitoris, that effectively blurred the hard lines of contention, that made it impossible to take issue with the irrepressible glory of his invasion.

"Yes, yes," she capitulated, her eyes shut tight, pleasure washing over her in waves. "I like it—I do . . . I do."

"That's what I thought," he drawled, tightening his grip. "Now let's see how much you can take . . ."

After that, nothing mattered. Lulu was beyond resentment, without pride or principle, inundated by fierce, ravishing sensation. She clung to him, melted around him, welcoming each hard, powerful thrust with feverish passion, almost senseless, gasping for air, coming quickly once, twice, three times before the man holding her captive with his cock and arms said in a tight, constrained voice, "That's enough for now. It's my turn."

He swiftly lifted her away, placed her on her feet, waited a millisecond to see if she could stand, then softly swearing, frustrated and restive, spilled his seed on the floor instead of where he would have much preferred—inside her. Short moments later, his forehead braced against the wall, he tried to catch his breath, tried to remember where he was, wondered if he'd entered some sorceress's hut because he wanted to fuck her—still . . . again— right now this minute, like a man possessed. Pushing away from the wall, he glanced at Lulu, thinking her hair might have turned to spun gold or she may have dissolved into a cloud of mist for surely this wasn't the real world.

"Hello . . ." There was gloating satisfaction in the whispered word and not a scintilla of strife.

"Hello back."

His half-smile had a sensual charm—like everything about him, she thought. "Feeling better?" She was braced against the wall, languid, content, thoroughly indulged. "No more dictatorial moods?"

Merriment lighted in his eyes. "We don't *have* to do this anymore, if you'd rather not."

Her voice was still warm with residual pleasure. "I must admit, I'm not *completely* averse to authority."

He looked amused. "Because your greed isn't yet assuaged?"

"It's your fault. You're much too beautiful."

"Forgive my bluntness, darling, but you're not looking for beauty."

"I disagree. Your penis is very beautiful."

His eyes flared wide for the briefest moment. "Most women aren't so frank. Not that I'm complaining. At the moment, I'm quite willing to fuck myself to death. Don't ask me why." He reached for the used towel. "I haven't a clue."

"Maybe it's the storm."

He glanced at her. "Only in fiction, darling. My sex drive is immune to poetic fantasy."

"Perhaps mine isn't."

His brows flickered in roguish response as he searched for a usable portion of towel. "That must be it. Although, whatever the reason, this is about as near to paradise as I've every come. Save for the lack of a bed," he noted, glancing at the wet pallet, "and maid service," he added with a grimace, selecting a small corner of the towel and wiping himself. "I wouldn't mind a cognac right now, but then that's not likely either." He dropped the towel on the dollops of semen on the floor.

"Will you settle for cider?"

His hesitation was infinitesimal; he didn't know if he dared considering his already rapacious mood. "Why not." So much for good judgment.

"We could talk."

Another small hesitation. She noticed this time.

"Is that frightening?"

"Sometimes. Not at the moment, however," he graciously added.

While Lulu poured their cider, William improvised, taking down the blanket, wringing it as dry as possible, spreading it on the floor on the side of the stove opposite the leak. "I'm so hot in more ways than one that this wet blanket will serve nicely." Lying on his back on the makeshift bed, he held out his arms. "Come sit on me."

It wasn't an offer any woman with a heartbeat could refuse, Lulu thought, surveying his powerful body. Broad-shouldered, long-limbed, all honed muscle and strength, surely he'd been fashioned by the hand of god. "What if I said no," she teased.

"Then I'd have to come and get you," he drawled.

"Umm . . . get me? Would that have a sexual connotation?"

"Everything about this encounter has a sexual connotation, sweetheart."

"I know. You're most unusual." Picking up the cups of cider, Lulu moved toward him. "Tell me about yourself."

"And you tell me about yourself," he pleasantly countered, taking a cup from her, offering her his other hand to help her sit.

Neither had any serious intention of discussing their lives, but the necessity for subterfuge was obliterated almost the moment she settled on his thighs. Her legs were spread in a most enticing way, his indefatigable erection was fascinatingly close, and sexual desire replaced any inclination for conversation. Setting her cup down on the floor, Lulu ran her fingertip down the prominent vein on the underside of his penis. "May I?"

It took him a moment to answer; he was distracted by the explosions in his brain. "I wish you would," he finally answered, sliding his palms up her thighs, slipping his thumbs into her damp slit, needing to touch her.

"I'm going to have trouble concentrating," she whispered, gently rocking on his thighs, absorbing the enchantment his fingers provoked.

"Don't worry. I'll tell you what to do."

Her eyes narrowed.

"You said you weren't averse to—ah—suggestions. And you always like it," he added in soothing accents, gently rolling her clitoris between his thumbs, tenderly massaging the tumid flesh, pleased to see her lashes drift downward. "Now, wrap your fingers around my penis. That's not so hard, is it?"

Her lashes lifted and she smiled. "Yes and no."

He grinned. "Let's focus on the no." Her flesh was liquid under his thumbs; she was more than ready. "You know you want it again, darling. Look, how wet you are." Lifting one hand, he held out his thumb. It was drenched with pearly fluid, tiny droplets trailed down its length. "I'm going to slide in real easily," he murmured. "Now all you have to do is make sure I'm big enough to make you climax."

"You're more than big enough already."

"But if I'm bigger, you'll like it more."

His erection lengthened under her gaze, and lured, captivated, she circled it with her fingers, the pulsing heat, the solid thickness triggering a convulsive spasm deep inside her. She tightened her grip, slid her fingers upward slowly, tracing the splendid breadth and length.

His eyes went shut, and for a brief moment, he found it impossible to focus on anything but the delectable pressure.

When she reached the flanged ridge at the top, she gently squeezed.

"Now I'm ready to die . . ." he sighed.

"Please don't." She circled the gleaming crimson head with delicate strokes. "Because I'm still hot, hot, hot."

His eyes opened, but slowly as though it took considerable effort, and shaking away his soul-stirring self-absorption, he delicately cupped her pelvic bone in the curve of his thumbs. "Lift up," he murmured, exerting upward pressure.

She smiled and rose to her knees. "You're *ever* so nice. I just want you to know how much I appreciate your . . . er—courtesy." She'd watched him unselfishly come alert for her.

"It's not a hardship, sweetheart, believe me." He smiled. "If you're hot, consider me here to put out the fire." Withdrawing his thumbs, he slid one hand under her bottom, began to ease her into place.

But she quickly shifted her hips, drew his erection to the pouty lips of her labia, and plunged down his rigid length in a swift, sudden descent.

"Is this a sprint?" he teased, but he was swelling inside her. She could feel it; he could too, clear down to his toes.

"Next time, I'll consider something more leisurely," she murmured, slowly rising up his lengthening erection.

"Next time." He smiled. "I like the sound of that."

"And I the feel of this . . ." She sank down again.

They were both momentarily bereft of air.

When the conscious world came back into focus, when they could breathe again, he lightly gripped her hips, his fingers splayed over her pale flesh. "In case you need help staying on."

Her brows lifted. "Or perhaps you want to control the ride."

He shook his head.

"So you don't mind a woman on top?"

The way she said it required a moment to digest, but in the present circumstances, he'd be a fool to offer demur. "Not at all," he said.

It turned out to be true for she proceeded to ride him with a fierce, unbridled passion, and he absorbed each blissful, shifting, writhing bit of friction with relish and pleasure. Heedless of all but her driving need for consummation, she was an opulent sight to see, bucking and plunging, rising, falling, her cheeks flushed pink, her lavish breasts bouncing, her auburn tresses bobbing, the damp curls at her crotch colliding with his in the most lascivious carom.

She was ravenous, insatiable, unrestrained, coming to orgasm in a wild, breathless rush, over and over and over again. Until finally, out of breath, momentarily sated, she came to rest.

"I knew there was some reason for staying in shape." His grin was roguish as he brushed her tousled hair away from her face.

"Oh . . . my—god," she gasped. "Thank you . . ."

"My pleasure." A tame word for his own hotspur lust. "Are you warm enough?"

Her brows flickered.

"I only ask because this blanket's wet and I was hoping you wouldn't mind the coolness. Strangely," he explained, bemused, "I wish to be on top. Call it a need for variety, or more to the point," he added, suddenly serious, "consider it an ungovernable compulsion to dominate and possess you. I apologize in advance."

In exceedingly fine spirits, she only smiled. "No need to apologize—really. Possess away."

He apologized again anyway, because if she wasn't alarmed by his aberrant proclivities, he certainly was. But understanding the irregularity of his feelings did nothing to control them, and promptly rolling her under him, he proceeded to engage in a *droit du seigneur* style of dominant sex he'd never even contemplated before. There was no excuse, no precedent in his former life. He said that to her, breathless, faintly bewildered, as he ravished her with an almost savage violence.

"It's all right," she whispered. "We're both out of our minds." And she met his next powerful thrust with a wildness of her own.

But if they were crazy, it was the most opulent, exquisite, unparalleled insanity on the face of the earth. And they explored their glorious outlandish Xanadu of pure, unadulterated sex all through the night—with reckless abandon, with creative ingenuity, with curious affection at times. Until, at last, enervated by pleasure, exhausted, half asleep in his arms, Lulu whispered, "You're the very best, my darling gypsy."

He gently touched her face, traced the downy curve of her brows, smiled a smile of rare contentment. "And you're the sweetest delight on God's green earth, my darling Sarah . . ."

Chapter Two

He'd been awake since dawn, holding her in his arms while she slept, smiling frequently whenever he recalled the memorable night past. Having enjoyed the lovely Sarah's hotblooded passions, he was contemplating a much longer stay than originally planned in Buckinghamshire. Time enough for his family duties once he had his fill of the delectable little vixen. She was insatiable, greedy, inventive, the quintessential fuck, and having amused himself with women from Pole to Pole, he recognized her unparalleled accomplishments.

At the sound of approaching footsteps, he briefly considered letting her sleep and dealing with the intruder himself. But he assumed she wasn't a stranger in the neighborhood and gossip was more of a liability in the country; morals were less licentious than in town. There was no point in putting her in jeopardy. But he woke her reluctantly; she was sleeping so peacefully. "We have visitors," he whispered.

Coming awake with a start, Lulu stared at him for a flashing moment and then color pinked her cheeks, recall of the night past flooding her mind. But more important than her embarrassment was waylaying whoever was approaching. They mustn't come in. Marshaling her drowsy senses, she rose on her elbows. "What time is it?"

"Close to eleven."

"Eleven!" she exclaimed, scrambling from the bed. "I thought you were going to wake me!"

"I didn't have the heart. Let me send this person away."

No apprehension echoed in his voice and he could, she knew, but that would only worsen her predicament. "I'd better, but thank you." She was already stepping into her drawers. "It's probably Thomas."

"He knows you?" Her bottom was luscious, her slender legs exquisitely formed, her breasts swaying slightly as she bent over, plump, inviting, also exquisitely responsive to sucking, he recalled. Only sheer will kept him from tumbling her back into bed, Thomas be damned.

"He's the gamekeeper and yes, he knows me, so please stay out of sight." Lifting her arms, she slipped her chemise over her head.

With luck, she'd send the man packing, he thought, watching her struggle to pull the sheer fabric over her large breasts. And quickly he hoped, his erection was standing at full alert.

In very short order, she was dressed, presentable, shutting the door behind her, and struggling to deal with her embarrassing behavior last night.

But her voice was composed as she greeted her gamekeeper from the porch. She explained how she'd found herself so far from home and had taken shelter from the storm.

"It were a right hard rain," Thomas politely agreed, his blue-eyed gaze open and friendly. "Did you keep yerself warm enuf?"

She tried not to blush. "Very well, Thomas. The firewood was more than adequate."

"I'll straighten up inside if you want—after I feed the youngins here."

"Why not leave it until tomorrow," she hastily suggested. "I'll be staying here a bit longer."

"Do you want me to bring in more wood then? Or carry fresh water from the well?"

"No, no . . . that won't be necessary. I'm quite comfortable." Time enough to mention the leak in the roof to him when she returned home.

"Good enuf, ma'am. I'll tell Angie you'll be back later today."

"Yes, please do." Young Thomas and her lady's maid, Angie, were planning to marry in June. "With everything so fresh and beautiful after the rain, I'll take a leisurely walk home," she said as though this were an ordinary day and she were an ordinary woman without a stranger—no—a lover, waiting for her inside.

"It is a right fine day, ma'am, sure enuf. The grouse are growing right fine too."

"Thanks to your excellent care."

"Thank you, ma'am." He touched his finger to his cap brim.

With a smile and a flutter of a wave, Lulu walked back to the cottage door, slipped inside, and leaning against the unpainted wood, slowly exhaled. Her guest was still abed, apparently not concerned with propriety *or* discovery.

"Come back here," he said softly, holding the blanket open, their bed having dried in the night. "And tell me why he called you ma'am."

"I can't. I have to go back now. I work at the main house." She didn't dare go near him or she'd never leave. She didn't even dare *think* about going near him or she would find her life impossibly complicated.

"Doing what?" He was beginning to wonder if a woman of such flamboyant sexuality might be some nobleman's mistress—or considering her celibacy—a discarded mistress.

"I'm a governess," she lied.

"You're sure you're not warming the master's bed and he's waiting for you? Is that why you won't come closer?"

"No, it's not, and no, I'm not. Rest assured, I'm not warming the master's bed," she briskly reiterated. With the exception of their first months of marriage, her ex-husband had always preferred new bed partners.

"You're sure?" She'd told the strapping young gamekeeper he'd glimpsed through the window that she was staying on at the cottage.

"Are you questioning my honesty?"

In the cold light of day, he was suddenly questioning everything about her. "I'm simply questioning how a woman of your—er—appetites goes a year without sex."

"It's really none of your business." But she nervously smoothed out the wrinkles on her skirt.

He noticed and, sitting up, skewered her with a glance. "How many children do you instruct?"

"Two," she replied, aware of his keen scrutiny.

"What ages?"

Her chin came up and she folded her hands together at her waist. "I don't have to tell you. I don't have to say anything more to you than goodbye. You and I both agreed to the brevity of this—"

"Marathon fuck-fest?"

"Whatever you wish to call it," she testily replied, frightened of the violent feelings he occasioned when she'd only recently brought her life into a semblance of order. "Don't look at me like that."

"Like what?"

"Like I'm under interrogation. You have to see to your automobile in any event," she added, changing the subject.

"It's not going anywhere." He didn't want to change the subject. She'd overlooked in the throes of passion last night how she detested men telling her what to do or thinking they had the right. "As soon as Thomas leaves, I shall be going. You should get dressed."

"Are you fucking Thomas?"

"If this is jealousy I'm hearing," she crisply remarked, standing ramrod straight, "it's not only out of place, but outrageous. Just because we made love doesn't give you ownership."

He had the grace to look sheepish. "You're right, of course. Please accept my apologies. My behavior was inexcusable."

"Perhaps you drank too much cider," she said, smiling because he looked not only disconcerted, but bewildered.

He raked his fingers through his hair in a restless gesture, and then smiled. "It must have been the cider. Or a moment of insanity."

One perfect auburn brow arched upward. "A different insanity from that last night?"

"Definitely." He grinned broadly. "Now that was quite another kind of insanity. One for the record books. Thank you, by the way."

"You're very welcome. You're quite magnificent, but I expect you already know that."

"Not in the least. You're very kind, ma'am," he murmured, dipping his head.

She laughed. "It's too late to put on airs of deference, darling. I know how poorly you take orders."

"Perhaps I could mend my ways," he proposed, full of grace.

"If my world would allow, perhaps I'd let you try," she replied with unfeigned sincerity.

He was thinking he could buy out any governess's contract if that was what she was, but as quickly he realized he wouldn't know what to do after that. Avoiding permanent relationships had been a prime motive in his life for many years. "A shame," he blandly said.

She recognized his withdrawal, however minute, and while she should have been grateful for his good judgment, she felt the smallest twinge of disappointment. But only fleetingly because such sentiments were ludicrous under the circumstances. She better than most understood the transience of sexual desire. "Yes, a shame," she agreed. "But I very much enjoyed your company, William."

She could have been talking to a servant, he thought, bristling at her tone. On the other hand, he wasn't looking for more. Was he? The disturbing thought jolted his psyche and, more importantly, his sense of security. "And I enjoyed your company as well," he urbanely affirmed, reaching for his trousers in a blatant act of self-defense.

The interval of waiting until Thomas departed was awkward. Both felt a paradoxical relief and resentment, their capricious sensibilities at once pleased and oddly displeased at the end of their brief, torrid affair. Neither, however, was willing to alter or reverse long-held habits on such short acquaintance, nor was either inclined to perceive of anything so fantastical as the possibility of love having entered the scene.

The lady in question was hardened against love for numerous reasons. The man didn't know what the word meant any longer, nor would he recognize the emotion if he met it dressed in gold lamé and riding a pink unicorn. So their conversation was stilted and constrained, punctuated with awkward periods of silence, or times when they both spoke at once like gauche adolescents. Before Thomas was finally seen walking away, the state of the weather had been thoroughly dissected and their nerves were on edge.

"If you want to leave first," Lulu immediately suggested, "I'll close up the cottage. And good luck with your automobile." Her tone was one a stranger might use.

"Thank you." He hesitated. "And thank you for the pleasure of your company." He found it impossible to pretend last night hadn't happened.

She nodded, her cool, imperious gesture spiking his temper. Abruptly turning, he strode from the room.

From his concealed position, Thomas watched the man clear the porch steps in a leap, turn left, and walk into the forest as though he knew where he was going. The gamekeeper had lingered out of concern. Everyone at the house had been anxious when their mistress hadn't returned last night, and Thomas along with a small army of servants had set out before dawn to search the estate. Thomas had caught sight of the man's footprints, or what was left of them after the rain, long before he reached the hut.

But he'd hesitated intruding, well aware that the aristocracy lived their lives by different standards.

Before long, his mistress, Lady Darlington, came out on the porch. He'd follow her from a distance, just to make sure she reached home safely.

Chapter Three

For Lulu, the following fortnight seemed to crawl by at a snail's pace, each hour of each day seemingly endless, her loneliness all the more intense after the enchanted night she'd spent with

William. She'd forgotten how it felt to be held in a man's arms. She'd forgotten how sweet it was to desperately want someone. As for William's expertise and stamina—she doubted she would ever again find anyone so fine.

As if her inexplicable sense of loss wasn't enough to lower her mood, she'd just received news that her son, Andrew, wouldn't be home for his spring holiday. Charles and his new wife were taking him on a Mediterranean cruise.

As if Charles's young wife hadn't caused her enough grief. The news of Arabella's pregnancy coming in her aunt's letter that day of the storm had been a bitter blow. It wasn't as though Lulu hadn't anticipated Charles having more children. She'd always understood the inevitability of such an occurrence. What she'd not anticipated was her reaction. After all the years she'd longed for more children, after all the years Charles had said he didn't want any more. Then, so soon after his marriage, his new wife was with child. She'd been surprised at her sense of abandonment.

And now, she wouldn't even have Andrew's company for the spring holiday.

Lulu redoubled her efforts at keeping busy, needing diversion more than ever. She sent for every new book published and read until she couldn't read anymore. She worked in the gardens with her gardeners for hours on end and had a new terraced garden for her efforts. She had all the furniture in all the drawing rooms rearranged, at which point she decided new drapes and upholstery were in order. The tradesmen from London had arrived yesterday to see to the improvements.

The house was full of workers now—and if her sleep had been erratic the previous fortnight, their influx further disrupted it. She rose at dawn and rode each morning, the long, solitary rides through the countryside offering her a degree of serenity. She oversaw the new decorating with a meticulous regard, even re-searching the old inventory records to see that authentic fabrics were reproduced for the rooms. But at the end of the day when all her contrived activities were over, when the house was quiet and the servants in bed, her nights stretched long.

If someone had inquired into the reason for her restlessness and insomnia, she would have blamed it on the news of Charles's coming child.

But the servants had come to their own conclusions about their mistress's unease after listening to Thomas's report on the events at the cottage. Perhaps they were more percipient than Lulu or simply more objective. Although, even had they wanted to mitigate her restlessness, the stranger from the cottage had left the village the next morning and his automobile had been hauled to London by Lloyd Danvers's Percheron team. The mechanic in London who received the car didn't know the man's identity either. Or at least he said he didn't; Lloyd had particularly asked.

So they treated their mistress with all the kindness of retainers who had known her from childhood and attempted to lighten her burdens as best they could.

But they were worried.

She'd barely slept in a fortnight.

Chapter Four

The gleaming black lacquer carriage with the foreign coat of arms bowled down the drive and came to a dramatic stop at the base of the twin staircase fronting the house. A tall, impeccably dressed man stepped from the carriage, leaned lightly on his pearl-handled walking stick, and surveyed the vast Elizabethan facade with a casual nonchalance. He turned, briefly answered a question from his driver, who was resplendent in a magnificent coat of deep crimson, and then returned to his contemplation of the huge expanse of windows, articulated bays, and vine-covered stone that overlooked the green, verdant valley.

The groom, Jem, said afterward in the kitchen that he'd seen him wrinkle his nose and mutter, "Bloody hell and damn," before taking a deep breath and moving toward the stairs.

By this time, Magnus, the butler, aware of the visitor, was racing down one side of the staircase. Halfway down, he recognized Thomas's stranger. Since everyone below stairs had been treated to a minute description, Magnus was absolutely certain. "It's him," he said excitedly to the footman running beside him, who whispered the news in turn to the footman behind him and so it went through the ranks of servants, the man's identity sweeping through the house with the force and speed of a gale wind.

Reaching the visitor, Magnus bowed with the deference normally reserved for royalty. "Welcome to Bishop's Knoll, my lord," he boomed, his enthusiasm prompted by his mistress's patent melancholy the fortnight past. "Might I say what a *great pleasure* it is to see you!"

When the visitor looked nonplussed, Magnus realized his ebullient greeting had overstepped the familiarity allowed servants. "I mean, my lord, Bishop's Knoll is always pleased to welcome visitors," he more calmly declared, casting a furtive glance at the carriage boot to see if the man had brought luggage. With several valises in evidence, it required enormous restraint to maintain his composure.

Lulu was well loved, you see; her ex-husband was not, and everyone had been deeply concerned with her recent sadness. The servants had suffered with Lulu through the travail of her marriage, as well as her divorce, and wanted only happiness for her now that she'd rid herself of the despicable baron.

"Is Lady Darlington at home?" the visitor inquired. Lulu had reverted to her maiden name after the divorce and had taken up residence at her favorite property.

"Yes, sir. She's in the drawing room. Whom may I say is calling?"

"Prince Rakovsky."

"Very good, sir. This way, please."

When Magnus entered the drawing room and announced, "Prince Rakovsky has come to call," Lulu thought he was referring to her mother's new husband. In a shocking act of passion she'd not thought possible, her exemplary, long-suffering mother had fallen madly in love with a Russian nobleman last year, promptly divorced Lulu's father, and married her new love. The newlyweds had taken up residence in St. Petersburg. Which just went to show you, Lulu thought, that truly anything is possible. She was smiling at the thought when she directed Magnus to show her visitor in. "And have tea brought up," she instructed.

Turning to the door, Magnus opened it with a flourish and stood aside so the man standing on the threshold could enter.

"You!" Lulu gasped.

"Lady Darlington. What a pleasure to meet you at last," the man from the cottage said with rich sarcasm, his bow faultless.

"That will be all, Magnus." Lulu was surprised her voice sounded so normal.

They both waited for the door to close.

"You were in Japan during the wedding," she charged, censorious and disapproving, as though he were at fault.

"My bad luck." He took a seat opposite her despite her gelid look. "I could have fucked you then." His smile was thin. "Apparently you make a habit of bedding anyone who takes your fancy."

"You could have told me your name and I wouldn't have touched you."

"Or *you* could have told me, *sis,*" he drawled. "Or should I say . . . *Sarah.*"

"Don't take that tone with me—*William,*" she tartly replied.

"You started it. Don't think I couldn't tell you were scrambling for a name when you introduced yourself. Had you been honest, at least I would have known whom I was fucking." There was a dry, cutting edge to his voice.

"From what I hear of your reputation, I doubt a name matters."

"You're not too particular yourself."

"If I had known, I certainly would have been! Good God, you're my *brother!*"

"*Stepbrother* and only recently. It doesn't count."

"Of course it counts! You can't stay here," Lulu firmly declared. "You must leave!"

"Au contraire, *sis.* No one's going to take issue with a brotherly visit." He settled back in his chair, stretched out his long legs, a wicked smile forming on his lips.

"Don't you dare do this," she whispered, unconsciously pressing into her chair back as though retreating that slight distance could save her from temptation.

"I believe my luggage is being brought to my room even as we speak," he smoothly noted. "I must admit, I've missed your—ah—distinctive style of friendship."

"You knew who I was," she hissed.

"Lord, no. I came to visit on my father's orders, and until this moment rather reluctantly, I admit. I shall have to write the *père* and tell him what a lovely new stepsister I've discovered," he said with a wink. "And thank him for reminding me of the courtesies required of family."

"This isn't funny . . ." She hesitated, not recalling his name.

"My name is Mikhail," he said, construing the reason for her pause, "Mischa for family," he added with shameless impudence.

"Prince Mikhail," Lulu coolly intoned, hoping to clearly impart her displeasure. "This is an impossible situation, as even a man of your rather irregular habits must know. You *cannot* stay here. We *cannot* be in this house—"

"Alone? Is that what you were going to say? But then I very much wish to be here alone with you." His voice was a low murmur, silken, familiar. "Very, very much indeed. And honestly, darling, but for my name, admit it—you want the same. So be sensible, sweet Sarah," he whispered. "No one knows and no one need know what went on between us or what might come to pass in our"—his tone lowered to a husky rasp—"friendship."

"It's impossible," she disagreed, scowling. "Someone would find out; they always do."

"How? Good God, I'm not going to strip you naked before the servants."

The way he said "strip you naked" struck her with particular intensity. She gripped the arms of her chair, forcing away the lush memories that inundated her brain. "I'm sorry," she said, her knuckles turning white at the necessary constraint. "But you can't stay. You absolutely *cannot.*"

He focused briefly on her hands, shifted in his chair, his expression grave when he finally spoke. "I've been miserable the last fortnight, if it matters," he quietly said, "and I'm not used to feeling miserable. I didn't know what to do. I couldn't sleep. I even talked to a detective about looking for you. So you see the level of my interest. Do me a favor, sweetheart, and act like a grown woman about this. Let me stay. I won't embarrass you. I promise to behave in front of the servants."

"And away from the servants?"

"I'll do whatever you want." His voice deepened. His dark gaze was compelling. "As often as you want. Wherever you want."

There was no mistaking what he was offering, nor her body's immediate heated response. But it wasn't right even if she could ignore propriety. The man was her stepbrother regardless of his equivocation. And so the world would view him. "What if I insist you go?"

He paused for a moment. "If you truly meant it, I would."

His beautiful dark eyes seemed to see right through her, and she found it impossible to dissemble. But how could she deal with the illicit nature of their connection? How could she justify giving in to her desires with a man whom the world viewed as her brother? She searched her conscience, but he was so alarmingly close and available. And utter perfection in bed.

Could she turn him away because of convention?

Could she be sensible and proper?

She would have to, of course.

"If you were to stay," she heard herself say as though conscience and propriety were defenseless against the force of desire. He leaned forward, taut, poised to move, and she put up her hand. "I would expect, indeed require, the most circumspect behavior. I have a houseful of tradesmen, not to mention my own staff."

He'd realized he'd triumphed the moment he'd heard the word "stay," her guidelines inconsequential against the prospect of fucking her again. His smile was full of lazy charm. "I will be most circumspect, darling. I promise."

"You can't call me 'darling.'"

"Of course, Lady Darlington." His long dark lashes lowered marginally. "It won't happen again."

"You must treat me like you would a sister."

He gazed at her over his steepled fingers, his soft exhalation a light wafting breath. "That's going to be slightly harder, but I shall do your bidding, Lady Darlington. At least outside the bedroom," he added in a roguish undertone.

"That's another thing," she crisply said.

He looked pained for a moment.

She sighed. "I'm not sure this is going to work."

Leaning forward, he reached for her hand. "Darling—Lady Darlington, I mean, you will find me the easiest of guests to entertain," he promised, gently twining his fingers through hers. "I require nothing but the pleasure of your company. This visit will go along swimmingly, you'll see." Releasing her hand, he blew her a kiss and lounged back in his chair. "I'll even cook for you if you like," he offered with a grin. "You may dismiss your staff and we'll muddle along without them."

She couldn't help but smile. He overlooked problems with aplomb and seemed to bring sunshine in his wake. "Who would wash the dishes?"

"We'll throw them away. I'll buy you more." He grinned. "I'm very rich, you know."

Everyone knew. The Rakovskys had gold mines. "You have an answer for everything, don't you?"

"Everything you want, my lady," he said, opening his arms wide. "Wait and see."

Magnus knocked and entered the room, a flunky with a tea tray in his wake, and the conversation turned to more general matters while a table was set between them and tea was served. After the footman left the room, Magnus addressed Lulu. "The prince's luggage is being unpacked, my lady. I put him in the west suite."

Lulu dropped the sugar tongs with a clatter. Quickly looking at her majordomo, she saw only the blank expression of a well-trained servant. She found it more difficult to display such composure, and her voice trembled slightly when she spoke. "Thank you, Magnus. That will be all."

"Very good, my lady." He bowed and, twirling on his heel with parade-ground precision, walked from the room.

The prince gazed at her with interest. "What the hell was that all about?"

"Magnus put you in my ex-husband's suite—next to mine." Her face was cherry red.

"Servants always know everything." He shrugged with a Gallic nonchalance. "Do you have something to drink?"

She glanced at him, at the tea table, then back to him, her brows raised high.

"Tea's perfectly fine," he quickly interposed, taking note of her expression. "And I'll be more than happy to move to a garret in the attic if you wish. You may creep up to visit me when everyone is asleep."

"This isn't humorous." Her voice was constrained, her hands clasped tightly in her lap, her mind in tumult. How much did her staff know? Or more to the point, *how* did they know?

"At the risk of offending you, does it matter what the servants think?"

"Maybe not to you," she crisply replied.

Undeterred by her disparagement, his tone was indulgent. "I've found my staff always has my best interests at heart. They like to take care of me. Doesn't yours?"

She slowly exhaled, unclasped her fingers, and smiled ruefully. "You're right. They do. But how did they know about *you?*"

"Young Thomas, I suspect. Servants always listen at doors, read your mail, know every bit of gossip. He probably did a little spying on us at the cottage."

Her embarrassment showed. "Oh, dear."

"Darling, they know about making love. They do it too. Maybe more than we do."

She cast him a look of rebuke.

"I've reformed. I swear, I haven't slept with anyone since you. I thought I was sick."

"Please, I'm not an ingenue. And your reputation is well known."

"Why would I lie?"

"For all the obvious reasons."

"So cynical, darling. Although Charles could give one cause for cynicism. You've heard the news, I presume."

"News?" Her expression was bland, but hypersensitive beneath her apparent calm, she couldn't keep the tears from welling in her eyes.

"You've heard of the child, I see," he said, gently. "Did you hear as well how furious Charles was at the revelation?"

She started, a flush of color rising up her throat. "How do you know?"

"He speaks of nothing else over the gaming tables. Apparently, his young wife surprised him. She's not entirely naive, it seems."

"Arabella Monmouth doesn't have a naive bone in her body. But she's very beautiful and very young, and Charles was intrigued enough to marry her."

"Was it a blow to you?"

"The marriage? No."

"But not the child," he said, prescient and kindly.

She shrugged and exhaled softly. "I was surprised . . . shocked, actually at my response. Charles and I had lived apart for some time. We'd both had our own lives. I didn't think I had any feelings left."

"Jealousy?" he posed.

"Over Charles?" She shook her head. "Perhaps I was jealous about the baby, though. Charles had never wanted another child during our marriage. Andrew was his heir and one was enough, he'd always said. So news of the child coming so soon in his marriage caught me unaware."

The prince smiled. "He was equally astonished."

She laughed, a lighthearted sound. "I can't believe it. Poor Charles, who always has to be in charge."

He playfully winked. "Feeling better now?"

"Curiously, yes. I have no explanation for my envy."

"You must want another child." His voice was smooth as silk, warm, inviting.

A small tremor of excitement streaked through her senses at the allure in his voice, at the imperceptible invitation, and it took her a moment to restore her equanimity. "No, of course not," she replied, but she wasn't quite able to meet his gaze.

"Not even a little?" His voice was teasing.

"We're not as cavalier about by-blows here in England." A modicum of stricture rang in her tone. "I understand Russian society views illegitimate children with more tolerance."

"If that was meant as a personal remark, my children are financially secure, well cared for, and loved," he calmly remarked.

She instantly looked stricken. "Forgive me. That was rude."

"You're forgiven. I'd made you uncomfortable." He poured milk into his tea.

"You're wrong. I wasn't uncomfortable in the least," she dissembled.

"Yes, ma'am." His smile was boyishly sweet, as was the warmth in his eyes. "I won't bring up the subject again. What are we going to do after tea?" he lazily inquired, stirring in the milk.

"What would you like to do?" Immediately as she'd uttered the unthinking politesse, she realized her error.

He set down the spoon, pushed away the cup, and slid a fraction lower in his chair. "You probably shouldn't ask me that," he murmured, looking at her from under the drift of his lashes. "I'm trying to be polite."

She should take issue with his bluntness. She should be abstemious if he couldn't. She should have more self-control. "But if I were to ask," she said instead, feeling the way she had the night they'd met when he looked at her like that. Feeling hungry for him.

He didn't move in his lounging pose, but a moody restlessness sharpened his gaze. "I'd say you could show me to my room. And then show me how much you missed me."

"Perhaps I didn't miss you at all," she said, but fevered memory was galvanizing her senses.

"I missed you so much, I've barely slept." He abruptly came to his feet and held out his hand. "So if I fall asleep, be sure to wake me."

She didn't move. "You're presumptuous."

He grinned. "Not yet."

"What will the servants say?" She couldn't so easily throw caution to the wind in her own home.

"They'll say nothing, like all good servants." He let his hand drop. "You aren't seriously concerned, are you?"

"They're bound to gossip." She was having second thoughts, or third or tenth thoughts. How far would the gossip spread? As far as Petersburg? As far as her mother, who wouldn't understand in the least?

"I'll see that they don't."

Alarm drew her brows together. "I won't have you threaten my staff."

"Acquit me, darling. I was going to pay them off with a handsome bribe."

She couldn't help but smile. "Does nothing faze you?"

"Waiting for you does." Covering the small distance separating them, he lifted her from the chair with effortless ease and placed her on her feet. "Do you want to hold my hand or should we pretend we're strangers on the way upstairs?"

"I didn't say I'd go."

"Then I'll have to carry you."

"You wouldn't." Her eyes flared wide.

"Of course I will. I've been waiting for you for two weeks."

"You could have found me if you'd looked."

"I don't want to argue. I should have looked; I'm sorry I didn't. But by some fortuitous hand of fate, I've discovered you again and here we are, both wanting the same thing. At least I'm honest about it."

"Men always are when it comes to sex. Where they find themselves less candid is afterward—when they walk away."

He scowled faintly. "You practically threw me out the next morning. Don't try to put the onus on me."

"You left easily enough . . . and then disappeared."

"I'm sorry, I couldn't read your mind."

"But you're quick to read my mind when it comes to sex."

He opened his mouth to speak, shut it again, and turning away, strode to the windows overlooking the valley. Leaning on the marble sill, he gazed on the distant landscape with unseeing eyes, frustration a tumult in his brain, anger racing like flame through his blood. She'd told him to leave that morning—explicitly, directly. How dare she take issue now that he'd left. Temperamental little bitch. He should walk away.

But he didn't. Couldn't. And lust alone wasn't the reason.

She was long past putting up with tantrumish men. She should leave the room, have his luggage repacked and brought down to his carriage. She should summarily send him on his way.

And if she had an ounce of sense, she would.

But she didn't move, nor did he, the silence so profound, a door closing below stairs echoed like thunder in the high-ceilinged room.

He wore houndstooth check pants, the smooth flow of fabric

down his long legs unwrinkled despite his hours in the carriage. His coat was charcoal gray and beautifully cut, although she wouldn't expect anything but the finest tailoring for a man of his wealth. She couldn't see his waistcoat with his back to her, but she remembered the braid-trimmed black velvet covering his hard, flat stomach. His black hair glistened in the sunlight, the heavy waves brushing his white shirt collar. Her fingers flexed at the memory of how the silk of his hair felt in her hands.

Suddenly, she felt unutterably deprived, as though she'd been in a nunnery the past fortnight. And now liberation was within reach.

She sighed softly.

He instantly swiveled around.

"I apologize," she said. "Although I hope this won't become a habit—me apologizing to you."

His smile was conciliatory. "It was my fault. I was too precipitous." His gaze briefly surveyed the room as though reminding himself of his surroundings. "This is your house, not mine. You know best how to deal with your staff."

She restlessly swung her arms, shifted in her stance, brushed an imaginary wrinkle from her skirt. "Now what?"

"It's entirely up to you, Lady Darlington." His manners couldn't be faulted, nor could the amiability of his expression.

She grimaced—all the objections and obstacles, the difficulties and drawbacks causing a furrow in her brow. "I need a drink." She sighed. "Or maybe two."

"Let me get you one," he offered, gracious and propitiating. "And if you don't mind," he added, recalling her reaction the last time he'd asked for a drink, "I'll have one myself."

She smiled faintly. "Do I look like I'm going to bite?"

His teeth flashed white against his bronzed skin. "Hopefully, not until later."

"You arrogant man."

He shook his head. "Only extremely grateful, darling. Believe me."

She dropped into a chair. "Did you really talk to a detective?"

He nodded from the liquor table. "I did. He was obstructive—stupid man. He made it sound impossible. Sherry, cognac?" He held up two bottles.

"Cognac. Enough to take away my conscience."

"Done," he simply said, and proceeded to pour a sizable portion into two glasses.

When he carried over the drinks, he offered hers with a bow and the familiar, intimate smile she'd missed, she realized, her sudden epiphany gratifying.

"How close am I allowed to sit?" Amusement gleamed in his eyes.

She pointed to his former seat. "There. Until I'm sufficiently unconcerned with appearances."

He wanted to say, *You surprise me.* Not only because of their former acquaintance when appearances hadn't mattered, but for the manner of her previous life. She wasn't an innocent. "Your servant, ma'am," he said instead, taking a seat opposite her.

He carried the greater part of the conversation, more comfortable perhaps with seduction. Maybe her divorce had been more traumatic than she'd admitted—her celibacy a case in point, or perhaps, reentering the world of amour in the broad light of day was cause for her apprehension. He'd already dismissed their familial relationship. Despite her concern, he considered it the most tenuous of connections.

After offering all the latest news of her mother, whom he'd seen just before leaving St. Petersburg, he spoke of his country estate where he raised barb horses renowned for their speed. She asked considerable questions when the conversation turned to his racers. She was a breeder of note herself. By the time the first drink was drained, she appeared less nervous, and by the second cognac, their conversation was relatively unconstrained.

Before long, shadows began filling the room, the sun only a glow on the horizon.

"Are you hungry?" Lulu asked, the role of hostess second nature. "I could have the supper menu altered if you have any preferences."

"I'm not hungry for food."

"Oh." A small, startled sound.

"Maybe we could eat . . . later," he said very softly, her artless response profoundly arousing.

She glanced at the clock.

"Are you expecting someone?"

"No." Her gaze swung back to him, then slid away. "No ... I mean—that is, it will be ... twilight soon," she finished weakly, the inanity of her remark bringing a blush to her cheeks.

"If you don't mind," he said, his voice deliberately mild as he came to his feet, "I'll go to my room and freshen up from my journey." Certain of what he wanted even if she was unsure, he wished very much to lift her into his arms and carry her with him. Understanding the lady was in doubt, however, he tempered his urges. "Which way do I turn at the top of the stairs?" he inquired, exquisitely polite. "Or should I ask Magnus? "

Temptation stood flagrant before her; desire flooded her senses. How to answer? She unconsciously brought her palm to her cheek. What to do? Dare she even consider the innuendo in his sudden leaving?

"Why don't I ask Magnus," he said into the silence.

"Left," she hastily responded, dropping her hand back into her lap. "I mean—turn left ... at the top of the stairs and go— ah—to the end of the corridor. The rooms overlook the lake ... as well as a Grecian folly and a linden allée—Capability Brown ... had a hand in the design like so many others ..." Her voice trailed away and she nervously bit on her lower lip.

"Maybe you could show me the view later." His voice was pleasant, a putting-at-ease tone. "I'll wait for you."

She understood what he meant, understood as well what awaited her should she choose to follow. With the cognac easing scruples, selfish longing overwhelmed more praiseworthy virtues, and he was so very competent, she thought, not to say, excessively ... large. She couldn't keep from glancing at his erection faintly lifting the soft wool of his trousers. Her nostrils flared and it took considerable effort to speak in a normal tone. "I'll come up after a suitable—interval."

"Maybe you could set dinner back."

A noticeable pause ensued before she could find the breath to speak. "For how long?"

She wasn't equivocating, he noted with satisfaction, and his erection, fully stretched and aching, was gratified as well. "Maybe we could dine *en suite* tonight," he suggested. "But you decide." Urbane, amiable words.

"If only I were capable of deciding anything," she whispered, lust coursing through her senses, feeling as though she might climax just looking at him. "Hurry and leave."

He caught the breathy note of urgency in her voice and instantly dismissed further discussion of dinner. "I'm very pleased I found you again." His voice was low, hushed, his smile warm as sunshine.

"While I'm still slightly in shock, as you can see." Her words were scarcely audible, irresolution in every syllable.

Knowing better than to debate the nuances of desire with a skittish lady, he sketched her a bow. "Take your time, darling. I'm not going anywhere." His smile was tolerant, beatific in a Russian icon sort of way, she incongruously reflected, and feeling better under its spell, she found herself able to say with equanimity, "Thank you for your understanding."

After the door had closed on him, trepidation returned with a vengeance, for now it was up to her to actually follow him upstairs and agree to what he obviously wanted and what she was less certain should happen. Feeling as though she needed additional absolution from her conscience or less conscience altogether, Lulu poured herself another drink. But too restless to sit still, she quickly set it aside and began pacing the room. Keeping one eye on the tall case clock in the corner, she contemplated the difficulties in making love to a man who was, first, clearly unsuitable and, second, too flagrantly visible to her staff. Unfortunately, the advantages he had to offer were a highly persuasive argument against all the reasonable caveats, and she found herself wondering what exactly would be considered a credible lapse of time before she might follow him upstairs. Conversely, should she do that, how strident would be the gossip below stairs? Did she care? she speculated, or more pertinently, how much did she care?

This particular situation was harrowingly new to her.

Her indiscretions in the past had always followed the accepted pattern of her class, where dalliances occurred at country house parties or discreet apartments or love nests. Where everyone looked the other way, where appearances were more important than the truth and affairs were never publically acknowledged. She was new to this flagrant openness of having a lover in one's home, not to mention the more horrendous transgression of sleeping with a man who happened to be her stepbrother. The scandalous reminder almost turned her fainthearted.

Her tumultuous qualms were curtailed by a knock on the door, and looking up, she saw Magnus entering the room.

"Prince Rakovsky has inquired after you, my lady." Her majordomo stood just inside the door, his voice unutterably calm. "He said you'd promised to show him the lake from the west balcony." He could have been saying, "Cook tells me we're out of eggs."

"Thank you, Magnus." She hoped her demeanor was as composed.

Her butler bowed himself out, and Lulu drew in a deep breath to calm her wildly beating heart.

She was expected upstairs, Magnus had said.

The servants knew.

There was no point now in continuing to cavil over the nuances of exposure or degrees of iniquity.

Although it would have been considerably less daunting had she not been going upstairs to meet her stepbrother.

If not for that, she would have gladly gone.

A smile slowly formed on her lips. Morality aside, the prince would make any woman immensely glad.

The word "immense" triggered further licentious thoughts, reminding her of his splendid erection and remarkable sexual repertoire. A shiver of anticipation raced up her spine.

He was waiting.

She must go.

If she didn't, she suspected he'd come for her.

As Lulu exited the drawing room and came out into the corridor, she noted an unusual absence of servants. Her household was normally a busy one, particularly now with the workmen on the premises, but not a single retainer or tradesman was in sight. Magnus had seen to it, of course; he was tactful to a fault. In her present agitated state, she was grateful for his thoughtfulness. Racing up the stairs, she ran down the corridor, slipped into her room, and leaned back against the door, waiting for her pulse to quiet, feeling like a child having escaped detection, feeling nervous and equivocal. Regardless of her participation in illicit amours in the past, this was surely the most inappropriate.

The connecting door between the adjoining suites opened, interrupting her tumultuous thoughts. Her houseguest stood limned in the doorway, the light from the balcony windows in her ex-husband's room framing his large form.

He was too tall, was her first thought. Charles was much smaller. Then he spoke, and her perceptions immediately altered. "I hope you didn't mind me sending Magnus?"

"Would it matter if I did?" Her words were faintly testy.

Her stepbrother—William, Mischa . . . her thoughts were as mutable as his designation—had removed his coat and waistcoat, his cravat. His shirt was unbuttoned at the neck, his rolled-up sleeves exposed his strong forearms, the dusting of black hair on his bronzed skin too conspicuously male for her peace of mind. His feet were bare, reminding her of when he'd gone outside the cottage to cool off in the rain, reminding her, too, of all that had transpired when he'd returned, that delicious memory explanation perhaps for why she was standing in her bedroom with a man she barely knew. His dark beauty was breathtaking, the amalgam of perfect bone structure and his Romany heritage sheer perfection. For a fleeting moment, she wondered how many times he'd stood like that, making small talk with a woman in her boudoir, knowing he was irresistible.

"Of course it matters."

"Then perhaps I'll make you apologize."

His dark brows rose, amusement in his gaze. "That sounds interesting."

"This isn't a joke. It's unnerving. All the servants know."

"They knew before."

"Well, they're certain now."

"And?"

"It's embarrassing for me."

"Then we'll go away somewhere," he replied. "We don't have to stay here."

"You have an answer for everything." She should have been saying, *You must leave.* "Where would we go?" Surely that wasn't her voice uttering such indefensible words.

He braced his hands high on the door jambs, leaned forward slightly, his smile indulgent. "Anywhere in the world you want."

He was offering her the world with unutterable casualness. Perhaps it was his largesse more than anything that appealed to her—his intrinsic Russianness that viewed excess as ordinary and self-gratification as a right. Unfortunately, she had commitments that wouldn't allow such an untrammeled existence. "My son is in England."

"Then we'll stay in England. Darling," he said, gentle, lenient, "all you have to do is tell me what you want, and I'll see that you have it. Anything, anywhere. I'm more than willing."

"You make everything sound so easy."

He dropped his hands. "It doesn't have to be difficult. Your servants adore you, I'm sure. The workmen won't say a word for fear of losing a lucrative contract, and I'm completely amenable to your every whim." Moving into the room, he walked toward her, understanding better than she that making love was infinitely easy, not hard. That making love to her was the sweetest of pleasures, one he wasn't about to give up, no matter how much she equivocated. "Let me see if I can make you forget—everything that's bothering you."

"If I were fifteen, perhaps it might be possible."

He came to a stop a few feet away. "Now that you're over fifteen, your problems require something more than sex to resolve?"

She took a deep breath and nodded.

"Then, I'll have to be especially creative." His smile formed slowly, warming his eyes and her soul in the bargain. "I've missed you very much."

Could she believe him? Dare she? He'd peopled her thoughts and dreams almost exclusively the fortnight past, and while she might wish for requited feelings, Prince Radovsky's reputation suggested otherwise. He was legendary for his casual amours. "Forgive me if I find your charm suspect."

"Because we're too jaded?"

She softly sighed. "I don't know. Perhaps being alone has made me overly critical."

"In that case, I shall have to perform to your exacting standards," he said with a beguiling raillery.

She suddenly smiled. "I don't foresee a problem in terms of

performance—unless you've had considerable memory loss since last we met."

"My memory is excellent, if that reassures you." His brows quirked. "Are we both agreed then? Finally? And I ask with the utmost respect."

Her gaze traveled slowly down his powerful form, then back to his amused countenance. "I suppose we are, you exceedingly smug man."

He laughed. "Such reluctance, darling. One would almost think you didn't like to climax."

She wrinkled her nose. "You make me like it too much. If not for that, I would have sent you on your way."

"I'm grateful you didn't." Closing the distance between then, he gently took her hands in his. "If you like, we could go for a walk instead, or have a drink, or you could show me your library or gardens or stables. We don't have to be here."

"*Now* you offer me alternatives."

He shrugged faintly. "I'm trying."

"But you'd rather—"

"Make love to you. I'm not the one in doubt."

"Nor would I be, if not for our relationship."

"I see." His voice was unutterably polite. It wasn't that she didn't want sex. Thankfully. The rest didn't matter. Leaning forward, he dipped his head so their eyes were on a level. "As I recall," he murmured, "you like to come more than once."

The rush of heat streaking through her body was instant, memory stark, any capacity for refusal dissipated by his reminder of how he could bring her to orgasm endlessly. The small throbbing deep inside her took on a new insistence. "You like to stay up all night, if I recall." Her smile was sensual, anticipation bringing a flush to her cheeks.

"I particularly like to stay up here," he whispered, slipping his hand between her legs, easing her thighs apart. "Way, way up here . . ." he added, cupping her throbbing cleft through the light dimity of her gown.

His gaze was close.

Perhaps too knowing and assured. "I might be interested," she murmured.

"I already knew that. The only question was when."

"If you annoy me, I might say no."

He moved his head faintly in negation. "No you won't."

"Don't be so sure. I've managed quite well without a man."

"But not without me. That's different. We're different. You and I fit . . . perfectly."

And they both remembered exactly how perfectly—how exquisitely, how wondrously.

Mischa was no longer capable of flirtatious play. He'd already waited two endless weeks, the politesse downstairs adding strain to his gallantry, not to mention having to deal with Lulu's fitful mood when she'd finally arrived upstairs. Fueled by potent memory, by long-suppressed urges, he said, "I hope you don't mind," and moving his hand, he lifted her skirt, exposing her silk-stockinged legs and lacy drawers. "Or if you do, I'm sorry," he added, forcing her back against the bed, unbuttoning his trousers as he moved.

"You don't actually want an answer, do you?"

His gaze flashed up, her warm undertone distinct from her sarcasm.

"I missed you—every day . . . every minute," she whispered, jettisoning masquerade or cavil, wanting what he wanted—as much . . . as desperately. "I thought of you . . . of this . . . of touching you like—"

"Good," he muttered, cutting her short because he didn't want to talk anymore; he wasn't sure he even could, focused as he was. Putting his hand over her mouth, he pulled open the tie on her drawers.

She should have taken offense at his gruffness, at his hand on her mouth, at his hurried stripping away of her drawers. But she was hot and wet with longing, hotter and wetter than she should be with a man who refused to take no for an answer, who had disregarded all her reservations, who was clearly going to have sex with her whether she wanted to or not.

"Lift your foot," he ordered.

She did.

"The other one."

And her drawers lay puddled on the carpet.

She shouldn't be so wet with a man who hadn't even kissed her once.

Her heart shouldn't be beating so wildly.

She shouldn't be wondering how it would feel when he first put his beautiful, huge penis inside her—oh, God—like that . . . like heaven—like pink-clouded, sweet-scented heaven . . . like waiting-for-two-weeks-to-feel-this heaven.

He drove in another small measure, then stopped—to catch his breath, to give her tight cunt time to yield . . . to allow himself to absorb the shocking pleasure.

The bed was high, the kind with a set of steps on either side and the mattress struck Lulu's back midpoint, even raised on tip-toe as she was. His hands were at her waist, supporting her weight, his legs flexed as he held her firmly on his erection. How tempting it would be to straighten his legs, thrust upward, lift her with his cock, and sink in completely. For a flashing moment, he gathered his momentum to do just that—until saner counsel reminded him that this was the first time he'd made love in a fortnight and he was in full ramming mode. Curbing his brutish impulses, he slid his hands under her bottom, raised her higher, wrapped her stockinged legs around his waist. "Don't let go," he warned. Standing upright, breath held, he eased her down his rigid length slowly, tense with his need for restraint.

Clinging to his neck, she softly sobbed in pleasure as he entered her by cautious degrees. Her tears wet his cheek, but he didn't stop because she didn't ask him to, and he couldn't have if she had.

"I thought about fucking you like this every waking minute," he muttered, forcing his way deeper. "I thought about fucking you a thousand different ways . . ."

"I know." Breathy, fevered need.

He heard and didn't hear, because he was almost there—almost. He took a small breath, flexed his powerful thighs. There—now . . . he was knocking at the mouth of her womb.

She whimpered, gasped, clutched him in a stranglehold.

Immune to her grip, he smiled faintly, in triumph and good fortune, in happiness.

He was incredible, sublime, every superlative known to man, and much, *much* better than any memory, however bewitching. She was trying not to come—or at least not instantly, wanting the splendor to last, wanting to savor the glory after her fortnight of deprivation.

But he lifted her just then, the merest few inches, pressed her back down, held her securely in place, and suddenly overwhelmed by an extravaganza of carnal bliss, all her notions of constraint lost their relevance.

"What if I were to come in you?" he murmured, two weeks of celibacy—two unheard-of weeks of celibacy screaming for release.

It was impossible to speak, she was so near climax. It was impossible to think with his enormous erection rammed in so far she was almost in shock from pleasure.

He wasn't sure what he'd do regardless of her answer; he wasn't sure he could keep from coming even a second from now.

But she suddenly climaxed with a high, piercing scream that would have brought the servants running if they didn't know better and liability became moot. Inexcusably, with the folly of a grass green youth, he met her orgasm, indulging himself without thought for consequences, forced himself hard against the mouth of her womb, and poured, pumped, flooded her with two weeks' worth of princely semen.

"I'm sorry," he gasped, the instant his brain began functioning again, and an instant after that, he castigated himself a thousand different ways for being so stupid.

"It doesn't matter," she breathed, her face still buried in his neck.

He stiffened at the casualness of her reply, too long the object of female pursuit. Now he *knew* he'd been stupid; no doubt her previous demur had been simply well-rehearsed drama. He almost asked, "How much do you want?" but he found himself loathe to leave her yet and curbed the impulse. His delectable stepsister incited an intense carnal hunger not easily sated. Time enough, he callously thought, to bargain over a price for a possible pregnancy once he'd had his fill of her. Right now, he felt like fucking her for another month at least.

"You're still hard . . ." Lulu's voice was a wispy purr, her mouth warm as she lifted her head, leaving a trail of kisses on his throat and face. "You're not going to make me wait . . ." Her violet eyes were half-lidded, her smile lush as she met his gaze.

"Why would I do that?" A modicum of disdain tinged his voice.

Leaning back, she raised her brows. "Are we angry about something?"

"No."

"At least your splendid erection still finds favor with me," she said lightly, ignoring the pique in his tone.

His frown was the merest compression of his brows. "Why aren't you alarmed about—"

"You coming in me?" she finished. "Would it help if I were? It's a little late for concern, wouldn't you say?"

"You don't care?"

"Don't scowl at me. I should be the one angry, not you. That was incredibly poor judgment on your part."

"Then why so *unconcerned?*"

"Because you're rich." She suddenly laughed. "My lord, don't eat me alive. I was only teasing. Do they *all* want your money?"

"More than money," he softly replied. "They want marriage."

"Acquit me, darling. After Charles, I've sworn off marriage forever. Nor could I marry you in any event"—her lashes lowered briefly—"considering our relationship. My menses just ended yesterday, darling," she explained. "That's why I don't feel imperiled today." She smiled. "Tomorrow, you'll have to be on your best behavior."

"Ah." His expression lightened.

"Relieved that I'm not out to capture you?"

"Forgive me. Force of habit, I'm afraid." He glanced at the clock. "Does that mean I have until midnight, or do I have a full twenty-four hours instead?" he inquired, with a grin.

"It depends how nice you are to me."

His dark lashes lowered, as did his voice. "I can be extremely nice."

"Don't I know it," she purred.

"Perhaps we could test your bed next."

"I was thinking of testing your stamina—in the next twenty-four hours."

"Or the next decade the way I'm feeling right now."

"Wouldn't that be nice." She brushed a kiss down his nose.

"By the way, I have plenty of towels this time," she said with a wink.

"So I won't have to tear the cupboards apart?"

"You found two more that night. I was impressed."

"Anything for my darling."

"Carte blanche from a man of your talents? Two weeks of missing you. I can hardly wait."

"Nor will you have to," he murmured, holding her impaled on his erection as he walked around the foot of the bed, moved up the two-tiered step, and carefully lowered her to the bed.

"You're a man of finesse," she whispered, kicking off her shoes and gently moving her hips.

"An obsessed man," he whispered back. "It seemed like longer than two weeks to me. And now that I can come in you for twenty-three hours, fifty-five minutes more, I intend to use that time to advantage."

She laughed. "The gods are definitely smiling on me."

He shook his head. "On us. Now point out the direction of the towels."

Scarcely an hour into the twenty-three hours and fifty-five minutes, after having availed themselves of the soft bed for a time, after having undressed in a particularly satisfying way, Lulu was currently pressed facedown over the curved back of her chaise. The prince was behind her, his hands circling her waist, his knees making deep dents in the down seat, his erection out of sight, buried deep inside her. Then his penis appeared again— shiny wet, massive, engorged—as he paused at the limit of his withdrawal stroke.

"No, no, no," she panted, frantic, swinging back as much as his firm grip on her waist allowed. "Mischa—please . . . please"— her last word lost in a gasp as he plunged back in again.

He began moving in a hard-driving rhythm, giving her what she wanted—again—what they both wanted again, one of his hands on her shoulder holding her in place, the other securing her hip to meet the strength of his downthrust. The atmosphere was highly charged, feverish, the odor of sex pungent in the air, the only sounds her soft, wild cries and his labored breathing.

A sharp knock on the door took a moment to register in minds benumbed by ecstasy.

With awareness, the prince's first impulse was to shout, "Go away." But he couldn't so flagrantly call attention to his presence in Lulu's room.

The second knock was more insistent. Reluctantly, he paused in his exertions. "You have to answer," he whispered, his mouth near her ear.

She couldn't. She could barely breathe, dizzying pleasure smothering her, every seething sensation focused in the melting hot core of her body.

The third knock was a hard tattoo.

Whoever was outside wasn't going away. "Tell them to come back later," he prompted, soft command in his tone.

Struggling back to consciousness, Lulu slowly opened her eyes, drew in a breath, and with effort, obeyed. She repeated Mischa's words in a voice not loud, but sufficient.

"Lady Harcourt is here!"

The shouted reply was Magnus's voice, clear and frightening. For a moment, Lulu thought her heart had stopped. Sheer panic cleared her brain. "I'll be there in a few minutes!" she cried, beginning to rise.

But Mischa gently pushed her back down, the sound of receding footsteps transient deliverance. He resumed his pleasurable rhythm.

"Don't," Lulu groaned, trying to resist the delectable friction. "It's my aunt."

He gently kissed the nape of her neck. "She'll wait."

The warm imprint of his mouth registered in every stimulated, fevered nerve, and it took enormous will to stem her passionate response. "Please, Mischa, I have to go."

"Hold still, darling—right there . . . there. Tell me how this feels."

She was lost; she always was when he was moving inside her, filling her, inflaming her passions. She could no more give up the intoxicating rapture than she could consider not breathing.

And he knew it. He knew what women liked.

With artful genius, with finesse and skill, with the unfaltering virility that had made him welcome in boudoirs around the world, he kept her there until they reached glorious climax once again.

Moments later, with panic assailing her senses, Lulu pushed him away. "I can't keep Lydia waiting."

Sprawled at the end of the chaise, he grimaced, selfish of his hours of orgasmic freedom.

"I'm sorry." Lulu offered him a rueful smile. "I'm probably more sorry than you, considering your profligate life and my nun's existence of late. But you have to go. I need to dress and I don't want you anywhere near me."

"I could help you." One brow lifted in roguish sport. "I could help wipe away that come running down your legs."

"No, you could not," Lulu said firmly. "You don't know Lydia. She'll be up here before long if I don't appear, and I'd prefer she not walk in on us."

He swore softly.

"But I *will* have to tell her you're here, since the servants may have mentioned it. So once I'm downstairs, join us at your leisure."

"You don't really mean at my leisure, do you?"

She shook her head, pointed at the door to the adjoining suite, and waved him away. "Hurry."

"Yes, ma'am."

"And don't pout."

"Yes, ma'am."

"Did I mention Lydia retires early?"

His smile flashed, his moodiness gone. "How early?"

"Early enough that I should be able to exhaust you completely before morning."

"You're on," he said softly.

Chapter Five

After quickly dressing without the services of her maid, who would have spread the news of her amour far and wide, Lulu descended the staircase and approached the drawing room. "Give me a minute," she said to Magnus, who was waiting before the door. Mentally reviewing her welcoming words, she nervously smoothed her hands over her skirt. Then straightening her shoulders, she nodded at her majordomo.

The door was opened, her aunt looked up from pouring tea, and Lulu hoped her smile didn't reveal the full measure of her unease.

Her aunt's bright gaze surveyed her. "I received a letter from your mother day before yesterday and decided you needed some company," she said briskly. "And from your pale color, I'd say you also need someone to see that you eat better and get a deal more fresh air."

"I'm in good health, Aunt Lydia. Really, I am. What a surprise to see you so far from Bath."

"So Magnus said. By the way, he doesn't look a day older than he did when I was a young bride. You're lucky to have him."

"I agree. He's irreplaceable. I'm grateful he's willing to stay on when he could have long since retired."

"No matter, though, darling, you need more than the company of servants, even if they're old friends. And that's why I'm here. I thought I'd take you visiting." Apparently not concerned with an answer, her aunt continued in a tone that indicated she'd brook no interference. "The Pugins have been wanting to see you and the Holcombs, too. You've been turning everyone away, I hear."

"I've been content to rusticate. But if you wish, we'll have them over." Lulu knew better than to argue with Lydia when she was in her Good Samaritan mood. "They might like to meet Mama's stepson as well. Prince Radovsky arrived this afternoon." She offered her aunt a polite smile and hoped Lydia wouldn't detect the state of her nerves.

"Prince Mikhail?" Her aunt's brows rose into her hairline. "He's an unbridled young rogue according to rumor—with any number of bastards," she added in a whisper. "Although your mother tells me it's *comme il faut* in Russia. All the young bucks there are populating the world."

"When he comes down, you may inquire after his progeny," Lulu sweetly said.

"Very amusing, my dear." Her aunt sniffed. "But he's full of charm, your mother also says. The reason, no doubt, for his busy love life. Has he been in England long?"

"I haven't had time yet to inquire," Lulu lied. "He only just arrived. His father asked him to visit me."

Her aunt's smile was tight. "With a man of his repute, it was fortunate I arrived so opportunely. It would never do to have you here alone with him."

"He's family, Auntie. No one will take issue with his visit. Especially when he came on his father's orders. I'm sure he wouldn't be here at all, save for that command." A modicum of truth in a web of deceit.

"Nevertheless, my presence will prevent any gossip."

"Isn't it a bit late for that? Between Mother's divorce and mine, all the gossip mongers have been heartily entertained."

"Your mother should have left your father years ago. As for Charles. *Hmpf,*" she snorted. "I don't know how you put up with his philandering more than a fortnight."

A pithy observation that didn't bear contemplation unless Lulu wished to cavalierly dismiss fifteen years of her life.

Taking note of her niece's afflicted expression, Lydia quickly made amends. "You were an absolute angel, my dear, to tolerate Charles for the sake of your son. It wasn't easy, I know, and everyone sympathizes with you. Absolutely everyone. Now that I'm here, I'm going to see that you get out a bit more and put that awful marriage of yours completely out of your mind. We're going to also put some roses back into your cheeks, my dear." She pushed her plate away. "I'll send a note directly to the Pugins and Holcombs."

Lulu smiled at her aunt's good intentions, although a houseful of company might prove vexing to her other visitor. She wasn't sure herself whether she would welcome or condemn the influx of guests.

As if on cue, the prince appeared on the threshold, his hair still in damp waves from his exertions, an incongruity in the perfection of his attire.

"Ah, here's Prince Rakovsky now." Lulu was careful not to meet his eyes, for fear of what she might see. "Prince Radovsky, may I introduce Lady Harcourt, my Aunt Lydia. She's my mother's sister. Lydia, Prince Mikhail Radovsky."

Lydia openly surveyed him through her lorgnette. "You weren't at the wedding."

"I'm sorry to have missed it," the prince replied, apparently not disturbed by female inspection, nor her lack of a greeting. "Papa's eagerness to marry didn't allow me time to return from Japan. But Marguerite has made my father very happy, for which I'm grateful. He'd been alone for so long."

"When was it that your—"

"Almost ten years." The prince's voice had taken on a coolness.

"I'm sorry." Even Lydia who wasn't known for her intuitiveness took note of the prince's reserve. "You must miss your mother."

"Very much." His gaze was shuttered as he moved to take a seat near the women. "Did you find your journey tiring?" he asked, preferring a subject other than the death of his mother.

"Auntie came up from Bath," Lulu quickly interposed, offering Mischa a conciliatory glance before turning to her aunt. "You must have had to leave at dawn."

"Douglas drove me to the station at five-thirty. Train travel is always tedious, but a necessary evil. I shall take a short nap before dinner—after I send off my invitations." She waved her hand at Lulu. "I refuse to hear any dissent. Tell her, Prince Mikhail, how much good the company of her neighbors will do her."

"Lady Darlington has been too much alone, I hear. In fact, my father sent me here on a mission of mercy." A hint of amusement underlay his soft drawl.

"There, you see." Lydia smiled at the prince before regarding Lulu again. "I'm not the only one who thinks you need a modicum more compassion and company."

"Your aunt and I will endeavor to take good care of you, Lady Darlington."

"Indeed we will," Lydia agreed, unaware of the innuendo in the prince's words. "The Pugins and Holcombs will enjoy meeting you as well, Prince Mikhail. Everyone has heard of the Tsar's new Minister of Finance who has brought so much foreign capital to Russia. My banker has invested in your railroad stock, it seems. You must enlighten us at dinner." She suddenly rose in a flurry of sea green silk. "Which means my notes must be sent out forthwith. Fortunately Bess and Winifred are old friends and will overlook our eleventh-hour invitation. Do I have the Rubens room?"

"Yes, Auntie."

"You're a sweet child." Lydia patted Lulu's shoulder. "What a waste—all those years with Charles." She sighed. "But never fear," she went on briskly. "I shall see that you're happy once again." She nodded at the prince. "Until dinner, Radovsky."

When the door closed on her aunt, Mischa slid down in his chair and surveyed Lulu with a waggish grin. "Do you think we can make you happy?"

"Over and above the scandal you might cause?" Her brows rose. "Speaking of which—my aunt thinks I need protection from your reputation."

He grinned. "Too late."

"I decided not to mention that to her. And another warning, darling. She spoke of your children. So she might ask questions."

Nothing moved in his lounging pose. "Let her."

"Unfortunately, she's not always the soul of discretion."

He shrugged. "If she feels compelled to question my life, I have no compunction telling her about it. Just for the record, I don't have scores of children as rumor suggests. I have two; Natalie is fourteen and Virgil is sixteen. Their mother died when they were very young and I've raised them." He was able to speak of Maiia with a degree of normalcy after all the years. It hadn't always been so. "And in case your aunt was wondering—or in case you were, my children are wonderful and I'm not intimidated by any questions."

He must have been very young when they were born, Lulu thought, but she spoke as casually as he. "You seem to have charmed Lydia in any event. She didn't take issue when you said, *We'll* take care of Lady Darlington."

He smiled. "Perhaps she recognized my sincerity."

The warmth in his eyes was disastrous to any latent sense of propriety she might harbor, as were the heated memories of their recent lovemaking. "I shouldn't say this . . . I shouldn't even think it—but"—her lashes half shielded her eyes—"I don't want to think of you leaving just yet."

"How fortunate. Because I have no intention of leaving."

"Be warned, though, once the Pugins and Holcombs descend on us, any possibility of privacy will be greatly curtailed. They're old friends of my mother and Lydia, and they consider me like one of their children."

"Since your aunt is already here, a few more guests won't matter. They may actually help keep her company."

Lulu's eyes brightened. "I hadn't thought of that. Her entertainment won't fall exclusively on us."

"Us?" he teased.

"I could make it worth your while."

"Did I mention how fascinating I find your aunt?"

"It might be a formidable task even for you, darling. She considers you a bit of a rogue."

"It shouldn't be too difficult to change her mind."

"Such assurance."

He gently shrugged, conscious that any answer would only provoke her. "Tell me about these neighbors of yours," he said instead.

"They're slightly stuffy. The men hunt and loudly deplore the rise of the middle class. The ladies gossip and loudly deplore the rise of the middle class. And," she added, exhaling in a dispirited way, "now that I think of it, you'll have to move to another room. You can't sleep in a suite adjoining mine."

"I'm not moving."

"You have to," she tersely replied. "How will it look otherwise?"

"I was here first. You gave me the best suite. That's how it will look, and if anyone dares take issue, I'll politely refute their assumptions."

"Lydia might insist."

"This is your home, darling. And last I heard, you were of legal age."

His succinct rejoinder couldn't have been truer. In addition, she'd spent the months since her divorce reprioritizing her life, reaffirming her independence. "Yes, I believe I'm old enough to place my guests where I wish," she firmly declared. "Thank you for reminding me."

"If you let the gossips run your life," he lazily drawled.

Her eyes took on a mischievous glow. "I suppose most would say, it's a little late for me to become concerned."

"That would be my feeling, but if you're anxious about what these new guests might think, I promise to be the paragon of discretion in public. And wait and see how well Aunt Lydia and I get along. I believe we're both intent on seeing that you're suitably entertained." His grin was wicked. "Although I have some auxiliary plans I don't propose discussing with your aunt."

"Promises, promises," she purred.

"Speaking of which," he murmured, "if Aunt Lydia is taking a nap, I don't see why we shouldn't follow suit. Entertaining your guests tonight could be exhausting. A little rest would do you good," he said, his dark eyes suggesting something else entirely.

She hesitated, still torn between desire and the possibility of scandal.

"First I'll take off all your clothes," he murmured. "Very, very slowly . . ."

"I'm not sure that will be restful."

"It depends. In some respects, it's the ultimate repose. If nothing else," he said with a grin, "you'll be lying down."

It was impossible to ignore the blatant temptation. "And where will you be?"

"Where I belong. Deep inside you."

A shudder raced up her spine and she gripped the chair arms as though needing safe anchor against his potent allure.

Sliding up in his chair, he leaned across the small distance separating them, and gently pried her fingers free. "You'll like it," he whispered. "Guaranteed."

"But now?" Lulu breathed. "Lydia might not be sleeping yet. She won't be. She'll know."

"We'll go up the servants' stairs."

Lulu's eyes flared wide. "That's worse. It will look like we're sneaking around."

He came to his feet, pulled her up, and drew her close so she could feel the extent of his arousal, so the hard length of his erection pressed into her stomach. So she knew how much he wanted her. "If your aunt happens to come out of her room and sees us together, I'll walk away." He dipped his head and gently kissed her. "But if she doesn't, if we can reach your room undetected, I promise I'll make you come a dozen times before dinner."

She took a small breath, her aunt's presence daunting. On the other hand . . . he moved his hips just then—a delicate light pressure—and she felt every engorged inch. "You can't touch me," she quickly said. At his startled look, she added, "Until we reach my room."

He immediately stepped away and gestured toward the door.

Midway down the second-floor corridor, they heard footsteps coming their way.

"I didn't know you had two Rubens's paintings," Mischa remarked, stopping before a portrait of a lady.

"Actually, I have four," Lulu replied, although her voice had none of the calm of the prince's.

"Really—four? You'll have to show them to me," he said in a conversational tone, glancing at a maid coming into view. "Along with your sweet, delectable pussy," he added in a low tone.

Lulu's gaze darted toward the maid moving toward them.

"My favorite Rubens is his 'Three Graces,' " he went on as though he had nothing else on his mind. "His handling of flesh tones is really quite remarkable." Mischa's glance flicked to the servant passing by. "On the other hand, his early portraits like this one have a freshness of color and line that charms—she's far enough away now," he whispered, surveying the servant's receding form. "I could even kiss you," he teased, "and she'd never know."

Terrified he might actually do something so brazen, Lulu swept past him and quickly walked away.

He followed, a half-smile on his lips. The amorous Lady Darlington wasn't an exhibitionist, it appeared. Although, in private, fortunately, she was delightfully uninhibited. But he took care to enter his rooms first, then use the adjoining door into Lulu's apartments in order to mitigate her trepidation.

"You have to be more discreet," she scolded the moment he walked into her room. "That could have been Aunt Lydia!"

"But it wasn't. Although I shall take care in the future," he quickly interposed at the sight of her frown.

She bit her lower lip and exhaled softly. "I'm not sure I'm capable of carrying off this subterfuge."

"You surprise me. Neither of us are novices."

"This is my home, though, with all my servants about. And regardless of the fact that Lydia is at the other end of the corridor, she's much too near."

"I'll muffle your screams when you climax," he offered with a smile. "Would that help?"

"This isn't humorous."

"Forgive me. But she's not going to walk in unannounced and I swear I'll be well mannered. On the other hand"—he pulled up a small gilded chair and sat—"I'm more than ready to listen to all your apprehensions."

"For one, you're going to break that Louis Quinze chair."

Quickly rising, he set it back in place. "I'll stand while you tell me," he offered, suavely deferential and conciliatory. "You'll find me sensitive to your every concern."

"As long as we end up in *bed*, you mean."

"We don't have to be in bed," he replied, in the gentlest of voices.

"If you don't stop being so unctuous, I'm going to beat you."

His mouth twitched. "I'm not sure that's incentive to stop."

She tried to suppress her smile. "You're impossible. You know that, of course."

"I also know a very good way to calm your nerves."

Her violet eyes held a hint of levity. "I'm sure you do."

"Would you like a demonstration?"

"Does it involve taking off my clothes?" she asked drily.

"That's up to you." He grinned. "I'm flexible about clothes. On the other hand," he murmured, moving toward her, pleased to see her temper was cooling, "I'd enjoy playing lady's maid. You wouldn't have to do a thing. Although I'd suggest you don't scream too loudly when you come. In the interest of prudence."

"Since when have you been interested in prudence?"

"Since it seems to matter to you." Reaching out—but slowly, so she could stop him if she wished—he began to untie the bow at her neck.

His hands at her throat triggered a familiar welcoming response, as though he had only to touch her and her body shifted into pleasure mode, as though her senses recognized the carnal promise. "How can you make me feel . . . instantly in a rut?" she demanded ruefully.

"I might ask the same of you. I've been in a constant state of arousal; I don't even mind being at your beck and call." He slid free the hyacinth-colored ribbon at her neck and carefully draped it over a chair back like a maid might. "Now, do you want your earrings on or off, my lady." He set one pearl pendant swinging with a brush of his finger. "I'm new at this job."

"Liar."

"I meant being a maid. The rest I know."

"From vast experience."

"Like yours."

"How would you know?"

"How would you?" He half smiled. "Are we done now with our mutual recriminations?"

Her smile matched his. "Yes. You're right, as always. Isn't that what men like to hear?"

Teasing or not, he knew better than to respond to her sarcasm. "Then we're back to the earrings," he blandly said. "On or off?"

"You decide."

"You have to." He waited, telling himself it shouldn't matter that she had a past or that there had been other men, reminding himself he was the least likely person to question anyone's prodigality.

"On," she replied, beginning to suffer from a familiar impatience when he was near. Or maybe all she had to do was see the extent of his arousal, she thought, glancing downward at the bulge in his trousers, and she was lost.

"Yes, ma'am," he replied, tactful and restrained. "Your blouse?"

She nodded. How beautifully large he was, the fine wool of his trousers lifted, stretched over his enormous penis. She felt her vaginal muscles flex in anticipation.

Lulu had dressed hastily in a simple silk blouse and a lavender taffeta skirt for her meeting with Lydia, and the prince began opening the pearl buttons on her blouse.

She felt the air caress her skin as he pulled her blouse open and slid it down her arms—a rush of coolness on her warming flesh.

Running his fingertip over her breasts pushed high into plump mounds above her corset and chemise, he found himself wondering how many other men had seen her like this, flushed and waiting, impatient for sex. "This is tight," he said, gruff and low, plagued by the disconcerting images of her other lovers. "How did you manage to put on your corset alone?"

"Practice," she whispered, only half listening, the searing path of his finger holding her attention.

"Practice from dressing yourself after your sexual rendezvous?"

Her lashes lifted at the resentment in his tone. Was he really interested in styles of corsets?

"You're not allowed to do that anymore," he brusquely said. "Fuck other men."

"Really." It was meant to be nonconfrontational, a putting-off-to-another-time response; clearly corsets weren't the problem.

"I mean it," he growled.

"What if I demanded the same of you?" A modicum of confrontation entered her voice.

"Fine. I won't. Now lift up your arms. I'll take off your chemise."

Wait, she wanted to say—wait just a minute, or more realistically wait a week or month on this particular discussion that had to do, irrationally, with fidelity and virtue. But he was pulling up her chemise and she lifted her arms, because at base, she wasn't interested in controversy at the moment. Her body was aflame with desire and selfishly she wanted surcease.

As he deftly stripped away her skirt and petticoats, she stepped out of them as directed. "You're suddenly docile," he noted, his gaze examining.

"Isn't that what you want?"

"*More* docility from the uncompromising Lady Darlington," he drawled. "Have I done something right?"

She glanced downward. "Actually you *have* something I need."

He grinned. "Greedy puss."

"Very."

He smiled, her insatiable desire a pleasant constant. "And to think I almost didn't come to visit. I would have missed these very large, luscious breasts among other things," he murmured, reaching around her to unhook her corset. "Do you like them sucked?"

She could feel her nipples grow taut, an answering excitement shimmer through her senses. "Only by you," she murmured, understanding how best to please him in this amorous game.

"How nice," he whispered, lifting away her corset, letting the wisp of lace and boning drop to the floor. Taking a half-step back, he surveyed her breasts, still quivering slightly after being freed from their unnatural constraint. They were luscious, ripe, and plump, his for the taking—his to keep, he thought, feeling autocratic. He lightly flicked a pink, peaked crest. "Would you like me to suck on this?"

She nodded, the pulsing heat of arousal having turned to a fierce drumbeat, her need for him now—as always—prodigious.

Slipping off his coat and cravat, he drew her with him to a chair. Sitting down, he leaned back and spread his legs. Too large for the lady's chair, perhaps overdressed, his dark trousers and waistcoat were stark contrast to the rose-patterned chintz-covered chair. He shifted slightly, making himself comfortable, looked up at her, and softly snapped his fingers. "Stand here."

Her gaze narrowed. "I'm not your trained pet."

But a delectable pet, no question. "I apologize."

"How much?" Provocative authority was one thing; masculine imperatives quite another.

"As much as you like," he drawled. "If you come a little closer."

"Say it," she insisted, not moving.

He lifted one brow.

"Say, I'm sorry."

"Say, I'm sorry."

"It's been really pleasant knowing you," she murmured, turning away.

He grabbed her wrist. "I'm sorry. Truly. Don't go." He smiled. "It's your room after all."

She shook his hand away. "You're much too annoying. I'm not sure you're worth it."

"You're much too sexy for my peace of mind and, unfortunately, very much worth it." He grimaced. "Damn your sweet allure," he whispered, pulling her closer.

She didn't or couldn't resist.

Smiling in satisfaction, he smoothed his palms down her arms, twined his fingers through hers, and drew her hard against his thighs. "If you were to bend over, your nipples would be easier to reach," he whispered. "I could make you come standing right there . . ."

"Damn you—that's not fair," she breathed, a surge of lust flooding her body.

Fairness wasn't anywhere on his list of priorities at the moment; it wasn't even a recognizable word in his current hot-blooded mood. "Just a little lower," he coaxed. "I can almost reach them . . ."

She slowly leaned forward.

Perversely, her submission wasn't enough. Driven by inexplicable feelings, he seized her breasts in a harsh grip and forced her lower.

Slapping his hands away, she jerked upright, her eyes hot with temper. "What's your problem?"

"What's yours?"

"Like you, I don't take orders."

"Sometimes you don't mind," he said silkily.

"And sometimes I do," she snapped.

"Am I supposed to read your mind?" She was nude from the waist up, her flamboyant breasts close, almost at eye level, lush, succulent, her nipples jewel hard, none of which was helpful to the state of his erection, his insistent cravings, or his unsettled state of mind.

"Maybe you'll have to if you want sex. I can be moody too."

"And not just craving cock."

"Is that a disparaging remark?" she asked with dulcet sarcasm.

He shrugged, began to answer, changed his mind, and with a sigh, slid lower on his spine. His dark gaze came up a moment later, his expression unreadable. "I'm out-of-my-mind crazy for you and I don't like it."

She smiled faintly. "So it's not something I said."

He grimaced. "Amusing."

"Would it help if you *could* suck on my breasts?"

His eyes turned cool. "I'm not fucking my mother."

"I have no intention of playing that role with you. Consider it a purely selfish request."

"I'm relieved," he gibed.

"If you'd let me sit on your lap, I'd be relieved as well," she noted, a sportive light in her eyes.

He suddenly shifted up in his chair. "Is that a fact?" he said, husky and low.

"A very relevant fact."

"How relevant?"

"I'm not begging, Mischa."

A familiar impudence met her gaze, his sullenness gone. "If you were to sit on my lap, your breasts would be conveniently near my mouth . . . you realize that."

"I do. But it's not every day that I have a houseguest like you. I thought I'd take advantage of your—er—advantages."

"So you're using me."

"That would be for you to decide." Her voice was soft, enticing.

He didn't answer for a moment and then he began unbuttoning his trousers. "How can I refuse a lady of your grace and charm . . ."

"And we can debate who wants whom the most later," Lulu noted, placing her hands on his shoulders, lifting first one leg then the other over his thighs and lowering herself down. "Plainly, we're both obsessed."

He grinned. "Now I feel better."

Her smile was benign. "If you'll just move a little forward, I can feel better too."

It wasn't as though they weren't in agreement on everything that mattered, he thought, helping her rise slightly, guiding his erection to her pouty lips. Their appetite for sex was in perfect accord.

As he entered her hot, silken warmth, he sighed, bliss overwhelming discord, any issues of authority suddenly irrelevant. And a moment later, when she glided up his erection, her breasts came conveniently near his mouth. Capturing one nipple lightly in his teeth, he held her prisoner, poised on the crest of his penis and leisurely sucked, nibbled, licked, softly, softly at first and then with more force until she didn't know if she was sobbing from frustration or near-orgasmic rapture. And as he finally released her elongated nipple and allowed her to slide down his penis once again, they both felt the wild, fierce pleasure like a jolt.

He serviced her as she rode him, with his mouth and rampant cock, with the finesse of much experience, with a rare affection and she came to orgasm countless times—with violent passion, with sobbing gratitude, with the giddy charm of an innocent maid. Driven by his own raging desires, by the provocative opportunity to climax in her with freedom, he met each of her unbridled orgasms with an explosive, self-indulgent profligacy that ruinously stained his trousers, the chair, that brought them after a time, panting and breathless, to collapse.

Resting against his arms, she cradled her aching breasts.

"I'm sorry." Bending his head, he gently kissed them both. "Do they hurt?"

"Ummm"—half-sigh, half-groan—"a little."

"I'll let them rest." He glanced at the clock on the mantle. "We have to dress for dinner soon anyway."

Her groan was clear this time. "It's going to be an incredibly dull evening."

"All we have to do is be polite for a few hours."

"For that degree of politeness, I'm going to need several glasses of champagne." Glancing at the clock, she sighed. "They're all going to be downstairs soon. Which brings up a sore subject; I'm going to need some help with my corset and evening gown. They're slightly more complicated."

"My pleasure." Numerous orgasms had painted the world with a rosy glow, issues of corsets dismissed.

"Just help dressing now," she cautioned. "Our time is limited—although that warning is probably more for myself than you."

"I disagree. But I might be able to last a few hours without making love to you if I really try."

As it turned out, however, neither could, their toilettes delayed the first time by Mischa's washing up. He'd undressed and Lulu couldn't long resist the sight of his splendid nude form and rampant penis. Her offer to help him with his ablutions led to an exceedingly pleasant delay that dampened the bed in more ways than one.

They managed to restrain themselves afterward for the time it took Mischa to fit himself out in full evening rig and even for the interval in which Lulu washed and dressed. But at the last, as he was standing behind her, doing his duty clasping the small silk-covered buttons at the back of her gown, the sight of her bare shoulders and opulent breasts nearly spilling over the low décolletage, the perfume of her hair and skin, brought his unruly penis to pikestaff attention.

She couldn't help but notice and she surveyed his jutting trouser front with a wistful expression. "Is there time?" she whispered.

"There's time," he said without even looking at the clock.

She held out her hand. "Just don't muss my gown."

He led her to a table, cleared off the top, eased her down on her back, and carefully folded the cream-colored silk muslin of her skirt over her waist with the precision of a laundry maid. "You're very good at that," Lulu murmured, his concentration charming to behold.

"I'm not buttoning another two dozen ridiculously small buttons tonight," he muttered, making another neat fold. "I'm keeping this gown pristine."

"Like me."

He grinned. "Exactly, my virginal little minx. I think that's what I like best about you—your sugar-sweet innocence."

"What I like best about you is—"

"I know what you like best, darling," he murmured, smoothing the beaded hem of the skirt flat, slipping his finger down the opening in her drawers, easing the fabric apart. "You like to be filled with my cock," he whispered, unbuttoning his trousers, freeing his erection. "Once more now, darling," he breathed, gently forcing the head of his penis past the lips of her labia, slightly swollen from their afternoon's ardor, "and then you have to wait until after dinner," he added, plunging forward.

Her eyes went shut as he buried himself inside her and she moaned softly, ecstasy flooding her senses, the aching pleasure almost too much to bear. She was addicted to his touch, her craving insatiable; all she wanted was to feel him inside her. Like that . . . God, like that, the lush rhythm, the size and agonizingly perfect feel of him—there . . . right there. She screamed as she came, but neither cared, carnal tumult eroding reason, his climax so intense, he felt as though he was being drained dry.

He no longer even questioned his insatiable lust for her. It was enough to keep her in his sight, to know he could fuck her again. But too soon, they were forced to recognize the reality of time. Putting their clothes to rights, they stood at the door a few minutes later, reluctant to leave. "I'll come down in a few minutes," he murmured, kissing her gently.

"I hope I can last 'til then." Reaching up, she touched his cheek.

His gaze was openly affectionate. "Just remember, you're mine," he whispered.

"I should like to be yours." Her smile was winsome.

"Good. Because you don't have a choice."

Chapter Six

Lydia, Lord and Lady Pugin, the Holcombs, Mrs. Holcombs's brother, Dean Stanley, visiting from his parsonage in Kent, were all assembled in the drawing room when Lulu joined them. After greeting her guests, Dean Stanley brought up the last time he and Lulu had met at the Ainsley Hunt. Since hunting was a popular topic of conversation with all the guests, the discussion immediately took on a convivial tone.

A footman brought round a tray with glasses of champagne, and before long, Lord Pugin was holding forth on his favorite harangue—that of the influx of the bourgeoisie into the local hunt clubs. "It wasn't more than ten years ago when one never saw a man of trade in a pink coat! Now, they're in every hunt club of note. None of them can ride worth a jot," he grumbled, "and as far as jumping a fence"—odium fueled his rising tone—"any noble stripling could do better! The only way to rid ourselves of them is to close them out," he exclaimed. "I say, blackball them, every one!"

"While I remind Harold," his wife interjected in a calmer tone, "that if we do, the churches will be the poorer for it. That London banker who bought Lord Crewes's property donated five thousand to the parish church for repairs. Although"—a small frown creased her forehead—"his wife felt as though she could take over the annual floral display at the church on the basis of that donation. I had to tell her," Lady Pugin went on in reproving accents, "that the Pugin family has been in charge of that parish event for centuries. I believe I made myself clear," she finished with a smug smile.

Winifred Holcomb viewed the rising middle class with equal scorn. "I completely concur," she said, supporting her friend. "I had to give that déclassé cocoa magnate's wife a set-down last week at the young ladies' seminary. She had the temerity to attempt to take precedence on the stage at the annual poetry awards. When the entire county knows I always present those awards and so a Holcomb always has," she added with uncompromising finality. She glanced at her brother. "Miles, tell them about your contretemps with that scandalous rug merchant over communion."

Magnus took that moment to enter from the dining room and announce dinner.

"But the Prince isn't yet down," Lydia noted. "A few minutes more, Magnus."

The hall door opened as she finished speaking and Mischa appeared.

With Magnus waiting and the footmen standing at attention in the dining room, the story of the rug merchant was forgotten. Introductions were quickly undertaken, the prince gracious in turn to each of Lydia's friends. At his last bow, he turned to Lulu and offered her his arm—as though he had the right to escort her into dinner.

His smile was benign as he waited, his arm extended. She couldn't take issue without calling attention to his audacity, and she placed her hand on his as he knew she must.

Considering the recent quenching of their passions, neither thought so trivial a gesture would cause such a shock.

The prince concealed his surprise. Lulu's cheeks flushed pink.

Quickly turning them away from any discerning gazes, he moved toward the dining room, his sidelong look amused. "You're adorable when you blush."

"You have to behave," she whispered, shooting him a flustered glance.

"Do I get a prize if I do?"

"Mischa!" Both fear and longing vibrated in her hushed exclamation.

"Don't worry," he soothed as they entered the dining room, lifting his hand to brush away a loose curl from her temple. "I'll be good."

Her senses leaped at the light pressure of his fingertips. "Don't touch me," she pleaded, "or I'll embarrass us both."

His smile was tantalizing and much too close. "Later . . . when we're rid of all these people, I'll touch you—everywhere . . ."

"Mischa, please . . ." Her gaze flickered toward the footman standing near her chair.

While the prince wasn't in the habit of worrying what footmen thought, he knew Lulu felt differently. "Your servant, ma'am," he said, his expression bland, his tone conversational, and gesturing the footman away, he pulled out her chair himself. If she were more dégagé or the party less staid, if she weren't blushing so furiously, he thought, gazing down on her bare shoulders so close and inviting as she sat down, he would have taken his place beside her. Or in a more perfect world—whisk her away entirely from the dullness of the evening ahead.

"Prince Radovsky, sit by me," Lydia called out, curtailing any further wishful thinking. She indicated a chair to her left at the opposite end of the table.

"Go!" Lulu muttered, sotto voce, and then quickly smiled at the Holcombs, who were approaching.

"As you wish." Mischa's bow was flawless, his smile obliging. He strolled away, seemingly untouched by the tremulous emotion gripping his hostess.

Dean Stanley had taken a seat on Lydia's right, the Holcombs sat on either side of Lulu, flanked by the Pugins, and the table was complete.

"There now," Lydia cheerfully exclaimed, surveying the seated guests with a benevolent smile. "Isn't this a wonderful occasion? All of us together once again!" There was a certain smugness to her expression as she gazed at her niece. "Lulu, darling, you must admit, this is so much more pleasant than keeping company with yourself."

There was only one acceptable answer and Lulu obliged. "Yes, Auntie. You're right, of course."

"I knew it," Lydia indulgently replied. "Your mother and I know best, my dear. It never pays to rusticate too long. Activity, companionship, a little excitement in our lives. We all need it. Don't you agree, Prince Radovsky?"

"I couldn't agree more. You must listen to your aunt, Lady Darlington. She seems to have the proper formula for satisfaction. A little excitement"—he dipped his head toward Lydia—"how astute."

"Hunting, now there's excitement," George Pugin interposed. "You must ride with us again, Lulu. Give that hunter of yours some exercise."

"I've been doing my share of riding, George." The double entendre struck her almost the moment she'd uttered the words and she dug her fingernails into her palms to keep from flushing a deeper red. "I take Volante for a ride each morning," she added with what she hoped was calm.

The temptation to interject a comment was almost overwhelming, but courtesy forbade it and Mischa took care not to glance Lulu's way.

"I expect you ride, Prince Radovsky." Harold Holcomb said.

Again. That blatant opportunity. "I occasionally ride some amateur races," the prince said instead. "We hunt in Russia as well, but with a degree less formality."

"Ah, the wild Cossacks," Lady Pugin pronounced with drama.

"Not exactly Cossacks where I live, but horsemen of note."

The footmen arrived with the first service, momentarily arresting the conversation, and after a prayer by Dean Stanley, the guests were served a choice of several soups. Hors d'oeuvres followed and then a variety of fish and meats. A discussion arose over the merits of cooks versus chefs as the second service began, Lord Pugin and Harold Holcomb agreeing that they fancied cooks. Their wives preferred chefs, although they were quick to remark that they liked those who were English-trained. The curate took a tone of virtuous constraint on the subject. "My village cook prepares unpretentious fare. But simplicity befits a well-ordered life," he righteously intoned, taking a second helping of pheasant served with a champagne and Seville orange sauce.

"You haven't expressed your opinion on chefs, Prince Radovsky," Lydia said with a smile.

"I like whatever my staff prepares for me." He gave a small deprecating shrug, not mentioning his various establishments had numerous chefs and cooks. "They know my tastes."

"And what are those, Prince Radovsky?" Winifred Holcomb asked, her curiosity piquant.

"Mainly what my mother used to cook for me."

"Your mother cooked?" Lady Pugin couldn't conceal the shock in her voice.

"She was a very good cook. I liked her outdoor breakfasts best. Wild mushroom and chive omelet cooked over an open fire always reminds me fondly of my childhood."

"My word!" Lady Pugin gasped.

"The Prince has a Romany heritage on his mother's side," Lulu explained, silently amused at Mischa's urbane provocation. "Don't you think he's inherited her coloring?"

"The Russians are exotic, you must admit," Lydia smoothly interposed, "with the Empire incorporating so many divergent peoples. Marguerite has found her life in Petersburg endlessly fascinating."

Since everyone at the table was well aware of the extent of wealth into which Marguerite had married, they restrained their comments concerning the prince's eccentric background.

"I previously asked Prince Radovsky about the tsar's new Minister of Finance," Lydia remarked, segueing the conversation to safer ground. "You have funds in the Russian railroads, don't you, Harold?"

"Yes . . . yes, I do," he quickly replied with heavy-handed politesse. "They're bringing me a first-rate return too. Can't say I have any complaints about Witte's foresight."

For the remainder of the meal, Witte's financial acumen was discussed and lauded, Lydia's allusion to the Radovsky wealth sufficient to remind her friends that the foreigner in their presence was a man of means and title. The English gentry tended to be isolationist in their politics and exclusive in their friendships, but a sizable fortune always made borders superfluous as well as erasing the taint of sullied bloodlines. So the conversation was extremely amiable, with everyone agreeing that no nation was building railroads with such speed and boundlessness as Russia. The Trans-Siberian Railway was nearly half finished—an indication of the rapid modernization of Russia's far-flung empire that they all viewed with approval.

In the course of the discussion, the prince was circumspect in his opinions, and particularly reserved in his remarks to his hostess. His tone was civil when he addressed her, never familiar. No one would have guessed from his demeanor that he'd only recently made love to her.

Before long, Lulu relaxed. She became a vivacious hostess, a role familiar to her friends, entertaining them all with favorite stories, reminding her friends of events they cherished, of happy times they'd shared. If the prince didn't know better, he wouldn't have had an inkling that Lulu had been in virtual seclusion for months. Lady Darlington was captivating.

It was unfortunate the rich array of dessert sweets reminded Winifred Holcomb of her brother's rug merchant story. The thin, crisp rounds of shortbread on the confection tray must have brought communion wafers to mind. Or perhaps the numerous glasses of wine she'd consumed had loosened her tongue.

"Miles, you simply *must* relate your tale of the"—her voice lowered to a thrilling whisper—"Manchester merchant who put you in such a frightful position."

Since Dean Stanley had had his share of wine as well, he willingly responded to his sister's prompting. Sitting up straighter, he surveyed his audience with a commanding air and cleared his throat. "There is one thing that all churchmen are agreed upon," he began, his voice resonating with authority, his thin mouth firming, "and that is that marriage is a subject upon which *the Church* has the last word. Despite"—indignation swelled faintly in his tone—"the continuing attempts by *certain* individuals to legalize marriage with—if you can imagine," he pronounced in censorious accents, *"a deceased wife's sister!* As you know, that heinous proposal has come before parliament *twenty-six* times since 1850. The entire notion of *affinity in marriage* is not only unquestionably illegal, but"—his gaze traveled around the table, emphasizing the seriousness of what he was about to say—*"forbidden* by Holy Writ." The Dean didn't actually use the word "Oedipus," but the implication was clear.

"My personal connection with this distasteful subject came as the result of being approached by a wealthy benefactor who had committed the unforgivable and married his deceased wife's sister. Perhaps the man hadn't realized the enormity of his incestuous offense, although," the curate said with a narrowed glance, "I doubt the merchant's barrister had overlooked the illegality. Nevertheless, this dastardly couple came to me requesting Holy Communion." He paused like an actor might before presenting his noblest lines. "I said to them"—he scanned those at the table with a righteous gaze—"as long as your *illicit* cohabitation continues, it is *impossible* to treat you as pious Christians. I quoted Leviticus eighteen: six—'None of you shall approach to any flesh of his flesh to uncover their nakedness, I am the Lord.' And I turned them away as would any moral, right-minded soul," he finished, his stern tone unflinching.

"The merchant owns one of the largest manufacturing plants in Manchester," Winifred whispered. "He'd moved to Kent with his new wife far from the site of his infamy. But people know," she added with raised brows. "They always find out."

The prince had surreptitiously glanced at Lulu in the course of the Dean's moral pronouncements, knowing how disconcerting such a tale would be to her, how little it would take to frighten her when she'd expressed her unease with their affinity numerous times. By the time the curate was finished, she was ashen. "As I understand it," the prince softly remarked, intent on assuaging Lulu's distress, "the proposal allowing marriage to a deceased wife's sister has passed the House of Commons numerous times only to be defeated by the churchmen in the House of Lords. Apparently, there are many in England who support such a proposal."

Dean Stanley's gaze pinned Mischa where he sat. "Are you suggesting something so hideous should be legal?"

The prince shrugged and his voice when he spoke was unutterably mild. "It is in many countries."

"Heathen countries," the clergyman spat.

"Those countries might take issue with your terminology. Since there's no blood relationship between the parties, the issue of affinity doesn't arise."

"The Bible is unequivocally clear on the subject."

Closely attached to pagan beliefs through his mother's heritage, the prince didn't take kindly to religious hair-splitting or more particularly those who knew him best might say—to dissent of any kind. But he was trying to be on his best behavior for Lulu's sake. "The bill will eventually pass Parliament." Mischa was controlling his temper with effort. "With or without the support of the clergy."

"Marguerite tells me Russia has a very diverse culture." Lydia smiled at Lulu and then at the prince. "I expect Prince Radovsky has been exposed to a broader religious experience than we have in England. Come now, Miles. Let us drop this subject. Don't you agree, Prince Radovsky?"

"Of course, Lady Harcourt. I apologize for my remarks. My father would be appalled." The prince's voice was full of regret. "Particularly when I was given express orders to show Lady Darlington every courtesy. My apologies, Lady Darlington, and to you, Dean Stanley—I beg your forgiveness."

"Hmpf . . . that is—I suppose . . . my apologies as well, Prince Radovsky," the curate grudgingly said. "We must agree to disagree," he uncharitably added.

"Whatever you say, sir." Mischa inclined his head in a faint bow.

"Here, here!" Harold Holcomb boomed. "Never discuss religion, my father used to say. And so we shan't." He smiled at Mischa, whom he silently supported for putting his toad-eating brother-in-law in his place. "Is the wolf hunting in Russia as thrilling as they say? I've only heard accounts secondhand."

"Then you should join me next winter at my estate in Livonia," the prince graciously offered. " You may experience wolf hunting firsthand."

"You don't say!" The bluff country squire was all smiles.

"But of course. You're all invited should you wish to come. Marguerite was with us last winter. You should join us, Lady Harcourt, and you as well, Lady Darlington. The sleigh rides over the moonlit snow are unforgettable." He glanced at Lulu and was comforted to see her color returning. "Have you ever ridden behind a speeding troika, Lady Darlington, with the harness bells ringing in the crisp cold air and the moon so close it looks as though it's going to fall into your lap?"

"It sounds charming," Lulu replied, her smile tentative but restored.

"Then come and visit your mother."

And you, she winsomely thought.

And me, he thought.

Chapter Seven

After the last offerings of dessert, dinner finally came to an end and the ladies retired to the drawing room for tea. The men stayed at the table with their port, although Mischa watched the clock, enduring the men's conversation with civility if not good humor, until finally, blessedly, Magnus arrived to summon them to the ladies.

Lord Pugin and Harold Holcomb grumbled, preferring their port, but Dean Stanley, obsequious and noticeably drunk, quickly rose. "Come now," he charged, his face red from drink, "Lady Darlington mustn't be kept waiting. The dear lady is in need of company after her painful, er . . . unhappy—ah, union and lengthy solitude. We must give her every consideration."

The prince immediately took issue, experiencing a novel sense of territorial rights as he came to his feet. "From all accounts, she's well rid of Charles," he remarked, more willing than the curate to call a spade a spade.

"Nevertheless, she's a fragile female without protection from the world and much in need of friendship and guidance."

Mischa's fingers clenched against an overwhelming need to lift the curate by his scrawny neck and point out that Lulu didn't need *his* friendship *or* guidance.

"She has friends enough, Miles," Harold Holcomb noted, frowning at his brother-in-law. "And Lulu has always done as she pleases."

"I can see the pain in her eyes, Harold, when perhaps you cannot. My calling makes me more perceptive of those afflicted, more able to offer them comfort and relief," Dean Stanley added with unctuous piety.

The phrase "over my dead body" came to the prince's mind, but curtailing the impulse to utter it, he bowed to the men instead and crisply said, "I for one feel the need for a cup of tea."

Pugin and Holcomb reluctantly rose from their chairs at his prompting, their steadiness at issue after two bottles of port. The prince, on the other hand, never displayed any sign of inebriation, save perhaps for an increased tendency to take offense. Which trait the dean was seriously taxing with his interest in Lulu. If anyone was going to give her comfort, it was he, Mischa sullenly thought. The dean would do well to restrain his charitable impulses for those in his parish.

* * *

When the men entered the drawing room and Lulu caught sight of Mischa, she felt a blissful pleasure quite distinct from any she'd previously experienced. She must have drunk too much champagne, she thought, and then he smiled at her and she understood how little champagne had to do with her delight. He made her feel as though they were alone in the room, in the universe, in the vast star-lit galaxy, his intimate smile unrivaled in its beauty. Life suddenly took on golden promise when he smiled at her like that, all the rapturous poetry of love taking on a new profundity or, perhaps more pertinently, taking on meaning for the very first time.

Her epiphany was frightening.

But exciting as well.

And thrilling.

It was almost impossible to feign complacency in the company of others with apprehension and joy running riot in her brain. Fortunately, Lydia was an engaging conversationalist as was Harold, who was known for his loquaciousness. No one seemed to notice Lulu's introspection. Dean Stanley's personal remarks went largely unattended, save for Lulu's occasional heedless rejoinders.

Her thoughts were focused elsewhere.

When they shouldn't have been.

When she should have forced herself to listen to the conversation.

When her aunt had to ask her almost every question twice, including whether she wished to have a picnic luncheon at the monastery ruins tomorrow.

Lulu made some excuse; she couldn't even remember how she responded. But the prince stepped in to give validity to her vague assertion of a previous engagement and suggested the party go on without them. He had some letters to write to his steward, he explained.

It seemed an endless interval before the guests finally departed, Lord Pugin and Harold staying very late, savoring their whiskeys. But at last, only Lulu and Mischa remained.

"That will be all, Magnus," the prince said.

Magnus glanced at Lulu for approval. She nodded and the door softly closed behind him.

"I hope you didn't mind me sending Magnus away. But your staff isn't going to get much sleep tonight."

"It's always difficult to send George and Harold to their beds if any liquor still remains in the bottles."

"While I've been waiting to see you in your bed since"—Mischa smiled—"at least half past eight."

"I doubt Lydia would have approved us disappearing so early."

The prince's grin was boyish. "I thought as much and restrained myself."

Lulu gazed at him from under her long lashes. "Except for your occasional rude remarks to Miles."

"He's a witless, drunken ass. I thoroughly dislike men of the cloth who proclaim their moral infallibility, not to mention how annoying was his excessive interest in you. If he had said once more that you needed his gentle hand to guide you, I would have throttled him where he sat."

"You feel you have the right?" she teased, inexplicably pleased with his jealousy.

"Damn his lecherous eyes, yes."

"And why is that?" It was the flirtatious Lulu of old.

He didn't answer, looking at her for a moment as though seeing her for the first time. "I'm not sure," he finally said with a slight disqualifying wave of his hand, hours removed from the passions upstairs, cooler reason holding sway.

"You just know."

"Something like that."

A sudden quiet filled the room. The prince shifted in his chair.

"Talking about your feelings makes you uncomfortable?" Lulu queried, a mischievous light in her eyes.

He shrugged. "Apparently."

"You don't sound sure."

He slipped lower in his chair, stretched his long legs out before him, and observed her from under his dark lashes. "I'd prefer talking about something else."

"Or not talking at all."

His smile was instant, the caution gone from his eyes. "How perceptive of you, Lady Darlington."

"Your reputation precedes you, Prince Radovsky, and then, of course, our previous acquaintance rather gave me the impression you preferred action to words."

"You must read minds, darling."

"Am I really your darling?"

His mouth quirked. "In contrast to Dean Stanley's darling, you mean?"

"I thought you didn't approve of that friendship," she sweetly returned. "Although I may have been mistaken. Are you going to tell me whether I'm your darling or evade the question?"

Despite his wanting Lulu in the most elemental way, it had been so long since he viewed anyone as his, darling or otherwise, he wasn't entirely sure of his feelings.

"Forgive me for pressing you," Lulu said lightly into the silence, recognizing he was different from the man upstairs, less impassioned. "It doesn't matter in the least."

"I don't mean to be ungracious."

"I shouldn't have asked." She lifted her bare shoulder in the faintest of shrugs. "It's the first rule of dalliance, isn't it? Never ask probing questions. I'd forgotten."

He inhaled, steepled his fingers under his chin, and slid a fraction lower on his spine.

"Good God, Mischa," she murmured. "I didn't mean to flummox you. It was a sportive comment, that's all." She mustn't forget, this was about sex.

"Did you know I'd been married?" His voice was almost inaudible.

"No." She suppressed her shock.

"My wife died."

"I'm sorry." Why hadn't she heard of his marriage?

"She died years ago."

"I see." His gaze was unfocused, his voice pained; she didn't know how to respond.

He suddenly looked up. "That's why I didn't answer you."

"I understand," she said, not understanding at all, only intensely aware of his unease. "There's no need to explain."

"Maybe there is." He drew in a deep breath. "Do you remember me telling you when I arrived that I'd been thinking of you for the entire fortnight since we'd met?" Not waiting for her response, he quickly went on, as though he might not if he hesitated, "You'd completely fascinated me; I couldn't put you out of my mind. No one has even interested me since Maiia's death. As for our time together now . . ." He slid up in his chair, leaned forward, rested his elbows on his knees, and looked at her directly. "I'm in deeper than I ever intended to be. So you see, I think you have flummoxed me. And I'm not sure what to do about it."

"There's nothing you *can* do about it."

"You're wrong." An obstinate phrase, firmly uttered.

"Didn't you listen to Miles tonight?" she softly exclaimed. "Good Lord, Mischa, he was almost apoplectic."

"You're not my wife's sister. I don't see how his apoplexy applies. In any event, don't you English make shrewd marriages with first cousins? So why should this connection between the sister of a dead wife and a husband be so scandalous?"

"Surely you're not suggesting marriage?"

He didn't answer for a very long time. "I don't know what I'm suggesting."

"That's a relief," she tartly noted. "I suppose I should be grateful for your indecision."

His eyes narrowed. "Bitch."

"I may be, but you're obviously out of your mind."

"Out of my mind for wanting you," he said, soft and terse.

She lifted her hand as though to arrest his words, but her heart was racing. "*Surely* you recognize the difference between lust and . . ." She couldn't bring herself to say something so outrageous.

"Love? Say it. The word is innocuous enough."

"It's not innocuous, Mischa—in this instance, it's *incredible*. We're not innocents. Far from it. More than anyone, we should understand the difference. I don't *want* to discuss this."

"What if *I* want to?"

"You didn't a few minutes ago. Let's just keep it that way," she said crisply.

"I've changed my mind."

"You can't."

"I can do anything I want." His gaze took on a glittering sharpness. "And I have for a good many years."

"Is that a threat?"

"Take it any way you wish."

"You can't force me."

"I doubt I'll have to force you," he silkily replied. "As I recall, you can't get enough."

She bristled. "I dislike arrogant men."

"And I dislike stubborn women." He rose to his feet in a surge of long-limbed grace and moved toward her.

Instinctively shrinking back in her chair at his overwhelming size and power, she looked up what seemed a very long way. "What do you think you're doing?"

"I was thinking about fucking some sense into you," he drawled.

"I won't allow it." Each word quivered with rebuke, her transient qualm overcome.

"But then I'm not asking for permission." Bending down, he plucked her from her chair with an effortless strength and swept her up into his arms.

"I'll scream," she warned, incensed at his coercion, shoving against his chest.

"I doubt it." Immune to her struggles, he moved toward the door. "Consider the nature of your guests."

"Put me down this instant!" she cried.

"Just a suggestion, darling," he calmly remarked as though she'd not spoken, "but you might like to stifle your affront or your aunt and guests might take notice." He smiled faintly. "I don't think you'd like your gallant, Dean Stanley, to see you being carried away."

"He's not my gallant."

"Damn right, he's not." The prince's voice was suddenly brusque. "Nor will he be," he added grimly, shoving the door open with his foot and striding out into the hall.

The public venue brought her mute, the possibility of discovery terrifying, Dean Stanley's pursed lips and horrified expression a graphic image in her mind.

Taking the steps in a run, Mischa swiftly moved down the hall to her bedroom with a single-minded determination that might have been arousing had Lulu not been so incensed at his effrontery. Carrying her into her bedroom, he unceremoniously dropped her on her bed in a heap of billowing muslin and sparkling beads and began unbuttoning his waistcoat.

She immediately scrambled to escape, but he promptly blocked her, catching her wrist, his long fingers biting into her skin. "I'm not in the mood to run after you," he said, action a viable substitute for resolution in the chaos of his mind. "You want this. I want this. Fuck Dean Stanley and his moral tale."

"I *don't* want this! I *distinctly* don't!"

"Let's just say, I have a feeling you'll change your mind." He jerked the bow loose on his tie. "You're a damned hot little piece, darling. Not that I'm complaining," he added insolently, stripping the tie free and tossing it aside. "I'm more than happy to accommodate you."

"I don't want to be accommodated. Damn you, Mischa!" She tried to shake off his hold. "You're always doing this! I dislike this coercion!"

"Give me a minute, darling." His smile was tight, his grip tighter. "It shouldn't take any longer than that to change your mind."

"So only men are allowed sexual desires? Is that what you mean?"

His dark gaze was bland as he kicked off his evening pumps. "Apparently not. Although, you do have a degree more—shall we say—impatience than most women."

"Fuck you!"

"Just as soon as I get some of my clothes off, darling, I intend to do just that."

"Even if I don't wish it?"

His smile didn't reach his eyes. "Even then."

"Do you do this often? Dragoon women?"

"Never." He began unbuttoning his trousers with his free hand.

"I'm the exception?"

"I doubt it."

"Don't take out your resentment on me because your wife died," she rapped out, brutal in her anger, as capable of insult as he.

He went utterly still, the color draining from his face, every muscle and sinew taut with restraint. His fingers were crushing her wrist. A pulse beat passed in the hushed stillness, then two, and he seemed to shake off his paralysis. Taking a shallow breath, he resumed his unbuttoning. "I don't suggest you move," he said in a voice so chill, her breath caught in her throat. "That's a good girl," he whispered, taking note of her sudden stillness, releasing her wrist to strip off his coat and waistcoat. "Now, do as you're told," he said in a voice devoid of expression, slipping his suspenders down his arms, "and you won't get hurt."

She launched herself at him, screaming insults, tearing a bloody path down his cheek with her nails, landing a hard blow to his jaw, before he managed to free his arms from his suspenders. He shoved her back on the bed, following her down in a lunge, crushing the air from her lungs, silencing her venom. As she struggled against his strength, he forced her flailing arms above her head and held her pinioned.

"I hate you," she gasped.

He rose marginally, easing his weight off her chest. "I'm not sure I don't hate you too," he said hotly. "You're fucking up my life."

"You started it."

"You did—the night of the storm."

"You couldn't resist?"

He snorted. "No man could. You were nude and more than willing."

"And you'd never turned down a woman in your life, had you?" she said bitterly.

Abruptly rolling away, he lay sprawled on his back, his arms flung over his head. "You're right," he muttered, his gaze on the pleated canopy above. "It's all my bloody fault."

But rather than enraged, he looked afflicted and miserable—alone—and Lulu suddenly recalled his earlier disclosures about his wife. What did Maiia look like, she wondered. How much had he loved her? How deeply did he miss her still? "It's not all your fault," she admitted, sympathy and atonement in her voice and gaze. "I could have said no the night of the storm as well." She sighed. "This evening was too long and nerve-racking—having to listen to all those misguided people . . . the pressure and anxiety were wearing for us both."

"Us," he said softly, as though seeing if the concept had credence.

She gazed at the red slash on his cheek. "And I'm sorry I hurt you."

He turned his head. "I'm fine. At least I think I'm fine," he said with a small smile. "I feel as though I'm standing at some damned crossroad." He looked away again. "I've never been here before . . ."

She touched his shoulder, and when he turned back, she saw the misery in his eyes. "What are we going to do," she whispered.

"I'm too deep in love." He tried to smile. "I can't think past my wanting you this second."

"And I don't want to think at all," Lulu said, tears spilling down her cheeks, wanting him too much, knowing they had no future.

"We're a good pair." He rolled back, wiped her face with his shirtsleeve. "Avoiding reason at all costs."

"I really have to right now, if you don't mind." Each word was filled with unease.

He nodded, certain and unequivocal. "Not another argumentative word. I promise."

"Call me weak and irresolute . . . immature"—she smiled— "but I'm just not up to dealing with any more problems."

He brushed her hair away from her temple, a gentle, protective gesture. "Then there's none to deal with."

"Thank you." The simplicity of his reply, his solid strength, was like a bulwark against the tumult of the world.

"You tell me what to do and I'll do it. Life will be simple." He glanced at the small clock near the bed.

She smiled. "You still have time."

His grin was boyish and cheerful. "Was I so obvious?"

"You needn't apologize to me. I'm your partner in obsession."

"And perhaps all the spirits and shamans are as well for bringing me to you."

He was beautiful as a god himself, she thought—a strong and perfect young god. "Having you here almost makes a believer out of me."

"So cynical, sweetheart."

She shook her head. "Not anymore." She blew him a kiss.

He caught it and then caught her, rolling onto his back, pulling her with him.

As she lay atop him, his arms light on her back, his palms resting at the base of her spine, she felt a rare, cloudless, unreserved happiness—like the unsullied joys of childhood. Framing his face with her hands, she kissed his smiling mouth. "You bring joy and gladness in your wake," she breathed.

He moved his head in the merest of negations. "I didn't bring it. I found it here."

"How long?"

He understood what she meant, what she needed to hear. "As long as you want," he replied gently.

"More," she said, like a child would, soft insistence in her voice. "I want more."

"Forever, then," he answered. "I'll love you forever and a day."

"Thank you," she murmured, an aching vulnerability in her eyes.

The ravishing beauty in his arms, dressed in a glittering beaded gown, with diamonds at her throat and ears shouldn't be looking at him like that. Charles should pay. And their privileged world, too, for giving too much credence to play and never to sincerity—for making Lulu, who had so much, afraid of love. "I can give you even more than that," he said with a smile.

She smiled back. "I know. You can do anything."

Chapter Eight

Blissful possibility was in the air when they awoke. In the course of their reconciliation last night, their contentions, if not resolved, had been set aside by mutual consent.

"Life is good," the prince whispered, holding Lulu in a gentle

embrace. "You in my arms, a new day dawning"—he grinned—
"you in my arms."

Half turning, she stretched upward to kiss his cheek. "I didn't
know I could be so happy," she said with a sigh. "Thank you a
thousand million trillion times." Brushing her fingertips over the
dark stubble on his face, she smiled up at him. "Would you like
me to help you shave, Your Highness?"

"I can think of something else I'd rather have you do for me,"
he whispered, grinning. "Something my valet isn't equipped to
do."

"So I'm just useful to you?" she teased, twining her arms
around his neck, melting into his muscled body.

"Not *just*, darling. You offer me innumerable pleasures."

"And you can't live without me." She was in paradise; reality
didn't intrude.

"I definitely can't live without you." Well aware of reality, the
prince meant every word.

"How nice," she purred, feeling awash in love.

"I guarantee, it will only get better," he murmured, having
begun to make plans last night after Lulu had fallen asleep in his
arms, wanting what he wanted.

"So all we have to do now is act like strangers at breakfast
and wait until our guests leave for their picnic."

He pulled her closer, liking her use of the phrase "our guests,"
liking more the prospect of having her to himself for the afternoon. "I'll barely notice you at breakfast, Lady Darlington," he
said with a smile. "See how aloof I can be."

"Until later," she breathed, moving her hips suggestively
against his thigh, licking a warm path up his throat.

He groaned softly. "Maybe it won't be so easy to ignore you,
after all."

The door suddenly opened and Lulu's maid hesitated on the
threshold. "Beggin' your pardon, my lady, I brought your morning chocolate."

The hairs on the back of Lulu's neck began to rise at the odd
reserve in Angie's voice, at her odder intrusion.

Mischa covered Lulu's bare shoulders with the sheet.

"I told your maid you wouldn't mind being wakened early, my

dear." The brisk cadence of Lydia's voice drifted in from the corridor. "I have some correspondence I wish to share with you before breakfast."

Lulu stifled the cry that rose in her throat, pulled away from Mischa's embrace, and sat up, clutching the sheet to her chin.

The prince swore softly, but didn't move from his lounging pose that exposed a good deal of his bare chest .

Angie whispered, "I'm sorry, she wouldn't take no," dropped the tray on a nearby table, and spun away.

"What do we have here?" Lydia said in awful accents, standing rigid in the doorway. "And not a word out of you," she ordered, shifting her wrathful gaze to the fleeing maid brushing past her.

In an oppressive silence, Lydia shut the door. "I intend to inform your father of your scurrilous behavior, Prince Radovsky," she declared furiously, her eyes hot with indignation. "As for you, Lulu, your mother will be appalled by your behavior," she added tersely. Her mouth set into a grim line as her gaze swung back to the prince. "You are without morals or honor, Radovsky, disgracing my niece in her own home. Leave this house immediately!" she commanded, pointing her finger at him like a vengeful wraith.

"With all due respect, Lady Harcourt," the prince remarked, "I'm well past the age where anyone can order me about. As is your niece." While his tone was well mannered, his displeasure was clear.

Lydia's face turned purple. "How dare you talk to me like that! Lulu, I *insist* you send this scoundrel away! Your acquaintance with him is not only disgraceful but forbidden!"

"She's wrong." Mischa gazed at Lulu, who was patently in shock. "It's not forbidden. We're only related in the most tenuous way."

"Don't you dare beguile my niece with your fiendish designs!" Lydia raged. "You are her step-brother as plain as plain can be! Tell him to get out of that bed, Lulu!" she ordered furiously. "Tell the vile man he must leave this instant!"

"Darling, we can resolve this like adults"—the prince glanced at Lydia—"without screaming at each other."

"I don't know, Mischa . . . please . . ." Lulu's eyes were bright with tears, stark fear in their depths. "I can't think . . . this is impossible—I mean . . . what will—"

"Let me deal with Lydia and then we can talk about this." His gaze swiveled to Lulu's aunt. "We need time to discuss this," he said calmly. "It would be helpful if you left us alone."

Lydia straightened her shoulders and glared at him. "I have no intention of leaving."

"Then I'll have to throw you out."

"Mischa, please!" Lulu clutched his arm.

"Darling, she doesn't have the right to interfere." He gently lifted her hand away, aware that Lydia playing avenging angel six feet away wasn't conducive to any reasonable discussion. "If you think me wicked and depraved, Lady Harcourt," Mischa noted, beginning to rise from the bed, "I'd be happy to oblige you."

Even a woman of Lydia's considerable boldness fled before the shocking sight of a blatantly naked man.

The door slammed shut a second later and disaster hung in the air.

Lulu groaned and fell back on the pillows. "You probably shouldn't have done that." The extent of possible scandal was horrendous with Lydia incensed and her house full of morally righteous and imminently dangerous guests. And when in the past she might have casually shrugged off such censure, since her divorce she'd discovered the merit in a certain degree of peace and tranquility.

"Your aunt can't tell you what to do." Mischa returned from locking the door; his voice was deliberately mild. "You're not a child." Sitting down on the edge of the bed, he took care not to touch her. "Nor can she order me about. And darling," he gently added, "I don't want to leave you. I'm not sure I even could."

Lulu slowly exhaled. "I knew this was going to be one horrendous mess."

"It doesn't have to be."

"Good Lord," she whispered as the sudden thought assailed her, "now my mother will know."

"I'll wire my father . . . explain everything. They'll understand."

"I'm not so sure they will."

"You're magnifying this completely out of proportion. People sleep together at country house parties all the time. In fact, protocol demands you don't walk into another person's room without knocking."

"Unfortunately, Lydia isn't always inclined to recognize the courtesies."

"Obviously. But that's not our problem."

"It is if gossip spreads about"—she hesitated—"you and me. What if Charles takes issue?"

"With what?"

"With Andrew being involved in this scandal."

Mischa snorted. "For one thing, Andrew isn't here. And secondly, Charles has never lived a life of respectability—nor is he now. He's still a regular customer at Madame Riviere's despite his new marriage. So that argument won't hold much weight in the court of public opinion."

"Is he really still going there?" Madame Riviere owned London's finest brothel.

"Darling, Charles is Charles." The prince shrugged. The aristocratic world was small and interrelated; everyone knew everyone. "You may discount any problems from that quarter. My word on it."

"Nevertheless." She sighed. "There's Lydia, et al., not to mention the outside world, which may not view our relationship with the same casualness you do."

He swore under his breath.

"Just because you've always done as you pleased," she said, a modicum of pique in her voice at his lack of understanding, "I'm not so inclined."

"Since when." His impatience was beginning to show.

"Must you always have your way?" Like a man, she thought.

"Must you?" Like a spoiled beauty who always has, he thought.

Their detente lay in ruins, their numerous disagreements front and center once again.

"Maybe Lydia is right." Lulu lifted her chin a fraction, Mischa's selfishness too reminiscent of a husband who had made her miserable. "Maybe it would be best if you left."

"Really," he growled. "And how would it be best?"

"We obviously can't agree on the serious consequences of this liaison," she enunciated with punctilious disdain.

His heated gaze pinned her where she sat. "We could if you had a spine."

"Excuse me if I don't live my life with the same disregard for convention as you," she shot back, flushing with anger.

"Excuse me if I don't believe a word of that drivel. You've lost your nerve. Did Charles taking a new wife break your spirit?"

"No more than your wife dying debilitated you, I suppose."

"At least you still have claws," he noted grimly.

"While your ruthless disregard for the world at large is unrivaled." She surveyed him with a scathing look. "I think perhaps it *would* be best if you left. I don't want to fight and I don't want to be miserable anymore. What I most desire is a measure of peace in my life and I'll never have it with you."

"Peace?" His mouth curled in mockery. "You're far from a nun, darling. I doubt so banal a life would engage your interest for long. Are you planning on giving up fucking too?"

"There's no need to ask *you* that. You couldn't go a day without it."

"It's not a measure of your worth whether you can or not."

"A convenient rationalization," she said tartly.

"Now that you've suddenly become a saint, you mean."

"Are you taking issue with my past?"

"Just pointing out that you and moral outrage aren't exactly compatible."

"This discussion is over." She made to rise from the bed.

He put out a detaining hand. "You rest, darling. You had a strenuous night, and unlike me, you're no longer used to hours of fucking," he murmured insolently, thin-skinned and chaffing at her abrupt surrender to Lydia's righteousness. In any case, he wasn't in the habit of pleading with a woman. He'd never had to. Quick-tempered and goaded, he had no intention of begging her. "If you come to your senses," he said brusquely, coming to his feet, "let me know. I'll be in London for a week or so."

She watched him, nude and splendid, walk out of her life, feeling simultaneously wretched and angry, unsure whether she wished to scream go or stay—at base, desperately wanting what she knew she couldn't have.

As he grasped the door handle, he half turned, the scratch on his cheek suddenly marked, like his anger. He opened his mouth to speak, shut it again, and then muttered gruffly, "I'm sorry." Pulling open the door, he moved into Charles's old bedroom and shut the door behind him with such finality, the soft click of the latch seemed to resonate like the voice of doom.

Sorry about what, she thought. That he hadn't had his way? That it was over? Sorry he'd ever come? While the sounds of packing next door insinuated themselves into her room, she lay prostrate, analyzing and reanalyzing their argument, his every word, the nuances and possible emotions expressed as though the minutia of comprehension mattered in the coming black void. As though anything in the entire world mattered, she morosely thought, now that he was leaving her.

Lulu didn't go down to breakfast; she sent her excuses with Angie.

Standing at the window a short time later, she watched Mischa walk to his carriage and enter it without once looking back. The black lacquer exterior gleamed in the morning sun as the light, fast brougham passed swiftly down the drive, the last ebony shimmer disappearing from sight behind the gaily blooming rhododendrons framing her gatehouse.

It didn't seem fair that anything could be gaily blooming when her heart was breaking. It was completely unfair that the sun was still shining when her happiness was destroyed. It was grievously unjust that she had the misfortune to fall in love or probably fall in love or maybe fall in love with a man so clearly, emphatically outside the pale.

And she hadn't lost her nerve—at least about everything—because within the hour she sent her guests away with the most transparent of excuses and not a scintilla of remorse. She even told her aunt with an unrelenting firmness that she would prefer being alone at Bishop's Knoll. On hearing the flinty hardness in Lulu's tone, Lydia knew better than to argue. In any case, her most important mission was accomplished. The highly unsuitable prince was gone and with him any possibility of scandal.

For that, Lady Harcourt allowed herself a measure of content. As for Lulu's happiness, Lydia had lived long enough to put little stock in passing liaisons. Lulu would soon forget Prince Mikhail. Her niece was still young, one of the great beauties of her time. Before long, her infatuation with the disreputable Radovsky would fade and she would find a more acceptable man to love.

Chapter Nine

Having been pricked by Mischa's criticism that she'd lost her nerve, Lulu decided to end her hermitage at Bishop's Knoll and partake of the Season about to begin. While she viewed life from a different perspective now, and no longer required the frenzied pace of society, she wasn't a complete recluse, nor a nun as Mischa had mocked. She would enjoy seeing all her friends again.

On the journey to London, however, she braced herself against the possibility of meeting Mischa at some future entertainment, rehearsing the casualness she would employ should the occasion arise. But when she reached the city, she heard that he'd precipitously closed up his house and left London.

So she was saved from any awkwardness.

She was pleased he was gone, she told herself.

It was for the best.

Throwing herself into the full array of festivities that season, Lulu attended all the society amusements from morning to night, playing her role with an apparent gaiety and cheer that would have passed muster by even the severest drama critic. Her divorce wasn't viewed with disfavor within the close and closed ranks of society, where everyone had been friends from the cradle and divorce was becoming more prevalent. A divorce really mattered only at court with the old queen, and no one went to court anymore.

Throughout the Season, various gossip columns linked Lulu's

name with numerous aristocratic lords, but rumor was only rumor, the connections of the most superficial, and no one but she understood what courage it took to maintain her lighthearted facade.

Gossip drifted back from the Continent. The prince had gone into seclusion at one of his country estates, it was said. He wasn't even going to race at Cowes, rumor had it, when his yachts had always been the ones to beat for the past decade. Then the on-dit that he'd married began circulating. Lulu first heard it at a country house party in July. She'd responded to the news with a bland casualness at breakfast that morning, but shortly after she'd excused herself with a very real headache. And later that day, after giving her hostess additional excuses, she'd returned to Bishop's Knoll.

She spent the rest of the summer there with her son, Andrew. They rode, fished, swam, worked together on estate business, took an occasional trip into the village for excitement, and fell into the comfortable companionship they'd always shared in a family that had been essentially without a husband and father. But as the summer came to an end, they set off for the Continent. She'd promised Andrew a trip abroad before he went back to school.

Paris was almost empty in August with everyone on holiday. Many of the shops were closed, but Andrew was infatuated with the Napoleonic wars, and the military museums and archives available in Paris enthralled him. So between their sightseeing, they perused all the military museums' nooks and crannies, studying uniforms and swords, military dispatches and captured regimental flags, battle maps, and officer portraits. They visited Père Lachaise cemetery, where all Napoleon's greatest generals were buried, and bought scores of military books to have sent back home. It was a full fortnight before they moved on.

After their busy round of sightseeing in Paris, Baden-Baden was peaceful. The spa town was small, self-contained, meant for repose. They rode each morning before breakfast, took the waters at the fashionable spa, gambled in the evenings, and in general did very little.

The constant round of activities since Mischa's leaving had allayed the worst of Lulu's regret, but she found herself thinking of him more than she liked now that she was without continual diversions. And no rationalization, however convoluted, lessened the intensity of her loss. She often wondered if she should have given in and allowed herself simply to love him without concern for the world. But then she'd think of her son and she knew she'd made the right decision.

One morning as she and Andrew strolled through the colorful gardens separating the village from the hotel, a figure in the distance drew her attention. A tall man, flanked by a boy and a girl, preceded them down the brick walk. The group was casually dressed in tennis whites, and the set of the man's shoulders, the gleam of his black hair, the rhythm of his gait struck a familiar chord. Lulu's heart skipped a beat. But the small party abruptly disappeared from sight behind a topiary hedge, Andrew began speaking of his win last night at the casino, the pitch of his voice echoing his excitement, and Lulu's attention returned to her son.

"Promise we'll leave early for the casino tonight, *Mama*. I feel really lucky!"

"You're lucky the croupier is friendly. He knows you're too young to be there."

"I'm only gambling a little, *Mama*. And I'm with you."

"No doubt the reason the casino is being so understanding."

"Say we'll go. Right after dinner."

"Of course, darling. But I don't want to stay long."

"Then I'll win quickly," Andrew said with the confidence of youth. "See if I don't!"

They'd just rounded the bend in the walk, the border of sculpted yews giving way to a vista of green lawn and willow-fringed stream.

Lulu came to a standstill.

The tall man that had triggered recognition was standing beside the stream, no more than ten feet away, watching the children toss scraps of bread to the swans.

Andrew stopped and glanced at his mother.

As if sensing the charged air, Mischa turned.

Lulu's first instinct was to run, but she tamped down the impulse because she was a grown woman she told herself with a degree of firmness she wasn't feeling, and she could meet an ex-lover with politesse. Had she not a hundred times before?

"Lady Darlington. I didn't know you were in Baden-Baden."

His tone suggested had he known, he would have been else-where.

The children had swiveled around when Mischa spoke.

Their resemblance to their father was striking, Lulu thought. There was no question of paternity. "Prince Radovsky," she replied with commendable calm, considering her heart was pounding in her chest, "may I introduce my son, Andrew. Andrew, this is Grandmama's stepson, Prince Radovsky."

"And may I introduce my children." Mischa bowed with a familiar grace. "Lady Darlington and Andrew, my son, Virgil, and my daughter, Natalie. Have you been here long?" For some perverse reason he had to know, as if knowing would allow him an appropriate defense.

"We arrived . . ." Her mind was in chaos, unable to sort through the necessary accounting of time.

"Monday," Andrew chimed in. "Don't you remember, *Mama,* you said we had to leave Paris right away because you needed new amusements?"

"You're right, darling." She smiled at her son. "We arrived on Monday. And you?" she heard herself say when she shouldn't care or ask or do anything but walk away while she still could. "Have you been here long?"

The prince's mouth had tightened at the word "amusements," knowing too well how she'd always amused herself, but his voice gave away nothing of his feelings. "We've been here a month. The children are taking tennis lessons."

"I just started yesterday," Andrew interjected, glancing at the youngsters. "Do you have Herr Kompf for a tennis instructor?"

"Virge has him, but I have an Englishwoman," Natalie replied with a dazzling smile. "Miss Somerset won two championships last year in England."

"Come play with us," Virgil suggested. "We're on our way to the courts now."

"I'm not dressed." Andrew gestured at his clothes.

"They have shoes at the club house and you can take off your jacket and tie."

"Perhaps some other time," Lulu remarked, sending a warning glance at her son. "We were on our way to the village."

"You don't need me for shopping, *Mama*. Virgil and Natalie are practically relatives, and I haven't seen anyone my own age for—" He paused at the look on his mother's face. "Maybe I could play tennis with you some other time," he said quickly.

"Lady Darlington has plans," Mischa remarked coolly. "We don't want to interfere." He offered Lulu a faint bow. "Come, children."

Chapter Ten

If she wouldn't have appeared craven, she would have left Baden-Baden immediately. But Lulu wouldn't give Mischa the satisfaction. So she passed the day with Andrew in their normal activities, hardly conscious of where she was or what she was doing.

At dinner, however, she did succumb to cowardice, using the balmy evening as an excuse to have their dinner served on their balcony. She couldn't bring herself to go downstairs to the dining room, where scores of guests might be spectator to her unease should she come face to face with Mischa again. Which didn't bode well for breakfast tomorrow, or lunch or dinner, where the possibility of meeting him in the dining room was likely. And daunting.

Meeting Mischa that morning had been devastating to her carefully wrought emotional stability. Maintaining a reasonable air of detachment about her irresistible stepbrother was only possible, she decided, if he was half a continent away. At close range, she'd felt like melting in a puddle at his feet—a staggering revelation.

But there it was. Impossible to ignore. And she must deal with it like an adult.

Lulu particularly didn't wish to go to the casino that evening, but she'd promised Andrew, and as they entered the gambling rooms, she nervously surveyed the crowds. Reminding herself that Mischa hadn't been at the casino on their previous visits, she glanced at the ornate clock. Were they too early for the serious players?

Or perhaps the prince didn't gamble when he traveled with his children.

A startling image—the devoted father—a very different one from the man she knew who played at life and love with unbridled passion.

Then again, he might very well appear at any moment since he was a well-known gambler, the prospect making her decidedly edgy. It was impossible for her to think of playing tonight, her thoughts were too unsettled, but she'd keep Andrew company. Hopefully, he'd be willing to leave before too long.

Unconscious of his mother's anxieties, Andrew tempted fortune at the tables with carefree abandon, placing his bets quickly, sometimes lavishly, often hazarding his money on a run of numbers as though the sequence were magical. Concentrating on a single number at other times. And if his wagers went bad, he lost as cheerfully as he won.

He'd glance over at Lulu occasionally and smile, and she'd be reminded of her grandfather, who had that same flashing smile and flare for life. Their looks were similar as well—Andrew's deep auburn hair and tall frame, coltish now in his youth, the firm line of his jaw and the light in his eyes reminiscent of Grandpapa Durr. Her adored grandfather had lived in northern Cumbria and was probably more Scots than English, if truth be told, with his blunt manner of speech and intolerance of fools. But he was the best of friends to a lonely little girl who spent her summers with him, and she was pleased that Andrew had his looks and character.

But she was conscious of her son's losses, comforted by the fact his pile of chips was diminishing. If *she* were lucky tonight, they might be able to leave before any possible disaster struck.

* * *

Prince Radovsky had every intention of staying away from the casino that evening.

Lulu gambled like so many of their class, and seeing her today had shaken him enough not to willingly put himself at risk again. His summer had been a dogged, day-by-day attempt to forget her. And until this morning, he'd thought he'd actually come to terms with his deprivation.

After dinner, in an act of prudence, he changed from his evening clothes to more casual attire. If he wasn't dressed to go out, he would be less likely to indulge such a whim, less likely as well to give in to the temptation and craving that had come back with a vengeance the moment he'd seen Lulu in the park.

"That's the second hand you've given away, Papa," Virgil chided. "You're not paying attention."

Forcing his thoughts back to the card game, he smiled at his son. "Maybe you're just getting better."

"Or you're being generous," Natalie proposed. "You needn't entertain us every night, Papa. We're not little children." She offered her father a warm smile. "You're allowed to go to the casino if you wish."

"I didn't know I needed your permission," he replied lightly, reshuffling the cards for another hand. But the harvest moon was huge outside the windows, and he found himself drawn to the sight as though the bright orange luminescence was luring him out into the night.

"Maybe Lady Darlington will be gambling tonight," Natalie remarked casually.

The cards flew from Mischa's fingers, spraying across the table in disarray.

"You really should go, Papa," his daughter urged, taking note of her father's discomposure. As the pet of all the servants, she'd been privy to their gossip about Lulu and thus aware of the reason for her father's black moods that summer. "Virgil, tell Papa to go to the casino. He can spend the evening with us anytime. And if you see Lady Darlington, ask her if her son can play tennis with us tomorrow." Her gaze turned sportive. "She might let him if you ask very nicely."

"You think that might work?" A faint smile curved Mischa's

mouth as he gathered up the cards, his shock overcome. "If I were to be very nice?"

"You certainly could be nicer than you were this morning."

"Was I rude?"

"Of course he wasn't, Natalie. You're meddling again," her brother rebuked, championing their father. "You're always meddling."

Having struggled against his ungovernable need to see Lulu all day—all summer—having his daughter suggest he go where he most wanted to go was tantamount to placing the apple from the garden of Eden in the palm of his hand. Taking a small breath, Mischa tried to speak in a mild tone. "You don't mind if I go out?"

"You always went out before, Papa. It's only this summer that you've been underfoot every minute. Even Vassily is complaining," Natalie pointed out. "He's barely had time to court the downstairs maid because you've been home every night."

"I can see I've been a problem to you all—my valet included," the prince replied drily.

Virgil glared at his sister. "You have not, Papa. Natalie doesn't know anything."

"Perhaps I'll walk over to the casino for a few minutes." Mischa's voice was calm but his adrenalin was spiking, even as he cautioned himself there was no guarantee he'd see Lulu.

"The concierge told me Lady Darlington's son won two thousand at the casino last night." Natalie made friends with the staff wherever they were. "Louis says they go every night."

Could his daughter read minds? Glancing at her, he saw Maiia's face at seventeen, when he'd first met and fallen in love with her, and a wave of sadness overcame him. "Maybe I'll stay home after all," he murmured, feeling disloyal and faithless because Lulu was so much more than a casual amour.

"Papa, you've been home every night! Go!"

Natalie's forceful rebuff reminded him of her mother as well. Maiia had always lived life to the fullest. A pagan to the core, he suddenly felt as though he'd been delivered a message from the grave. "You're sure now?"

"I'm giving you permission, Papa," his daughter replied with a grin. "For heaven's sake, Papa, you're getting on my nerves!"

"And you're getting on mine, Natalie," Virgil noted irritably. "Leave Papa alone. If he wants to go out, he will!"

"Actually, I think I might." Abruptly placing the cards on the table, Mischa came to his feet. "I shouldn't be gone long."

"You're nothing but trouble," Virgil muttered, giving his sister a censorious look as their father left the room. "You're always telling people what to do."

"You never do what I tell you anyway, so I can't see how it matters," she retorted brightly. "I think I'll go downstairs and see if the kennel manager needs any help. The cutest little goats came with the Turkish minister's family. His wife likes her own goats' milk."

"Good. Then I'll have some peace and quiet."

"The Comtesse Gallemont's daughter might be on the veranda too, just in case you're interested," Natalie observed slyly. "She told me she would be there if she could slip away from her mother."

Virgil's dark gaze lifted. "What makes you think I care?"

"Let's see . . ." Natalie placed her finger to her chin. "Maybe the way you fawned over her during our tennis lesson, or perhaps the looks you cast her way at dinner gave me a clue. But if you don't want me to meddle," she remarked, relaxing against her chair, "I shan't."

Virgil scowled at her. "Which veranda?"

Natalie grinned. "The south one, darling brother, and you're welcome."

His mouth slowly curved into a smile. "Thanks, Birdie. I guess I owe you."

So much for his attempt to ignore Lulu, Mischa thought, entering the casino a short time later. Although he was probably pursuing a lost cause—if he was even in pursuit . . . a tumultuous unknown in his current frame of mind.

Acknowledging the greetings of employees and acquaintances alike as he strolled through the anterooms, his reputation as a high-stakes gambler of long standing, he felt a measure of comfort and exhilaration at the familiarity of his surroundings. His mood lightened.

He saw her first when he entered the main room. Lulu was

talking to her son and unaware of him. Deliberately keeping his distance, he stood in the shadows of a small embrasure, not certain how he wished to proceed. Andrew was playing roulette; Lulu looked small beside her son, but splendid as usual, her beauty outshining the gilded opulence of the casino a hundred-fold. Although he might be prejudiced, he noted ruefully.

She wore black lace tonight, in stark contrast to her glorious red hair and seductive pale skin. Potent lures to every man there. Not that he was likely to allow any rival near her, he decided, instantly territorial. Her shoulders and slender neck were bared, her upswept coiffure crowned by a coronet of curls, her upper arms gleaming white above the black satin of her elbow-length gloves. Diamonds sparkled on her ears and at her throat, and twinkled from the silken waves of her hair. And he fiercely wished to unclip and unclasp, pull loose every pin and bit of jewelry, slip her gown free . . . and hear her sensuous sigh of surrender as he entered her.

If he'd been uncertain of what to do before, he no longer was. Driven by sharp-set desire, he pushed away from the wall.

As Mischa approached the table, Lulu's son served as a blunt deterrent to his predatory impulses. Coming to a stop, he debated his options.

The boy gambled with the rashness of youth, Mischa noted, overly impulsive and quick in his decisions, and while he may have won last night with an amateur's luck, he was going to lose if he insisted on putting his money on the same number every time. Deciding to intervene, the prince moved toward the table, leaned over, and slid Andrew's stack of chips to the red nine. "Try this," he murmured, straightening and smiling at the boy. Drawing several more chips from his pocket, he added them to the wager, directed a swift glance at the croupier, nodded faintly, then turned and winked at Andrew. "Nines tend to be lucky here."

Lulu's heart had lurched when Mischa had suddenly appeared or so it seemed. And she wondered if it was possible to expire from shock. Although she still seemed to be breathing, she noted a moment later and her vision wasn't affected because he was as beautiful as ever—dark, sensual, powerfully male . . . although his hair was noticeably longer.

And he hadn't looked at her once.

The croupier gave the wheel a spin, the ball rolled around wildly, gradually slowed, and eventually came to rest on the red nine. Andrew let out a whoop of delight before turning to Mischa and grabbing his hand. "Thank you, sir! Thank you ever so much!" he exclaimed, vigorously pumping Mischa's arm. "That was the last of my quid tonight!" He glanced toward Lulu. "Look, *Mama!* I just won a fortune! Thanks to Prince Radovsky! Isn't it great!"

"Thank you, Prince Radovsky." Lulu's voice was composed only with effort. "We're in your debt. Now give the prince back his winnings, Andrew."

"I have to talk to you." Mischa's voice was hushed, his gaze over Andrew's head sharp.

Lulu quickly looked around as though she needed permission from someone, but the strangers at the table, the croupier, even Andrew, who had begun gathering up his chips, were all unconcerned. "I don't know." Her mind was suddenly blank of suave disclaimers or politesse when what she wanted most was standing, magnificent and virile, only a small distance away.

"Give me a minute," Mischa said sotto voce, taking a step closer. "A minute can't hurt."

"It might." In some deep recess of her bruised psyche, she wasn't sure it was enough simply to want something anymore.

Yanking a handful of chips from his pocket, Mischa shoved them at Andrew. "Here. Try playing the reds. I have to talk to your mother."

"Wow!" Andrew's face lit up at the largesse—the markers were all large denominations. Then his sense of duty prevailed and he looked at his mother. "May I, *Mama?*"

"Say yes . . . *please.*" Mischa's voice was low and impassioned.

At the gravity of his tone, Lulu met his gaze fully for the first time and saw the longing in his eyes. "Very well," she whispered, thinking even as she spoke that she should know better than to trust a man who could charm women at will. But she didn't care, or she didn't care enough, or perhaps she'd been without him too long to be swayed by logic. "I'll be right back," she said to her son.

Immune to all but his huge windfall, Andrew hastily glanced

up at his mother, murmured, "Take your time," and turned back to the table.

Mischa lightly gripped her arm. Nodding to the croupier, the significance of his gaze verified with the faintest tip of the man's head, the prince guided Lulu toward the door.

"I can't leave Andrew for long. The croupier won't appreciate it."

"Johan will take good care of him. Trust me. We'll just go outside the door where we won't have an audience."

She surveyed him with raised brows. "Why?"

"Because I'm going to humiliate myself and I'd prefer doing it in private."

She put her hand out to stop him. "Are you married?" She needed to know that first or she'd be the one humiliated.

"Are you?"

Her gaze was unwavering, cooler. "I asked first."

"No. You?"

She exhaled, relieved. "No."

He wasn't so easily relieved; his possessiveness got in the way. "I heard rumors of your numerous lovers this summer," he said more curtly than he intended.

"You heard wrong. I heard you'd married."

"Which just goes to show you how irresponsible gossip is." But knowing her so well, he was skeptical that she'd been celibate since he'd left, and drawing her forward, his voice was a distinct growl when he said, "Come outside into the garden."

"I'm not sure I want to when you sound like that."

"I'm sorry. I'm jealous. What did you do all summer?"

Her gaze lifted to his. "Was I alone, you mean."

A muscle twitched over his cheekbone. "Yes."

"Were you? I can be jealous too."

"Answer me." He guided them around a knot of people. "Or?"

His gaze swiveled back. "Or I might lose what little self-control I still possess."

"Am I supposed to be frightened?"

"You're supposed to answer my question. And the last time I saw you, you *were* frightened, but not of me—of what people would think . . ."

"If you're trying to charm me," she said, bridling, "you're not succeeding."

"If you're trying to antagonize me," he replied, his voice silky with temper, "you're doing extremely well."

She suddenly halted and jerked away.

He jerked her back, his grip on her hand punishing. "I shouldn't have said that, but you've been in my thoughts every moment since I left Bishop's Knoll." His mouth twisted into a faint grimace. "And not always in a benign context."

"I thought of you every instant as well. My feelings are as tantrumish, and you're hurting me."

His grip loosened marginally. "So we'll have to do our best to act like adults."

"Is that possible?" Her voice was oversweet and provoking.

"I can't speak for you," he said gruffly.

She hit his chest with her closed fist—hard. Too hard. Grimacing, she pressed her stinging fingers to her mouth.

He suddenly smiled. "I love you when you're out of control." His grip loosened to a more benign pressure. "Actually, I love you any damned way at all."

"Do you really?" Her eyes were huge, her words faintly muffled by her fingers.

Mischa glanced at the doorman, who was listening with undisguised interest. "Could we go outside with this?"

Her hand dropped from her mouth. "You can't say you love me except in private?"

"I love you." He turned to the doorman, who was trying to repress a grin and not succeeding. "I love her. Did you hear that? He heard it, darling. Do you want me to raise my voice and let the rest of the casino know?"

"That would be sweet."

He glared at her for a moment, then turning back to the mirrored gallery alive with patrons, he took a deep breath, opened his mouth, and just as he was about to oblige her, her gaze turned benevolent. "I believe you."

He shot her an acerbic glance. "You're sure now."

"I'm sure."

"Now may we go outside?"

"Why?" She wasn't entirely certain she could behave like a lady, and his ego was outrageous enough.

"Because I have some details of our convoluted relationship I'd rather not have the doorman hear—if you don't mind."

"How convoluted?" she asked warily.

"All sorts of legal and lawyerly convoluted."

"That sounds ominous."

"It's not in the least. See, our doorman wants you to listen to me."

The man was holding open the door and smiling.

When even the doorman was insisting, she had little choice short of making a scene. Lulu allowed herself to be escorted outside.

The evening air was cool, but she scarcely noticed, her overwrought senses warming her blood as Mischa moved purposefully down the loggia.

Her pulse was racing like that of a naive young maid. She was instantly in love again—all the months of separation, the hurt and anger, dismissed without a thought . . . like a complete and irrational fool, she thought. Although fool or not, irrational or not, she wanted to throw her arms around him, kiss him, tell him she didn't care about any of their disagreements or obstacles or hindrances so long as he truly loved her.

But she didn't because she'd been married to Charles so long she'd developed a deep-seated suspicion of charming men and their facile words.

Mischa came to rest before an ornate iron bench and offered her a seat. Taking his place beside her, he gently enclosed her hands in his with a small awkwardness so out of character, she searched his face for some clue. "Are you all right?"

He took a small breath and nodded.

"I'm not angry," she said, as one might to an apprehensive child.

"I wish I were capable of flowery phrases," he replied, as though he'd not heard her, as though his thoughts were on some dissonant track. "But I'm not." He blew out a breath. "So I'll just say it. I want to marry you—I think I have almost from the beginning—don't," he added quickly, gainsaying her response.

232 / *Susan Johnson*

"Hear me out before we argue again." He took another sustaining breath. "I spoke to several lawyers and barristers. I know you were concerned about our relationship since our parents are wed so I had all the legalities researched. I was told there are no legal barriers to our marriage. I almost wrote a thousand times to tell you, but"—he shrugged faintly—"I've never begged before. And you hadn't been overly receptive when I left."

"I almost wrote to *you* a thousand times, but I didn't know what to say, save for telling you I loved you and I was miserable without you." She offered him a rueful smile. "But then reason always prevailed."

"I don't care about reason. I'm not sure I ever did with you or whether I'm capable of reason when it comes to loving you. Just marry me, Lulu—please! Put me out of my misery."

"If I should—if we were to do this," she murmured, finding it difficult to focus on the staggering possibilities with the choir of angels trumpeting in her ears, "we'd be the scandalous topic of conversation for months. Not to mention the shock our marriage would be to our children."

"If you don't mind my saying so, neither you nor I will shock anyone if we're involved in scandal. As for our children, I have the distinct feeling Andrew likes me and my daughter practically pushed me out the door tonight, so she, at least, won't be surprised."

Lulu half smiled. "So I should just throw caution to the winds?"

One dark brow rose faintly. "As I recall, that's not exactly a new concept for you."

"In general or in particular?" she queried, smiling in a seductive, teasing way that triggered numerous lush memories for him.

"Both," he replied pleasantly, "although I confess to having a partiality for the particular instances when you threw caution to the winds. And keep in mind, while you debate your decision, now that you're in my clutches, I'm not about to let you go."

"So I don't have a choice?" Her voice was playful.

His was not; it was princely. "No."

A sudden silence fell. She pulled her hands away or he let her, all the dynamics of independence and authority potent in the air.

She nibbled on her bottom lip, grimaced faintly, surveyed him for a telling moment, and then smiled very slightly. "I always did have a penchant for the big bad wolf . . ." she murmured, "but of course, it will be up to you to amuse me," she added pointedly, "or I won't stay."

"You just let me know . . . how big and . . . how bad . . . and how often," he drawled, holding her gaze, "and we'll see what we can do about amusing you."

Her smile broadened ever so little, a touch of mischief shown in her eyes. "It seems . . . my luck . . . has turned," she said in a tantalizing, heated undertone.

"*Our* luck," he amended softly. "And come morning, provided you're sufficiently amused in the interim, I'm finding a priest to marry us."

"A priest?" It was challenge however hushed.

"A minister," he corrected, well bred and urbane. "Will that suit you better?"

"You can be such a darling," she said, sweetly, "and at the risk of disturbing this delightful rapport, I have one small warning." She leaned back slightly to better see his face. "If you dare to look at another woman, I'll bring the next man I see home and bed him in front of you. I won't have another husband like Charles."

"In the interests of peace and tranquility and an aversion to seeing you bed some man in my drawing room, I promise never to so much as look at another woman."

"Just so we understand each other," she said firmly, his tone a modicum too easy and obliging.

"I'll expect as much from you." His casual drawl dropped away. "Should you renege, however, I'll do my whoring less conspicuously, but with equal determination." His gaze in the moonlight was direct. "I won't have a wife who's unfaithful."

"Done."

"We're agreed then?"

A small dead silence, their gazes locked.

"Perfectly," she breathed.

He exhaled softly, gently took her face between his hands, and gazed down at her with adoration in his eyes. "Over and above all the sound and fury, darling, and quite separate from your radical need for sovereignty," he said with a grin, "I promise to do my very best to make you happy."

Tears sprang to Lulu's eyes. "No one's ever promised me happiness before, and if I wasn't so filled with joy, I'd take issue with your word 'radical'—she sniffed away her tears—"because you know as well as I do—"

"I'm not Charles," he gently interposed. "I'm not like him. I won't be like him."

"Thank you," she whispered, sniffling again, trying to smile.

He knew how difficult her marriage had been, knew as well how perfect a marriage could be. "You're the best thing that's happened to me for a very, very long time," he murmured, pulling his handkerchief from his pocket and wiping her cheeks and nose. "We'll be happy, you and I. My word on it."

His simple words and tenderness warmed her heart, a roseate bliss filled her soul, and she thought of how close she'd come to losing him. "I can't thank you enough for coming here tonight."

"I couldn't stay away." He took her hands in his once again, compelled by an overwhelming need to touch her after being without her so long. "I tried." He grinned. "I really did . . . and here I am. Deep in love, wildly in love, probably slightly crazed in love, so once we see our children into bed, if you don't think me too precipitate, I'd like to find us a room somewhere far away from any interruptions—where I can hold you and kiss you and perhaps see if I can remember everything you like."

"Perhaps?" she purred archly.

"Without fail, darling. I was being polite."

A small heat flared in her eyes. "You needn't be *completely* polite."

He glanced at his wristwatch. "Just as soon as we can drag Andrew away from the gaming tables and see our children to bed, I'll show you just how *impolite* I can be," he breathed, brushing her lips lightly in a kiss. Gently pushing her away, he rose to his feet. "That's all I dare . . . in my current state of very tenuous control. And in order to avoid an embarrassing spectacle here on the loggia, I suggest we get the hell out of here . . ."

In short order—the prince was munificent in his bribes—the children had all been cajoled into bed. His offer to take them on the honeymoon—the destination one of their choosing—was additional incentive for their cooperation. A man on a mission, he would have quite willingly offered them the moon.

A brief time later, Mischa was escorting Lulu to the bridal suite hastily readied for them. "The children were genuinely pleased, don't you think?" Lulu squeezed his hand. "I'm so glad."

"Me too." Mischa smiled at her. Although he would have found a way around their displeasure had it come to that. He wasn't about to give up Lulu on anyone's whim. "I hope you didn't mind that I invited them on the honeymoon, but I wanted you alone tonight, I didn't want to discuss this at length, and it seemed the quickest way to put an end to all their questions. They can pore over maps tonight. The manager is bringing some up and we'll have plenty of time on our travels to all become better acquainted."

"You were very masterful . . ." She fluttered her lashes in flirtatious parody. "I found myself fascinated by your resourcefulness."

"I'll show you resourcefulness"—he glanced down the hall— "in about a minute and a half," he said with a grin, pulling her close.

"That long?" she cooed. "I'm not sure—"

Sweeping her up into his arms, he arrested her teasing with a hard, unrestrained kiss and, seconds later, carried her over the threshold of the bridal suite, strode through the sitting rooms into the bedroom, and deposited her on the bed. "Now then, my darling princess-to-be," he murmured, kicking off his evening shoes, stripping off his coat, and beginning to unbutton his trousers, "let me show you some of the Radovsky resourcefulness. And if you have any special requests," he added, swiftly brushing aside the yards of ruffled black lace skirt, easing her drawers open with the finesse of much practice, and settling between her legs, "you just let me know . . ."

Enchanted

Nikki Donovan

Chapter One

She should have listened to her mother. Why, oh why, hadn't she listened to her mother! Esmay choked back a sob, then winced as the horse beneath her broke into a pounding gallop, jostling her body as she lay helpless over its bony withers.

Too late now. Too late to recall her mother's warnings to be careful when she went into the forest alone. Now she was a helpless prisoner, captive of the huge, armor-clad knight who grabbed her out of nowhere and was now carrying her off to some hellish fate. She briefly contemplated what that fate might be.

It was said that, in the old days, Lord Blackhurst had constantly roamed the forest looking for victims. Sometime he merely raped the women and left them for dead. Other times he set his hounds upon them to tear them to pieces after he'd had his pleasure. A gasp of anguish rose in her throat.

But Blackhurst was dead, many years dead. And his son, the Beast Lord, although said to be monstrous and hideous-looking, never left the castle. The thought failed to reassure her and she knew a fresh wave of despair.

The knight must have been waiting for her. He must have known that she often went to that hidden glade to gather hare-bells and poppies for their bright beauty, and meadowsweet and bell heather to scent her bed. She'd heard no sound of the knight's approach, and yet he was a big man, clad in cumbersome armor. He had planned this, stalking her like a predator.

A shiver of fear wracked her. What did he want with her? If he'd planned to ravish her, why had he dumped her over the back of his massive horse and ridden off? Where was he taking her?

She sought once again to lift her head and catch a glimpse of her surroundings. Not foliage, but dark stone walls filled her vision. Blackhurst Castle.

Her terror increased tenfold. The castle was a cursed, evil place. Even the people who lived in the village in the valley below the fortress avoided going there. They brought their produce to the seneschal in a market area outside the castle walls, not daring to cross the drawbridge and enter the gate. She knew no one who had ever been inside, only tales of the inhabitants' cruelty.

It was said that the knights of the garrison there had once played a game of tossing a baby in the air and then catching it on the end of their swords. There were tales of female servants staked out on the trestle tables and raped by each man in turn while the rest watched. Of children left in a pen with starving dogs and torn to pieces while Lord Blackhurst and his knights laughed.

Blackhurst Castle—lair of demons. First Old Blackhurst, that master of cruelty and depravity, and now his son, the Beast Lord. And she was being taken there.

For the first time, Esmay considered trying to wriggle off the horse and escape, but at the speed they were traveling, she would face certain injury and possibly death. But might that not be preferable to the fate that awaited her? A swift end, rather than torture and lingering agony?

But the fall would probably not kill her, only break bones and render her more helpless. The knight would be certain to double back and capture her once again. There was nowhere to run, no sanctuary. She was as defenseless as a coney slung from a huntsman's belt and destined for the cooking pot.

Yet the horse was slowing. Perhaps if she could . . . She lifted her head, then gritted her teeth as the horse clattered across the drawbridge, jolting her body with every step. The castle entrance loomed ahead of her, the portcullis like teeth in a menacing dark maw ready to swallow her up. Swiftly, so swiftly, they were inside and she was well and truly trapped.

Dread paralyzed her. She closed her eyes, trying to shut out the overwhelming horror. Rough hands dragged her off the horse. The knight threw her over his shoulder like a sack of grain and started off.

Being carried this way was a little less uncomfortable than being draped over the back of a galloping horse. But not much. Her head ached and she felt dizzy. She opened her eyes but could see no more than the ground moving swiftly past. First, churned-up mud, then stone steps, then they were inside a chamber with rushes on the floor. More steps. Up and up. She closed her eyes as the winding climb made her even queasier.

Then a thought came to her, blotting out all the discomforts of her body and filling her with terror so stark she could scarcely breathe. It was said that Blackhurst had a tower room in the upper part of the castle where he liked to torture his victims, then leave them chained to the wall to literally rot there. She drew in a gasping breath, imagining she smelled the putrefying scent of decaying corpses, the foul reek of blood. When she dared to open her eyes, it seemed there was some sort of dark stain on the stairs.

A shudder swept through her. *Mama! Someone! Please help me!* The tremors grew more intense. She was shaking like a leaf in a storm. Her captor paid no attention, but continued to climb. She could hear his harsh, rasping breathing. It must be arduous to climb stairs wearing all that armor.

But he did not slow his pace. It was almost as if he was afraid to. Even he—this immense, fiercesome knight—did not want to displease whoever, or whatever, waited at the top of the stairs. Not the old Lord of Blackhurst, but the new one, the Beast Lord.

They called him that because he looked like a monster, his face deformed and repulsive. It was said that one of old Lord Blackhurst's victims had cursed him before she died, cursed him with a son who had a countenance so loathsome that it made hardened knights shudder and turn away.

The Beast Lord. That was her destination—the den of a hideous being. For all she knew he really was half-animal, living on human flesh. Was she to be his next meal?

Or was his purpose even more sinister and depraved? Would he ravish her, fill her body with his own grotesque flesh?

Her captor finally paused and she heard a latch being lifted, a door opening. She longed to faint, to escape the horror of what she faced by lapsing into senselessness. But as disabling as her terror was, she remained perfectly aware. Acutely aware, as if her every sense were honed to extreme receptivity. She heard footsteps, felt another presence close.

"Is this the one?" the knight holding her asked. There was anxiety in his tone. He feared to displease this dread being he faced.

"Aye." Another voice. Deep, rumbling. She squeezed her eyes more tightly shut. If she pretended to have swooned, perhaps he would leave her alone, for a time at least.

"She looks half dead." The Beast Lord spoke again. "What did you do to her?"

"Nothing! I swear it," the knight responded. "It's her fear that has rendered her senseless. I could hear her gasping and sobbing as we rode. You can't blame her, considering the tales they tell of—"

"Enough!" She flinched at the furious sound of the Beast Lord's voice. *Nay, stay still,* she pleaded with herself. "Put her on the bed and leave!" he ordered in thundering tones.

She gritted her teeth, expecting to be dumped down upon the hard surface of some torture device. But the knight laid her gently on something that felt as soft as a cloud.

Her spirits sank further. She feared rape more than she feared torture and death. And what other purpose was there for a bed in a torture chamber?

Her resolve deepened. She would remain unmoving and senseless no matter what he did to her. If he was like his father, part of his pleasure came from observing the terror of his victims. But she would not give him that satisfaction. She would remain inert, and cheat him of his enjoyment.

She tried to breathe deeply and evenly, feigning unawareness, but she could feel him looming over her. Hear *his* breathing. Harsh, a little fast. He was agitated about something. Perhaps excited by the prospect of ravishing her. She winced inwardly at the thought.

She could smell him. Not an unpleasant odor. Indeed, a strangely appealing scent. Fragrant herbs with a deeper, darker smell beneath. Intriguing . . . She wondered at her own thoughts. All she had to do was open her eyes and see his revolting visage and know unspeakable terror. She could not find his smell entrancing.

It was a trick. He was trying to get her to awaken so he could torment her. That was his purpose. The soft bed, the pleasant, intoxicating odors . . . he meant to lull her into a false feeling of safety. Then he would pounce on her!

What a subtle, clever fiend he was, toying with his victims. Like a cat that bats its prey around with velvet paws, then kills with sharp teeth and brutal claws.

She felt the subtle disturbance of air near her face. One of his hands—she envisioned it, covered with warts and disfigurements, with nails like claws—was only inches above her face. She imagined his hoary, repulsive flesh against her skin, caressing . . .

As the image flooded her mind, she managed to remain still, but only barely. She must not let herself anticipate what was to come, or the fear would unhinge her and she would betray herself. She wanted with every fiber of her being to jump up and try to flee.

But there was no escape. Somehow, she must continue her deception. If she thought of other things, pleasant things, she might be able to manage it. She would pretend she was back in the forest, lying in the tall grass of the meadow, surrounded by birdsong, a gentle breeze on her face, the sweet scents of the wildflowers filling her nose, the warmth of the sun making her sleepy and content . . .

She was so beautiful. Like a flower. Her skin as smooth and perfect as the rarest, softest petals, suffused with a pale, transparent glow, magically alive and wondrous. An enchanted being, born of sunlight and dewdrops and lush, green growing things . . .

Alexander took a deep, convulsive breath. The most exquisite woman he'd ever beheld lay on the crimson satin coverlet of his bed. He held his hand inches from her divine perfection, longing to touch her. To stroke his fingers over her silken, elegantly curved cheek, glide his hand through her masses of hair, spilling like coils of dark, gleaming honey over the satin.

Before this, he'd seen her only from a distance, as he crouched in a thicket a good dozen paces from the meadow where she came to gather wildflowers. Even from that far away, her beauty had left him breathless. The slim grace of her body, moving lightly among the colorful blooms. The rich, burnished warmth of her hair, tawny gold in the sunlight, flowing down her back like a waterfall. Her face, a small creamy oval with pale pink mouth, pert nose, and those saucy, bewitching eyes. They were neither brown nor green, he knew, but some mixture of both. Hazel, they called it, but that term hardly did justice to the shifting magic her eyes possessed, as if all the hues of the sunlit forest danced in her gaze.

One time she must have heard him, for her head came up like a startled doe's and she looked directly at him. He had held his breath, both for fear that he would betray himself and also in amazed wonder at her loveliness. She embodied the wild beauty of the woods. The innocence and elusiveness of the shyest forest creature. The heartbreaking beauty and promise of a tiny dewdrop flower glowing pearl white among the dark moss of a secret glen.

If only he had been able to admire her beauty from afar. But he had wanted more, desired more. To touch the butterfly's wing softness of her skin. To kiss the nectar-sweet, budding rose of her mouth. To—heaven help him—join his damned flesh with her pure, untainted beauty. His gaze trailed down her body, thinking of her breasts. They would be round and firm with nipples as pink as her delicious mouth. And he thought of her cunny, soft, delicate, petal-like folds of rose, surrounded by maidenshair of deep, amber gold. He would fill her deep and feel her wet, welcoming flesh close around him . . .

He turned away from the bed, overcome with self-disgust. Here he was, contemplating crude sexual acts with this ethereal beauty. He was no better than the heinous, corrupt monster who had sired him. He had no right to have this young woman abducted and brought here. But he knew that he would, eventually, carry out the rest of his plan.

He turned back to the bed, drawn like a moth to a candle's flame. His gaze raked the slender form sprawled over the blood red covers. He wanted to ruck up the plainly woven, russet gown she wore and view her nakedness, but he fought the urge with all his strength. He had no right to take such liberties with a helpless, unconscious maid. The selfishness of such an act reminded him all too keenly of his father's crude amusements.

He inhaled sharply. What if she never woke? Worse yet, if once she did, she began to scream in terror and would not stop?

What would he do then? Would he let her go? Or would he remain committed to his plan?

He told himself that he had no choice. If there was even the tiniest chance that he could somehow make her care for him . . . and if her acceptance could shatter the curse, or at least lessen it a little . . . How could he not try, against all odds, to pursue the only hope he had to ever know a normal life?

Perhaps it would be better if he had not overheard the servants talking that day, gossiping about a remedy to the curse. The story was that if he could manage to entice a woman to his bed and make her fall in love with him, the spell that caused him to appear so monstrous would be broken. Of course, the servants tsked sadly, such a thing was unlikely to happen. For what woman could ever fall in love with a man so repulsive?

What woman, indeed? Alexander had considered the matter extensively, telling himself that he should find the homeliest, poorest, most wretched female in his domain and have her brought to the castle. Shower her with gifts and treat her like a queen and hope that somehow she would be grateful enough to fall in love with him.

But the trouble was, he did not want such a woman. He wanted this one.

Ah, how he wanted this woman. Wanted her with a craving that took his breath way. He leaned nearer to the bed. She was perfect. Every part of her. His gaze fell to her hand. So small, barely half the size of his. The fingernails were cut short, the skin slightly tanned. The shell-like delicacy of her fingernails affected him. He wanted to envelop that small hand in his own. Hold her, possess her, protect her forever.

Again, he drew away from the bed. His longing for her was too strong. Overpowering. He did not intend to ravish her, but instead, seduce her, entice her, make her weak with desire.

It could be done. He had heard some of the bolder knights talking of their conquests, of the things they did to earn the favors of the women. Few fighting men had enough coin to tempt their paramours with extravagant gifts, but there were other means. Techniques of lovemaking. Secrets to making a woman sigh with longing. Ways to make a woman experience such ecstatic pleasure that she would return to a man's bed again and again.

And if a woman desired a man, surely she would eventually come to care for him. Even if he *were* a grotesque, bestial monster.

But . . . the dilemma was . . . He gazed again at the bed, aching with hunger and need. How did he convince this woman to even let him touch her, when it appeared she was so completely overwhelmed with terror at the very thought of being in the same room with him?

He closed his eyes, overcome with agony. He had no right to do this, to attempt his own salvation at the expense of this woman's peace of mind. Was he a beast in truth, as black-hearted and cruel and selfish as his father?

What was he doing? Why didn't he just grab her and get on with it! Esmay repressed a sigh of exasperation. She did not know how long she could pretend unconsciousness. Her nose itched fiercely and there was a crick in her neck from remaining in the same position. But she dare not give up the ruse. That was what he was waiting for. He wanted her awake and terrified when he began his torture.

He had moved away from the bed. It was strange how she could sense when he was near. Partly it was his scent, distracting and confusing her. And partly it was some instinct that alerted her when he brought his hand near her face. As if he were fondling her without actually touching her. She knew when he was looking at her, his gaze like a tangible caress.

For now, he had moved away. She could hear his footfalls, pacing, some distance from the bed. This might be the only chance she had to shift position.

With infinitesimal care she moved her head so her neck did not ache, then listened. When there was no indication that he had seen her movement, she dared to open her eyes.

She could see him, silhouetted against the light from a high arched window. His back was turned to her. Exhaling in relief, she lifted her head and scratched her nose, then swiftly resumed her prone position. When he did not turn around, she dared to glance around, taking in her surroundings.

She was in a round tower room, but it hardly looked like a

place of torture. More like a lavishly furnished bedchamber. In addition to the massive bed she lay upon, there was a high-backed chair near the window where he stood, a large table covered with books, several large chests, two stools with cushioned seats, and a smaller table holding glass jars and drinking vessels. On the floor of the chamber was some sort of heavy, plush fabric, a rich red with a pattern that reminded her of gold leaves. The walls were covered with hangings bearing a similar pattern, but red upon gold.

The room was beautiful, the most dazzling sight she had ever beheld. Rich colors and exquisite textures everywhere—polished wood, gleaming fabrics, sparkling glass. It took her breath away and, for a moment, made her forget her fear. Then there was a knock at the door and the figure at the window slowly turned around. In the split second before she snapped her eyes shut, she saw him, as big as the knight who had captured her but dressed in black clothing rather than armor. His face was completely covered by a mask of black leather.

The image stunned Esmay and all her dread returned. He *was* a monster, a dark, hulking shadow out of her nightmares. She went rigid once again, anticipating her horrible end.

Alexander narrowed his eyes as the stoop-shouldered, white-haired serving woman entered the chamber carrying a tray. "Mabelle, what are you doing here?"

"I've brought you your supper, of course."

"I told Drogor that I was not to be disturbed."

"You will still need to eat," Mabelle replied placidly.

Of all the servants at Blackhurst castle, she was the only one who treated him as if he were no different than any other man. Despite the fact that she had seen him without his mask and knew what a monster he truly was, she was always utterly fearless around him.

Sometimes it irked him that she had no dread of him, although it was rather comforting as well. With her, he did not have to guard his tongue and keep a rein on his temper. One harsh word did not send her running in terror for the door. Indeed, when he raged and roared, she merely looked at him with her one good eye, startlingly green in that wrinkled, wizened face. Under her unflinching, clearly disapproving stare, he always began to feel a little foolish. And she ofttimes reminded him that, despite his deformity, he enjoyed a comfortable and easeful life. He should be grateful for that, she told him.

It made him think. To consider that perhaps he was not so unfortunate after all. But then his hands would go to the mask covering his face and he would remember the looks of dread on the faces of the people he encountered during his rare excursions out of the castle, and he would know the despair of the curse all over again.

Mabelle was fussing with the tray of food, taking her time in arranging it on the table. He knew she was aware of the woman lying unconscious on the bed. Although it made him angry to think that he should have to explain his actions to a servant, he decided he had to say something.

"She swooned." He jerked his head towards the bed. "I haven't touched her. Nor do I intend to."

"Oh, indeed, what *do* you intend to do with her?"

His mouth twitched in irritation. There was no reason to tell a servant his plan. Except . . . he really had no idea what the needs of a young woman might be. He was going to need Mabelle's assistance in making his lovely captive comfortable.

"You've heard the tale that there is a way for me to undo the curse?" he said. "Well, I thought I would try it."

Mabelle raised the brow over her good eye. She looked toward the bed, then back again. Although she didn't say it, he knew what she was thinking. *You—a repulsive, beastial monster—think to make the fairest maid in creation fall in love with you?*

It was absurd. Utterly mad. Thinking about the hopelessness of it made him want to weep. He turned away, clenching his hands into fists and gritting his teeth in misery.

"Well," Mabelle spoke softly. "I think for now it's best if you take your leave of her and let the poor thing recover her wits. I'll tend to her while you're gone."

He turned back to the bed. He didn't want to leave her. Ever. Yet Mabelle's advice was sound. The maid needed time to adjust, to get used to Blackhurst Castle, let alone to him. He approached the bed, wanting to get one last look, to drink in his fill of her. It was as if her very presence fed his soul, made him feel strong and whole and hopeful.

It also aroused his deepest, darkest, most primitive cravings. Just looking at her gave him a rock-hard, raging erection. He imagined one of those small, delicate hands touching him, enclosing his heated cock in cool, smooth fingers.

The idea almost made him gasp aloud. Damn Mabelle, if not for her, he would try it, despite his vow not to touch the maid until she grew used to him. Unconscious, she would not even be aware of what her hand was holding, but it would afford him so much satisfaction. He'd probably come in seconds.

He glanced over his shoulder. Mabelle was still there, waiting for him to leave. He could order her to go, but if he did that, she would know how truly base and crude he was. She might think of his father and wonder if he were not a lot like his sire after all. He had abducted an innocent young woman to use for his own ends. Hardly a noble scheme, for all that he intended to give her was the greatest pleasure imaginable.

Pleasure. That was the key to it. Unless he could make this woman sigh with contentment and moan with ecstasy, he would never make her fall in love with him. And then he would be locked in this hellish prison of his deformity for the rest of his life.

Chapter Two

She heard heavy footsteps, the Beast Lord leaving. But someone else was leaning over her. Once again, Esmay concentrated on remaining perfectly still. *Ouch!* Something sharp poked into her arm and she jerked reflexively.

"Ah, so you are alive after all."

Furious at being tricked, Esmay opened her eyes. Then she let out a scream. The old woman staring down at her was almost as horrific-looking as the Beast Lord. Where one of her eyes should have been, there was an ugly knob of flesh and the rest of her features were twisted and disfigured. With her scraggly white hair, wrinkles, and hunched-over body, she was a sinister-looking old crone. But it was her one sound eye that terrified Esmay. The bright green orb regarded her with fierce disapproval.

"Just a bit of a thing, aren't you?" The old woman shook her head. "And not much backbone either. Afraid of your own shadow. But I suppose that's part of why he fancies you, thinks he can bend you to his will, he does."

Esmay licked her dry lips. She'd heard them talking, and this woman was clearly a servant. She would not be afraid of her. The woman's comment about "no backbone" penetrated her fear and replaced it with anger. She sat up straighter.

The woman shook her head again. "Well, we'd best get you to eat something. Fatten you up a bit."

Esmay went rigid. Fatten her up? What did that mean?

"Oh, don't look so wretched. I just mean that no man wants to lie down with a little stick of a woman and have her hipbones poke into him."

Esmay swallowed. She took these words to imply that the Beast Lord *did* intend to ravish her. And this old hag wanted to make sure she gave him a comfortable tumble! She sat up even straighter, glaring at the servant.

The woman smiled. "Now, that's better. Don't make it too easy for him." She laid a platter of food on the bed next to Esmay.

Esmay regarded the food, cheese, ripe apricots, and a big chunk of bread with a rich brown crust and a center of dazzling whiteness. It looked delicious.

"I put the wine over here." The crone pointed to the table. Her one green eye regarded Esmay piercingly, then she shuffled toward the door. "I'll return in a short while. In case you wish to bathe or otherwise tidy yourself up."

Esmay stared after the servant. She was obviously being prepared for the Beast Lord's enjoyment. He wanted her clean, well fed, alert. The idea made her shiver, but did not altogether ruin her appetite. She would need her strength if she were going to fight him.

Alexander made his way into the hall, trying not to notice the sudden tension his presence aroused. In the next few moments, everyone in the hall, from the maidservant scrubbing the trestle tables to the churl stoking the hearth fire and the senschenal's wife weaving near the one window—everyone would suddenly find some excuse to leave. He sighed heavily, wondering what it would be like to enter a room and not feel like a wolf stalking a herd of deer.

He spied Drogor and approached him. The knight was drinking ale at a table near the hearth. Alexander took a seat beside him and poured himself a cup. Although he knew that Drogor was not exactly easy with him, at least the knight was too proud to show his discomfort.

Drogor looked at him. "Hasn't she come around yet?"

Alexander shook his head.

"Maybe...." Drogor traced the rim of his cup with one scarred finger. "Maybe you should bed her now, while she's yet unconscious. That way, she wouldn't struggle."

Alexander sighed. Drogor obviously misunderstood his intent. It wasn't his plan to rape her.

"Because ... the thing is ..." The knight shot him a glance. "The first time isn't usually much to the woman's liking. Especially with a wench so small."

Drogor, bless him, was trying to help him. "You think I'm going to hurt her?"

Drogor raised his brows. "You're a big man, milord."

Alexander took a deep breath. "Is there any way around it? I mean, if I ready her ... arouse her ..."

"Even then. The first time is painful for a lot of wenches. Which was why I was thinking if you did it to her while she was unaware, she would not come to associate the pain with you."

Meaning that Drogor thought that he already had enough things to overcome. Like the fact that he was a terrifying monstrosity.

"Do you have any other suggestions?" He could not help

speaking sharply. The pain inside him was too intense, the familiar hopelessness beginning to take hold.

"Well, I . . . Nay, not really. Probably best to get it over quickly, that's all."

Dear God, he didn't want it to be quick! His fantasies of their first coupling did not involve speed. It involved long hours of fondling, of skin to skin, his cock deep inside her, savoring the feeling of her wet flesh surrounding him, her soft femaleness yielding to his hard male need.

Drogor pushed his chair away from the table and stood. "You might ask a woman for advice. One of them might have a better suggestion." He waited a heartbeat, then strode off.

Pain stabbed Alexander. Drogor couldn't help him. No one could.

He finished the rest of his ale in a morose mood. He wasn't certain he even wanted to go back up to the tower, if it was going to be like that.

But he would. The lure of his prisoner was simply too great. The needs of his body too demanding. Even if he was going to hurt her, he knew he would eventually go through with it. The only alternative was to have Drogor fetch her and take her back to the forest. Forget the whole notion and live out the rest of his damned, hopeless life as the Beast Lord.

"I've been thinking."

He turned to see Mabelle standing next to him. For a shuffling half-cripple, she moved with amazing stealth. She was forever sneaking up on him.

"What?" he demanded. He was in no mood for her tart, insulting comments.

"There's no way to turn her into a robust, buxom wench overnight. A big man like you . . ." She shot a quick, wry glance at his crotch. "You're bound to hurt her."

"Drogor has already spoken of these things," he hissed out through clenched teeth.

"Oh, well then. I just thought you might want to think on it. Consider that causing her pain is hardly going to—"

"Enough!" he growled. "Go tend to her or something. Anything. But get out of my sight!"

"Of course, milord."

Her voice was meek, but he knew better. She took pleasure in bedeviling him.

He picked up his leather gloves and slapped them hard against the table. Then he paused and looked them closely. He put one glove on and examined his leather-clad fingers, from the smallest to the thick shape of his thumb. It might work. It might. But who to get to make them for him?

The room was lit with candles, dozens of beeswax candles. They filled the small, round chamber with a warm, beneficent glow. Esmay had never seen such amazing extravagance. It was like the food. Hard to imagine that people dined on bread like that every day. Soft, chewy, fine-grained, sweet-tasting bread as white as new-fallen snow.

And there was her gown. She glanced down at it, a swirl of gossamer fabric, the very shade of a wild dogrose. It felt like a swan's down against her skin, and she was aware of her body as never before. Of the way the soft fabric caressed her nipples and swished over her buttocks and thighs, gliding over her body like warm liquid.

Indulgent. Enticing.

She paced across the small room, wondering at her own weakness. Despite her resolve to fight her captor, she'd given in and allowed the crone to bathe her, wash her hair, and comb it out in an herb-scented cloud that floated over her shoulders. She'd even succumbed to the crone's urging and taken a handful of the sweet-smelling creamy salve the servant had offered, then rubbed it on her skin until it glistened and her nipples looked like shiny, ripe berries.

The crone had also advised her to anoint her private parts with the stuff, but she'd refused. Too horrible to contemplate making herself alluring for a brute, a beast.

Yet even though she had not used the salve there, she was intensely aware of that part of herself. She was naked beneath the luscious gown and so vulnerable, so excruciatingly *accessible*.

The thought made her turn on her heel and pace back the other way, tense with dread and agitation.

The servant had advised her to be no meek, willing victim. But she knew as soon as he strode into the room, her knees would go weak and her resolve vanish. He was huge and powerful and . . . *he was the Beast Lord.*

She thought about what he must look like, under the mask. What deformity, what repulsiveness the black leather concealed. She shuddered, then paced back across the small chamber. The thick carpet felt soft and soothing beneath her bare feet, and she paused a moment to knead it with her toes. Then, she whirled around as the door opened.

Sweet heaven, what had Mabelle done to her? Alexander gaped at the vision in front of him. A phantasm of pink silk, creamy skin, and honey gold hair. He'd left behind a demure, innocent-appearing waif, and returned to find his rawest fantasies come to life. The gown clung to her body, highlighting each curve and contour. And the color—the voluptuous, rosy shade seemed to him the very hue of a woman's vulva. Her vulva, flushed with the heated blood of her passion, sleek and slippery like silk.

Nay, Mabelle had not aided him in this, not at all. His control was already tenuous. Faced with this impossibly erotic creature, he could feel the fine, thin threads of his restraint begin to snap.

Help! Please, help! The silent plea formed in Esmay's throat, but there was no point speaking aloud. She was utterly trapped, at the mercy of this man.

If he *was* a man. A huge, imposing figure filled her vision, power and threat emanating from every aspect. The stark black mask, the black garments that covered the sleek, well-muscled torso, the long, formidable limbs . . . Then she saw his bare hands. Big, long-fingered, but still recognizably human. She regarded them with interest. All of him was not deformed. Her glance moved upward. Perhaps only his face was monstrous. Perhaps that was why he wore the mask.

He took two steps towards her, then paused. This close, she could finally see his eyes. They were gray, a wintry, bleak gray, and . . . undeniably human. Filled with awareness, with emotion. He was not looking at her as a beast regards its prey. There was something so vulnerable, so compelling in his expression.

The mask also revealed his mouth. It appeared normal as well. His lips were quite nicely shaped.

The thought startled her, and she remembered that she should be afraid. This man had brought her here for some vile purpose.

He was the Beast Lord, the cursed offspring of a man renowned for his depravity and cruelty!

At the thought, her body went rigid and her breath quickened. She wanted to run, although there was nowhere to run to.

He watched her face change, her eyes turn wild-eyed with fear. He saw the tension overtake her body. Her breathing accelerated and become shallow. What had he done? For a moment, she had gazed at him with a kind of wary interest. Sizing him up, evaluating her adversary. What had she seen that suddenly provoked her terror?

He released his breath in a sigh. This was going to be more difficult than he had expected. He didn't know how to accomplish even the most basic aspects of seduction. Getting close to her, removing her clothing . . . touching her.

His whole body ached with longing. His skin throbbed with awareness of her incredible sexual allure. He would not be denied. *Could* not be denied.

He took a step towards her. Her chest heaved in agitation. The slight motion made her breasts quiver beneath the thin fabric of the gown, emphasizing how soft and full they were, liquid, shivering flesh. All the aching, wild hunger rose up inside him. He wanted this woman beyond reason or sanity. Somehow, he had to begin.

He reached out and seized the low neckline of the gown, then pulled on the thin fabric until one of her breasts was revealed.

One perfect breast. Lush, exquisitely rounded, the nipple gloriously pink. The skin as fine and fresh as rose petals.

He took a deep, ravaged breath, wanting more, so much more. With trembling fingers, he grazed her nipple. She did not move, but her eyes widened. He held his hand against her breast, then spread his fingers and surrounded the soft flesh, enclosing her perfection in his hand. Then he bent his head and brought his lips to her nipple.

She tensed in dread, then relaxed by slow degrees. His mouth was on her, but he was not hurting her. Indeed, it felt good. Like a babe suckling must feel. His mouth was wet and warm. The pressure of his lips even more provocative than his hand felt.

She closed her eyes. She could feel the strange sensations deepening, fanning out from her breast. Her body was still rigid, but not with fear, but a yearning ache that made her arch her back.

He was licking her nipple. Running his tongue over it, flicking lightly. The feeling maddened her, making her want to writhe, to squirm . . . made her want . . . something.

A fierce urgency overtook her. She was exceedingly uncomfortable, but not from what he was doing. She wanted, needed . . . something. Perhaps for him to suckle her other breast. Or to touch her all over.

Her body felt hot, her skin prickly. A heated, feverish feeling that demanded soothing.

She opened her eyes and looked down. The mask did not cover the back of his head, but was fastened there with straps that went under his hair. Black hair. Long and silky, with a slight wave. She wanted to touch that hair, feel the softness in her fingers, feel the slight movements of his head as he sucked and licked her breast.

She reminded herself of the mask, and what it concealed.

Her legs were growing wobbly. The gnawing urgency inside her making it difficult to remain still. She closed her eyes again. The pleasure flooded her, at the same time arousing a burning craving that was almost too much to bear.

She was responding. He could feel it. Her nipple was hard and engorged, like a succulent fruit ripening in his mouth. She was trembling, but not with dread. He felt her sway, heard her harsh, rapid breathing. He had reached her, made her forget who and what he was. But it was only a beginning.

He drew away. Her nipple was wet, swollen, and such a deep, vivid pink it reminded him of another sensitive part of her. Her vulva, her woman's flesh, the sweet, hot flower between her thighs. And he was drawn there, like a bee to a nectar-laden bud.

Such thoughts made his cock throb. It was hugely engorged and aching, pressing painfully against his braies. When he considered how long it would be before he could find release, he felt he would go mad. His body began to tremble and he took a step back. His control was as thin and frail as spider's silk.

He concentrated, breathing slowly and deeply, trying to dispel the heated, mindless lust that held him in its grip. He would not have her think him a crude beast. Somehow, he must hold back, forget his own harsh, raw desire and concentrate on arousing her.

But the sight of her was too much for him. Her body, curvaceous and female, partially revealed by the loose, bright gown. Her bare breast, teasing him to taste and suckle once again. Her face, wild-eyed and flushed. His need was too great, too overwhelming.

He reached out and grabbed the thin silk with both hands. It ripped easily, falling away like gossamer wings floating to earth, revealing her splendor.

Beauty beyond imagining. An enchanted form of exquisite grace . . . and consummate sensuality. Though he might admire her beauty in his mind, his body had a cruder, more visceral response. The swollen pinkness of her nipples reminded him of other rose-colored sentient flesh. The smallness of her waist accentuated her rounded hips—curving and substantial hips to clutch as he thrust into her. The slim, white thighs led upward to a secret, hidden haven of bliss. The mossy tuft of tawny brown hair guarded the deep pool of his lustful imaginings.

With effort, he brought his gaze back to her face. He could see her embarrassment and her fear. No man had ever seen her naked before. He half pitied her, guessing how vulnerable and helpless she must feel. But he could hold back only so much. His restraint could endure only so long. Besides, he did not intend to hurt her, but give her intense pleasure.

He took a step towards her. She did not move, but her eyes widened. With a quick motion, he swooped her into his arms. In three long strides he was at the bed. He lay her there, then moved back so he could look at her.

She lay gazing up at him, her legs held tightly together, her eyes even more anxious and full of dread.

Fierce need fought with reason. Go slow, his mind said. But his body was ready to pounce on her, to forget all subtly and seduction. His braies felt like an iron band around his pulsing, raging cock. He fought desperately for control.

Now. Now he was going to rape her! Esmay's body went taut with the instinctive urge to flee. She imagined pain, imagined her tender, private parts invaded, wrenched apart and battered.

He was so big. So powerful. He had picked her up as if she were a little wisp of a thing, as if it took no effort at all.

Of course. He was the Beast Lord. Half-animal, half-man. Or was it, half-monster, half-man?

She looked up at him and the stark black mask filled her vision and her thoughts. What did he look like beneath it? How horrible was his disfigurement?

The gray eyes watched her. The eyes of a hunter, a predator. And yet they were not an animal's eyes, but distinctly, startlingly human.

She shifted on the bed, wishing she dared try to cover herself. She felt so exposed, so defenseless. But she feared to make him angry. And she knew in the very core of her being that he wanted her naked, wanted to look at her. That was why all the candles were lit. That was why he had torn off the beautiful gown, reducing it to rags.

And the way he gazed at her made it clear that he desired something more. She felt like a plump roast piglet on a cooking platter, waiting to be devoured.

Yet, he was fully clothed, she thought in puzzlement. *How could he rape her if he did not free his penis?* Her gaze went to his groin, then she realized in horror what she had done. She glanced nervously at his face and saw that his eyes had changed.

That swift, unconscious glance, an instinctive awareness of the thing she most feared, somehow had affected him. In recognizing his sexuality, the weapon of his lust, she had triggered some change in him. She could sense the difference in the way he looked at her. A kind of caution and calculation.

He moved away from the bed. Esmay waited, wondering breathlessly what would happen next.

Alexander took a deep breath and stared at the tapestry on the wall. It was exactly as both Drogor and Mabelle had warned him. He was too big for her. She knew it, and that was why she had shot him that look of panicked dread, her gaze straying ever so briefly to his crotch. Instead of arousing him, that one look had quelled his desire. He wanted her to *want* him, to long for the feeling of his cock inside her—not to regard his member as some sort of instrument of torture.

He released his breath in a sigh. He'd never had a virgin. Indeed, the few worn-out slatterns who were desperate enough to allow him to bed them were about as far from virgins as possible. For enough coin, they would spread their legs for any man, even a monster like him. They had been used so much and so often that they were flaccid and well stretched. Fucking them had been rather like trying to fuck a deflated pig's bladder. He'd known release, but it had been of the most unsatisfying, futile sort. Even his desperate body had known that it wasn't supposed to be like that. That a woman's cunny was supposed to be snug and tight and afford a delicious friction that could send a man over the edge in seconds.

And he knew, *knew* that it would be like that with his beauty, his lush, perfect Esmay.

But he also knew that no matter how wonderful it would feel to be inside her, he did not want to do it if it was going to cause her pain. She had to care for him if the curse were to be broken, and a woman was unlikely to care for a man who hurt her. Beyond that, he knew that if she still regarded him with horror and dread after their coupling, he would not be able to endure it. He would want to die.

He pushed the agonizing thought away. All was not lost. He would find a way to make her accept him, to experience their lovemaking as pleasure. If only he could convince her to go along with his plan.

He reached into the pocket of his braies and withdrew the first small leather phallus. He'd had Elen, the senaschal's wife, sew it for him, using the smallest finger of one of his gloves. He wondered if she guessed what it was for, but he doubted it. She thought him such a beast, she would never imagine him conceiving of such a clever plan.

It would work, he knew it. Today, he would put the phallus inside her and order her to keep it there. Tomorrow, he would replace it with a larger one. At the end of a sennight, she would be stretched and ready for him. The only thing that bothered him was how to explain to Elen the size of the larger phalluses. He was far bigger than a finger.

But he would worry about that when the time came. For now his challenge was to get Esmay to allow him to insert the first one. The thought of it aroused him unbearably. Although he might not be able to fuck her, at least he would be able to touch her, to fondle her, to spread the lips of her vulva, to play with her sweet, tender flesh . . .

He took a deep breath. His cock was so agonizingly hard that he thought he would burst. He steadied himself, preparing himself for the incredibly sensual act he was about to perform. Then he moved toward the bed.

Chapter Three

She looked like some sort of heathen sacrifice, her pale, perfect body spread out helplessly on the crimson silk of the bedcover. The thought of her being so vulnerable disturbed him. Yet he *had* ordered Drogor to capture her and bring her here against her will, giving her no choice in being part of his plan.

But he dare not give her a choice. No woman would come willingly to his bed, certainly not this beautiful virgin. Did she have a sweetheart, some gawkish village boy to whom she planned to someday give her maidenhead? The thought made him furious. She was young and naïve and did not know what she wanted, what was best for her! No village churl could offer her what he did, luxury and leisure for the rest of her life. And no rude peasant could know how to make love to her like he would!

He could imagine some red-faced lout grunting and groaning over her, pawing and groping her exquisite body. Nay, he would not let that happen! What he was doing was best for her. He would treat her like a queen, fulfill her every wish, if only . . . only she would come to feel something for him.

He repressed a sigh. Once again, he felt daunted. His plan appeared so simple, but it was not at all. How did he get her to spread her legs for him, to fondle her intimately so he could insert the phallus?

What was wrong with him? Why didn't he get on with it? Esmay regarded the man looming over her with a mixture of dread and frustration. She was weary of feeling hunted, like a mouse batted around by a cat. It would better if he would just mount her and get it over with. Then she could grit her teeth and endure.

Obviously, rape was his scheme. He had ripped off the gown, carried her to the bed. There could be no other logical purpose for his actions. Unless he meant to torture her first.

A quiver of warning shot through her. As her body tensed, she thought she heard him sigh. Her gaze met his. Those expressive, oh-so-human eyes watched her, filled some emotion she could not fathom. *What did he want?*

He sat down on the bed next to her and reached out his big hand. She watched, rigid with fear as his fingers touched her neck. But then, gently, oh so gently, his fingers grazed her skin. He began to stroke her, moving upward to trace the line of her jaw, then caressing her neck. Subtle, soft. His hands were warm. The light calluses on his fingertips felt tantalizing, rough and stimulating.

It was odd to be touched like this, as if he were petting a cat or dog, soothing it. Some of the tension in her muscles had begun to ebb. His hand glided along shoulder and down her arm. It was as if he were exploring her, discovering how each part of her felt. His movements were so gentle, tender. He seemed to know the exact amount of pressure to use to make her skin feel alive and tingling. It was pleasurable, no doubt of it.

He covered her hand with his own, then fingered it front and back, testing the sharpness of her nails against his palm. She tore her gaze away from the sight of his big hand enveloping her smaller one and looked up at him. His eyes were rapt as he rubbed her hand, and a strange sense went through her.

She enchanted him, every part of her. Her hand seemed so cunning, almost magical. Small and yet every detail so perfect. The slight tan of her skin and blunt, short nails touched him. This was no pampered, white-skinned lady, but a wild wood nymph who spent her days in the dappled sunshine of the forest. She seemed so real and alive, a part of the earth, sensual and free.

He released her hand, then noticed that a lock of her hair had fallen over her shoulder. He fingered the lustrous curl, admiring the glints of bronze striking bright in the dark gold depths. A skein of the finest silk was not so lovely as this. Someday he would like to feel her hair against his naked body, against his face.

That reminded him of his mission, and he began to fondle her again. He wanted to make her used to his touch. So at ease with him that she would not fight him when he put his phallus inside her. He stroked her breasts, exploring their beauty in a way he had not earlier. Their graceful shape, so bounteous and yet delicate. Her nipples were like jewels set in the creamy mounds.

His hands glided downward. The dainty shape of her ribs, her narrow waist, the teasing indentation of her navel. He caressed her there, then moved his hands back up to brush the lower curves of her breasts. Making slow, lazy circles, he explored the smooth skin of her torso, feeling her delicate ribs beneath, then the plush softness of her belly, then down, down, almost to the patch of curling hair that beckoned him. His fingers grazed it, briefly feeling the springy curls, then he withdrew. Nay, she was not ready for that yet.

He was driving her mad! Who would have guessed that having a man rub her stomach could arouse such peculiar, fluttering feelings? It was as if a bird were trapped inside her, struggling to be free. But there was worse. She could feel a hard, almost painful ache between her thighs.

This could not be happening! She gritted her teeth, feeling slightly frantic as his fingers barely touched her pubic hair, then moved away. It was growing more and more difficult to keep her legs together, to remain still. This was not rape, but some kind of torture!

Her breath came in harsh, uneven gasps. Her whole body tingled. Her skin felt like it was on fire. She wanted to moan and cry out. Clamping her lips together, she quelled her outcry. She could not be feeling these things, not with this man, this monster.

She glanced up at the mask, trying to remind herself of what he was. A beast. A monstrosity.

But his hand was human and, oh, so incredibly skilled.

She closed her eyes. He'd shifted position and began to stroke her feet, rubbing them. It felt so soothing, delightful. Then, as she'd anticipated, he moved his hand up her leg. She held her breath and her every sense seemed focused on the throbbing flesh of her crotch. His caressing, teasing fingers moved closer. He stroked her thighs, making the skin prickle. The sense of being hot and feverish grew more intense. She was ablaze. Her nipples hurt and there was hot wetness between her thighs.

His fingers edged closer, easing between her legs. Although she fought surrender with all her strength, her thighs slid apart. She was suddenly limp and weak. A muffled moan escaped her lips.

By all in heaven, she was beautiful! And so responsive. Against all hope of hopes, she'd spread her thighs for him. Willingly. Almost eagerly. Alexander took a deep breath, then gazed in wonder at his conquest. Her eyes were closed, her long, dark lashes quivering faintly against her cheeks. Her creamy skin was tinged with a delicious rosy flush. Her nipples thrust up like plump berries. And between her thighs . . . Taking another deep breath, he gently spread her legs wider, then gazed on paradise.

Flowery, mysterious folds surrounded by curling. mossy hair. A wet, tender mouth to swallow his cock. A secret cavern leading to rapture. With one trembling finger, he began to explore, fondling her delicate flesh.

He was touching her! Stroking the outer lips of her vulva. Esmay flinched, expecting pain. It was almost as intense as pain, but edged with a different sort of fire. She gritted her teeth, wanting to writhe, to squirm. And yet, she didn't want him to stop. His fine, delicate caresses made her hungry for more. She knew that she'd lifted her hips, spread her thighs even wider, wanting him to increase the pressure of his stroking, to probe deeper and tease the inner lips. Her body, of its own will, was begging him to somehow soothe the squeezing, tormenting hunger inside her.

With horror, she realized that she wanted him to take off his clothes and mount her. Fill her with his penis. That seemed to be the only thing that would ease her.

She told herself that she could not want such a thing. He was the Beast Lord, the embodiment of her worst nightmares. But her body would not listen. She heard herself gasp with pleasure.

She forced herself to open her eyes, hoping the sight of the terrifying mask would jar her body into awareness of who was touching her. He loomed over her, a sinister vision in black. It did not matter. Whatever he was, her body had learned to know his touch, to respond. Then she saw that he held an object in his other hand. Her eyes widened. What did he mean to do to her? Her gaze jerked to meet his.

"I . . . I . . . must stretch you," he whispered.

It was the first words he'd said to her. She remembered that deep, husky voice when he spoke to the servant and the knight. Then he had sounded harsh and commanding. Now he seemed to be pleading.

She looked at the thing in his left hand. Made of black leather, like his mask. What was it?

He spoke again. "I'm a large man. I could not penetrate you without causing pain. So, I will stretch you first." He held out the black object. "I'm going to put this inside you, so you will get used to the feeling. Even this may hurt, when it breaches your maidenhead."

Her desire seemed to evaporate. Reason reasserted itself. She did not want him to do this. He had said it would hurt and she feared it would. Gone was all sense of wanting him to mount her, to fill her with his penis. She had never wanted that. Nay. He had done something to her, muddled her wits. She tried to move her legs together, but his hand was in the way, spreading her apart.

She stared at the black thing. It reminded her of his mask. Soft, black, leather. "Please," he whispered.

She remembered the servant's words. *Don't make it too easy for him.* "Nay," she said. "Nay."

She heard him sigh. He removed his hand from between her legs.

Had it really been that easy? If she had said "nay" long before, would he have left her alone? *Not* torn off her gown? *Not* touched her all over?

He got up and walked away from the bed. She could sense his dejection. It startled her. To think that she had some power. Some say over what her captor did to her.

She lifted her head and watched him across the room, observing his tall silhouette. What would he do now? Have his knight return her to the forest? Could it really be true, that all she had to do was say "nay" to him and he would leave her in peace?

She thought about going back to the forest, going home to her mother, her brothers and sisters. That life seemed bland and colorless now. She glanced around the room, observing the beauty of the furnishings. The soft, lovely glow of the myriad candles. She felt the incredible softness of the bed beneath her.

Then she looked at the man across the room. She remembered how he had touched her, the gentleness and skill he had used. The truth was that she wanted him to touch her some more. For a brief moment, she had wanted him . . . desired him.

If he always wore the mask, she would not have to think about that part of him. And if his hands were normal, perhaps the rest of him was also. She gazed at him assessingly, wondering exactly what all that black clothing concealed.

He was a coward, and a fool, Alexander thought bitterly. One word of protest and he was defeated. But he could not give up. Having proceeded this far, he could not turn back. Too much was at stake. Like his sanity. His peace of mind for the rest of his life.

It was not as if she had fought him. For a moment, she had seemed acquiescent, willing. It was the phallus she feared. He opened his hand and looked at it. It was the size of his smallest finger. Surely she could endure that much the first time. Women were meant to stretch, else they would never be able to bear children.

He turned back towards the bed, resolute once more. She might experience a little pain, but he would make it up to her.

He was coming back. Esmay adjusted her position on the bed. Would he force her now?

A huge black-shrouded presence. So close to her, so very close. She felt a thrill of excitement. Was it fear? Or something else?

"Spread your legs for me," he ordered.

She liked his voice. It was rich and deep. It made something throb inside her. Her thighs slid apart. She was on the fine edge between fear and the odd craving she'd experienced when he touched her earlier.

He put his hand between her legs. Stroked her. Her body reacted with a jolt. Closing her eyes, she spread her legs wider. Her body was yielding to him. It trusted that hand, had felt nothing but pleasure at the touch of that hand.

She felt him spreading her, fondling her innermost lips. The feeling was excruciating, intense pleasure intermingled with the threat of pain.

Abruptly, his hand left her. She opened her eyes, bereft. In amazement, she watched as he licked his fingers. Watched the movements of his mouth, his tongue. He put his moistened fingers on her vulva, adding to the moisture that was already there.

She closed her eyes again. Her body was taut with anticipation. She felt something push inside her. His finger. She could feel the rest of his hand pressed against her. He pushed the finger deeper. She gasped, then instinctively arched her hips, easing his way. Intense pressure. Her body trembled, then began to relax. It felt good. Soothing and yet arousing at the same time.

She wanted him to rub his hand against her, to use his other fingers to fondle her even as the firm pressure filled her. But he did not. He remained still, his finger buried inside her. Unmoving, almost rigid.

He was afraid to move. Afraid he would hurt her. He had never guessed that she was this small. He was using his littlest finger and it was only halfway in. How long would it take to stretch her? How would he bear it? He'd waited years to bed this woman. To sheathe himself deep inside her. Now, how many more days would he have to delay?

The sense of impatience he felt was almost unendurable. His cock ached with need, with the desperate urgency for release. Glancing down at her, naked, exposed, he could barely stand it. The urge to fill her—but not with his finger—overwhelmed him. Panting, he withdrew his hand. *Now, put the phallus in now, then leave her!* his mind screamed. *Leave her before you become a ravening beast, a fiend in fact as well as appearance.*

Grabbing the phallus, he pressed the small, rag-filled sheathe of leather against the wet, pink lips of her cunny, then eased it in as far as it would go. "I want you to keep it inside you," he whispered, hearing the harsh desperation in his voice. "Until I return." Then with one last glance at her enticing body, he strode to the door and went out.

Esmay let out her breath in a sigh, feeling restless and discomfited . The thing he had put inside her contributed to her turmoil. She was still aroused, uncomfortably so. Like his finger had, the leather object vaguely soothed her but, at the same time, inflamed a kind of craving.

She touched herself, feeling the end of the thing, spreading her slightly. Around it, she was wet. Moisture from her, moisture from his mouth. She played with the outer lips as he had. The leather object seemed to slip in deeper. But not deep enough. The tension that gripped her body did not ease.

She exhaled a sigh. When would he return? Would it be a few moments, or hours? She wanted him to come back. Wanted him to touch her some more. Her skin was still hot and tight. Everything seemed to throb, to ache. She touched her breasts, remembering how he had stroked them. It felt different when she touched herself. Much different. She missed his big, warm hands with their slight calluses.

She shuddered with delicious pleasure at the memory. She wanted those hands on her again. Wanted them to cup her bottom, to play with her vulva. Then she wanted him to . . . something. She was not sure why she felt so unsettled and quivery. What, exactly, did she desire? For him to mount her, ravish her, to put his member inside her?

She stood, clutching her arms around her body. The leather thing rubbed against the inner lips of her vulva, reminding her all too keenly of its presence. She wanted to take it out but she worried what would happen if she disobeyed him. Would he punish her? He was, after all, the Beast Lord.

Her mind turned again to his deformity. His hands were normal. It seemed strange that his hands should be like any other man's if his body were disfigured. Would she ever get to see his body, *his penis?*

She'd seen animals mating, knew that men were like them, that when aroused and ready to couple, the man's member grew big and rigid, not the little wobbly stem of flesh that her younger brothers possessed. Exactly *how* big was the Beast Lord?

She thought of his finger inside her. Bigger than that, certainly. That was why he'd put the leather thing inside of her, to stretch her. To ready her for him.

He wanted to mate with her. Her mother told her that men were always eager for coupling. Alyce, Esmay's mother, had not made much of it, saying that being tumbled was not that pleasant, no matter what men might say. It was messy business and not very satisfying for the woman. But it was the only way to get a babe, and she did love her children after all.

Esmay's mind wandered back a few years to the time before her father had been killed in a hunting accident. She vaguely remembered her parents making noises in their bed. Her father grunting and breathing heavily. In some part of her mind she knew they were coupling, like the animals did. She had accepted it as perfectly normal but not very interesting.

And then there was the notion of rape, a dread instilled in her, that if she were alone and saw a man whom she did not know, she should run away as fast as she could. Especially if it were a knight. She was told that such men would prey upon her, couple with her so brutally that she would be injured or even killed.

That was what she had expected when the knight grabbed her. And even worse when he brought her to the castle.

But what she had experienced with the Beast Lord was an altogether different thing than either her parents' nighttime activities or the barbaric ravishment she'd been warned against.

She glanced around the luxurious chamber. She was in a beautiful, almost magical place, and what he had done to her was like that, sublime, miraculous, something out of a dream. Hazy and vague, but entrancing.

She stood, intensely aware of the leather thing inside her. Then she heard the door creak open. The crone shuffled in, one green eye glinting. She gave Esmay a shrewd glance, then saw the pink gown on the floor. "Men," she said in disgust as she went to pick up the ruined garment. "They are such beasts."

Esmay thought it a very odd thing to say. But then, everything about the old woman was odd. After gathering up the gown, the crone turned back to Esmay. "Well, he obviously has not had his way with you yet. Told me to come back here and to ready you for bed, he did." She tsked, tsked. "I suppose I must find you another garment to sleep in."

The crone—Mabelle, she was called—went to a chest in the corner and pulled out a long garment made of creamy white fabric. She approached Esmay. "This should do for sleeping. Lift your arms."

Esmay obeyed and the woman pulled the garment over her head. "Huh," she said, looking at Esmay.

Absurdly, Esmay felt herself blushing. The fabric was so fine as to be almost transparent, revealing her nipples and the shadow of her pubic hair. Yet it was a beautiful gown, edged with some sort of embellishment around the low neck, as fine and delicate as the tiny white clusters of the angelica flower.

Mabelle went around the room, snuffing candles. Then she went to the bed and pulled the covers back. "Now, what else do you need?" she asked. "Some wine?" She nodded to the glass ewer and goblets on the table. "Perhaps we should braid your hair so it does not tangle?" Esmay started to nod, but Mabelle added, "Nay, I don't suppose he would want that. He desires you to look as you did when he first discovered you, 'a lovely wood nymph' is how he described you." She made a horrible grimace, distorting her grotesque countenance even more.

Discovered her? What did that mean? Hesitatingly, Esmay dared to ask the question that haunted her. "What . . . what does the Beast Lord want with me?"

Mabelle rolled her good eye. "If you haven't guessed that yet, you must be even more hen-witted than I thought!"

Esmay bristled. "Aren't you his servant? And did he not tell you to see to my needs?"

"Aye, anything you want, you should have, he said."

"Then perhaps you should not insult me!"

Mabelle gave a cackle of laughter. "Oh, indeed." She started towards the door. Esmay wanted to stop her, to plead with the servant to tell her a little more about her captor. But then she considered that such questions would only incite the old woman's contempt.

The door shut with a loud noise. Esmay heaved a sigh.

She crossed to the bed, feeling the leather object inside her with every step. It seemed to have worked its way down while she was standing and was halfway out of her now, pressing on her tender opening, almost hurting.

She lay on the bed and, pulling up the gown, tried to push it back inside of her. She stroked herself, feeling the little flutters of tension inside her body. How would she ever sleep? Did she dare take it out? What if he came for her in the night? What if he found that she had disobeyed him?

She gave a shudder. No matter the gentleness with which he

had touched her, he was still the Beast Lord. And his intentions toward her were not exactly benign.

Mabelle's mocking words rang out in her mind. Obviously, he meant to couple with her. But why was he being so careful, so cautious? Was it because he knew he was going to hurt her?

She wondered again about his penis. He had said he was big and she did not doubt him. The rest of him was not small, so why should that part be?

But what if it were also horribly deformed—like his face?

An image flashed into her mind—a thick, hideous member, covered with lumps and scaly skin, with a claw-like appendage on the end. Her heart began to race. Was he was preparing her from some truly awful, loathsome thing? Something so terrible that even he—a bestial, deformed monster—felt sorry for her!

She climbed out of the bed and went to the door. As she expected, it was locked. She went to the windows. They were all filled in with glass, fine, dazzling, expensive glass. She managed to open one of them, but found it too small a space to crawl through. And even if she could, she would surely fall to her death. She remembered the endless stairs the knight had climbed.

Her sense of panic intensified. Her legs trembled. Her hands shook. There was no escape.

She went to the table and examined the ornate glass ewer full of deep red liquid. What if she drank enough to make herself witless, like the men at the tavern at the crossroads? Then she would not be so aware when he hurt her. She shuddered at the thought.

She filled one of the goblets to the rim, took a large swallow, then grimaced at the taste. Not as sweet as cider. Tarter and fruitier than ale. She swallowed quickly, then took another drink.

It seemed to be warming her, making her limbs tingle. Abruptly, she remembered the leather object inside her. She put down the goblet and went to the bed and lay down. Pulling up the soft, fine gown, she reached between her legs and withdrew the thing. It was saturated with wetness. She dropped it on the bed. Then she got up and returned to the wine.

After the second glass, she found that the drink was relaxing her. Her legs felt wobbly, her skin, warm and flushed.

Clutching the goblet, she went back to the bed and lay down.

She took another swallow. The bed seemed to move beneath her. She was so warm, so very warm.

Sitting up, she pulled the shift over her head, then lay down again. She remembered him touching her, the delicious sensations he had aroused. Her fear began to ebb. Maybe he intended to hurt her, but before he did, perhaps he would touch her like that once more.

She arched her hips and began to fondle herself. Her eyes were closed. She concentrated, trying to move her hand the way he had. Her vulva was slick with wetness, hot moisture. Little ripples of sensation built inside her as she touched herself, exploring. She'd scarcely been aware of this part of herself before. Now it seemed to be the center of her.

She frowned in frustration. The more she touched herself, the more restless and dissatisfied she became.

She decided to put the leather thing back in. It slid in almost easily. His plan was working. Her body had already stretched a little. How much more would be necessary before he . . .

Nay. She would not think about it. She'd go mad if she dwelled on what was to come.

A vague sleepiness was overtaking her. Perhaps it was the wine. Or all the turmoil.

The candle by the bed flickered, guttering in wax. She blew it out and lay back.

In another part of the castle, in a different tower, Alexander paced, on fire with restless anticipation. How long must he wait before he went to her? How long before he could once more gaze upon her beauty and touch her? The night was passing so slowly. The hour candle burned with tedious, maddening sluggishness.

He went to the window and stared out into the darkness. Seeing no light in the tower across the ramparts, he decided she must be asleep. Abruptly, he headed for the door. If she was asleep, she would not even know he was there. What would it hurt to watch her while she dreamed?

Chapter Four

Alexander closed the door with slow deliberation. The latch fell into place with the faintest of clicks. He turned, holding out the candle, and started toward the bed. A few paces away, he halted. Her hair was strewn over the pillow, forming a dark nimbus around her face. Her delicate, feminine features held such an expression of serene innocence it made his breath catch. He could scarce believe that she was truly there, that the object of his longing was within his grasp.

It had been over a year ago that he'd first spied her walking in the woods, swinging a basket at her side and humming some playful melody. It was in the very early fall, when the leaves were beginning to turn. All winter, he had dreamed of her, that one memory warming him, transforming his long, cold, dark days into bright reveries of summer. As soon as the thaw came, he had ridden out wearing Drogor's armor, searching for her. He had discovered the places where she went and spent more than a few hours spying on his love, watching her from where he was hidden among the foliage.

But now she was his. He would possess her at last.

A twinge of guilt afflicted him but he shrugged it off. He was taking every possible precaution to make certain he did not hurt her.

He edged another step closer to the bed. Although the covers obscured most of her body, he could see that her arms and shoulders were bare. At the thought that she was naked beneath the silk coverlet, he swallowed thickly. Overwhelming desire seized his body, suffusing it with savage heat. He should not have come. *Just a moment or two longer,* he argued with himself. *All I want to do is look at her.*

Esmay came abruptly awake. A chilling sense immediately gripped her. Someone was standing by her bed. The candle he held dazzled her sleepy eyes, and it took a few seconds to realize that it was *him.* Her body went rigid.

He did nothing. Merely stood there, holding the taper. With the mask obscuring his face, he was a black, formless wraith, blending into the shadows. A scream rose in her throat. Yet she did not give vent to her cry of terror. For who would aid her, if she did scream?

"I . . . I'm sorry to disturb you," he said. He sounded genuinely distressed. "I couldn't sleep. But I shouldn't have ruined your slumber as well."

She saw him turn, as if to leave. "Wait!" she called.

He did not move at first. Then, by infinitesimal degrees, he shifted so he was facing her and waited. Esmay searched her mind, trying figure out why she had stopped him from leaving.

It was the fear of the unknown that so unnerved her. If she could confront what he meant to do to her, *what he was*, then perhaps she could overcome this suffocating dread. She raised herself to a sitting position, holding the coverlet protectively around her body. "I want to see your . . ." What should she call it? Penis, prick, dick, maypole, cock—she thought of all the terms she knew for a man's member. None of them sounded right.

"My . . . what?" His voice seemed huskier than she remembered. Dark and smoky and raw.

She licked her lips. "Your . . . penis." It was the most proper term she knew. This man was a lord, not some smirking village boy.

The silence was palpable. She heard him exhale. "My cock?" His voice was harsh, almost strangled sounding. But the way he said the word changed it, made it seemed intimate and . . . sexual. Not crude, but mysterious . . . intriguing. Rather like how he'd made her see her own body, experiencing it as something altogether wondrous, capable of astonishing pleasure.

Then his next word jarred her, made her consider what she'd asked. "Why?" he whispered.

She felt her face grow hot. How could she be talking about this . . . with *him*? But she had begun and there was no turning back. She *had* to know. "You said it was big. I want to know exactly *how* big." A lie. But better than the truth.

She heard him release his breath in a kind of hiss. Warning prickled down her spine. He was obviously reluctant to honor her request. Why? Did he fear what she would do when she saw him? Had he hoped that by caressing her and petting her that when he revealed his deformity, it would not matter?

But the longer he delayed, the more lurid and horrifying her imaginings grew. She thought of the skin of a toad, bumpy and uneven, of scars she'd seen, raw, red, and hideous, of Mabelle's twisted features, of putrefying sores . . .

He placed the candle in a holder on the table near the bed, then began undoing his belt. She forced herself to remain still.

He was very close to the bed. The light from the candle revealed his torso. He unlaced his shirt and pulled it over his head. His chest came in view. A man's chest, not a beast's shaggy body. Swirls of black hair, but no more than was normal for a man grown. Thick muscles flexing beneath the bronze skin. She released her breath in a sigh of relief.

Then he began to unfasten his braies. She swallowed.

His cock seemed to spring out of his clothing as if it had a life of its own. Long and thick, with a blunt, knobby tip. A maypole, indeed.

The sight affected her strangely. She felt apprehension at the thought of that huge thing being inside her. But her alarm was edged with a kind of tingling thrill. He was not deformed, not at all. He was . . . well shaped, symmetrical, if overlarge. The skin covering his cock appeared smooth, sleek. The tip was round and glossy, like a ripe damson plum.

Heaven help him, the way she looked at him! Alexander paused with his braies half undone, gritting his teeth, in a state of agonized arousal. Her gaze roved over him, as if she were fascinated by what she saw. Her breathing had quickened; her nostrils flared. At this moment, she looked less than innocent. Oh, aye, far less than innocent.

He had to remind himself that she was a virgin, that she had no idea of the effect she had on him. She knew nothing about a man's crude sexual appetites, could not imagine the thoughts that were going through his mind.

He imagined thrusting his cock into her mouth and feeling those plump, soft lips close around him. He thought of tearing away the covers that she held so carefully over her breasts, then lifting her legs high and pounding into her with hard, ruthless strokes. His cock quivered at the thought, and he considered that it was likely he would simply burst, ejaculating like an arrow shot from a crossbow. He fought to restrain himself. His fantasies did not include losing control like some oafish squire dandling a maid for the first time.

But then he saw her reach out her hand. He closed his eyes, not daring to watch. Her fingers traced the length of him, then touched the engorged, aching tip. Only with the greatest effort did he keep from exploding, clenching his fists and digging his nails into his hands so hard he could feel them pierce the skin. Focusing on the pain, he could almost block out the ecstatic sensations rioting through his brain as the hands of his angel, his consummate dream of a woman, caressed him.

She was unskilled, uncertain, handling him as if he were some delicate, precious thing. What he really wanted was for her to squeeze hard, to clasp him tight, to fill her hand with him. Someday, he would teach her. Someday.

He jerked back, pulling away from her, then opened his eyes. It had been a mistake to come here. She tested his determination, threatened all his noble intentions. And she had no idea of what she did to him. That was part of her incredible allure. That she was so naive, completely unaware of the delightful possibilities that a man and a woman could share. He meant to show her all those possibilities. Explore every one of them. Do to her every tantalizing thing he'd ever imagined doing to a woman. Share every mystery.

But not tonight. He'd only barely put the first phallus inside her. By his reckoning, it would be days before she was ready for him to fuck her.

A disheartening thought. But had he not waited nearly a year already? What were a few more days?

An eternity, his frustrated body complained. A veritable lifetime.

He began to rearrange his clothing, forcing his engorged cock back into the painfully confining clothes, fastening his belt, putting on his shirt. His skin was glazed with sweat. His hands trembled.

But once he had dressed himself, the devilish thoughts began to haunt him once more. *Just one look,* the inner voice taunted. *Make her drop the bedclothes, make her spread her legs and show you that the leather phallus is still inside her.*

A wave of carnal hunger rippled over him, so strong he felt his whole body convulse. "Now, it's your turn," he said. "Show me your sex." He knew he sounded hard, implacable. He couldn't help himself.

Her face changed, became wary, almost fearful. He wondered if she'd disobeyed him and taken the phallus out. Sudden anger mingled with his arousal. She was torturing him, whether she knew it or not. If she'd removed the phallus, it might have cost him another day of waiting. *Another day of going mad trying to restrain himself.*

"Show me!" he commanded.

What do I do now? The panicked question rose in her throat like a silent scream. Shortly before falling asleep, she'd taken out the stretching device. It bothered her, made it difficult for her to relax. With her wits muddled by the wine, she had not really thought about the consequences of removing it. She'd assumed he would not return until morning, that she would have plenty of time to put it back in. But he'd caught her unawares. She'd been so obsessed with *his* body, she had not considered that he might ask to see hers.

Slowly, she dropped the coverlet. Perhaps she could distract him with her breasts. She hesitated, watching him. In the dim light, his features obscured by the mask, it was difficult to guess his mood. Yet, she sensed that he was impatient, that he would not be easily deterred. There was no help for it, she decided. Better to do as he wished rather than angering him by stalling.

She threw the bedclothes aside and started to lie down.

"Nay," he said. "Sit on the edge of the bed and show me."

Taking a deep breath, she obeyed.

He moved close to the bed and dropped to his knees between her flexed thighs. Reaching for the candle, he moved it to the floor in front of him. She could feel the flame's heat against her skin. But it did not scorch her the way his gaze did. She felt like she was melting, her whole lower body as liquid as candle wax.

"Spread your cunny lips."

She closed her eyes, touching herself. Her vulva was wet and slippery. She wanted to tell him that she was already stretched, that all the barriers inside her had dissolved, that she did not need the leather object distending her.

"Where is it?" His voice was smooth and soft as ermine fur, yet she dreaded answering him.

"I took it out," she whispered. "I could not sleep."

Long moments passed. The tension built inside her.

"You must listen to me in this. I'm trying to spare you. I vow, I can't wait forever. I'm going to put another phallus inside you. A bigger one. Much bigger."

His words aroused her. She both dreaded and dreamed of being filled, stretched, penetrated. The memory of his cock teased her. Sweet, hard heat. Steel overlaid with soft, fluid skin. She wanted to tell him this, to advise him to use his own beguiling flesh to stretch her wide, to breach her innocence with the proud shaft of flesh between his thighs. But she was still afraid of him.

She heard him rising; she opened her eyes. He strode to the door and went out. She waited, breathing rapidly, not daring to move. If she did, he would be even angrier. Her thighs were wide open, the tender, wet opening of her sex exposed. She hoped he would return soon. Her whole body felt taut.

In moments, he was back in the room. He returned to the bed and seized the taper in the holder on the floor, then began to light the candles arranged around the room.

When the chamber was a blaze of light, he returned to the bed. He knelt down between her thighs. Esmay shivered with mingled fear and yearning.

He put his hand between her thighs. His palm felt warm and smooth against her vulva. Then, using his fingers, he began to stroke her. He teased apart the sensitive lips, playing. She closed her eyes and arched her hips.

"Aye," he murmured huskily. "Open for me, my love."

Her mind registered the endearment, while her body responded to the command. Streaks of fire coursed through her lower body, making her legs tremble. She shifted, writhing. Pleasure tinged with torment. With every stroke and caress, her restlessness grew more intense. She wanted, needed . . . something.

She felt him open her and ease his finger in. Hard, rigid, not exactly what she yearned for. Yet it soothed the worst of her craving.

But then the finger was withdrawn. She opened her eyes, fighting back a moan of protest. He held another leather device in his hand. It was nearly twice the size of the one he had put in earlier. Remembering the discomfort the other one had caused, she tensed. He placed it against her opening. Stroked her with it. The device felt soft, but not as soft as the skin of his cock. With one hand he spread her. With the other, he pushed the device against her inner lips.

Her body seemed to fight him. She did not want him to do this. This was not what she wanted at all.

He stopped pushing against her. She stiffened even more, wondering how he would punish her for refusing to accept the stretching device. But it was not exactly *her*. It was her body that refused it.

Alexander released his breath in a groan of frustration. He didn't want to hurt her, yet he surely would if he pushed the phallus inside her before she was ready. What was wrong? He'd fondled her, teased her, made her wet. Then, as soon as she saw the phallus, her arousal faded.

He sat back, considering. Somehow he had to excite her even more intensely, make her so weak and helpless with need, she would not fight him.

Dear God, she was beautiful! His aggravation faded as he stared at her, at the sublime vision she made, naked, legs spread, sex exposed. The sight made his throat go dry and his cock twitch with longing. His gaze focused on the wild rose blooming between her thighs. He wanted to kiss her there, to lap the nectar from her sweet, lush petals.

Drawn by the irresistible urge, he leaned forward. The thought of the mask almost deterred him, but he considered that if he ate with it on, then he could surely manage this.

Esmay tensed as the Beast Lord put a hand on either thigh. He brought his face near her crotch. Sweet heaven, he was not really going to . . . The half-finished thought dissolved at the feeling of gentle pressure on her most sensitive parts. His mouth was against her, kissing her. Then he was licking her. She experienced a tiny dart of embarrassment, then her doubts were overwhelmed by a tide of exquisite pleasure.

Reason, fear—all thoughts dissolved. She was nothing more than a trembling mass of fantastic sensation. Dimly, she was aware of different textures playing upon her exposed, stretched flesh. Soft lips, hard teeth, the edges of mask, rough yet tantalizing. And then his tongue. Gentle, exhilarating, provoking. She felt as if her body would turn itself inside out, so aroused and hungry she was. Each touch of mouth and tongue drove her closer to the edge of some abyss. She fought going over and being swallowed by the consuming passion. And yet the pull was irresistible, and when he thrust his tongue inside her, her will gave out. A dark, violent oblivion, but suffused with sweetness and lit with pricks of starlight.

She came to herself, weak and panting. When she opened her eyes, she saw that he held the leather device in his hand. As he pushed it against her quivering, dripping opening, she lay back, utterly passive. Then the pressure inside her stirred something to life. Incredibly, she felt the arousal building once again.

He stood and adjusted his clothing. His breathing sounded hard and fast. She sat up, aware that he was leaving her. The idea made her feel bereft and empty. She wanted to call out, to say something to make him stay. But no words formed in her fuzzy, half-coherent mind.

The click of the door latch made her jump. She let out a long sigh as she realized that she was alone. A musky, animal odor filled the air. It took her a moment to decide that it was the heated scent of her own release. Suddenly, she was cold, although the room still blazed with candles.

Alexander leaned against the wall in the stairwell below the tower room, trembling all over. It had taken all his will to leave her. To abandon the very embodiment of his erotic dreams. Oh, how badly had he wanted to finish what he had begun. To fill her quivering, juicy cunny. To fill her deep and hard, lunging over and over and then pouring his come into her, deep, deep, so deep inside her.

He took a ravaged breath. The tiny shred of reason remaining to him assured him that he had done the right thing. His fantasies were very close to rape, and that was hardly the means to make her fall in love with him. *The curse,* he told himself, *remember the curse. Don't squander what trust you've won from her for the sake of your unholy passion.*

But there was another reason he held back. She was so young and lovely, so pure. The thought of hurting her, frightening her, horrified him. He didn't want her to think him a beast . . . even though he was the Beast Lord. He wanted her to care for him, not only because of the curse but because he needed her to love him. Needed it with his whole soul.

Exhaling, he gathered himself together and began to stagger down the stairs. He must get away from her, far, far away.

Esmay climbed from the bed and, holding her arms around herself, began to blow out the candles. With every step, little tremors shook her, but it wasn't from cold. She could feel the leather device inside her, tormenting. It was so much bigger than the first one, big enough to almost hurt, to push her sensitized body to the edge of arousal but no further. She wanted it out, wanted to be able to sleep.

Either that, or she wanted *him* to come back and touch her and kiss her cunny some more. Why had he left her? Was it some plan to torture her? To make her go mad with craving?

He said he must stretch her or he would hurt her, but she knew his plan was not the way it was usually done. When a man took a woman to wife, there were jests at the wedding about the size of the man's cock, but when the couple went to bed together, the man just did it, thrusting into the woman and tearing her maidenhead. She might feel pain and there would be some blood, but then it was over and she was as well as ever.

Esmay stopped blowing out candles. Had the device torn her maidenhead? Was she bleeding? She took one of the candles and went back to the bed. Sitting on the edge of it, she pulled the device out and examined it. There did seem to be some blood. She put down the candle and touched herself. More blood.

She felt a sense of sadness, realizing that she was a virgin no more. Except . . . she still felt like a virgin. She still didn't know what it felt like to lie with a man. Sadness was replaced by frustration. If she were going to lose her maidenhead, she wanted to know all of it.

She looked at the device. Should she put it back inside? What if he returned and found she had disobeyed him once again? Would he put another, larger device inside her? And would he kiss her and mouth her cunny to make her wet and open first?

A tremor of remembered ecstasy went through her. The way he "punished" her for removing the first device had been extremely satisfying. As far as she was concerned, he could do it anytime he wished!

With shock, she realized that she was no longer afraid of the Beast Lord. Perhaps knowing that his body was normal had lessened her fear. Or maybe it was the fact that so far he had not hurt her, had barely even caused her discomfort. But whatever it was, her dread of him was completely gone. If anything, she missed him. She wanted him to come back. She wanted to stroke his cock some more. For him to kiss her cunny and put his tongue inside her.

She shivered again, breasts tingling, groin aching. Then she blew out the rest of the candles and went to bed.

In the morning, the crone brought her food. Esmay, wearing the shift, sat at the table and ate the honey and bread on the tray while Mabelle tidied the room. She stripped the sheets off the bed and replaced them with clean ones and put out new candles. After Esmay had eaten, the crone brought her water for washing and left again. Esmay washed her face and hands and then her crotch. She felt vaguely sore, but also extremely sensitive, almost aroused. She hurried to finish, not wanting Mabelle to come in before she was done.

Mabelle returned and combed out Esmay's hair. She dug in the clothing chest and came back with a gown of pure creamy white. Like the pink garment, it was made of silk and was soft and fine and beautiful. Then Mabelle brought her jewelry—earbobs and a necklace of round beads as lustrous as the gown. "They're pearls," she told Esmay. "They come from the sea." Mabelle helped her put on the necklace and earbobs, then stepped back. She gave a low cackle. "I wonder if he will manage the rest of his scheme. I just wonder."

Esmay was startled. "What scheme?" she asked.

Mabelle cackled again. "Your maidenhead is not all he desires. You've hardly served your purpose yet." She turned and left the room.

Esmay stared after the servant. If ravishment was not the Beast Lord's goal, then what did he want? She glanced around the beautiful room. Her captor had gone to a great deal of trouble to bring her here and arrange everything—the clothing, the leather devices, the long drawn-out way he coaxed her to accept his touch, his body. Why had he done all this, planned every detail so carefully? *You've hardly served your purpose yet*—the crone's word echoed in her mind, making her uneasy. Esmay began to pace. What did he really want of her? She touched the beautiful garment she wore. White, the color of purity . . . and of sacrifice.

She went to the window and looked out. Staring at the view of the peaceful valley beyond the castle, she tried to calm herself. In the distance, the rich green of the forest floated off into the mist at the edge of the horizon. As she gazed at it, her hand crept lower, touching her breast. Her nipples immediately went taut. It was as if he had taught her body to be keenly sensitive to the merest touch. Remembering the feel of his hands on her, she relaxed slightly.

Then another thought came to her—what if he loved her slowly and carefully, then used those same strong, capable hands to break her neck?

Alexander paused at the rain barrel at the edge of the practice field and, using the wooden dipper, sluiced water over his head and torso. The cool water washed away the sweat and dust, but did nothing to ease the fiery craving in his groin. Nothing eased it. Nothing.

He tried riding until he was exhausted, galloping his destrier over the open country, jumping the thorn hedges between fields, testing the absolute limits of his mount. Then, when the beast was lathered and blowing, he'd returned to the castle, gone to the practice yard, and engaged Drogor in a fierce bout of swordplay. The exertion had tired his muscles, but did nothing to relieve the tight, painful ache in his balls.

He turned and gazed at the castle, feeling himself drawn inexorably towards that one tower room. There was no help for it. He had to go to her, had to see her.

He went to the bathing chamber. After soaping and giving himself a good dousing, he dressed in clean garments. Still feeling as fresh and eager as he had that morning, he made his way to the other end of the castle and climbed the stairs to the tower.

Chapter Five

Esmay sat at the table, staring at the goblet of wine in her hand. At the sound of the door opening, her nerveless fingers released the goblet and it toppled over and spilled. She turned to face the door.

She had forgotten how big he was, how terrifying. The mask, the black garments he wore—he entered the room like a specter of death. She came slowly to her feet, wanting to flee. But there was nowhere to run.

For a time, he simply seemed to look at her. She was acutely aware of the thin fabric of the gown she wore, then she reminded herself that he had seen her naked already. Nay, more than that. He had seen her innermost parts and probed the deepest secrets of her body. A spasm of remembered pleasure throbbed between her legs. She ignored it. In the long hours that she'd waited for him, she had come to a decision. She was going to make him tell her the real reason he'd brought her here.

He took a step nearer. "Nay," she said. He froze instantly. There was not a sound in the room, except for her pulse thudding in her ears. To her, it sounded like thunder. "I want to know," she said, "I want to know what you want from me."

His voice was throaty, harsh. "I would think that would be clear. When the time is right, I will penetrate you . . . fill you with my flesh."

His flesh—that hot, thick rod between his thighs. A quiver of need echoed inside her. She forced her desire aside. "But then, after that . . . what will you do with me after that?" He did not answer, and her dread intensified. "Is there something else?" she demanded. "Some other reason you've brought me here?"

"I can't tell you what it is."

"Why?"

One heartbeat passed. Two. "I can't tell you because . . . it's forbidden."

Forbidden. She took a step back, the hair on the back of her neck prickling. He'd had her abducted, imprisoned her in this tower, now he would not tell her what he wanted with her. It was all so sinister. Her breath came hard and fast. The urge to flee became overwhelming.

He held out his hand. "Please," he said. "Don't be frightened of me. I mean you no harm. I vow it."

She wanted to believe him. The sight of his hand, that hand that had touched her with such consummate gentleness, made her want desperately to accept his words as true.

He took another step toward her. "Let me touch you," he whispered. "Let me caress you and love you as I did before."

Impossible desire. The sound of his voice, so soft and tender, yet so male, so dark and rich and full of lust, tore at her will and inundated her senses. He took another step nearer. She could feel her resolve slipping away, feel her body surrendering. Her body knew this man, accepted him, hungered for him.

He came and stood next to her. She wished he weren't wearing the mask. She wanted him to kiss her, to feel those skilled, arousing lips against hers. He reached out and his fingers gently grazed her neck. For a second, she thought of those hands clutched around her throat, then the image was forgotten as his caress moved lower. He rubbed her breasts through the soft fabric of the gown, teasing her nipples to tautness. Then he bent down and mouthed them, sucking first one nipple deep into his mouth, then the other. Tremors of anticipation coursed downward, striking arrowtips of pleasure in her groin.

She arched her back, offering herself. He gave a kind of growl, a low rumble of need and hunger, then he began to ease up the gown until he could cup her bare buttocks. He kneaded them, making her legs go weak and her cunny clench with longing. At last he moved his fingers down the crack of her bottom. He spread her slightly, then began to play with the wet, heated, sensitive flesh of her vulva, even as he still gripped her buttocks in his strong, hard hands. He was opening her, making her ready.

Ahhhh, she was so ready! She twisted and shivered, moaning.

"Where is it?" he murmured. "Where is the phallus I put inside you?"

She went rigid, then released her breath in a sigh, beyond caring what he thought of her disobedience. "I took it out. I don't like it. Please, please fill me with *you*. I want it. I'm ready . . . please . . ." The last word was a gasp.

"I don't want to hurt you."

"You won't hurt me," she pleaded. "I've already bled. My maidenhead was breached when you put the second device inside me." His hands still fondled her, tormenting. "Please . . ." she begged. "I will die if I don't have it."

He groaned. "I won't be able to be gentle. I won't be able to hold back."

"Give it to me! Fill me! Fuck me!" Hearing her own words, she was shocked. But her need was that great, that overwhelming. The way he touched her was excruciating. She could feel her cunny lips, dripping wet, enflamed and distended, feel her body screaming for release.

She jerked away from him and pulled the gown over her head. Then she went to the bed, lay back, and spread her legs. With both hands she framed the V of her crotch, spreading the outer lips of her vulva. Wordlessly, she waited.

He unlaced his shirt and shrugged it off, then undid the fastening of his braies. She watched with delight as his cock sprang out. He started to approach, but she shook her head. "Nay, take off everything." Even the mask. Although she thought the words, she did not say them. She was not certain she was ready for that.

He sat down on a stool to remove his braies and boots. As he undressed, she stared at his cock, thrusting out between his thighs, greedily surveying the satisfying length and width of it, the thick, yet sleek tip, like the head of a lance.

Finally, he stood and approached the bed, gloriously naked. She could see his balls beneath his upthrust cock. They were big and heavy and swollen-looking, full of his seed. His seed that he would put inside her. She wondered briefly if there would be a babe, and if it, too, would be a monster. Then he climbed on the bed and all rational thought left her. He braced himself over her and took his cock in his hand. She closed her eyes, wanting nothing to interfere with the sensation.

Sweet fulfillment.

She felt the pressure of his thick, firm flesh against her tender parts, the exquisite sense of him entering her. She helped him by opening her legs wider and lifting her hips. Her body stretched around him, drawing him deeper, deeper and deeper. She gave a gasp, suddenly realizing the limits of her own body. But then he began to touch her with his hand, rubbing the outer lips of her cunny, tantalizing them, making her stretch even further. She could feel him at the entrance to her womb, and she opened her eyes to see how much more of him she must take. A good three inches had still not breached her. She closed her eyes, arching her back and willing herself to take more of him.

Alexander gritted his teeth. Torment, but of a delightful kind. He could feel her squeezing him tight, his cock clasped in a most enthralling embrace, surrounded by silky, hot flesh. He wanted to move, but he was not near in yet. Somehow he must arouse her even more, make her yield to him, utterly surrender.

He was fondling her already, but now he did so with a purpose. Finding the places where she was most sensitive, the areas that when touched made her whimper. There seemed to be a spot at the very apex of her cleft. Aye, that was it. The slightest pressure there made her whole body jerk. And with each movement his cock slid in a little deeper.

He kept up his caressing until he felt her go rigid. As she screamed her release, he thrust himself all the way. She seemed to melt beneath him, and as she did so, he gave in to his own need and began to stroke deep and hard.

Violent ecstasy. His every dream fulfilled. She was so soft and lithe and female. Her cunny tight, miraculous perfection. She met each thrust with a hungry urgency of her own. He would not have believed it, but she did want it! Wanted his cock deep inside her. Wanted to be fucked!

Madness tore through his brain. A white hot heat of unbelievable gratification and pleasure. And then his release, blinding him. He felt himself pour into her. Hot, thick, gushing deep. . . .

He awoke in paradise, sprawled on her soft, lovely, female body. A sense of sublime completion washed over him. He savored it a moment, then moved onto his side next to her and reached to stroke her cheek. She was so beautiful, and never more so than at this moment. Her skin seemed to glow. Her eyes were a misty, wild golden green.

She was watching him, but he could not discern her mood. "Are you satisfied?" he asked. "Was it all that you thought it would be?"

How could she answer? Esmay wondered. It had been incredible. Overwhelming. Her body still sang with bliss. First, he had brought her to her peak with his hand, then as the aftermath of that climax still shimmered inside her, he had driven her over the edge yet again, thrusting and pounding inside her, making her feel things she had not dreamed possible. She had been right in thinking that his cock was the secret to her deepest pleasure. The feel of him inside her, the incredible intimacy, it had made her see him differently.

Which was why there was no easy answer to his question. If she told him that she was satisfied, what would he do? Send her back to the forest? Proceed with the rest of his plan—whatever it was? She did not want things to be changed between them.

So, she said nothing, just looked at him as he lay beside her. After a time, he murmured thickly, "There *is* more I can show you." She could sense his gaze on her crotch. "Now that you are properly stretched, there is no point not taking advantage of the situation."

A thrill of desire went through her. He wanted her again.

Her thighs slid apart, as if they had a will of their own. She could feel how wet she was, slick with his seed as well as her own juices. He fondled her lightly, dipping his fingers in the wetness, using quick strokes to make her breathing catch. "Mmmm," he murmured. Then he rose from the bed.

She watched, admiring the backside of his body as he moved across the room. The broad, well-muscled shoulders, the narrow hips, the tantalizing shape of his buttocks. From this angle, with the mask out of sight, he seemed like an ordinary man. Nay, not ordinary. She'd never known a man's body could look so sleek and strong and beautiful.

He turned and approached the bed. Her gaze focused on the mask and she realized she wanted him to take it off. After what he had shown her, what he had done to her, it really did not matter what he looked like, how repulsive his face might be. She could see his mouth and eyes already, and they were pleasing and attractive. Even if the rest of his countenance was scarred or deformed, she knew she could get used to how he looked.

As he neared the bed, she saw that he had a cloth in his hand. He leaned over and used it to wipe the wetness between her legs. The damp linen felt deliciously rough against her tender flesh. She looked up at him. "Take the mask off."

He went completely still, his hand frozen between her thighs. Then, without answering, he finished cleaning her.

He returned the cloth to the wash basin in the corner, then came back to the bed. She saw that he was not aroused anymore. It startled her to see how much smaller his cock was when flaccid. His whole demeanor had changed. He appeared uneasy, almost distressed.

"Please," she said. "Take the mask off."

"Nay."

"Why not."

"Because . . ." His voice was ravaged. "I don't want to ruin this."

"You won't," she whispered. "The rest of you is beautiful. Even if your face is not . . . perfect, it will not matter to me."

He slumped down on the bed. "You don't understand. When the curse first came upon me and my father saw my face, he ran off screaming. The servants were the same."

"When was this?"

"I was thirteen when the curse took hold." His voice grew even harsher, raw with pain.

"Tell me about the curse."

"My father raped my mother, a witchwoman in the village. Afterwards, she laid a curse upon him, that when I—his son— reached manhood, I would turn into a monster."

"But that's so unfair! Why punish you for your father's evil?"

He shook his head. "I don't know why. My mother died when I was born, so there was no way to ask her. I know I looked normal as a baby, as a young boy. It's only when my voice and body began to mature that I took on this hideous appearance."

"So cruel." She touched his arm, thinking of how shy and embarrassed she had been at thirteen. It was a terribly uncomfortable age anyway, but he had been forced to endure this added misery of turning into a monster.

Yet, how monstrous could he be? Every part of him was visible except for his face. His nose, forehead, chin, and cheeks, that was all that the mask covered. How could those few inches of skin matter so much?

She gazed at the rest of him, admiring the fabulous beauty of his body. He was like an animal, so gracefully made, so formidably, intriguingly male.

She moved her hand to stroke his chest, delighting in the feel of the coarse hair and the smooth skin beneath. The little bump of his nipple also enticed her and she rubbed it until it grew hard beneath her fingers. He released his breath in a gusty sigh.

She explored further, easing her hand down his belly. She expected to find soft, dangling flesh, but he was already growing hard. As she stroked him, he swelled and grew, becoming that sleek, massive rod she had fondled once before. She heard him catch his breath as she played with the tip, running her finger over the opening at the end, like a little eye, feeling him shudder and twitch as she caressed him.

She moved her hand to cup his balls. They felt as solid and fascinating as she had expected. Big, solid, the prize of his manhood. She moved her hand back to his cock and traced the long, glossy-skinned length of it. Back to the tip, so different in texture, silky soft, as tender as her own private parts. She thought of him mouthing and kissing her there and knew she wanted to do the same to him. Without letting go of him, she went down on her knees between his legs.

"What are you doing?" he rasped.

"I want to . . . kiss you . . . suck you." She could sense the tension in his body, then all at once, he relaxed. He put his hands behind him and leaned back on the bed. His cock jutted out, tempting, magical.

She licked the opening on the end, tasting him, then she drew the big, plummy tip into her mouth. He gasped. She sought to draw him deeper, to see how much of him her mouth could take. A bare half of that thick shaft could she swallow.

She sucked at him, then drew back and teased the tip, using her lips and tongue and teeth to play upon him, as he had done to her. He groaned, then made several unintelligible sounds in his throat. At this moment, she realized, it was she who had power over him. His cock grew harder and harder. When she started to fondle his balls as she sucked him, he took hold of her head and pulled her away from him. "Stop! No more!" he cried.

"Why not?"

"Because . . . I . . . can't . . . bear . . . it," he panted.

"What do you want?" she asked coyly. She knew full well what he would say and that it was what she wanted, too. But first she would bargain with him, to take off the mask.

"I want to fuck you," he said hoarsely. "I want to spill my come deep inside your hot, tight cunny."

Her body clenched with desire at his words. But she said, "First, you must take the mask off."

"Why?" He was still breathless, gasping.

"So I can see you, all of you."

"I've told you—"

"And it changes nothing," she insisted.

Moments passed. She could sense him struggling with himself, his arousal and need fighting the agonized self-loathing he felt. If he refused to take off the mask, she could do nothing. If he were determined to fuck her, she would not deny him. "Please," she said. "I pleasured you as you did me. But I want you to do this one other thing for me. I promise I will not run away screaming."

There could be nothing so terrible under the mask that she

could not deal with it. It might take her a moment or two to adjust, but she believed she would be able to hide any dismay she felt for that short while.

"All right," he said. "But I will not take it off until I am inside you."

She nodded, satisfied. That way, it would be easier for her to bear as well. The rapturous pleasure she felt when he was inside her would overwhelm any other response.

He stood and, taking her hands, drew her up with him. He embraced her, leaning over her to stroke and knead her buttocks. In seconds, she was limp and helpless, leaning against him for support. He backed her slowly across the room until her hips bumped against the table. He leaned over her and pushed everything off the table, then abruptly turned her around so she was facing the table. He slid his hand between her buttocks and began to play with her. She clutched the table for support, clinging to the cloth-covered surface as waves of pleasure sang through her body.

For a moment he left her. She tried to catch her breath. Her thoughts were ajumble, her body pulsing with sensation. Before she knew what was happening, he was behind her once more. He put a pillow on the table, then lifted her onto it so her buttocks faced him. His hand found her vulva, teasing and stroking. She spread her legs to give him better access. The sensation of his cock against her engorged, aching opening thrilled her, but only as he slid into her did she realize what he had done. He would take the mask off now and she would not be able to see him.

His trick angered her, but she could not focus her thoughts to protest. He pushed in deeper, impaling her, spreading her wide. The pressure was almost unbearable. She feared she would faint from the pure overwhelming sensation of his huge cock inside her. But then he reached around and began to play with her cleft. As he fondled her, the pressure seemed to ease and the unendurable fullness gave way to ecstatic pleasure. She heard herself shriek. Her body convulsed. Her thoughts dissolved into a swirl of light and dizzying color.

When she gathered her wits once more, he was still inside her, unmoving, deep. "Now you are inside me," she panted. "You must take the mask off."

"I already have."

She started to turn, to look at her, but at the same time, he began to thrust into her. With each thrust, her will, her reason whirled away. Once again she was caught up in a maelstrom of sensation. She peaked again. And then again. Gasping, sweating, her body trembling. And still he moved inside her.

But this time, she fought the rising tide of her climax, fought the urge to close her eyes and stiffen with rapture. Even as the deep strokes of his cock inside her grew faster and more intense, she twisted her body to catch a glimpse of him . . . and froze in stunned amazement.

He was dimly aware of startled gold-green eyes meeting his own gaze. But he was too far gone, too caught up in his own burgeoning climax to react. At this moment, nothing mattered but the furious, violent need wracking his body. The abyss of pure, mindless pleasure loomed ahead. He plunged in, drowning, sinking deep, deep, deep.

Only as the lapping waves of sensation faded did he have the presence of mind to pull himself out of her and turn away. He still clutched the mask in his left hand, and he hurried to pull it over his head. She was suddenly beside him, grabbing his hand. "Nay," she said. "Don't put it back on. I've *seen* you."

He sighed, recalling the startled expression he'd seen on her face right before he climaxed. It was too late. He sighed again.

She touched his arm. "It's all right. In fact, it's better than all right. There's nothing wrong with you. Nothing."

What an angel she was. Only someone so innocent and tenderhearted would seek to spare his feelings like this, to pretend that he was not a monster. But he had seen the shock. No matter what she said, he would not believe her. He knew the truth. The curse was still in effect. Which meant that she did not love him. And now she never would, now that she had seen him. He wanted to weep.

"Please. Believe me. Whatever people have led you to think about your appearance is a lie. Have someone bring a mirror. I'll show you."

"A mirror?" Alexander went rigid. He remembered the last time he had looked in a mirror. The face staring back at him had horrified even him. Disgusting, repulsive, that's what he was. The Beast Lord. And so he would remain to his dying day. If Esmay could not come to care for him, then no woman could. They'd shared so much pleasure together. He'd hoped that would be enough. The realization that it was not, shattered his dreams.

"A mirror," she prompted. "We need a mirror."

"There are no mirrors at Blackhurst. I had them all destroyed years ago."

"Have Mabelle ask among the women of the castle. I'm certain one of them has a mirror hidden away."

"Nay." He shook his head. "I can't bear it."

"You're being silly. Here, I'll ring the bell for Mabelle." She went to the bell rope and pulled it. "We'll ask her to fetch a mirror. Or you can show her your face and ask her if there is anything wrong with it."

"Nay." He hurriedly pulled the mask over his face and began to fasten it. "I won't let anyone see me but you."

She gave a sort of laugh, then shook her head.

Mabelle appeared and Esmay told him what they wanted. The servant shot him a quizzical look. Alexander turned away.

While they waited for Mabelle to return, Alexander went over things in his mind. He knew what he would see in the mirror, but maybe it didn't matter. If Esmay could accept him for what he was, then his life would not be so terrible. It hurt that she didn't love him, but maybe, over time . . .

He went to her where she sat on the bed. She had put the gown back on before Mabelle came in. He reached out and touched her breast through the thin fabric, waiting for her to flinch. She smiled and said teasingly, "Not had enough yet? Goodness, but you are insatiable."

He withdrew his hand, considering. His touch did not seem to distress her. Could it be true that she really didn't care what he looked like?

He heard the door open. Mabelle came in, carrying a wooden-backed mirror. Alexander knew a twinge of irritation to realize that someone at Blackhurst had defied his command. "Give me the mirror and leave us," he told the servant. Mabelle gave a kind of smirk and went out.

Esmay stood. "I'll hold the mirror. Now, take off your mask and look."

He handed her the mirror, then took a deep breath, bracing himself. He unfastened the mask and pulled it off, but still held it in his hand, ready to put it back on as soon as he'd had the barest glimpse. Esmay held the mirror up, near her face. He looked at her, admiring her beauty, thinking that it was a kind of abomination that someone like him should get anywhere near such loveliness. Then, with his heart in his stomach, he gazed at his reflection. A wave of shock went through him.

Nay, it could not be true! It was a trick!

He brought his hands to his face, feeling the smooth skin, the aquiline nose. He looked . . . normal, completely normal. Giddy excitement swept him. He gave an exultant laugh, then looked at Esmay. The delight on her face was real. Of course it was. She feared she'd bedded a monster, only to find out that he looked no different from any other man. "The curse," he said. "The curse is broken."

He wanted to dance around the room, to run around like an excited child. Then he thought of his people, all the servants and knights and retainers in the castle. He wanted them to know that the curse was over, that he was himself again. He embraced Esmay and ran from the room. On the stairs he almost stumbled. He caught himself at the last moment, thinking how terrible it would be if he ruined his newfound attractiveness by falling down the stairs. He gave a half-crazed laugh and continued his rapid descent.

He ran into the great hall, gesturing wildly. "Look at me! Look at me! The curse is finished! I look like myself again." Servants paused in their tasks and stared at him. The knights seated at the tables stopped eating. Drogor's wife, sewing by the window, stood up and let her handiwork drop to the floor. No one moved for a time, and Alexander froze, wondering for a moment if he were mistaken. Had it been some magical apparition he'd seen in the mirror? He started to reach for his face, to reassure himself, then all at once the people in the hall began to cheer. Drogor rose and came to Alexander, beaming. "My lord, this is wonderful! Simply wonderful! Not only are you no longer repulsive, but I would say in fact, you were downright comely!"

Elen, Drogor's wife, approached, nodding. "Aye, my lord. You are handsome, quite handsome."

Alexander gave a giddy laugh. "I must show everyone. "Where's Mabelle? She's always told me that I should not let my deformity rule my life. But she was wrong. Now, look at all of you. You smile at me instead of flinching. Approach me instead of fleeing." He laughed again.

"I saw Mabelle leave the castle," Drogor said. "She probably went to the herb garden, where she's always fussing."

Alexander nodded and hurried off in search of the old woman. He didn't know why it mattered so much that she knew about the curse, but somehow it did. She'd been such a constant in his life since he could remember. She was the only person—besides Drogor, who shaved him—that he'd ever allowed to see him without the mask. Although she irritated him much of the time, he was fond of Mabelle, and he wanted her to know about his good fortune.

Esmay got up from the bed and began to pace around the room. It seemed like a long time had passed since her lover left. Was he ever coming back?

She came to a halt, struck by the thought that now that the Beast Lord—or the man who used to be the Beast Lord—was no longer deformed and repulsive, he would be able to get any woman he wanted. Not by abducting her and holding her prisoner as he had with Esmay, but by seducing her with his handsome face. He had everything any woman would want—wealth, power, and now extreme good looks. Why should he settle for a penniless village girl when he could have an heiress?

The pain twisted inside her, and she jerked as she heard the door open. Was he finally coming back? Did he care for her after all? Her hope sprang to life, then faded when she saw Mabelle standing there. The old crone smiled at her, but it wasn't an entirely pleasant expression. "They say you've broken the spell," she said. "That milord is normal again."

"The curse?" Esmay exclaimed. "How did I break it?"

"You haven't heard the tale? Of how if milord could find a woman to fall in love with him, the curse would be broken and he would look as he had before? Did you not know that was why he brought you here?"

Esmay turned away. So that was why he had been so careful with her, had tried so hard not to hurt her. He had not wanted her maidenhead, but her heart.

Tears filled her eyes. She'd thought that he'd cared for her, that he'd chosen her because he felt something special for her. But it was more likely that he'd simply thought her so young and naïve and unimportant that she would be easy to seduce, easy to manipulate.

With a half-sob, she realized that she'd reacted exactly as he hoped. At first she'd felt mostly pity, wanting to help him, this tormented, vulnerable man who seemed to need her so much. But gradually, pity had turned to love. She was beguiled by his gentleness, the way he behaved as if she were the most beautiful woman in the world. And then there was the enthralling way he'd touched her, the incredible things he made her feel. He'd suborned her heart even as he captivated her body.

It was all very clever, his subtle manipulation of her feelings. Yet even knowing what he'd done changed nothing. She still loved him. There seemed to be no way to alter what was in her stupid, foolish heart. Sighing, she said, "What's going to happen to me now?"

"What do you mean?"

"He doesn't need me anymore. He could have any woman."

"You'll have to ask him when he comes back. Right now, he's busy showing everyone in the world his stunningly handsome face. Like a child with a new toy." Mabelle gave a snort of disgust. "I worry about him, if he's learned anything at all from this. Or if he will end up like his wretched father after all."

Mabelle's words puzzled Esmay, but she was too caught up in her own concerns to think much about them. She glanced around the room. He was likely not coming back for a while, having better things to do. When he returned, she would not be there. She had her pride left, even if he'd taken everything else. She motioned to the clothes chest. "Is there anything in there that I could actually wear outdoors? Something sturdy and practical? And I'll need some shoes as well."

Mabelle cocked a brow. "You're leaving?"

Esmay nodded, feeling her heart break.

Chapter Six

"There you are!" Alexander burst into the tower room. "I've been looking all over for you, Mabelle." As she continued to fuss with the things in the chest, he added impatiently, "Come on, look at me, you're the only one who hasn't seen! The curse is no more! Can you believe it?"

Mabelle got up slowly and turned to gaze at him. There was no expression on her twisted countenance as she said tonelessly, "Aye, the curse is over."

"You aren't happy for me?"

Mabelle shrugged. "We'll see if being handsome does you any good."

Alexander stared at her, puzzled, then suddenly looked around. "Where's Esmay?"

Mabelle shrugged again. "Gone."

"Gone? Gone where?" Some of his elation vanished, and he felt a stab of guilt. For a time, he'd forgotten Esmay.

"Back to her home, I suppose."

"But why?" Why would she leave now, when the curse was over and he had a chance at happiness?

"I imagine she feels that she's served her purpose."

He approached Mabelle. "What do you mean? What did you say to her?"

"I told her about the curse and that you had brought her here to end it."

"But there was more to it than that!" he protested. "I love her. And she loves me. She must, or the curse would not be broken!"

Mabelle gave him a strange look. "Are you so sure?"

"Of course! The spell can only be broken when a woman falls in love with me!"

"Hmmm," Mabelle said. "What if I told you that I am the one who started that tale about there being a remedy to the curse? That, in fact, the curse can only be lifted by the sorceress who cast the spell."

He was really puzzled now. Why was Mabelle talking about things that were no longer important? The curse was over. What did it matter how the end had come about? "The sorceress who cast the spell was my mother," he said coldly. "And she is dead, so there is no way she could have lifted it."

"Are you so certain she is dead?"

"Of course. She died at my birth. Everyone knows that."

"And who raised you? Who fed you and cared for you?"

"Why, you did. But what does that have to do with it?"

"Perhaps I am your mother."

Alexander gaped at her. Had the old crone lost her wits? "You can't be. My mother was beautiful! Everyone says so!"

"And I am . . . grotesque? Repulsive? Hideous? Just as you were until very recently." Mabelle's good eye fixed on him with a coldness that seemed to reach inside him. What was she saying? What did she want from him? "I did not say that," he protested. "I have never called you those things."

"Yet, you have *thought* them, despite your own disfigurement." She sighed heavily. "Have you learned nothing these past years? Are you still the selfish, arrogant boy that your wicked father raised you to be?"

"Nay, I'm not anything like him! I'm not!"

"If so, then it is because I have given you a chance to be a better man, a compassionate and caring one." Her green eye glittered. "*I'm* the one who cast the spell. And I'm the one who lifted it when I finally thought you had learned to care more for someone else than for your own needs."

"You! But that's not possible!"

"What will it take to prove it to you? Ah, I think I know the means." Mabelle moved her hands in front of her face. As

Alexander watched, her features seemed to twist and change. At the same time, her body altered its form. She grew taller, tall and straight. Suddenly he was looking at an older woman with the same white hair as Mabelle but with a fine-boned, elegant face and *two* piercing green eyes. The woman's bearing was regal, her whole manner refined and graceful.

Alexander gasped. "What . . . how . . . ?"

"Everyone knew I was a sorceress. Except for your father. He thought to crush and brutalize me, to prove he had no fear of my powers. But I was the one who prevailed in the end. He raped me, but I left him with a curse that forever changed his life."

"But . . . the curse . . . the curse was on *me!*" Alexander said angrily. "I was the one who suffered, not him!"

"Oh, he suffered. And he did change. He was never so ruthless and cruel after I finished with him. He stopped raping helpless women and abusing the servants and villagers. He was still a selfish, evil man, but he was much subdued."

"How could you?" Alexander muttered through clenched teeth. "How could you do this to me? All these years of misery!" He took a step towards her, wanting to throttle her.

She glared at him defiantly. "Has it occurred to you that I have had to endure the same torment as you have? That I have been trapped in the hideous form of an ugly old crone for even longer— since a few days after your birth? I have also had to endure shudders of disgust behind my back, to face the world as a kind of monster. But *I* never hid behind a mask. I lived not only as an outcast but as a servant. I did it so I could be with you, my son, to help you and guide you, to try to make certain you grew up humble and kindhearted and compassionate. I thought it had all been worth it, but now, looking at you, seeing the hate and fury on your face, I wonder if I gave up my beauty and suffered for naught! I wonder if you are not your father's son after all!"

Realizing what she was saying, he was ashamed. She had suffered as much or worse than him, had given up her beauty, her youth, to try and help him. "I'm sorry," he said. "I didn't think. But I vow to you, I'm not like my father. I'm not! I *am* capable of love, of compassion."

"Good." Mabelle smiled, a dazzling smile. And yet, he knew that she was not more dear to him now because she was beautiful, but because he knew what she had done for him, what she had sacrificed. She loved him, and that was what made her precious to him. He reached out for her and hugged her fiercely. The feel of her slender form reminded him of Esmay. He released her, feeling the old dread, the loneliness and fear resurface. "Esmay," he said. "You're telling me that she doesn't care for me?"

Mabelle shrugged. "Who knows? Maybe you should ask her what she feels."

"But she's gone."

Mabelle surveyed him up and down. "And it appears to me that you have two sound legs. You *could* go after her. Of course, that would be admitting that you care, that you are not too proud to pursue her."

Her appearance might have changed, but Mabelle's acid tongue was still the same. ALexander laughed wildly. There was no way he'd ever end up the arrogant, thoughtless bastard his father was—not with his mother around!

Esmay sat down in her usual spot in the meadow. Most of the wildflowers were going to seed, the grass turning brown. The first hints of autumn colored the forest—the red, scarlet, and purple of ripening berries, brown and gold leaves intermingling with the green. Yet it was not the approaching winter that gnawed at her heart, but the memories. She had only to close her eyes and she could feel his touch, remember the splendor they had shared.

It seemed like a dream, and perhaps that was the way to remember it—a beautiful, enchanted dream. The exquisite furnishings and clothing. Her fantastic lover, the personification of both her darkest fears and her deepest desires. For a time she had been part of a magical tale, such as a traveling troubadour might sing about while the villagers gathered breathlessly around him.

But there could be no happy ending to this tale. Not for her at least. She had done her part. The spell was broken. Her maidenhead, and her heart, had been sacrificed to save the Beast Lord, to give him a chance at a normal life. Now that he was no longer a monster, he would marry some elegant noblewoman and beget an heir on her.

The thought made pain lance through her. She did not want to think of him touching another woman, caressing her, making her sigh with rapture. Of his body joined with someone else's. Oh, she was glad that the spell was broken. She did not want him to be unhappy. But then again, if his scheme had not worked, if he had remained the Beast Lord, then perhaps she would have been able to make him happy anyway. She did not care if his face was handsome. It was his body that enthralled her. And those intense, gray eyes, so full of need and longing. And that mouth—skilled, sensual, miraculous. It had not mattered to her if the rest of his face was deformed. She loved him anyway.

A sob rose in her throat. Then a sound behind her made her stiffen. The hair on the back of her neck stood up as she realized that someone was watching her. Her gaze scanned the forest. She saw him and grew alarmed. It was the same knight who had abducted her. She recognized his helm and mail. What did he want with her now? Had he brought her a message from the castle? Or were his intentions more sinister?

Dread gripped her body. What if now that he was cured of the curse, her lover wished to be rid of her? He might not want her telling tales to the other villagers. She'd served her purpose; now he had no use for her.

She stood slowly, preparing to run. This time she was not caught unawares. She had a chance at escape. The knight took a step nearer. She whirled and dashed into the underbrush.

She could hear him behind him. He was surprisingly fleet, despite his cumbersome battle gear. But she knew the forest much better than he . . . and she was running for her life! Then, suddenly, a fallen branch loomed in her pathway. She tried to jump but her foot caught and she went down.

She closed her eyes, ready to weep with despair. It was all over.

"Esmay." The way he said her name aroused a memory. She opened her eyes and stared at the knight crouched over her. Gray eyes watched her through the slits of the helmet. She gave a gasp. Had he come himself to kill her? Could he really bear to take her life after what they'd shared?

"Esmay," he said again. He reached out his hand. She hesitated. What if she asked him, nay begged him, to love her one more time before . . . before he did was he was going to do to her? If only she could make him remember what they'd known together, make him care for her as she did for him.

She took his hand and let him help her up. He seemed even bigger than she remembered. Massive, formidable. She reminded herself that he had once desired her, needed her. Reaching out for his gauntleted hand, she brought it to her breast. He drew in his breath sharply. "Love me," she whispered. "Love me now."

She released his hand and he started to remove his helm. "Nay," she said. "Leave it on. It reminds me of the mask. It reminds me of the first time."

He began to undress—removing the mail shirt, the padded jacket beneath. His chest was bare, gloriously bare. She approached him and helped him undo the fastening on his braies. His cock sprang out and she filled both hands with the long, sleek rod. He stared at her, his eyes wild and hungry, full of the impossible yearning she remembered. "We have no blanket," he said.

She watched his mouth move, admiring those beautifully shaped lips. "We don't need a blanket," she whispered. She was intensely aware of the heated, live thing she held in her hands, the way his cock twitched and pulsed as she stroked it. "We can lie down in the tall grass of the meadow."

He took a deep breath, fighting for control, then shook his head. "Nay. I have another idea."

He took her hands in his and guided her backward until her hips met the trunk of a small birch tree, then he pulled up her skirts and began to fondle her between her legs. She was already wet and aching, and at his touch, her knees grew weak. He moved his hands to cup her buttocks and lifted her. Then, with her braced above him, he held her skirts out of the way with one hand and lowered her down onto his thick, heated length with the other.

She gasped. The weight of her body drove him deep, so deep inside her. Then, with one hand holding her and the other gripping the tree for support, he lunged upward. She shrieked in ecstasy, then cried out again and again as each thrust of his cock struck the entrance to her womb and sent spirals of keen pleasure shafting through her body. She peaked in waves, over and over, relentless and thrilling. Then at last, he collapsed against her.

She held him tight, feeling the rise and fall of his chest as he caught his breath. Peace, utter peace. She could stay here forever, resting in his arms, enjoying the aftermath of their incredible coupling, her face cradled against his neck, fragrant with his rich, deep, male scent. But then she remembered it was the last time. She did not think he would hurt her after this, but he would still want to be rid of her. Now that the curse was over, he had his whole life ahead of him, the life of a normal man, a lord.

She pulled away, gently disengaging his arms from around her.

Despair shafted through Alexander. She was leaving him. Even after what they'd shared, she didn't want him. He glanced around. Was it this, the wild beauty of the woods that called to her so strongly that she would not leave it even for him?

He watched her rearrange her clothing. Her face was sad, although she wouldn't look at him. She must regret their parting, at least a little.

His heart twisted in his chest. How could he let her go? How could he live without her? He grabbed her arm, feeling the desperation take hold of him. "Nay! I won't let you leave. If I have to drag you back by force, I will have you as my wife." She stared at him, her eyes wide and confused. "Don't you understand?" he whispered fiercely. "Having you, being near you, it was always more important than ending the curse. I *love* you. I *need* you. And although I know it isn't right for me to do this, I am your lord, and I *command* you to come back to the castle with me!"

Her eyes grew wider, deep pools of gold and green and umber, like autumn leaves reflected in a quiet pool. Then she laughed suddenly, a glistening, crystalline sound. "Of course. Of course, I will come back with you." Her gaze grew smoky. "I would go anywhere with you, my beloved Beast Lord."

He embraced her passionately and bent his head to kiss her. Then he remembered his helm. He jerked it off and grabbed her once again. For the first time, their mouths met. Honey sweet, as intoxicating as mead.

With His Promise

Liz Madison

Chapter One

England, 1250

The massive stone curtain wall shook but held firm as the fifty-pound rock, hurled from a catapult, slammed into its side.

"Assault tower—eastern end! Crossbowmen, light your arrows and fire!" Victoria Woodville issued the order to her knights from her position atop the watch tower, where she had an unobstructed view of the besieging army on the ground.

Suddenly the dark shroud of impending nightfall was streaked with orange color as hot, flaming arrows hailed down on the attackers. Shrieks of pain echoed from below as some of the arrows hit their targets. Victoria's knights were not as successful in their attempt to destroy the high wooden assault tower as it was pushed ever forward toward the castle's outer walls. Damp animal skins nailed across the front and sides of the mobile wooden structure doused the flaming arrows with the efficiency of a monsoon.

Despite the knights' best efforts, the month-long siege was taking its toll and the marauding army had made alarming steps toward penetrating the ancient fortress. The hours ticked on with an air of desperation.

"Hold your positions," Victoria commanded, then raced through the arched passageway and down a narrow stone stairway toward the inner courtyard, where activity was frantic. Every servant employed in the castle, along with the hundreds of serfs and peasants who had managed to take refuge before Hamlin Port's invading army sealed off the village, rushed about the courtyard aiding the battle. Armorers furnished and repaired broadswords, shields, and metal lance tips, fletchers carved and feathered arrows. Along the courtyard's north wall, in the kitchen, huge iron cauldrons were heating hot oil which could soon be poured down upon the invaders' heads through murder holes in the castle's thick walls.

Victoria's sharp green eyes took a swift look around, seeking Jonas Auber, the newest knight within Mistbury Arms' prestigious force. He had left his position behind the south wall battlement over three-quarters of an hour ago, stating that he needed to check with the fletchers on their stock of new arrows as the crossbowmen's supplies were nearly extinguished. But as Victoria scanned the frenetic inner bailey she saw not a trace of Sir Jonas. Her eyebrows furled with irritated concern. Where *was* her knight? Had something happened? But as the questions leaped to the forefront of her mind, they were just as quickly cast aside. In the farthest southern corner of the inner bailey, the earth had moved.

"Invasion! Southern corner!" Victoria screamed, pointing toward where she'd seen the movement as she bolted across the courtyard as fast as her legs would carry her. Over and over she sounded the alarm, generating a flurry of movement as pages, squires, and knights surrounded the southern corner, swords drawn, ready to ambush the invaders.

It was the one and only small section of Mistbury Arms' solid rock foundation where the earth had turned into a softer subsoil, and thus the only possible area that could be invaded by troops tunneling underneath the ground. How had Port's army discovered that? Dumb luck? Unlikely, since the south end of the castle abutted steep, sheer cliffs that descended into a frigid river some hundred yards below. It was one of the many features that made Mistbury Arms nearly impenetrable. Not that it mattered now, for however the knowledge had been discovered the damage was done, and Victoria's knights were now forced to divide themselves between warding off the land invasion and capturing the soldiers who'd tunneled underneath the castle's ground. With a sinking heart, she knew her men's chances of success were whittling down to near impossible.

Unexpected tears stung her eyes and threatened to dissolve her into a heap of despair, but with the tenacity of a wild boar, Victoria trampled them down and instead focused on the raging battle ahead. Running back up the winding narrow stairways to the watchtower, she mentally calculated how long her people could withstand this siege. The castle's food supplies would yet hold out for many months, so there was no imminent danger of starvation. The same was true for the fresh water, supplied by wells dug within the inner bailey. The armory was well stocked, and skilled craftsmen had the raw materials to furnish and repair all her knights' weapons. But what of the emotional toll this battle was taking? Mistbury Arms was seldom invaded, and within Victoria's lifetime had yet to withstand a siege of this magnitude. Her men were weary; spirits sagged as Hamlin Port's army continued to press and gain small advantages. Their invasion of the inner bailey through an underground tunnel was just the latest victory to spur those soldiers on, but had cast another shadow on the souls of Victoria's men. Was it truly possible that she may lose her beloved ancestral home?

Not while I've breath to draw, she affirmed, emerging through the arched doorway and onto the watchtower. She alone ruled Mistbury Arms, and while there was life within her she would never give that up. This was her home, just as it had been her father's home, and his father's before that. It had been earned through the blood and sweat of generations of Woodvilles, and Victoria did not intend to relinquish that heritage to the vile likes of Hamlin Port.

Fueled by determination, she commanded her knights to battle onward, and the fire in her voice brought with it the energy and will to go on. Though they were now enveloped in the darkness of early evening, the army below had lit torches, enabling Victoria's knights to pick them out as moving targets and fire their crossbows with deadly accuracy. More archers fired through the arrow slit windows. An hour passed by; then two. The fighting continued with neither side gaining or losing ground. Victoria fired her own crossbow from her vantage point atop the watchtower, and continued calling out encouragement to her knights and ensuring that their spirits remained high. She was still worried about the elevated assault tower that Port's army continued to push closer and closer toward the outer curtain wall, but for the moment it was at a standstill.

A momentary lull settled over the besieged castle and Victoria wondered if Port's soldiers were halting the fight for the evening. Leaning her crossbow against the stone parapet, she eased away from the watchtower over toward the eastern corner where the assault tower stood. The knights guarding that wall remained tense and watchful, ready to resume battle the moment Port's soldiers again took up arms.

"No movement for over half an hour, my lady," one of the soldiers whispered to Victoria as she approached the wall. "But we're ready whenever they are."

"They've extinguished their torches near the castle," Victoria noted, "and the only light I see is in the far distance, toward their camp. I daresay the grumble of their empty bellies will occupy their time for a while."

The knight nodded his agreement. It had been over ten hours since his own men had last had a meal, a fact of which Victoria was all too aware.

"Divide your men into shifts and send them down for food," she ordered. "One shift at a time; half an hour per shift. Then we'll discuss who takes the first night watch."

The grateful knight was swift to follow the orders. "Right away, my lady. We'll start with—"

Screams of terror severed the vespertine calm. A surge of heat blasted Victoria's face, and as she turned toward the left, she saw an inferno of white-hot flame consuming the assault tower. The fire crackled with rampant zeal as it feasted on the sturdy wood. The damp animal skins covering the outside of the tower failed to extinguish the blaze that had been set by an unknown multitude of torches. Within minutes the flames reached the top of the tower and the entire structure became a raging conflagration, lighting up the lurid sky like a blaze of morning sun. Seconds later it collapsed, turning the once ominous and imposing tower into little more than a useless, smoldering heap of rubble.

The assault continued, with the new army of invaders turning ever more ferocious in their battle against Hamlin Port's men. The saviors arrived in droves, surrounding the countryside outside Mistbury Arms, and in savage hand-to-hand combat cutting down the army that had terrorized Victoria's castle and people for more than a month.

Without knowing who these men were, or why they were helping her, Victoria resumed her role of commander and organized her soldiers to join the battle.

"Lower the bridge," she ordered, "then charge! Not one of Port's men shall cross into our home. The minute the bridge is down I want an all-out assault against these marauders. Prepare the mounts and attack!"

The instructions were followed without hesitation. The most proficient crossbowmen remained atop the battlement, but Victoria's army of brave knights descended into the courtyard to ready their warhorses and weaponry. As soon as the drawbridge was lowered, they would be ready to stampede across the moat surrounding Mistbury Arms and join the invading army to crush Hamlin Port's men. Victoria herself rushed down below, for she had her own horses and arms and would not for a minute exclude herself from the danger. This was her castle, and she would defend it.

Already she could hear the grinding of the huge chains holding up the drawbridge as they were unwound in order to lower the bridge. The snorting and stomping of the destriers indicated that the knights were mounted and ready to charge. Hundreds of lit torches illuminated the night sky. Squires had prepared Victoria's gelding as well. After donning her armor, she mounted the beast and took her position at the head of the group.

As soon as the drawbridge was lowered, she gave the signal and the entire army of mounted knights, followed by foot soldiers, raced over the bridge and into the midst of the raging battle. The smoldering assault tower still gave off enough light for Victoria to decipher where the majority of knights were fighting. As previously decided, Victoria and her army rode straight out into a wide semicircle, surrounding Port's men, then turned and rushed back toward the castle, forcing Hamlin's army into a defensive mode while they pressed their advantage from the surprise offensive attack. With lethal precision Victoria slashed through the horde of Port's marauding knights, then assumed a strategic position just outside the circle of battle, where she could command her army from a superior vantage point.

Again and again the hard metal of broadswords clashed against one another. The sharp whinny of the destriers pierced the air, intermingling with the stomping of their hooves against packed earth. Amid the furor were the sickening groans of fallen men.

Though her eyes swept over the entire battle scene, more than once Victoria's attention was magnetically drawn toward the phenomenal prowess of the largest knight she'd ever seen. Though darkness and the armor he wore obscured his features, it was clear that the man was built like Goliath. He wielded his sword and shield with colossal power, making every swing and thrust a movement of fluid beauty. Atop his snorting destrier he battled Hamlin's army and commanded his own men, his deep voice of authority ringing across the battlefield.

Almost as soon as it had begun, the battle ended. Victoria gave one last command to press forward, but as her knights moved in, it was clear that there was no one left with whom to fight. The siege was over.

An eerie silence blanketed the countryside. For a moment, not a word was spoken. Every man remained in his place, whether standing upon the earth or mounted on a destrier. Stark, plenary exhaustion stole into the soldiers' veins, leaving them hollow and drained of emotion. The faintest whisper of a breeze stirred the air, like a giant victory flag waving over the triumphant knights.

Victoria surveyed the battle-ravaged countryside surrounding Mistbury Arms. Dead and wounded knights were strewn about the area like so much discarded debris. Her heart squeezed with pain, knowing that some of the fallen men were her own.

The thud of horse hooves against the packed earth shattered the quiet and caught Victoria's attention. She shifted left in her saddle and turned her head toward the sound. It was the great knight. He sat ramrod straight upon his snorting mount, yet there was a relaxed nature about him as he rode toward Victoria with his visor turned up, revealing piercing, midnight blue eyes staring at her from a startlingly handsome face.

He pulled his mount alongside hers, though the beast faced the opposite direction of Victoria's own in order that she and the knight might face one another.

The giant of a man bowed his head toward Victoria, as if paying obeisance to a queen, and informed her, "Stephen de Burgh at your service, my lady."

A flame of recognition lit Victoria's eyes upon hearing the man's name. Though she'd never met him, the de Burgh family's castle, Blenleigh, had been neighbor to Mistbury Arms ever since the fortress had been built over a century ago. Victoria's father had been acquainted with the senior de Burgh and had spoken of the family with great respect. The ride to Blenleigh was but a three days' journey, though up to this moment Victoria had never met its imposing ruler.

"Victoria Woodville, my lord," she said, extending her hand as she responded to his greeting. " 'Tis a blessing that you came along when you did. You and your men have saved my castle, and for that I'll be forever in your debt."

Upon hearing her words, the faintest of smiles touched the corner of Stephen's mouth. Before answering Victoria, he removed his helm and shrugged back the mail hood attached to his hauberk. Though his hands were still covered in stiff leather gloves, Victoria felt as though she could feel the heat from his skin seep into her own hand as he lightly grasped her extended fingers and raised them to his lips. The light from the still-smoldering assault tower blaze was adequate for Victoria to gaze upon his magnificent, chiseled features. The aura of masculinity carried upon his powerful body graced the features of his face as well. His strong, high cheekbones looked as though they were carved from granite. They were offset by eyes set deep within his face and framed by a fringe of long lashes that would be envied by any woman. His hair was long, brushing just past his shoulders, and though shadows played about the night, obscuring the clarity of Victoria's vision, she thought his hair appeared to be blond. Overall he gave the appearance of an ancient Norse warlord, and Victoria remembered once hearing something about Vikings within the de Burgh ancestry. Whatever the truth of the matter, Stephen de Burgh certainly looked as though he could conquer countless nations.

His eyes gleamed in the dying firelight as he said in a rich, deep voice, "Dispense with such foolishness, Lady Woodville. Give my knights some stout ale and a hot meal and consider your debt paid in full."

Victoria's cheeks warmed with the stain of an embarrassed

blush. The immense knight had a way of distracting her normally flawless etiquette.

"I beg forgiveness, my lord. You and your men are the guests of honor in my home. Please, enter and stay the night. I shall have the cooks prepare us all a celebration feast."

Turning away before de Burgh could respond, she signaled for her soldiers to gather the fallen men, both hers and Hamlin Port's, to prepare them for burial.

When she turned back to face lord de Burgh, Victoria noticed a second man on horseback had drawn up alongside him, somewhat smaller than Stephen but as powerful in appearance.

"May I introduce my brother, Hendrick de Burgh," Stephen said. "Hendrick, Lady Victoria Woodville."

Hendrick de Burgh crossed his arm against his chest and bowed toward Victoria. "We've known of your family for years, my lady," he said, "and a pleasure it is to at last make your acquaintance in person."

There's a silver-tongued devil, Victoria thought, extending her hand to the younger de Burgh. His manners were impeccable, yet she sensed the virility beneath his suave exterior. His brother, on the other hand, made no show of pretense to disguise his true identity. Stephen de Burgh was raw male power, coiled within the fierce body of a seasoned warlord. What surprised her was why knowing that about him sent a shiver of excitement rushing through her blood.

The three nobles turned their mounts in the direction of Mistbury Arms and began riding back toward the drawbridge.

"As I told your brother," Victoria said to Hendrick, "my people and I are indebted to your assistance. Once the feasting begins, we must speak of how you knew of our plight, and why you came to our rescue."

"Anything you wish, my lady," Hendrick responded. Stephen remained silent, but Victoria could sense his watching eyes upon her as if he were a hawk and she, his prey.

They reached the drawbridge and ceased conversation as the destriers' mighty hooves pounded against the rock-hard English oak. They rode underneath the raised portcullis to pass through the gatehouse, and then entered the inner bailey, where the frantic activity of early evening had been replaced by jubilant celebration and preparations for a hearty feast. Acrid smoke poured through the chimney of the kitchen, where meat slowly roasted upon iron spits. The smell of the food made Victoria's stomach rumble. She had not eaten since early morning. Young maids drew water from the well to fill the cauldrons and make soup, and the pounding of the cooks' knives upon chopping blocks filled the air.

Crossing the inner bailey, they reached the outside door of the keep, and it was here where Victoria, Stephen, and Hendrick dismounted.

"Welcome to Mistbury Arms," Victoria said to her guests as she gestured toward the great hall. "Come inside and quench your thirsts."

"Grateful indeed, my lady," Stephen replied, and as Victoria turned toward him she could see by the light of the burning rushes that her earlier assessment of him had been only partly correct. His ancient Scandinavian heritage was evident within his sculpted features, but she had seen a mere shadow of his beauty, which was now apparent in the light. Stephen de Burgh was like Adonis, come to life.

Servants had already laid out tables along the length of the great hall and spread white linen cloths upon the tables. At each side of the table they placed trenchers for the meat, and on either side of the trenchers was a steel knife and spoon. Before each place setting were silver cups and mazers, and scattered across each table were dishes of salt. The servants rushed about making preparations for the feast like an army of worker ants. Orchestrating the arrangements was a slender, dark-haired man whose effete mannerisms nevertheless commanded authority. When he spotted Victoria, he glided over to her side.

"Welcome back, my lady, welcome," he said, the light in his eyes showing the respect he held for his mistress.

"Esmond," Victoria said, grasping his hands in a familiar show of friendship, "these lords have saved Mistbury Arms, and for that we are indebted to them. Please welcome Lord Stephen de Burgh and his brother, Lord Hendrick. Lords de Burgh, this is my steward, Esmond Bele."

Esmond bowed low in front of the brothers. "We are at your service," he said, his arm sweeping wide to indicate that the entire household of servants was included in his statement. When he rose, he walked toward the high table and pulled out the large wooden chair in the middle. "My lady," he said, then indicated that Stephen and Hendrick should sit on either side of his mistress. As they settled into their chairs and Victoria spoke to Esmond about arranging drinks for her guests of honor, Stephen at last had an unobstructed opportunity to look upon the face of the woman who single-handedly ran the prosperous castle of Mistbury Arms, and about whom he had heard much over the years.

'Twas said that Victoria Woodville possessed the fighting prowess of the best-trained knight. Naturally Stephen knew that the truth had a way of becoming exaggerated over the repeated telling of tales, yet he had to admit that the courage she displayed on the battlefield this evening lent credence to her reputation. Though she possessed not the strength to wield the heavy broadswords knights used in battlefield combat, stategically she was a first-rate commander. She'd kept her wits about her throughout the fiercest fighting, ordering her men to move when the exact right moments became available. No wonder she was held in such high esteem by every servant within her household.

As she looked up from her seated position to speak with Esmond Bele, her long arched neck was illuminated by the burning rush mounted on the wall behind her head. An unexpected yearning to trail kisses along the delicate smooth skin of that neck forced Stephen to shift his position in the chair. His eyes roamed over the rest of her face. Her complexion was flawless; smooth like fresh cream, although there was a touch of bronze within her skin tone. Doubtless she spent a great deal of time outdoors, demanded by her position as head of the household. She had wide eyes the color of a lush, green forest. Her mouth was small, but her plump, full lips looked as soft and inviting as twin pillows. Her crowning glory was the thick chestnut hair that hung down her back in a wild tousle of curls, highlighted by streaks of red that blazed within the flames of the rush. Her beauty was not that of the classic maidens in the songs of troubadours, but instead a reflection of Victoria's personality: strong, independent, untamed. Stephen felt his blood begin to simmer.

At that very moment she turned, having finished her instructions to Esmond. Stephen did not make even the slightest attempt to mask the fact that he'd been staring at her. His eyes, Victoria noted, as heat rushed to stain her cheeks, were as piercing as the tip of a dirk. For the space of a heartbeat their gazes met and held, then it was Victoria who broke the link and shifted her attention to Hendrick.

"My lord," she said, deliberately casting her undivided attention upon Stephen's brother, "you must tell me how it is that you came to be aware of the siege upon our castle."

Hendrick was not blind; he had noticed Stephen's perusal of Victoria while she spoke with Esmond, and was aware that the lady had captured his brother's interest. It was also clear that Victoria, for whatever reason, chose to ignore it. Hendrick knew she would not be able to resist him for long. Maidens flocked to Stephen as readily as beggars to food. But until she fell prey to her brother's smoldering sensuality, Hendrick would enjoy Victoria's attention for himself.

"There is kin between our two households," he replied. "The daughter of your brewer is married to one of my villager's sons, and they have recently born him his first grandson. There had been talk of them making the journey here in order that your brewer might see the child, but when a messenger was sent ahead with word of the visit, he spotted the siege upon your castle."

He paused when a footman approached the table to serve tankards of ale. By that time the room was overflowing with Victoria's household staff and the de Burghs' knights, all shouting and laughing as the celebration got under way. A hearty fire crackled and popped from the massive hearth in the middle of the room, the smoke rising some thirty feet to the vaulted ceiling above. Squires, men-at-arms, porters, watchmen, ladies-in-waiting, all gathered within the jovial great hall to eat and drink and toast to victory. Tankards knocked against one another in hearty salutes, some tables sang songs of triumph. Hendrick raised his voice above the exalted din.

"We've had our own threats from Hamlin Port," he continued, "and when the messenger spotted his flag amidst the invading soldiers, 'twas no difficult decision to want to help." Hendrick leaned forward to look past Victoria and catch the eye of his brother.

"What say you, Stephen? Were we right in aiding the fair Lady Woodville?"

A lazy smile touched the corners of Stephen's mouth as he acknowledged the truth of his brother's words. "A more just decision could not be had," he responded, his gaze never wavering from Victoria's face. She felt the heat of his stare but did not meet it, unwilling to again become mesmerized within the midnight blue depths. How was it, she wondered, that after knowing a man for a mere couple of hours she could sense a current of desire running between them both. True he was a feast for the senses, his startling sculpted looks coupled with the manly smell of leather and the untamed forest. But there had to be something beyond mere superficial beauty that would account for the way Victoria's blood stirred whenever she felt his magnetic eyes upon her. Perhaps it was his recent heroics? He and his men had saved her castle, doubtless her very life. Yet if that were true, then the younger de Burgh would cause the same reaction in her.

Victoria shook her head and looked again toward Hendrick as she raised her hand to signal for more ale. There was a clear similarity between Stephen and Hendrick, with the younger de Burgh possessing the same Nordic traits as his brother, from the shoulder-length blond hair to the prominent high cheekbones. His features were perhaps a touch softer than Stephen's and his eyes a paler blue, but he drew attention from the ladies within the great hall just the same. Yet when Victoria looked upon him, she felt only the admiration that one would give to a fine tapestry, or perhaps a purebred stallion. She appreciated his beauty, but he did not stir her blood.

The footmen rushed back with refills of strong ale while servants proceeded from the kitchen to the banquet hall, laden with platter after platter of steaming hot food. The aroma of richly seasoned dishes filled the great hall, teasing the hungry bellies of all who awaited them.

Though pairs of diners at the lower tables shared dishes between them, Victoria and her guests each had a trencher to themselves. For several moments no further words were spoken, conversation being replaced by the festive noises of eating. But once the initial edge was taken off their appetites, Victoria asked

Stephen and Hendrick to elaborate upon the comment Hendrick had made earlier.

"You hinted that Port's skullduggery has besieged Blenleigh as well," she said. "Have you suffered many invasions in recent years?"

Stephen took a quaff of ale before answering, then lowered the tankard upon the linen-covered table while keeping his tanned fingers curled around the base of the steel cup. "We've not suffered a siege upon our lands from the likes of Hamlin Port," he said. "But the black-hearted knave has made threats, and our men know to expect trouble from him at any time."

Victoria felt a surge of ire toward Hamlin Port churn and twist her stomach into knots. Were it not for that evil baron's depraved gluttony, the brave men who had died saving Mistbury Arms would be enjoying this festive evening with their wives and children. Instead the villages upon her land were now dotted with grieving widows and fatherless babes.

"I would know what possesses that man to constantly raid and plunder the peaceful lands of our countryside," she said, her genteel voice not masking the anger behind her statement.

"Greed," Stephen replied, the lone word as cold and harsh as Port himself. "Your lands are enviable, and he wants them for himself."

"Especially with the immense tract of forest under your jurisdiction," Hendrick added. "It's no doubt left Port seething into his cups on many a fine evening, trying to figure out how he can get his villainous hands on it."

Victoria knew the brothers spoke the truth. For an avaricious brute like Port, the wealth of her estate must be a bitter pill to swallow.

The meal being finished, bustling servants were quick to clean away the trenchers and replace them with bowls of fruits, figs, and dates, as well as honeyed desserts and sweetmeats. Generally Stephen did not care for sweets, preferring wine and ale to sugary confections, but his heart lurched into his throat when he saw Victoria bite into a ripe plum and then sweep her tongue across her full lips to catch the juice that had dripped from the fruit. It was a simple, swift gesture, done with no more thought behind it than breathing, yet it was the very essence of that purity which quickened his pulse and hardened his groin. He leaned back in his chair, stretching his long legs as he studied her profile. She was an interesting mixture of contrasts, he decided. On the battlefield she was a study in valiance, allowing not a whisper of fear to impede her determination as she led her men to victory against Hamlin Port's army. But she was also a feminine feast for the senses, with her lush body and cascading chestnut hair. Against his better judgment, Stephen allowed his imagination to roam, thinking of how her soft skin and ripe breasts would feel pressed against his chest, her arms entwined around his neck as he pulled her into his embrace to feast upon her lips. He played out the scene in his mind, hearing her breathy sigh of acceptance turn into moans of desire as his hands stroked and caressed her dusky rose nipples, transforming their silky softness into stiff rigid peaks. He could lead her over to the bed, pressing her gently down upon the mattress as he nudged apart her thighs . . .

He became aware of silence surrounding him, and by the looks upon Victoria's and Hendrick's faces, it was obvious he was expected to answer a question he did not hear.

"Forgive me," he said. "My attention was captivated by your mummers."

From the seductive embers in his eyes as he looked at her, Victoria knew he did not speak the truth. Nevertheless, she allowed his statement to pass without comment. Instead she dipped her fingers in the small ewer placed in front of her, wiped her hands with a linen cloth, and prepared to depart.

"My lords," she said, acknowledging both Stephen and Hendrick, "it has been an understandably long day and were I to remain any longer, I would have to prop my eyelids open with sticks. Instead I will bid you good night and see you on the morrow. The pages will show you to your rooms when you are ready."

She rose from her chair and turned away, hearing the grating sounds of chairs being pushed back from the table as all the diners within the great hall stood to acknowledge the departure of their mistress. As Victoria moved away from the table, she was startled to realize that Stephen walked with her. She stopped as she turned to face him, craning her neck upward in order to meet his eyes.

"My lord?" she said, confused as to why he stood by her side. " 'Tis unnecessary for you to escort me to my room. I believe I know the way quite well."

Her humor made him smile, dazzling his features like the morning sun upon a clear mountain lake.

"On the contrary, my lady," he replied. "I'd hoped you would do the honor of escorting *me*." His voice was low, as if confiding a secret, and the impropriety of his request caused Victoria's heartbeat to quicken. Stephen de Burgh was a powerful, virile man, and his dominating presence exuded sensuality. It was clear that he desired her, and Victoria could not deny her attraction toward him as well. But if the man thought to hoodwink her into sharing his bed, his gloating male pride was about to get bruised.

"Very well," she answered. "Lord Hendrick, will you accompany us?" She flashed Stephen's brother her most charming smile, and although Hendrick found her as captivating as did Stephen, he knew his older sibling had already staked his claim.

"Thank you, my lady, but I am not quite ready to retire and should like to remain with our men awhile longer. You have my gratitude for a wonderful banquet."

Victoria acknowledged Hendrick's praise with a bow of her head. "And you have mine for helping to save our castle. Good night, Lord de Burgh."

She and Stephen stepped down from the high table, Stephen following behind her as silently as a shadow. No words were spoken between them as they walked through the great hall toward the ascending staircase that would lead them to the guest rooms and Victoria's solar beyond. She began climbing the clockwise spiraling stairway ahead of Stephen, her torchlight held out in front of her to guide the way. The flames hissed and popped as they burned the rushes, and cast dancing shadows across the cool stone walls. She could not see Stephen behind her, but his presence was undeniable. It was as though she could physically feel his heated gaze upon her.

When they reached the block of private rooms in which prestigious guests were housed, Victoria halted their progress and turned to Stephen once again.

"Make your way down this hallway, my lord," she instructed,

lifting her face toward his. "The third room on the right is yours."

"I am obliged," he answered, bowing his head once with gratitude. He made no movement toward the hallway.

By the light of the flames she could see his eyes glint as he studied her face. His gaze was magnetic, drawing her into him even as she felt her body take a shaky step backward. With panther-like stealth he followed her, stride for stride, until she could move no more as her back pressed up against the immovable stone wall. His left arm moved up behind her to set the burning rush into the wall bracket, then he propped his hand against the wall beside her right cheek. She felt like an animal caught in a trap, but her heartbeat raced with irrepressible excitement. She knew she should walk away from him and continue up the stairway toward her own room, but she could no more command her feet to move than she could fly to the shadowed heavens above.

His warm breath caressed the flushed skin of her cheek as he brought his head closer toward her face. Victoria could now clearly see the hot desire smoldering within the depths of his eyes. His supple full lips were close, so very close, and she fought the irrational desire to place her hand behind his neck and close the distance between them. She wanted to feel those lips upon hers; hot, moist, sensual lips belonging to a warrior knight who could invoke fear among men by his very presence.

Instead, out of the corner of her eye she saw his right hand lift up toward her face, and in the next instant his strong, scarred warrior's fingers were lightly caressing the creamy skin of her neck. His touch was like fire, scorching her skin as his fingers stroked upward, toward her face. She felt his thumb trace the fine bone of her jaw line, while his fingers brushed her cheeks, her eyelids, her nose, then her lips.

Their eyes melded into one another as he explored the contours of her face, and she could not hide the wild leaping of her pulse nor the trembling of her legs. With his mere touch he evoked heady, erotic sensations within her that she'd never before experienced, and left her trembling with desire. She shifted her head ever slightly, lifting her face even closer to his, straining for the kiss she knew he wanted to give her. Yet just when she thought he would at last capture her mouth with his own, his hand dropped down to his side and he took a step back.

"Your beauty takes my breath away," he murmured, then bowed before her. "Good night, Lady Woodville." Without another word he turned in the direction she had pointed to earlier, walked down the hallway, then went through the doorway and into his room. The click of the lock was a lonely echo in the dark, still hall.

Victoria waited for her breathing to calm and her heartbeat to slow before she could at last move her feet and climb the stairway to her solar. Her chambermaid awaited her, and within minutes she was undressed and in bed. Yet it would be several hours before the welcome arms of sleep could claim her, for her mind was too riddled by a myriad of emotions swirling about her head, like a pile of autumn leaves blowing and twisting in the wind.

"Your silence will only make this more difficult." The prisoner to whom Stephen's comment was directed merely shook his head and refused to speak. It had been that way for over two hours, and Stephen's patience was wearing thin. He had no taste for torture, but he was also not about to release any of the prisoners until they gave him the information he required.

At his side stood both Victoria and Hendrick, who had accompanied him to the drum tower dungeon following their morning meal. They had chained roughly two dozen prisoners in Mistbury Arms' dungeon, all soldiers who had fought in the siege against them. All soldiers of Hamlin Port's.

"We could beat your face to a bloody pulp," Hendrick informed him. "Perhaps that would aid your memory?"

The soldier recoiled from the giant men, shrinking his body against the dungeon's cold walls. Still he refused to speak. Victoria could not help but admire his loyalty, however misplaced it may be.

Now it was she who confronted the soldier, standing before him with compassion in her eyes.

"Don't die a fool for Hamlin Port," she said calmly, "for you know within your heart that he'd do naught for you. Think instead of your family, soldier. Of your wife, your children. If you choose to remain silent, they will hang their heads in shame, tears of sorrow streaming down their cheeks, mourning the pointless loss of a brave soldier who fought battles for a hateful, vile, gluttonous lord."

The prisoner remained silent, yet Victoria knew her words had struck a chord within his soul. How could anyone, she thought, place loyalty to Hamlin Port above the love of family.

"Tell us what we want to know and you'll see your wife and children once more. But spite us and you'd best pray that your memory shines brightly within them, for 'tis all they'll have left of you."

She saw the glistening shine of tears shimmer in the brave knight's eyes and knew he'd made his decision. "He'll kill us," he croaked in a parched, pained voice. "If we say one word, he promised to kill us all."

Stephen and Hendrick had walked toward the soldier when they heard him begin to speak, but it was to Victoria that the knight directed his words. "Please, my lady. Please understand. If we don't speak, you'll kill us. If we do speak, Hamlin Port will. What choice do we have? Our only hope is that you'll have more mercy than he will and spare us the suffering."

Victoria's heart cracked as she heard the stricken pleas of her prisoner. Such a poor, desperate man.

"Listen to me," she commanded, willing the man to believe her. "If you tell us everything we need to know, you, your men, and all your families may remain on my lands and pledge fealty to me. You need not serve Hamlin Port ever again. Your life will be your own, in exchange for your loyalty. *But only if you tell us everything.*"

The strong words hung in the air like a threat, yet wrapped around them was the promise of hope and new life. The knight realized that his decision was simple, and the barest of smiles cracked his dry lips. "What do you want to know?"

A cool wind shook the heavy branches of the apple trees, laden with ripe fruit ready to be picked. Overhead Victoria could see thin clouds scudding by, driven by the late summer wind that foretold autumn's lurking presence.

Despite the chill and the impending evening dusk, she enjoyed walking in the quiet calm of her castle's vast orchards. It was a place where she could collect her thoughts and find peace, and after spending the better part of her day in the dungeon hearing heartbreaking tales from Hamlin Port's knights, it was a place she needed to be.

She walked nearly three-quarters of an hour, then sat upon one of the stout wooden benches used by the peasants when they took breaks from picking fruit. Pulling her fur-lined mantle closely about her body, she closed her eyes for a moment, arched her head back, and breathed in the clean, smoke-scented air.

"May I join you?"

Victoria's eyes flew open. Casting a shadow upon her as his towering frame blocked out the sun, Stephen stood there, shrouded in a fur-lined mantle, blond hair ruffling in the breeze.

"Of course you may," she responded, masking the unexpected rush of desire that coiled in her stomach. A memory of last evening flashed before her mind, a memory of Stephen standing before her, trapping her within his massive arms, lowering his head as if to kiss her . . .

She had seen him since then, of course, having been in the dungeon beside him and Hendrick as they probed Hamlin Port's knights for information. But that had been a different setting entirely, hardly a place that would induce thoughts of intimacy. Now she was with him in the serenity of the apple orchard where no one else was about. He settled down beside her.

He said nothing more at first, seemingly content to share with her the brilliant glory of the setting sun; luminous splashes of pink and red glowing in the twilight sky.

After a few moments he turned toward her, shifting his body so that their knees brushed against one another as he did so. She assumed he would slide away to correct the impropriety. He did not.

"Did you believe them?" he asked, his blue eyes intently studying her profile as if committing every detail to memory.

"You mean the prisoners?"

"Yes."

"I did," she nodded, meeting his gaze. "Most of Port's knights are hired mercenaries, deserters from Crusades, and my heart bears little respect for anyone whose loyalties are for sale to the highest bidder. Yet be that as it may, I don't think these knights speak lies when they tell tales of the murderous raids Hamlin Port pays them to lead."

"Nor do I," Stephen agreed. "Port's only ambition is to expand the vast holdings he already claims as his own, and he'll do whatever it takes to accomplish his goals." The breeze had become stronger, shaking and bending the apple trees' branches, plucking away some of the unpicked fruit so it rolled and tumbled upon the ground. Stephen pulled his mantle tighter around his muscled shoulders and moved ever closer beside Victoria, blocking her from the frigid wind.

"Do you want to go inside?"

"Not quite yet."

She felt so small and feminine beside this colossal knight, so comfortable and safe, and she discovered with some surprise that they were feelings she quite enjoyed.

"Did you know about Hamlin's relation to the king?" she asked, admiring the way Stephen's eyes sparkled in the last rays of the dying sunlight.

"No," he admitted. "Not for certain. I had heard talk once amongst some knights at Blenleigh, but they were merely repeating the gossip of village peasants."

Victoria nodded. "The kinship is not close."

"But kinship nonetheless. 'Tis no doubt why Henry turns a blind eye against Hamlin's plunders and raids."

"And why Hamlin has no reason to stop." An icy finger of fear crept up Victoria's spine, raising the hairs on her skin. But her voice was strong, symbolizing her resolve to keep fighting him for as long as she was able.

Stephen's gaze swept the vast landscape, now cloaked in darkness as the sun slid beneath the ground. He thought of the beauty of Blenleigh, his home, in many ways quite similar to the lands surrounding Mistbury Arms. His castle's location was a strategic masterpiece, high atop a cliff and surrounded by natural barriers. But also like Mistbury Arms, Blenleigh had captured the attention of Hamlin Port, who yearned to include the fortress among his vast holdings. As he had told Victoria, they had yet to endure one of Port's raids, but Stephen knew it was only a matter of time.

He glanced back over at the strong-willed beauty before him. He had not lied when he told her that she took his breath away, and even as his eyes brushed over her now, he felt a tightening in his loins. How demure she looked, her eyes focused upon her lap as she shivered against the cold. But Stephen knew this outward softness masked steely strength beneath. Victoria was like a gladiator shrouded in femininity, and she stirred him as no other woman ever had. Without a second thought, Stephen made a decision.

"Port has no reason to cease raiding our lands because neither of us has the means to stop him. The jurisdiction he controls is larger than either mine or yours, and as long as he can raise an army, his ruthless invasions will continue. It's only a matter of time before he succeeds and one or both of us loses our holdings. We cannot ward him off forever. At least not alone."

He saw her eyes widen, perhaps guessing at what he was about to propose.

Stephen breathed deeply, filling his lungs with the crisp evening air as if he were drawing in courage to say what he needed. His eyes never wavered from hers; deep and serious, matching his words. "I would take you for my wife," he said. "Marriage between us will unite our lands, our armies, and our villages, and our combined strength will be able to fight off armies twice the size of the one Port brought against you this past month. We shall be victorious together, and preserve our families' legacies for generations to come."

He paused before saying more, allowing her time to think. Her face was serene, not allowing him room to speculate upon her reaction. After a time she rose from the bench and walked a few paces from where they sat. The breeze was still strong, blowing Victoria's hair away from her face so that it streamed behind her like a lustrous veil. The faint smoky aroma of nearby cooking fires perfumed the air, and off into the distance arose the faint sound of servants' voices as they prepared the evening meal. At long last Victoria walked back toward Stephen, her shoulders squared as if ready to do battle.

"You're correct that we'll have a much better chance against Port's invasions as a united front," she said. "Our combined holdings would be larger than what he currently rules, and the lands would be preserved—for *your* family alone."

Stephen rose from the bench and in two long strides stood directly before her. " 'Tis not what I meant," he said, an angry scowl creasing his face. "You dare liken me to a vile opportunist like Port?"

His piercing blue eyes had darkened to the color of midnight, and he towered more than a foot and a half above her. But Victoria was not about to cower in fear when the fate of her family's legacy was being threatened. Every woman knew that once married her entire ownership of property and lands automatically forfeited to her husband. No more would Victoria rule Mistbury Arms, and its fate and history in her family would not be hers to pass along. It was a fact of which Stephen de Burgh was all too aware.

"I liken you to none other than who you are," she replied. "If we marry, Mistbury Arms becomes yours. I fail to see how that would preserve *my* family."

She stood firm while she spoke, her voice soft but unyielding, and despite his anger, Stephen could not help but admire her courage. Men had oftentimes trembled before him, intimidated by his massive size. Yet here was this small, graceful woman refusing to so much as bend. A stab of desire heated his blood.

"Despite your lowly opinion of my character," he said, "I am no more interested in ruling Mistbury Arms than you are in forfeiting your rights of ownership. But if we do not unite, there will be nothing to rule—for either of us." Stephen's hands reached out and grasped Victoria's, encasing her fingers in his warm powerful grip. "I will have papers drawn up and signed by me guaranteeing that you retain ownership of your property. Would that satisfy you?"

She hesitated, then nodded once in agreement. She withdrew her hands from his and walked back over to the bench, though she did not sit. Stephen sensed her unease and wondered at the reason behind it.

"There is something else you are not telling me," he said, his voice insistent. "Something which prevents you from agreeing to my proposal."

The dark shadows prevented him from clearly seeing her face, yet he sensed that he had hit upon the truth. "What is it?" he probed. "You know the idea is sound, and I've agreed to let you keep ownership of your lands. Why do you not agree to this arrangement?"

Victoria was thankful for the cover of night so that the flush of her cheeks was hidden from Stephen's view. How could she dare speak the truth behind her unwillingness to marry, especially since he had agreed that she would retain control of her castle? She looked away from his probing gaze, chiding her own foolishness. Though Stephen's marriage proposal was far from the romantic ideal of young girls' dreams, Victoria knew his reasoning made perfect strategic sense. But in her mind she could hear the hushed whispers of the wives within her castle, reverberating over and over like the tolls of a warning bell. They spoke of pain, of having to endure, of foul breath and sweaty bodies and filthy rutting like hunting hounds. All this, they said in knowing, ominous voices, was what women must tolerate when men claimed husbandly rights. Victoria had heard such conversations ever since she was a girl, and never once did anyone disagree with the wives. *A dreadful business*, they would say, shaking their heads and clicking their tongues. And though sometimes a young woman about to be married would express doubt as to the veracity of the older wives' words, Victoria would see that young woman after she was wed and her former doubts would be voiced no more.

Still, she was strong, and if other women could bear it, then so, too, could she. It was inevitable anyway, for she needed heirs if she were going to pass along the legacy of Mistbury Arms. But was Stephen de Burgh the man she would choose to father her children? She looked up at him, standing directly before her, immobile as the Rock of Gibraltar. His stature was that of a king; proud and imposing, capable of commanding great armies of men. The thick mantle wrapped around him could not disguise his broad shoulders and muscled chest, nor hide the power behind his panther-like grace. Her physical attraction to him was undeniable, and she even wondered whether coupling with this man could be the horror she had heard described. But she still harbored doubts about him, doubts which made it difficult to accept his proposition.

"I must believe unconditionally in the man who would be my husband," she said, answering him at last, "and I know you not at all. How can I be certain of your true intent?"

Stephen's darker eyes narrowed when she finally began speaking, angered by her skepticism. His jaw clenched, and she saw a small muscle jump beneath his seemingly calm persona. He leaned into her so that his face came within inches of her own.

"My intent, Lady Woodville," he breathed, "is to thwart any future raids upon my lands and yours by a corrupt, opportunistic barbarian who will stop at nothing until he gets what he wants. Is that so difficult for you to believe?"

"I cannot yet answer that question, my lord," she said, far from being intimidated. "It seems there would be other ways for you to reinforce your army other than taking me to wife."

He expelled a sharp breath. "Certainly there are, Lady Woodville," Stephen replied. "For instance, I could stop accepting scutage from the vassals on my land and demand their military service instead. But that would not get me any sons, now would it? For that I require a wife!"

His reminder that he would claim his husbandly rights brought to the forefront of Victoria's mind the warnings of the wives in her castle, and she was not capable of hiding the blush that stole upon her cheeks, or the embarrassment that flickered in her eyes.

Stephen noticed at once, and his anger melted away like ice in the heat of summer, replaced by surprise and the dawn of understanding. So it wasn't only distrust stemming from not knowing him which caused the fair Lady Woodville to not accept his proposal. It was fear. This strong, independent ruler who aptly and bravely commanded her own army was frightened of the intimate coupling between man and wife.

"You're afraid."

"No."

"Don't deny it." His voice was quiet. "I saw it in your eyes. When I said that I want to mate with you, that I want you to bear my children, I saw your fear."

" 'Tis not fear," Victoria insisted. "It's just that—"

"What?"

She ran her tongue across her lips, moistening them as if it would help her to explain.

"I've heard talk amongst the wives in my household. They speak of how appalling it is to mate with a man. Of the pain, of the mess, and of the inexplicable loneliness after the deed is done. They make it seem as though women are nothing more than vessels for men's lust. Most likely 'tis only foolish babble, but I . . . I've not heard anyone contradict them. Ever."

The honesty of her confession infused him with sympathy. He also could not help but admire Victoria's caution. She would be a fool to blindly trust a stranger, despite the history between their two families. But he had an idea that might help to erase her doubts and fears. He guided them both back down upon the bench.

"So you fear that I'll steal your lands by day and rut against you like a stag in heat by night."

Heat stained her cheeks. "My lord," she protested, but Stephen held up his hand to silence her.

"I did not say that I blame you for your doubts. In fact, I admire them. You would not be where you are today if you trusted like a child."

He grasped one of her hands in his, and his thumb began stroking against the back of her hand, while he rested his other hand upon the top of her thigh. Victoria had to force herself to concentrate on what he was saying, and she idly wondered if he were trying to seduce her to get what he wanted.

"I will prove to you that I am trustworthy, Lady Woodville, and not the fortune-seeking brute you imagine."

She was about to defend herself from his taunting accusation, until she saw the twinkle lighting his eyes and the faint smile that curled one side of his sensual mouth. Victoria's heart sprang into a backflip.

"How will you prove it?" she asked, her voice becoming thick.

He looked into her wide green eyes and saw the stirrings of desire within their mesmerizing depths. How easy it would be to wrap his arms around her soft, lush body, pull her tightly against him, and capture her lips in a soul-stirring kiss. He could imagine the sweet, hot, wet taste of her mouth, and then the salacious rapture of her nipple as he suckled it like a hungry child. His cock, hard as marble, begged for release from the confines of his braies. But he could not give in to his carnal hunger, not here, not now. Instead, with indomitable self-control, he focused on what he had to say and in getting her to agree to what he wanted.

"Mistbury Arms is built upon a solid foundation of rock. At least, that is the appearance and it's what most would assume when they see your castle. The fact that there is one small section of softer subsoil is a well-guarded secret. I did not know about the area myself until we questioned the prisoners."

"It's true," Victoria agreed. "That small area of soft terrain has been a family secret for generations."

"But Hamlin Port knew about it, and he knew exactly where to command his knights to dig so that they gained entrance to the inner bailey underneath the ground."

She knew what he was going to say next, had even thought it herself. But it was still a difficult thing to accept.

"You've got a loose tongue among your staff, Lady Woodville. Someone is betraying you."

The words sank her heart as if they were weighted with stone. Yet even as Victoria felt her head shaking back and forth in denial, the movement seemed false, hollow, and she realized that she had suspected the exact same thing herself. How else was it possible that Hamlin Port's army knew just where to dig amid the enormous area of land surrounding her castle, and where they would end up once they had reached the other side? The idea of a traitor among her beloved staff was as difficult to accept as the death of a child, but she knew deep within her soul that it had to be the truth.

"Perhaps what you say is true, Lord de Burgh, but how does my apparently deceitful staff prove your own trustworthiness? Am I to presume that since you are drawing this to my attention, I should judge your own character to be without reproach? Is that my 'proof'?"

Something about the tone in her voice when she made that statement, at once both presumptuous and vulnerable, caused Stephen to smile. There was a feminine spark within this woman that he found irresistible.

"On the contrary, Lady Woodville," he replied. "Your proof shall come when I reveal to you the traitor."

The surety in his words forced Victoria to look back at him. "How can you be so certain you'll find him?"

"Because in doing so I will obtain you for my wife."

His eyes darkened as he answered her, lending an air of seduction to his stark, simple answer. His hand reached out to caress her face, the backs of his fingers gliding along her cheekbone as smoothly as a skater across a flawless sheet of ice. His touch was gentle, like the whiff of a summer breeze, floating in silent exploration over the delicate curves of her face.

Despite her hesitancy to accept his marriage proposal, Victoria could not ignore the waves of sensuality washing over her with his every caress. She felt heat rise to the surface of her skin, flushing her cheeks red with evidence of her desire. Her pulse quickened and began trembling, tiny beats that fluttered against her neck like an excited bird in its cage.

His fingers followed a trail back up toward her mouth, then again skimmed across both her top and bottom lip. She had no idea her lips could be so sensitive; it was as if every nerve in her body originated from them. He dropped his fingers away until only the forefinger remained. It rested upon her lower lip for a moment, then slowly he eased it between her lips and into her mouth.

Against her will Victoria's eyes fluttered shut, drawing all her attention to the taste and feel of Stephen's intimate touch. His finger grazed the tops of her bottom teeth, and then moved forward to sweep over the tip of her tongue. He collected some of the warm dew inside her mouth, then he withdrew his finger and swept it around her lips as if he were painting them.

Victoria opened her eyes just as Stephen took his finger off her lips, and she saw him rub the tip of his forefinger against his thumb as if he were sampling the juice of an exotic nectar.

"Your other concerns will be addressed as well," Stephen said, moving still closer beside her, the heat from his body flowing into her like sunlight.

"My concerns?" she asked, although she knew what he was talking about.

"The wives from the castle and their whispered gossip. The pain. The mess. The horrors of coupling."

"My lord, I hardly think—"

"I shall prove to you the futility of listening to gossip. I shall prove to you how baseless their words are. When I am finished, Victoria, you will know the unbelievable wonders that occur when men and women mate."

His words were sharp and intense, and Victoria saw a flash of anger cross his face as if he were personally affronted by what she had told him.

"You will give me one month," he continued. "For one month I shall stay at Mistbury Arms and discover who it is that has betrayed you to Hamlin Port. And for one month I shall visit you in your solar and teach you the ways of love. You will know pleasure as you've never known it before, Victoria, and you will discover things about yourself that you never knew existed. I want to give this to you, as I want you to give it back to me in return."

She cleared her throat. "I don't know . . ."

"I know."

His voice did not waver for a moment. "If at the end of one month you still feel that walking barefoot atop the burning logs in your hearth fire would be preferable to sharing my bed, I will withdraw my marriage proposal and leave."

"And what of Hamlin Port?"

"Hamlin Port be damned. We shall have to fight him alone and hope he does not trounce the lot of us."

Stephen's final words were like a warning bell, reminding Victoria of all that was at stake should Hamlin Port's army conquer her lands. Was that a risk she was willing to take? When she had become head of this household five years ago, she vowed to uphold the dignity and honor of the Woodville name. And she also vowed to pass along those traits to her heirs. To maintain her pledges she knew she must marry sooner or later, and partnering with Stephen de Burgh would fortify her lands and naturally enable her to bear children. But it would also mean forfeiting her independence and relinquishing sole control of her estate to someone she had only just met. Was he telling her the truth? Could she trust him? Victoria took great gulps of calming breath deep into her lungs, exhaling slowly, clearing her mind. She asked herself the question a second time. *Could she trust Stephen de Burgh?* Her eyes swept over his lean, massive body, strength surging from every pore, his strong jaw set, his face a powerful mask of determination. Without doubt, she would have to.

"Very well," she said, rising to her feet. "I shall accept your proposal, my lord." She shook the folds of her mantle as if to rid herself of crumbs, then pulled the thick fabric tightly around her body. "Find me a traitor. The month begins as of sunrise tomorrow."

Stephen allowed a smile to touch his lips as he noticed how she deliberately avoided addressing the second part of their bargain. "And at sun*set* tomorrow, I shall see you in your solar."

Victoria's face flamed at his candid remark, but she could not ignore the spark of desire that raced through her veins. Stephen de Burgh was the most striking man she'd ever laid eyes upon, exuding a bold sensuality that made certain his promises of pleasuring her were more than heady words. She felt suddenly like a traveler about to venture into an untamed, savage jungle.

Chapter Two

Fire was everywhere. Flames crackled within the fireplace, rushes were anchored to the wall, and atop the private dining table was an elaborate centerpiece of wax candles. Light danced throughout the room, creating a myriad of intricate shadows upon the walls and ceiling. Her apartment had never looked so beautiful.

Victoria entered at precisely half past six, as Stephen had requested. She was dressed as though attending a formal affair, though she knew it would be only the two of them in attendance. The pale blue tunic she wore had full-length lace sleeves from elbow to wrist. Layered over it was a sleeveless dark blue surcote, drawn up around her waist with a linen belt and fastened at the top with a sapphire brooch that sparkled in the candle flames. Her long chestnut hair was plaited and fashioned into a bun, and covered with gold netting.

Stephen was already in the room, overseeing the servants, when she entered. Her transformation from the strong warrior he'd first met two days ago to the ethereal goddess standing before him now was astounding. She radiated the delicate beauty of an angel, but with an underlying aura of vibrant self-confidence.

"Leave us," Stephen commanded the servants, who immediately whisked themselves away at his behest. For a brief moment Victoria was taken aback, seeing the proof before she and Stephen were even wed of how easily he would rule. But just as quickly as the thought had come she brushed it aside, refusing to dwell on that which she could not control.

Stephen rose from the chair upon which he sat, his long legs bringing him to stand before her in seconds. She tipped her face up to meet him, smiling as she saw the effect she had on him.

"You're stunning," he said simply, making no effort to mask his desire. With one arm he reached out to take her hand and draw it up to his lips. He brushed a kiss upon the back of her hand, and Victoria's breath caught in her throat when he leaned closer toward her. For one wild moment she thought he would kiss her, and she felt the leap of her heart as she imagined how his lips would feel upon hers, his hot breath caressing her cheek as he bent his head down. But instead Stephen clasped his hand around hers and drew her gently toward the table.

"I've had the servants prepare us a special feast," he said, pulling the chair out for her as she sat down. "A celebration of sorts."

He took his own seat and poured them each a glass of wine from the jug by his side. When he was finished, he grasped the stem of his glass and raised it to Victoria. "A toast," he said, with a twinkle lighting his midnight-blue eyes, "to the beginning of our relationship. May we both enjoy years of happiness."

"Lord de Burgh," Victoria said sharply, refusing to lift her glass in response. "I hardly find that appropriate. If you'll recall our agreement, I have one month to decide whether or not I can trust you and wish to take you as my mate. That is far from a sealed bargain."

Stephen drank deeply from his wineglass and picked up the jug to pour a refill. "Like you, Lady Woodville," he said as the wine splashed into his glass, "I admit to having a healthy dose of self-confidence. I've no doubt that our agreement will lead to the outcome I desire."

He smiled as he made his declaration, but its brilliance failed to achieve the hoped-for response in Victoria that it had in so many other women.

"That, my lord," Victoria said, at last lifting her glass, "will be for me to decide."

She trained her eyes upon his face as she drank her wine, testing the effect of her words. No doubt Stephen de Burgh had had his share of willing females falling at his feet, but Victoria refused to play into his hand. It would take much more than smug arrogance for him to make her his wife.

She noted that he remained silent for a time, not responding to her last statement with words, but instead answering it with the dark look in his eyes. He stared at her with a sharp intensity that was becoming familiar. She had issued him a challenge; one he was all too willing to accept. She felt the hairs raise on her arm.

He pushed his steely body away from the table and walked over to where covered dishes rested upon a sideboard. Lifting a copper tureen by the handles on its side, he carried it back to where Victoria still sat. He stood next to her so closely that his fine wool tunic brushed against her arm, and she could smell the faint scent of his bathing soap mingling with his own unmistakable aroma. It drifted over to her like a curl of smoke, enveloping her as if she were being branded as Stephen's own.

Then it was replaced with a different aroma, that of the fragrant lamb stew he ladled into her bowl. The thick broth was filled with onions and garlic, peas, beans, and turnips, along with the seasoned meat. With the stew Stephen also served fresh bread and cheese. Small bowls of dried fruits and nuts accompanied the meal.

Once they'd both been served, Stephen resumed sitting and they began to eat. The food was delicious, but Stephen was more interested in learning about Victoria's background than he was in their meal.

"My father knew your sire," he said. "Tell me of him."

"He was a wonderful man," Victoria answered, the memory of her beloved parent lighting her face with joy. "Strong in his convictions but always willing to listen to the voices of others. He had great respect for the people who dwelled within his castle, and for his serfs and villagers." She paused for a moment to cut some meat from her stew and take sips of the broth. "He taught me all I know about being a leader and gaining respect from those you lead."

The fire from the candles shone in her eyes, making them sparkle like priceless jewels. "The main thing I remember my father teaching me," she continued, "is that respect is earned, not demanded. You can order your servants and your knights to respect you, but it will be given only grudgingly and won't be genuine. If you earn it, it can last forever."

She fell silent after that, and Stephen hoped he had not upset her. He knew both her father and her mother had died from the pox within days of one another.

She set aside her spoon, no longer interested in eating, and a tenuous silence settled between them. But as Stephen regarded the woman seated opposite him who might one day become his wife, he again noted the calm, inner strength she radiated. Even the tragic loss of her parents did not shake the foundation of that strength. It was almost as if she gathered spiritual energy from sharing her memories with him.

"What of your family?" she asked, breaking the silence. "Have you any siblings?"

"A cartful." Stephen smiled. "I am the eldest of eight. My sire yet lives as well. In fact, he resides at Blenleigh."

"But you are lord there."

Stephen nodded, stretching his long legs out before him as he turned sideways in his chair. "My father was always a strong man, but the years have taken their toll on him."

His right arm rested atop the table, the linen sleeve of his tunic doing nothing to conceal the swell of muscles beneath. He sat with a relaxed, easy posture that bespoke of his confidence.

"I would imagine," Victoria said, scrutinizing him as if trying to solve a puzzle, "that being the eldest of all those siblings has thrust you into the role of leader for a very long time."

"I suppose it has," Stephen agreed.

"You've grown accustomed to giving commands."

"It's part of the role."

"And never, ever being denied from getting what you want."

He rose from his chair, flexing with tension like a lion about to spring. Before Victoria could blink, he stood at her side, breathing down upon her with sparks in his eyes. "I would have no more of these crafty hints," he growled. "Say what you mean."

A flash of anger crackled the air between them. Victoria stood as well, refusing to cower before this hulk of a man.

"Any ruler used to having his own way would naturally want to expand his empire so as to command even more power. Might that be the real motivation behind your wanting to lay claim to Mistbury Arms?"

She stood so close to him that he felt her warm breath upon his cheeks as she issued her challenge. He could see the quick steady beats of her pulse, evidence of her irritation. But beneath her willful exterior he sensed a trickle of uncertainty, as if she were reluctant to believe her own accusation. Then what would be the motivation behind her words? Was it masking her fear?

As they stood face to face before the snapping fire, Stephen felt an unexpected jolt of raw lust burn within his loins. Reaching down to grasp her small hand within his, he drew it to his lips and branded a kiss upon it. "You don't think that, Victoria," he said, his voice thick and low, "and both of us know it. 'Twas not at my behest that Port's army tried to overtake your castle."

She said nothing in response, absorbing his words, unresisting as he continued to grasp her hand and lead her through the arched, narrow doorway that separated her apartments from her solar. Though the room was now devoid of servants, their earlier presence was clear. The fireplace crackled with a blazing fire and burning rushes were mounted to the wall. A thick tallow candle was also lit, set upon the small wooden stand beside her oak bed. It was covered with layers of thick, vibrant covers, and surrounded by velvet curtains, drawn back and tied to the bedposts with narrow velvet cords. It was toward the bed where Stephen was headed.

Realization of where he was leading her cleared Victoria's thoughts like a bucket of icy water. She stopped walking, planting her feet to the floor as if they'd grown roots. Stephen noted her resistance, but was not in the least dissuaded from his mission.

"I do not bite," he said, pulling her against him and circling his arm behind her back, "nor will I be persuaded to change my mind."

She gave him no response, but he could feel the slight trembling of her body against his, and he realized that she had not been bluffing when she'd expressed her concerns about being with a man. But as he looked down upon her face, he also noted the lustful darkening of her forest green eyes, and he smiled with appreciation of how strongly she desired him. The feeling was mutual.

They sat together upon the bed, supported by layers of pillows with their backs against the headboard. Reaching over to the stand beside the bed, Stephen lifted the two wineglasses that had earlier been filled and passed one to Victoria.

"To our first night together," he murmured, touching the rim of his glass to hers.

"To our first night together," she answered, drinking deeply of the wine and allowing the fermented juice to calm her nerves. It was warm and spiced; a drink she'd never before tasted.

"It's gløgg," Stephen said in response to her unasked question. "A drink from my Nordic ancestors. It will help to relax you." And after her third glass of the sweet beverage, Victoria was aware that the drink had accomplished its purpose.

Stephen set aside the glasses and turned his body so that he could face her. His hand reached out to caress the silky skin of her neck, then trailed downward to the fragile area around her throat and collarbone. His touch was soft, sensual, almost reverent, as if sampling the delicate petals of a rose.

"How beautiful," he said, moving his hand ever downward until it met the neckline of her tunic. Undeterred by the cloth, his fingers glided on top of it until they met the beginning swell of her breast. He reached his other arm behind her to pull her forward, aligning their bodies so that they faced one another. Then he moved them both down upon the expansive bed so that they were half-sitting, half-lying, resting against the pillows. He heard the sharp intake of her breath, her awareness of their intimacy.

"The foundation of any relationship is trust, Victoria. Trust within your soul that I will not harm you, even as I make you burn with passion."

Was that a threat? A *promise?*

"I've given you one month, my lord," she answered. "It's up to you to convince me that I was right to do so."

He nearly groaned aloud from the flood of ecstasy that surged within him as she granted her acceptance. Blood raced through his veins; he felt his body harden and tremble with unfulfilled lust, and it was only with enormous restraint that he managed not to rip away her chemise and tunic, part her legs, and bury himself in her. But he knew that would ruin everything and only confirm her worst fears. If he allowed his primitive, overwhelming hunger for her to take control of his senses, the pain and humiliation she would feel could never be erased. So it was that he reined in the wild, ravenous beast that was desire, vowing to unleash it as soon as he was able.

"And so I shall," he answered. He brought around the arm that had been behind her so that he could use both hands to untie the cloth belt around her surcote. The fabric was easily undone, and he tossed it aside. Then he reached down to grasp the bottom of her surcote, drawing it over her legs. He could go no further without her assistance. "Lift your hips," he instructed, wondering whether or not she would resist. She did not. He brought the woolen fabric up and over her head and then, as he had done with the belt, tossed it aside.

She felt the coolness in the air without the extra layer of clothing to protect her, but she knew that the goose bumps on her arms were not strictly the result of being chilled. Stephen's attention excited her. When his strong, sensual hands caressed her skin, it was as if every one of his fingers were a smoldering torch, heating her blood and inflaming her passion. She felt herself opening up to him, her unease peeling away like the clothing he tossed aside.

He took hold of her hand, positioning her fingers so that they were pointed toward him, then slowly, very slowly, he drew her first finger inside his mouth. He swirled his tongue around her finger, bathing it, consuming it like a morsel of succulent fruit. He did the same to her next finger, and the one after that, all the while staring into her eyes, gauging her reaction. At first she did not look at him; her eyelids had closed in rapture from the rush of exotic sensations he introduced. But he had to see her, he had to know what she was feeling, and the only way he could be certain was to gaze into the depths of her soul.

"Look at me, Victoria," he commanded, though his voice was barely above a whisper. Her eyes opened, responding to his words, fixating on him as if drawn by magnetic force. He could see the evidence of her arousal, her forest green irises stained dark with passion. Her lips were slightly parted, expelling shallow breaths, quickened by her stirring desire. The tip of her tongue darted out to moisten her lips.

Lust heated his loins when he saw the simple gesture, hardening him, pressing his erection so that it strained painfully against his braies. He yearned to free both of them from every restrictive stitch of their clothing, discarding hoses, chemises, tunics, and surcotes so they would feel nothing but the silky cream of skin against skin as their bodies stroked and caressed one another, rubbing hotly together like two sticks of wood, igniting fire between them.

"You're exquisite," he breathed, releasing her hand and wrapping his arm behind her back, then pressing her body against his and bringing their faces toward one another so that their lips were mere inches apart. He continued looking at her, noticing the way her body had become pliable and unresisting, trusting him to do as he pleased.

With his free hand he pushed aside the linen tunic and chemise from her shoulder, baring the creamy bronzed skin beneath. He tipped her head back so that he also had access to the arched elegance of her neck. He pulled her even closer, then dropped his head down and brought his lips upon her shoulder. He nibbled and kissed the delicate skin, noting the shivers of goose bumps that ran down her arm as he did so. With his tongue he licked the area he had just kissed, moving slowly along her shoulder and up toward her neck. His hand reached out and pulled away the gold net from her hair, then shook out the pins holding up the thick braids encircling the back of her head. He worked his fingers through her thick chestnut mane, undoing the braids until her hair flowed across the pillows like a sable river. He plunged his fingers into the silky depth, caressing the strands, massaging the back of her neck and her scalp. His lips and tongue continued their journey along the side of her neck, moving ever upward, until they reached her ear. With small, facile sweeps of his tongue he traced the swirled outline of her ear, then dipped inside the delicate chamber.

Victoria trembled in response to his invasion; so hot, so intimate. No longer chilled from when he had removed her surcote, her body ignited like tinder. She burned with an insatiable longing for him to crush her closer against his broad chest. She moved her left hand so that it rested atop the side of his body. Despite the layers of clothing from his undershirt, tunic, and surcote, she could feel the raw power of his muscles as they rippled and bunched beneath her fingers. Her hand stroked the length of his body, down the side, against the narrow curve of his hip, then back up again. She moved her hand as far behind him as she could to caress his back. She still felt the hot, wet exploration of his tongue inside her ear, and the sensual strokes of his fingers as they played with her hair. She started to shake against him, her body trembling with burgeoning need. There was a slight sting on her earlobe as Stephen nipped the tender flesh, followed by the soothing, erotic wash of his tongue. She tipped her head back and arched her neck, wanting, needing his lips upon the vulnerable skin, drowning her with his kiss. He hungrily acquiesced, burning a trail of fire along her throat. She uttered a breathy moan of acceptance, at the same time aware of the growing, insistent throbbing centered between her thighs, and the flood of moisture like liquid desire.

She moved her hands to wrap them around his forearms, thrilling to the sinewy force flexing beneath her fingertips. Stephen uncoiled his fingers from her silky chestnut mane and began trailing them along her throat and then moving lower still, slipping beneath her clothing, until he reached the beginning swell of her breasts. Using only his fingertips, he grazed them lightly across the sensitive flesh, skimming over the nipples. He glanced over at her, but Victoria could not look at him for her eyes had fluttered closed as his fingers stroked and teased her nipples. She gripped his forearms tighter and arched her back toward him, desperate for his touches, wanting him to caress her breasts with his entire hand. Instead she felt one of his arms circle her waist while his hand withdrew from underneath her chemise to support her back. He then lifted her toward him, bringing her face a whisper away from his.

He paused for only a moment, his eyes drinking her in, absorbing every detail. She felt his breath upon her cheeks, sweet and spicy from the wine, and the heady, woodsy smell of him. Off in the distance she heard the crackling of the fire, then suddenly she could hear no more save for the roar of her own blood rushing in her eardrums as his lips came crashing down upon hers.

His kiss was forceful and powerful like the man himself, erupting into her as if the tenuous hold on his lust was suddenly unleashed. She opened herself to him, parting her lips and allowing his tongue to enter her. He tasted every inch of her mouth, running his tongue along her teeth, drawing her into him. He pulled away just for a moment, licking the outside of her lips, leaving a trail of his moisture and then sealing their mouths together once more.

His hands were all over her, roaming, caressing. Over her clothing he stroked the lush mounds of her breasts, pinching and teasing her stiff, engorged nipples. In sensuous circles he rubbed his palms over and over her bosom, and then kneaded the flesh until Victoria thought she would go mad from the passion he inflamed in her. The center of her thighs was flooded with her moisture, and she ached from the insistent throbbing in her groin. Her arms were wrapped around his neck, pulling him closer, wanting him to crush her under his weight. The evidence of his arousal was pressed against her thigh, and with age-old instinct she parted her legs.

The kiss was broken as abruptly as it had begun. As he pulled away from her, Victoria's eyes flew open in confusion. What was happening? Had she done something wrong?

"The rest of your clothing comes off now," he said, making her shiver from the force of his tense, possessive words.

Seeing her tremble, Stephen held her against his chest and breathed into her hair. "Do not fear me, Victoria—enjoy the power you have over me. You make me burn for you. You're a woman of uncommon passion. But before I make you mine, I must know that you trust me, body and soul. You need to feel relaxed in my presence without the barrier of clothing, because I will have you naked before me many, many times."

She expelled a long, calming breath, knowing he was right. His caresses excited her and had already chipped away at some of her fears. But coupling was not done while wearing clothing, and she must learn to trust him. She had given him one month.

"Stand beside the bed."

"Remember your manners."

He smiled at her reproach, knowing she was right. He was so used to commanding and leading his army at Blenleigh that he was sometimes coarser than he needed to be.

"*Please* stand beside the bed."

She swung her feet over the mattress and stood before him. Her hands rested calmly by her sides, waiting, trusting. He sat on the edge of the bed and reached down to grasp the hem of her tunic and chemise. He then rose to his feet, dwarfing her with his height, making her feel like a young girl. But her body belied that thought, evidenced when Stephen at last pulled away the remaining garments and her full, ripe breasts came spilling forward, the dusky nipples tempered to stone from the fire of her passion. He studied her for a moment, lost in her breathtaking beauty.

As instantaneous as a streak of lightning, her naked body ignited fire within him. He became painfully aware of the blood racing within his veins, hardening his manhood until it was like a granite rod stuffed within his braies. He raked his eyes over her, feasting on the stiff, dark nipples of her breasts, her smooth, flat stomach, and the curly triangle of black hair at the apex of her thighs. He could feel his heartbeat slamming against his chest as his body trembled with untamed lust.

He sat her back down upon the bed, then bent to remove the light leather slippers upon her feet. When he stood back up, he noticed the stubborn lilt of her chin, as if daring him to make her feel embarrassed by her nudity. He sat next to her, stroking her shoulders, her arms, caressing the silken wonder of her supple skin. He dipped his head down to kiss her neck, pleased by the way she leaned her head back to accommodate him.

"Lie on your stomach, Victoria," he said, then added a hasty "please" when he saw her eyes narrow. She did as she was asked, settling her head upon her hands. Her back had a beautiful curve to the spine, enticing his eyes to travel downward toward the firm twin mounds of her buttocks.

"Have you ever been massaged?" he asked, picking up a small glass vile from the nightstand.

"The servants sometimes—"

"Other than by your servants."

Victoria gave a start as she felt the drizzling of warm liquid upon her back, and then Stephen's large, splayed hands moving sensuously along her spine.

"No, I suppose I haven't," she said, her eyes closing as Stephen stroked and kneaded the muscles in her back. His hands glided along both sides of her spine, warming the oil beneath them and easing away every drop of tension. With his fingertips he made small circles against the back of her neck, then his hands stroked downward once again. He massaged the sides of her body, and his fingers made contact with the luxurious swell of the sides of her breasts. Her heard the instant change in her breathing as he did so—deep, calm exhalations became the quick, shallow breaths of arousal. He continued to tease the sensitive skin, fluttering his fingertips against the swollen mounds. Without realizing it, her buttocks began to squirm, inviting his hands to stroke and caress her. His hands traveled downward, along the slope of her spine and up to the curve of her ripe, supple bottom. He was not as gentle with her here. He pinched and squeezed her teasing, squirming backside, instinctively knowing how much force he could use to arouse her without causing pain. He dipped his finger inside the crevice of her bottom, testing her to see whether she would tense at the invasion. But she lifted herself toward him; an invitation for more.

His fingers strayed between her legs to sample the moist petals of her labia, caressing the velvety softness. She was drenched with moisture and hot, so hot.

"Spread your legs for me," he whispered, while his fingers continued to stroke the lush folds of her sheath. She complied without comment, moving her legs apart and allowing him unrestricted access to the most intimate part of her body. She kept her head resting to one side with her eyes closed; embarrassed, perhaps, by the intimacy of his request. Though he wanted her to look at him, he respected her feelings and kept quiet. For now.

With her thighs opened, he could engulf his fingers in the slick fire of her womanhood. He foraged through the slippery petals, stroking, petting, amazed by the flood of her juices. He brought his finger toward the front of her vagina until he nuzzled her swollen nub of pleasure. She began panting as he stroked her, moaning into the bed as her hips writhed and twisted against his hand. He continued to fondle and caress her clitoris, relentlessly stroking back and forth, inciting her with unbearable passion. The folds of her labia were engorged with lust, and she spread her legs wider, imploring him to continue.

But he would not give her release, not just yet, and he stopped, momentarily, from caressing her swollen kernel. He drew his fingers down toward the opening of her flooded passage, swirling them outside the rim, preparing her for his entrance. When she responded to this contact with all the ardor and passion of his previous caresses, he knew she was ready for him and he slipped his finger inside.

"Stephen!" she gasped, alarmed, enthralled by what he was doing to her.

"Enjoy," he murmured, his low voice as soothing as chocolate. "Learn your own body, Victoria. Know what gives you pleasure. Feel my finger inside of you. Feel as I stroke and caress your beautiful body. Do you like it? Do you like what I'm doing to you?"

She said nothing at first, too steeped in the overwhelming rush of erotic sensations as his finger plunged in and out of her. But he inserted another finger, stretching her wider, and repeated his question, demanding an answer.

"Do you like this, Victoria?"

"Yes!" she exclaimed, bearing down, meeting every thrust as he penetrated her wet, burning chamber. She kept her eyes squeezed shut though her desire was evident by the deep red flush of her cheeks. He could wait no longer for her to look at him.

"Turn over," he said, withdrawing his fingers from their moist, salacious shelter. She opened her eyes, unsure why he deprived her when her body still throbbed with need, but hoping that he would continue, she quickly complied.

In one fluid movement she rolled onto her back, displaying her smooth, pliant body like a sexual offering. Stephen could feel trickles of sweat coursing down his chest as his body flared with the heat of his desire. She was beautiful, exquisite, perfect, and needed to know it.

"Bend your knees and part your legs for me, Victoria," he whispered. As she did so, he again slipped his fingers inside of her, but when she began to close her eyes, he spoke to prevent it.

"Look at me," he implored, "and watch what I do. Look down at my fingers as they thrust in and out of you. Understand how beautiful you are, Victoria. Flaunt your body for me."

He drew her in with his dark eyes, forcing her to watch him by the sheer power of his mesmerizing words. He urged her legs farther and farther apart, wanting her to hide nothing from him, reveling in her nudity.

"I want to devour you," he growled as his fingers continued to penetrate her slick vaginal walls. He captured her with his gaze, pleased as her face flushed red and her eyes glazed over with passion. He knew that her earlier embarrassment had vanished as she understood the intimate, sexual bond that formed when a man and woman coupled.

She ground her hips against him, seeking release, and as she approached climax, he bent over and with the tip of his tongue licked her straining clitoris to drive her over the edge.

She screamed as the carnal waves broke over her, bucking her hips and driving his fingers deeper inside of her. At last the throbbing began to subside, and as she looked at Stephen, he slowly withdrew his fingers from inside of her and inserted them into his mouth, licking away her juices, showing her how much he craved the essence of her. Then he bent over and kissed her moist, open lips, still swollen from their earlier passionate embrace. This time it was Victoria who first plunged her tongue within his mouth, licking and stroking him, tasting herself.

Stephen began to shake with the force of his desire for her. Saints be damned, but he wanted her. He was rock-hard with painful, throbbing lust. Every nerve in his body cried out for him to take her, to bury himself to the hilt within her, thrusting, pounding, over and over, until they both screamed and wept with the joy of their release. He could do it, and she would let him. But that time had not yet come. He had never hungered for a woman as badly as he did now, his body imploring him to take her. Her succulent, sweet femininity was naked before him and throbbing from the force of her passion. So what was stopping him? Why didn't he shove down his braies and hose and bury himself to the hilt, mindlessly pistoning in and out until his hot seed erupted inside of her?

He pulled away, knowing the answer almost before he asked himself the question. He could barely maintain control over his need for her. How would that possibly equate to making love? He did not trust himself to be unlike those brutes she'd heard stories of, those who simply slaked their lust on women, heedless of whether there was pleasure—or pain—on her part. This was what Victoria feared, and this was what he vowed not to do to her. His fingers were one thing, but his manhood was quite another. He had to leave her wanting more, so that she would permit him to come to her again.

He exhaled deeply, moving away from her and sitting at the side of the bed. In an instant Victoria knew that something had changed, something she did not understand. She covered herself with a blanket and scooted into a sitting position.

"Is anything wrong?"

He said nothing at first, only stared at her as if to imprint her memory on his brain. "You're an able student, Lady Woodville," he said at last, "but that's all I need to teach you for tonight."

For one brief moment he saw the confusion—the hurt—within her eyes, almost as if he were rejecting her, and it stabbed his heart like the arrow of a crossbow. Then she glowered at him, disliking the way he seemed to dismiss her. "I am not afraid of you, Stephen," she said. "Surely you realize that?"

He did not answer her, but instead moved off the bed, causing the ropes beneath the mattress to lift as they were unburdened with his weight. He walked to the doorway and unlatched the heavy lock. "Until tomorrow evening," he said, barely moving fast enough to dodge the pillow Victoria hurled at his head.

She did not watch him go, but she knew when she was alone in the room by the absence of his footsteps against the wooden planks on the floor. Her breathing was once again calm; her heartbeats strong and steady rather than slamming within her chest as they had while Stephen brought her to climax. She thought back on the hours that had just transpired, remembering the way her body reacted to his touch, inflaming her passions until she squirmed against him like a bitch in heat. But she was not mortified about her behavior; there was no flush of shame that heated her cheeks. She had agreed to let Stephen teach her about love, and lust, and the intimacies created between a man and a woman, and despite all the bleak stories she'd heard in the past, she already looked forward to what tomorrow would bring.

Shouts and laughter from the multitude of people breaking their fast in the great hall created a riotous din, but Stephen and Hendrick paid no more attention to the noise than they would a fly as they discussed their progress on finding who had betrayed Victoria.

"So far I've spoken to the head cook, the butler, numerous pages and men-at-arms, the porter, and the chamberlain," said Hendrick, washing down the last of his bread with a hearty swig of warm ale. "Not one of them has given me a whit of information, and they all say the same thing. Lady Woodville has the courage of a gladiator and the compassion of a village priest. She leads her people, she provides for their welfare, and they can't imagine anyone wishing her ill will." He shook his head, baffled that not the whisper of a clue had yet to come forth. "I don't know, brother. Perhaps we're wrong to think she was betrayed."

"And that Port just had the luck of the devil on his side?" Stephen's fist gripped the base of his ale mug, choking it as though it were Hamlin Port's neck. "I don't accept that, Hendrick. That thin strip of subsoil is hidden from view, and as difficult to access as a conference with the king. There's no way Port would have just discovered it by accident. Someone had to have told him."

Hendrick only nodded, knowing that there was nothing he could say to change Stephen's mind. He had a stubborn streak once his mind was made up, but the truth of the matter was, he was usually right.

"So what's next?" the younger brother asked, plucking a fig from the fruit bowl in front of them.

Stephen finished off the last of his ale and wiped his mouth with the linen napkin. "We talk to Esmond Bele."

"The worthless fool can rot in hell!" Hamlin Port snarled, slamming his ale tankard upon the wooden table as spittle flew from his lips.

His chief knight, Jonas Auber, used to his master's frequent high temper, said nothing until Hamlin stopped ranting, albeit momentarily, in order to gulp more ale.

"De Burgh's army caught us off guard," he admitted. "But I'll speak with Melina to learn when we can plan another raid."

Hamlin smacked his hands together toward the pages hovering nearby. "Keep these glasses full!" he shouted, "and bring some bread and a wheel of cheese. This minute!"

The pages, already shaking in fear from Hamlin's previous outburst, ran toward the butlery as if fire licked their heels.

Port turned back toward Jonas and pointed an accusing finger at the knight. "Let me make one thing perfectly clear, Auber," he said, the ragged scar down the left side of his face flushed an angry red with his temper. "That wanton whore who warms your sheets had better get her information right this time, or she'll have me to answer to. No matter how much she despises Victoria Woodville, she'll get no revenge if we don't succeed in taking Mistbury Arms."

Jonas fumed at Hamlin's base description of his lover. "Melina is no whore," he insisted, "and her information was correct. We found the subsoil and dug through it, clear into the bailey. She couldn't have known about de Burgh."

The pages arrived bearing the requested food and drink. They served Hamlin, then Jonas, careful not to splash one drop of ale lest the castle lord's powerful hand smack their young faces. Once they were gone, Hamlin broke off a hunk of bread from the loaves the pages had brought, and stuffed his mouth full.

"Spare your excuses for someone who gives a damn, Auber," Hamlin said through a mouthful of bread, "and get me the information I want. Tell your little garment scrubber to do whatever it takes, speak with whomever she wants, but find out what's going on in that castle over the next month so that we can plan our move." He swilled the remainder of his ale and snapped his fingers for the page to refill his tankard. "And if she doesn't come through, perhaps a sampling of my thick cock in her quim will prompt her to find out what I need."

He was a hateful, vile, repulsive man, more loathsome than the devil, but Jonas was powerless against his lord, so he held his tongue and refused to acknowledge Hamlin's depraved threat. Instead he steered him toward another subject.

"If de Burgh is still at Mistbury Arms, perhaps we should raid Blenleigh," he proposed, thinking that revenge against the man who had thwarted his last effort would appeal to Hamlin. But Port shook his head, not even considering his knight's suggestion.

"It wouldn't be worth the time or expense," he answered, staring off into the distance as if his mind were far removed from the words he spoke. "De Burgh's got an enormous, loyal army at Blenleigh, so it's protected from invasion whenever he leaves. Besides," he sneered, as though a dark enemy stood before him, "it's Mistbury Arms that I really want."

Chapter Three

He had not visited Victoria for the past two evenings, telling her he did not want to rush things, although Stephen knew that he questioned his own self-control whenever he was with her. He thought to let his passions cool for her by taking a break, but it only increased his fervent hunger. Victoria's own desires had unfurled and grown stronger, and he knew that her earlier fears waned every day that he was with her. It was impossible for him to wait any longer to claim her. Tonight she would be his.

He descended the winding stairway and walked down a long, narrow hallway toward the south end of the castle to where he could access a second set of stairs leading to the buttery. Winter's cold nip was in the air and he had decided to head toward the buttery to arrange for gløgg for this evening. The route he took was a long, circuitous one, but the shorter way would have involved going outdoors and cutting through the bailey. Since it had begun to rain, Stephen didn't mind the longer walk.

The hallway was dark no matter the time of day, and seldom used by Victoria's staff as it tended to be musty. Thus it was with some surprise that Stephen heard the unmistakable sound of voices some thirty paces ahead of him and around a narrow bend. He proceeded slowly, edging himself along the wall until he could make out what the people were saying.

"What a hot, lusty wench you are. Wrap those sweet thighs around me and let me drive my cock up your juicy quim. That's right, my sweet. Take *all* of me." The voice grunted and heaved, the breathing becoming heavier and more pronounced. Then Stephen heard a woman's voice moaning low, but increasing the volume in time to the rhythmic slapping of flesh against flesh.

"Give it to me, Jonas, give it to me," she pleaded. "I'll ride you like a stallion, I will. Now fuck meeeee!!!"

The tempo increased, along with the sighs and groans of their efforts. So engrossed in one another were they that the couple did not even notice Stephen as he came around the corner in plain view. It was obvious that the man was one of Victoria's knights, as his lance was propped up against the damp stone wall awaiting him once he had finished with the serving girl. The girl's back was up against the wall and her thighs were wrapped around his waist. The knight heaved and bucked against her, holding her buttocks in his hands to support her weight. Faster and faster he rammed in and out, approaching his peak. Finally he unleashed a roar as he spilled his seed, and they collapsed against one another, gasping from exertion.

As the girl uncoiled her legs from around her lover's waist, Stephen cleared his throat to alert them of his presence. Their heads whipped around toward the noise, and they sprang apart the second they spotted him. The girl pulled up her chemise to hide her exposed breasts as she floundered about to collect her discarded clothing. The knight was more cavalier about being caught; he would not let the other man make him look like a fool.

Once the girl had pulled her tunic over her head, Stephen addressed them both.

"Give me your names."

"I'm Melina. Melina Vesli," the girl said, a hint of obstinacy lacing her voice. "The laundress's assistant. And this is . . ." she gestured toward her lover, who scowled at Stephen but was not bold enough to argue.

"Jonas Auber. One of my lady's men-at-arms."

"You've a unique way of guarding the castle," Stephen observed dryly. "Does Lady Woodville have a problem with intruders along this damp stretch of corridor?"

The knight had grace enough to flush from embarrassment, but he declined to answer. At first.

In a few long strides Stephen stood before the belligerent knight, eclipsing the man by over a foot. His superior height was matched only by his Herculean strength as virile cords of muscle flexed across his chest and arms. His eyes snapped with anger as he glowered at the knight, looking every bit like the Viking marauder of his ancient ancestors.

"I asked you a question, Jonas Auber, and I would have my answer." Stephen did not raise his voice when angered; the eerie calm tone of his words was far more effective.

"I don't suppose she does, my lord," the knight answered, his voice trembling.

"Then get out of here now, the both of you. You do your mistress's faith in her serving staff a grave dishonor."

Their faces were impassive as Stephen rebuked them, and they did not apologize. But it took no further encouragement from him to get them to leave. Both Melina and Jonas gathered the rest of their things and walked down the opposite direction from where Stephen had come.

He watched them go, curious by what had just transpired. Most would have been shamed by the discovery of their behavior, particularly when their employer is as admired as Victoria Woodville. Yet these two appeared almost angry when Stephen mentioned her name. Did they hold any clues to the traitor in Mistbury Arms? Stephen vowed to keep a close watch on the both of them.

* * *

"Fifty bushels of malt and twenty-seven of grain, four hundred eggs and twelve gallons of beer from the villager Porter," Esmond said, noting down the tally. "Vinegar and mustard and four bushels of oats from the villager Cotter." His reckoning continued, although he knew his mistress's interest waned by the minute. Finally Esmond could no longer maintain the pretense of going over accounts.

"You're more quiet than I've ever seen you, my lady," he said, inviting Victoria to unburden herself.

She closed the ledger and pushed it aside. She could never hide anything from Esmond. "It's Lord de Burgh," she said.

"You do not like what he does to you?"

A ghost of a smile crept to her lips. "Perhaps that's what troubles me, Esmond. I like it very much. Too much."

Esmond reached across the table and grasped one of Victoria's hands between both of his. He lightly stroked the back of her hand, a comforting gesture he'd done ever since she was a child.

"If I may speak plainly, my lady?"

"You're the only one I rely upon, Esmond. Of course you may."

The steward looked at her earnestly, knowing she would consider what he had to say. "Have you coupled with him yet?"

Her eyes looked down at the table, unable to meet Esmond's gaze during such intimate talk.

"No. He . . . I . . ."

"I know, my lady. You are to develop trust in him, and that will—should—take time. You've ruled this castle with a successful hand because you are not naive and do not trust too easily. But your guard toward this man is breaking down, far more quickly than you'd like, and it troubles you."

It was as if the servant could read her mind. "I still don't know if I can trust him not to overtake my lands should he become my husband. Or even whether he's linked with Port in some devious way. I just don't know, Esmond. But when I'm with him, and he . . . does certain things to me . . . it's as if my body betrays my mind. I can't think, and I feel as though nothing matters except being with him. Every standard taught to me by Father and Mother, which has helped me become who I am today, vanishes like dewdrops in the morning sun. But after he leaves, and I am alone with my thoughts, the doubts about whether to allow him as my husband come racing back."

She dropped back in her chair, slumped against it like a defeated warrior. But Esmond knew there was no reason for her turmoil.

"You are independent and strong-willed, my lady. Accepting someone else into your life will require that you relinquish some of that independence, and it won't be easy. But rather than agonizing about whether or not you can trust de Burgh, you must realize that you can trust yourself. Remember, my lady—you would never do anything you don't want to do. When the time comes for you to make a decision about de Burgh, you'll know what's right."

The trestle tables were disassembled and stored back along the walls, the middle of the great hall was clear, and everywhere one looked brightly costumed ladies danced carols with knights and other servants. The jongleurs played lively tunes on lutes, vieles, and harps, accompanied by joyous singing and laughing. From their vantage point at the high table, Stephen and Victoria were in prime viewing positions to enjoy the evening's festivities.

Stephen had agreed to sup with her in the great hall rather than arrange a private dinner, but as the evening wore on he had twice suggested that they retire to her chambers upstairs. Thus far Victoria had declined, reminding him with a sly smile that his time in the castle included finding out whether or not there was a traitor among her staff.

"Have you any clues at all?" she asked above the reverberation of the music.

"There may be one," he said, and then told Victoria about Melina and Jonas. She agreed that their reaction was strange, but it didn't explain why either of them would betray her.

"I don't know them very well," she admitted, "but I don't see how they would know Hamlin. And even if they did, why would they betray me, or Mistbury Arms for that matter? It's their home as well."

"On the surface it doesn't make sense," Stephen agreed, "but they're worth watching."

"Whatever you think, my lord," Victoria said with a jaunty smile. "After all, you're the one who needs to find me a spy."

Stephen enjoyed this playful side of her; it was something he hadn't yet seen. "And *you're* the one, my lady," he said, whispering into her ear, "who needs to continue her lessons. Upstairs. Right now."

His low voice vibrated within her ear, and seemed to singe every nerve with his blatant desire.

She rose from the table, bidding good night to the others who remained, then walked through the arched doorway and up the stairs to her solar. Stephen was right behind her.

Her legs felt weak and trembly, as if she had walked for miles, but she knew it was apprehension, excitement—yearning—that caused her steps to falter. With the metal key hanging from the belt around her waist, she unlocked the stout wooden door and led him inside.

Anchoring her torch on one of the metal brackets on the wall, she looked around the room. It was swept clean with fresh rushes strewn about the floor, perfumed with lavender and rose petals. A blazing fire burned in the fireplace and a full jug of gløgg and two glasses were set on the nightstand.

"You've made preparations again, I see," she remarked to Stephen, who was already filling the glasses.

"I am not such an ogre that I would allow my lady to be either thirsty or cold," he answered, handing her a glass. She did not bother pointing out that she had not yet agreed to be "his lady," for in truth, she enjoyed the endearment.

They stood before the fire, warming themselves as they drank their wine. They said nothing for a while, but then Stephen walked over to the bed and set his glass down on the nightstand. "Come here, Victoria," he said, never taking his eyes away from her.

Suddenly she was shy, feeling like a rabbit being led into a lion's den. She knew she wanted him, and it very obvious how badly he wanted her, but once she gave herself to him there would be no turning back. Then Esmond's cool voice of reason echoed within her head. *You would never do anything you don't want to do. When the time comes for you to make a decision about de Burgh, you'll know what's right.* Would she, really? Victoria inhaled a large, calming breath, then let it out. It was time to find out.

She stepped across the floor to where he stood, the swish of her shoes against the rushes the only sound within the still room. As she reached him, he plucked the wineglass from her fingers and set it down on the night table. Turning back toward her, he rested his massive hands atop her shoulders, lightly caressing the delicate bones as if they would break from too much pressure. Victoria could feel the heat seeping from his fingers into her skin, relaxing her like a warm, sensual bath. He moved one hand up to cup her cheek, and placed the other behind her back to pull her into his embrace.

His lips merely brushed hers at first, a soft, lilting kiss that stirred her soul with its tenderness. But in seconds he was deepening the kiss, sliding his mouth across hers, dipping his tongue into her mouth, drawing her into him. He crushed her against the wall of his chest, gliding his hands down the curve of her back until they squeezed and caressed the plump mounds of her buttocks. Victoria rose up on her toes and circled her arms around his neck, lifting her breasts so they molded lushly against him. He dragged his lips from her mouth and slid them down her neck, kissing a hot trail of fire along her skin. Victoria closed her eyes and swept her head back, emitting a low moan as his tongue licked the hollow curve at the base of her throat. His kisses stirred fiery embers within her, making her body ache and throb. She writhed against him, wanting more, needing to be closer. His hands grasped the backs of her thighs and she was lifted in the air and molded against him. She wrapped her legs around his waist, anchoring her body to him; clinging to his heat. Again he kissed her, branding her with his mouth, their tongues gliding against one another in a lustful duel. The throbbing at the apex of her thighs grew stronger, more insistent, the agitation all the more extreme by being positioned right against Stephen's rock-hard cock.

He turned and brought her to the bed, laying her down upon the pillows as gently as if she were made of glass. His massive body covered her, pushing her into the mattress with his weight. He continued to kiss her, his lips traveling sensuously down her neck, then back up to her cheeks, forehead, eyelids. He propped himself up against her with one arm, while his other hand reached out to caress her breasts, sliding his palms over the swollen globes and teasing her nipples through the fabric of her clothing.

She twisted and writhed against him, passion roaring through her blood like madness. Without realizing it, her hips undulated against the bed, rubbing her throbbing, aching mound against his erection, seeking the relief she knew he could give her. She heard him groan aloud, then he broke their kiss.

In one swift movement he lifted her chemise, tunic, and surcote over her head and tossed them to the floor. With lightning-fast fingers he unbuckled the leather straps on her shoes, then pulled off her woolen hose. In seconds she was naked, her young, voluptuous body tormenting him beyond reason. Passion had stained his eyes nearly black. He stared at her, drinking her in, losing himself in the lush splendor she offered.

"You're perfect," he whispered, standing up to pull away his own clothing. It took him less than a minute to remove his surcote, tunic, undershirt, and braies, and then she had her first look at a naked man.

He paused before joining her back on the bed, allowing her to learn his body. Her eyes took in every inch of him, from his broad sinewy shoulders, arms, and expansive chest to his flat, chiseled stomach. His thighs were as massive and brawny as tree trunks and his muscled calves looked chiseled from a solid block of granite. But it was to the thick stalk of jutting manhood where her stare lingered, knowing this was the lance that would soon impale her.

"Do not be afraid," Stephen said, worried that she would shy away from him. But Victoria's face held no fear, only curiosity and a wicked excitement.

"You're larger than I imagined, my lord," she said, knowing he would understand exactly to what she referred.

Stephen stepped closer toward the bed. "And have you spent much time imagining it?" he grinned, climbing atop the mattress to settle down beside her. His hands immediately began to once again caress her breasts, stoking her inner fire.

Victoria arched her back against him, filling his hand with her bounty, gasping as his fingers teased her nipples.

"Perhaps I did spend a bit of time pondering the subject," she breathed, looking at him with eyes glazed over with passion.

His hands moved down to stroke her soft, flat stomach, and then his fingertips grazed the thatch of dark hair between her legs.

"I hope I haven't disappointed you," he said, dipping one finger between the folds of her sheath. She was dripping with juices, so ripe, so ready to take him. But first he would pleasure her.

"Part your legs for me," he whispered. She obeyed him at once, bending her knees so that her feet rested on top of the mattress, and then opening herself to him. Her heartbeat slammed within her chest, her pulse raced wildly in tiny beats against her neck. She felt her body begin to tremble with the heat of her passion, and the hot, persistent throbbing between her legs. Suddenly she felt a jolt of erotic rapture as Stephen's finger grazed her tiny pleasure bud.

"Tonight you will be mine," he promised, his low voice thick, almost guttural, "but you must be primed to take me. So relax and enjoy, my lady knight."

"I always do," she responded, purring like a cat. She sank into the pillows as his fingers rubbed the slick, pulsating kernel at the top of her slit. His touch was gentle at first, no more than a whisper, but as her arousal increased, so too did the pressure and speed of his finger as it swirled and rubbed against her throbbing clitoris. Somewhere in the room Victoria heard a low moan, almost like a sob, and realized with astonishment that the sound came from her. Heat coiled within her groin, growing, burning, tormenting her with erotic agony. Her legs fell farther apart, exposing everything to his lustful gaze. But she did not care about that, she didn't care about anything except finding relief from the raging fire between her legs. Her hips bucked and gyrated against his hand, shamelessly grinding herself against him, and when he plunged his finger into her slick passage it only incensed her more.

"Please, Stephen, please," she sobbed, helpless against the dizzying, sensual haze that consumed her. He inserted a second finger, stretching her, preparing her to accommodate his massive length. A third finger slipped in and then he thrust all of his fingers in and out, stroking her slick walls while his thumb continued to rub her pleasure point. Her head whipped from side to side against the bed and her moans increased until at last her climax erupted, ripping through her body like wildfire.

Stephen waited until the shudders subsided before he withdrew his fingers. They were drenched with her juices. He put his fingers into his mouth, tasting her.

"You're ready for me," he said, lying his body on top of her and gliding his iron-hard penis between the slippery folds of her sheath. "And I'm on fire for you."

He kissed her lips, her neck, her delicate collarbone, then traveled farther down, licking her supple skin until he found her dusky pink nipples. His tongue swirled around her nipple and the dark areola, and then he took the rigid peak into his mouth.

"Oh!" Victoria gasped, thrusting both hands into Stephen's silky blond hair and pressing his face into her lush mound.

He feasted upon her, suckling the nipple and grazing his teeth against it. She cried out with pleasure and her inner fire began burning once more.

He could no longer prolong their mating. His erection was so stiff it was painful, and he knew Victoria was ready. He raised himself up on both arms and positioned his penis so that the engorged head was pointed directly at the opening of Victoria's sheath. A drop of his pre-juices glistened on the tip.

"There will be some pain," he warned her, "though it won't last long. You must trust me."

"I do."

He eased into her, stretching her inner walls to accommodate the head of his thick shaft. She took him easily, but he knew there was no simple way for her to adjust to the rest of him. In a single, powerful thrust, he buried himself within her.

Her eyes popped open in surprise and she shoved her hands against his chest in a desperate attempt to rid herself from the sizzling pain. He dared not move a muscle, knowing she would adjust to his size, would adjust to *him*. When she stopped struggling, he pulled himself partly out of her, then plunged back in, slowly, slowly, allowing her juices to flow, slickening her passage for him. He moved in and out, a gentle, methodical pace, until he felt her creamy thighs wrap around his waist as her hips thrust against him.

His arms encircled her, drawing her against him, hungering to be closer, wanting to lose himself in her. He increased the pace as he heard her groans of passion, grinding himself so deeply that their pelvic bones touched. His orgasm began to build, a hot coil of fire within his loins, but he would not release himself until she found her peak. He stroked in and out, faster and faster, her fiery juices flooding him, drowning him in a hot, salacious sea of passion. He felt the sharp tips of her fingernails scoring his back, then her hands dropped lower to squeeze the taut muscles of his buttocks and drive his cock into her.

Their bodies were slick, moistened with the salty sweat of their exertion. Stephen could hear the sharp slapping of their skin as he rammed Victoria with his burning length. At last her body shook, trembling with the rush of her orgasm, and then Stephen exploded, filling her chamber with his seed like molten lava erupting from a volcano.

He collapsed on top of her, gasping like a fish out of water, his sweat mingling with hers as he gathered her in his arms and they spiraled back down to earth.

The room was nearly dark, the fire having died down to smoldering embers and the torches nothing but smoking stalks of charred wood. Under the cloak of that darkness, snuggled within Stephen's warm embrace, Victoria smiled. The gossiping wives within her castle could speak of the horrors of coupling until their faces were blue, but Victoria knew she'd just experienced a taste of heaven.

She took a final sip of her ale and was preparing to leave the breakfast table when Victoria spotted a profusely sweating young page who had just entered the great hall from outside.

"Lucca," she called out to the boy, "what have you been doing that you perspire so? The first winds of winter have begun blowing. Why are you so warm?"

The young boy stood before the high table and bowed to his mistress. "Aye, my lady," he replied, "the winter winds had begun to blow. But the weather is queer today and 'tis so warm outdoors that my garments became damp when I practiced with the crossbow."

"Perhaps the gods are in a good mood and will hold off winter's chill for a bit longer yet," she replied with a smile. "But you keep practicing your crossbow, Lucca, and you'll make a fine knight one day."

"Yes, my lady." The boy flushed red from the praise and went on his way.

"They look up to you," Stephen said, having observed the boy from the lower trestle table where he broke his fast with Hendrick and some of the other knights. Normally he would have joined Victoria, but despite what they had shared last evening, he sensed that the glaring light of day had made her a bit uncomfortable with her own passionate nature. Luckily, he had a plan to remedy that.

"Lucca is right about the weather," Stephen said, stepping up to the table and taking a seat next to her. "Hendrick and I were out early, and there are warm winds blowing like the heat from a hearth fire."

"A little tease before winter sets in."

"My sentiments exactly. But why not enjoy it? I would be honored if you rode with me through your forest. Hendrick and I have explored very little, and the land is vast."

Why not indeed? Her heart fluttered at the thought of spending the day with him, knowing that the night would be theirs to enjoy as well.

"Very well, my lord. I'll have our horses saddled."

"Already done." At her surprise he hastily added, "I had big hopes."

Commanding my servants already, Victoria thought, though she refused to allow silly doubts to cloud the beautiful day.

Their ride through the thick, dense forest was accompanied by lively conversation as they learned more and more about one another. Stephen spoke of his family, and the troubles he and his siblings had gotten into when they were young. The stories soon had Victoria shaking with laughter.

They turned north into the densest, least traveled part of the forest. Here the ancient oaks spread their branches so wide that the earth below them remained carpeted in shade. It was quiet and tranquil, much the same as it had been for centuries.

"Let's stop for a moment," Stephen said. "We'll let the horses rest."

They reined in their mounts next to one another although with each beast looking in the opposite direction so that Stephen and Victoria could face one another. For a time neither of them said anything, consumed by the beauty of the forest and the uncommon stillness surrounding them. Not even the scampering of forest creatures or the rustling of leaves upon the trees disturbed the silence. It was if that tiny corner of the woods had gone undiscovered until the moment Stephen and Victoria arrived.

He looked over at her now, her straight yet graceful posture exuding natural confidence. She had left her long hair undone and it flowed down her back in thick, lustrous waves. Stephen wondered if she had done so on purpose, knowing it was what he preferred. He noticed that her lips were fuller than usual, still slightly swollen from their hungry kisses last night. The memory was like a fuse, lighting a fire within him. In his mind he could see her writhing beneath him and moaning in ecstasy from their frenzied coupling. As he relived her shuddering cries when she peaked, his manhood hardened like granite and Stephen knew he must have her again. This minute.

"Have you ever ridden a destrier?" he asked, breaking the silence.

From his high vantage point atop the massive warhorse, Victoria was forced to look up at him as she shook her head. "Never," she said. "Father didn't want me to learn to ride them or even be around them very often. They're so enormous that he was afraid I'd lack the strength to control them and would get hurt."

"He was a wise man," Stephen agreed. "But I've got this beast under control so you'll be safe. There's plenty of room for two. Come and join me."

"I have my own mount," Victoria responded, though tiny frissons of excitement accelerated her heartbeat.

"I'll help you up," Stephen replied, his low voice ignoring her feigned protest. Victoria slid down from her horse to the tiny space that separated the beasts and stood next to Stephen. "Place your foot in the stirrup, then reach your arms toward me and I'll pull you up." She did as he asked and in seconds she was airborne, being lifted as easily as a grain of pollen floating in the wind. He placed her in front of him, then wrapped his arms around her waist and pulled her back against his chest.

"Comfortable?"

"Quite."

She sighed in the still air as she felt his lips beginning to nibble the sensitive skin behind her earlobe.

"Is this why you wanted me to join you?" She shivered as his tongue foraged inside the warm chamber of her ear.

"You've read my mind, Lady Woodville." His hands reached up to cup the heavy globes of her breasts, squeezing and kneading them together, pinching the erect nipples between his fingers.

"And here I thought it was so we could admire the view together."

Stephen pulled away the surcote and tunic from Victoria's right shoulder, revealing her golden, satiny skin. "I'm admiring the view," he breathed, licking and kissing her collarbone, "and it's stunning."

She let her head fall back against his chest and placed her hands on top of his thighs, stroking the trenchant, sinewy muscles. His hands had slipped through the sleeveless arms of her surcote and now caressed her breasts and nipples with only the thin layers of her tunic and chemise separating his fingers from her downy skin. She arched her back, filling his hands with her lush mounds, but the cloth still denied her the pleasure of his intimate touch. She expelled a frustrated whimper and for one wicked moment wished she were rid of the clothing and could lie naked with him in their private woodland paradise. She craned her neck behind her, seeking his kiss, and was rewarded with the hot, burning ecstasy of his lips as they sank down upon her. Their hungry mouths mated, tongues paring and thrusting, exploring sweet, wet orifices. One of Stephen's hands dropped down from Victoria's breast to the gentle rise of her pelvic bone. He gripped the layers of clothing she wore, already bunched up around her legs as she straddled the destrier, and pulled them up around her waist, exposing the dark thatch of hair on her pubis. He slipped one finger between the wet petals of her sheath, grazing the engorged clitoris. She moaned into his mouth as she pressed her hips against his finger, encouraging him to continue. He stroked her pleasure point, heightening her arousal, but when he sensed she was near her climax, he abruptly withdrew his finger.

"Why . . . why did you stop?" she asked, her eyes glazed with passion.

Stephen said nothing but he grabbed the material bunched

around her waist and in one swift movement pulled it over her head and tossed it on top of her stallion. Save for her boots she was naked.

Her head whipped about in a panicked frenzy. "What if someone sees us?" she whispered, lowering her voice as if she'd already spotted intruders.

"What if they do?" he responded, shedding his own clothing. His thick, pulsing member, freed from the confines of his braies, pressed into her back.

"Turn around," Stephen said. "I want you to face me."

She shifted in her seat, a quarter turn around, and then Stephen's hands grabbed hold of her right thigh and lifted it over his head, resting the inside of her knee atop his shoulder.

"What are you doing?" Victoria asked, her cheeks blushing a rosy hue from having her sheath wide open and in front of Stephen's face. It was, however, right where he wanted it. He lifted her left leg and placed it on the other side of his shoulder. Victoria's back now rested against the destrier's mane, while her legs straddled either side of Stephen's shoulders. She let her arms fall against the warhorse's muscled flanks to hold herself steady while Stephen buried his face between her legs.

In a million years she could never have imagined the sheer erotic bliss of having a man's lips and tongue kissing and stroking her most intimate area. She became mindless, aware of nothing but the rapturous sensations washing over her. She didn't care that she was outdoors, naked with a man, straddling his shoulders like a common trollop. She didn't even care whether or not they were discovered. The only thing that mattered was the euphoric ecstasy of Stephen de Burgh's tongue thrusting into her sheath and licking her swollen clitoris. It was only minutes before she climaxed, crying out his name as she did so.

When the pulsing subsided, Stephen lowered her legs and pulled her into a sitting position. She could see his engorged manhood jutting out like a battering ram from the patch of dark curls between his legs. He wrapped his arms around her, encircling her in his embrace, and kissed her with feverish passion, all the while pulling her forward until her stomach and breasts were crushed against his chest.

"What, Stephen?" she breathed, arching her head back as his

mouth dropped down to swallow one of her nipples. "What do you want?"

"Ride me," he commanded, his hands squeezing her breasts together as he tongued her lush cleavage.

"I don't understand," she gasped, close to reaching her peak once again.

He raised his head to gaze into her eyes, and she saw how dark his pupils had become. "Ride me," he repeated. "Sit on my lap with your thighs over mine. Put your feet on top of mine for leverage. And then ride."

She was beyond blushing at things he said and did, only wildly excited by what he wanted. She moved into the position he instructed, then impaled herself on his thick, throbbing member. The walls of her passage were drenched with her juices, and they moved easily together. He placed his hand beneath her bottom to guide her up and down, and she understood what he meant when he asked her to ride.

"More," she panted, incensed with desire. "I need more." In response he inserted a finger inside her second orifice, causing her to emit a gasp of surprise and pleasure. His finger thrust in and out in time with his cock as he pumped harder and faster, raising her up and then slamming her down on him, their pelvic bones grinding against one another, skin slapping together with every thrust.

The destrier snorted as they mated atop his back, and he walked a few paces, his undulating movements imitating those of the couple who rode him.

Victoria reached her peak for the second time that afternoon, squeezing her eyes shut as the waves of pleasure crashed over her. In seconds Stephen followed, his hot, sticky seed filling her love chamber. They held each other as they shook and trembled, only parting once sanity finally returned.

Stephen looked at her with a wicked glint in his eye, knowing he'd pleasured her.

"Now, that wasn't too bad, was it?" he teased, referring to the wives' gossip.

Victoria smiled as she lay her head against the warmth of his chest. "Not bad at all," she replied.

* * *

"Happy Birthday, my lady." Esmond greeted her at the high breakfast table the next morning with a wrapped gift in his hand.

"Oh, Esmond. How kind you are," Victoria answered, charmed by the steward's thoughtfulness. She unpeeled the delicate tissue that enveloped the gift, revealing an elaborately carved English oak box roughly the size of a bread trencher.

"It's beautiful," she breathed, admiring the intricate work of the artist who had carved it. "I shall treasure it always."

"It's actually a gift from your parents."

Her jaw dropped open to form a tiny, surprised O, and her eyes grew as round as a shilling. "My parents," she stammered, lines of disbelief etched across her forehead. "But I don't understand."

"There is something inside that box that they wish you to have, my lady," Esmond explained, "though I know not what it is. The box was given to me five years ago, when your parents were ill, with the strict order that it was to be given to you only in the event that something happened to them, and not until you reached the age of twenty. That day has arrived."

Victoria's eyes swam with tears as she thought of her beloved parents, taken from her far too early. She would examine the box's contents at another time, when she was alone, and when the shock of receiving it began to fade. For now she bade Esmond to take it to her chambers, and left the great hall to attend the day's meetings with her staff. Stephen was out, saying that he would be gone during the day but would return in the evening with a surprise for her. She felt her heart quicken at the thought of him, and a smile touched the corners of her lips.

"I can't accept this, Stephen."

They were in familiar territory, propped up in her bed. Earlier in the evening the servants had prepared a sumptuous banquet and Stephen surprised her by arranging for a troupe of mummers and jongleurs to entertain them after the meal. He said that was the first part of his birthday surprise for her. The second part she held in her hand, sparkling amid the torches and candlelight.

"You can't *not* accept it, my love," he murmured, his teeth grazing her bared nipple as he suckled her breast. "It's my gift to you. And so is this." He slid down in the bed, kissing her stomach, until he reached the moist slit between her thighs. Slipping two fingers inside her, he lathed and tongued her clitoris, pleasuring her until she cried out his name and shuddered in ecstasy.

After she had recovered, Victoria again protested the extravagance and generosity of Stephen's gift. "It was your mother's brooch," she said. "It should go to one of your sisters."

"It was given to me," Stephen said, "to do with as I wish. I wish to give it to you."

For one crazy moment she felt as though she would cry, something she rarely did since becoming mistress of Mistbury Arms. But Stephen had caused her to do many things she'd not done before.

"I love it, Stephen," she said, clearing her throat as she accepted the gift. "But since it is still my birthday, I think I should be able to do what I want. And what I want"—she ran her tongue across her lips, knowing how it aroused him—"is to do for you what you've done for me."

"What are you speaking of?" His brow furrowed in confusion until she pushed away from the covers and slid down the bed as he had done earlier. "I'm assuming women can do the same thing for men as men do for women," she replied, kissing the ladder of sinewy muscles across his stomach then dropping her head down until she reached the wiry swatch of dark curls nestled between his legs. His manhood, flaccid after their recent lovemaking, had begun to swell when he realized her intentions. She grasped the thickening stalk with one hand, while the other cupped the tender flesh of his testes. She caressed the twin sacks, rolling them gently in her hand, as her head dipped down to take him into her mouth.

Stephen hissed as he felt the scorching moisture of her lips and tongue envelope his swelling member. She licked away the glistening drop of fluid on the tip of his penis, then expertly glided her mouth up and down the length of him. He soon was as hard and hot as a fireplace poker, and low groans of pleasure rumbled from his chest. He weaved one hand into her thick chestnut hair, playing with the silky strands while she continued to devour him.

With the first trembles of his peak, he tried pushing her head away, unsure of whether she would want to taste the salty seminal fluids. But Victoria shook her head, wanting to give him everything he had given her, wanting him to shoot his pleasure into her mouth. At last he could hold back no more, and with a mighty roar he erupted. She continued to suckle, coaxing the last bit of moisture out of him, licking away every drop of his seed as if she were ingesting his very soul.

Afterward they lay wrapped in each other's arms, sated for the moment, so drowsy that they failed to hear the faint brush of footsteps outside their door as the eavesdropper moved away and slipped through the castle's shadowy corridors.

Chapter Four

"We've no choice but to kill him," Hamlin growled, teeth clenched in fury.

"My lord?" said Jonas, alarmed as never before at the depth of his master's rage.

"You heard me, Auber," Hamlin replied. "Make the arrangements for Stephen de Burgh's murder."

When the knight failed to respond, Hamlin's beefy fist slammed upon the table. "God's teeth, you worthless sot! Didn't you hear me? I want Stephen de Burgh's cold dead body lying at my feet! The bastard is taking what rightfully belongs to me. If he marries Victoria Woodville he'll inherit every square inch of her property, and he'll inherit *her!* That girl was once betrothed to me, Auber, though I doubt she knows it, and if not for her lily-livered parents reneging on the deal, Victoria and Mistbury Arms would be mine today!"

He exploded with vehement fury, crashing his chair to the floor and stalking around the room as if possessed by demons. Jonas remained silent, shaking like a leaf in a violent windstorm.

"If they're lovers—and it seems they are from what you heard outside the door of her bedchamber—then there's no chance that I'll ever get back what was mine to begin with. The only choice we're left with is to eliminate de Burgh."

Killing in battle was one thing, but the very thought of murder left a foul taste in Jonas's mouth. Still, he was not about to contradict a raging madman.

"Tell me what you need, my lord, and it shall be done."

His knight's subservience seemed to pacify Hamlin, and after refilling his tankard with ale, he righted his chair and sat back down. He was quiet for a moment, devising his plan, and when he bared his chipped teeth in a menacing grin, Jonas knew his lord had formulated an idea.

"That comely little scrubbing wench of yours is going to prove very handy," he said. "Especially with those luscious titties of hers."

A streak of hatred toward Hamlin flashed through Jonas's veins, but he remained silent.

"Here's what she'll do, Auber. Have Melina seduce de Burgh, or at least try to seduce him. It matters naught to me. What must happen, however, is that she works it in such a way that if Lady Woodville were to find the two of them together, her sorrowful little eyes would well up in tears and she'd order de Burgh out of Mistbury Arms at once."

"And I'm assuming I'll make certain she does find the two of them together."

"Glad to know there's something between those ears of yours, Auber." Hamlin took a long draught of his ale. "De Burgh will be forced to leave immediately, without time to gather his entourage for protection. As he does, our knights will be positioned just outside the castle walls, ready to ambush the unsuspecting, unguarded traitor as he tries returning to Blenleigh. Bring his body back to me. Once I'm certain of your success, our army will be standing ready to march to Mistbury Arms and attack. With de Burgh out of the way, victory will be mine." He rubbed his hands together in greedy anticipation, and his eyes sparkled like flames from the fires of Hell.

The door clicked shut as Stephen left the room the next morning, leaving Victoria sleepy but sated as she remained in bed. She refrained from summoning her chambermaid, deciding instead to perform her morning ablutions alone. She needed time to think about her relationship thus far with Stephen.

She washed her hands and face in the basin, donned a dark blue tunic and surcote over her white linen chemise, then sat on the edge of the bed, hairpin between her teeth, plaiting her hair and winding it into a bun at the nape of her neck. Tiny shivers of delight coursed down her spine as she recalled how last night Stephen had slowly kissed the very spot where she now pinned her hair. He pleased her in ways no man ever had, and she was aware that she'd developed feelings for him. True, he was a master of sensual pleasure, yet Victoria knew in her heart that the physical gratification was ancillary to the stronger, deeper emotions she felt. During the hours they'd spent together—alone in her solar, eating in the great hall, riding in the deep, lush forest—they had talked, they had shared, they had gotten to know one another. She had learned of his family, of his upbringing, and the path in Stephen de Burgh's life that had led him toward becoming the man he was today. Yet did she know what kind of man he was—really?

Victoria rose from the bed and strolled toward the fireplace. The morning was cold, and she stirred the embers and then held her hands toward the regenerated flames. Her troubled thoughts tumbled over and over in her mind like an acrobat trapped in a never-ending performance. She expelled a frustrated sigh. What concerned her most is that part of her knew she was falling in love with Stephen, while the other part still questioned whether or not she could trust him.

Their bargain had been sealed on gaining that trust. Certainly he had dispelled the falsehoods about husbandly rights whispered among the married women in her castle. Each time she joined with him, it was as if the doors of paradise were flung wide open, welcoming her into a world spun from erotic bliss. But the other half of their bargain was that Stephen would uncover who within her castle had turned traitor. Yet after nearly three weeks of time he had uncovered very little, and uncertainty began to irritate Victoria's thoughts like a tiny grain of sand within an oyster's shell. But rather than forming a pearl, she felt a seed of doubt germinate in her mind. Why did he have no clues? Was it more difficult to find the traitor than Stephen had anticipated? Surely with all the gossip among the servants he would have found out something, wouldn't he? Unless . . .

Victoria shivered, and this time it had nothing to do with the chill in the room. She hadn't wanted to think it, had even shoved the thought away when her mind began forming it, but she knew the time had come to consider the worst. Maybe the reason Stephen hadn't uncovered her traitor was because there simply wasn't one, and his "bargain" with her had been a ruse all along to get to know Mistbury Arms, *and bring the information back to Hamlin Port himself.* Could it be that Stephen was involved with Hamlin Port? Had that been the case all along? Had she been duped by the best trickster in all of England?

The idea was heinous, and Victoria squeezed her eyes closed as if the ensuing darkness could block out the thought. She didn't want to believe that Stephen was in any way connected with Hamlin Port, and she was nearly certain that he was not. But that tiny seed of doubt, her ominous black pearl, couldn't help but wonder why Stephen had said almost nothing about his investigation.

Hendrick raised his hand to greet his brother as he strode across through the great hall to join Stephen at the breakfast table.

"All's well at Blenleigh," he reported, helping himself to dark bread. "The messenger we sent out there returned this morning."

" 'Tis good to hear," Stephen nodded, "especially with the cold weather arriving."

"Indeed. And since we'll soon feel winter's sting, Father wonders when we'll return. As do our men."

Stephen signaled for ale. "We need to find Victoria's traitor first."

"And you've got to convince the fair lady to become your bride."

A smile touched Stephen's lips, spreading joy across his face. "I don't think that will be a problem," he confided.

Hendrick had never before seen his brother so happy. It was quite obvious that he was in love.

"To your upcoming betrothal," he said, lifting his glass toward Stephen's. "Congratulations."

They drank in a silent toast, sharing the joyous moment, but all too soon it was over and Stephen was back down to business.

"I want to find out everything we can about Melina and Jonas. The more I think about it, the more I'm convinced that they're involved with Port."

"There just doesn't seem to be anyone else," Hendrick agreed. "We've spoken with everyone in this castle."

"There could be peasants living in the village, I suppose. Someone having intimate knowledge of Mistbury Arms."

"Who'd share that information with Port? To what gain? So their homes can be plundered and burned by his marauding army?"

Stephen nodded. "That's exactly how I feel. There's no obvious reason to betray Victoria. She's more than fair to both her servants and villagers. But maybe something happened in the past with one of those two, something of which Victoria is unaware. Or maybe there was nothing, but Melina and Jonas are spies for Port. Whatever it is, I intend to find out. Today."

He finished the last of his breakfast and rose from the bench. "I've found out that it's Melina's day off, so I'm going to speak with the laundress and learn what I can about the girl. Make inquiries about Jonas. There's got to be something."

Stephen left his brother and made his way downstairs, his mouth set in a hard line. He was as sure that Melina Vesli was involved with Hamlin Port as he was that the sky was blue. There was something about the way she had acted when Stephen discovered her with Jonas that gave him certainty in his gut that she'd betrayed the woman who would soon be his wife. He just had to prove it.

He turned the corner toward the storerooms and the door leading to the outer bailey and washroom when he spotted the object of his musings leaning against the stone wall. This time she did not act surprised to see him. It was almost as if she'd been awaiting his arrival.

"Good day, Lord de Burgh," she said, fluttering her eyelashes at him in a coquettish flirt.

Stephen inclined his head. "Not working today, Miss Vesli?" he asked, knowing full well the answer.

" 'Tis my day off. And I . . . I've been waiting for you." She stepped forward until she was only inches away from him, purposely brushing her ample bosom against his chest.

What game does this tart play? Stephen wondered. *And why?* "Indeed? And what would such a lovely young girl be needing to speak with me about?"

They were alone in the corridor, a fact of which Melina appeared to be well aware. She lifted her hands and placed them against Stephen's biceps, appreciating the taut bulge of his sinewy strength as she ran her fingers along his arms. "I've been wanting to apologize to you, my lord," she purred, her blatant attempt at seduction almost amusing if not for the fact that Stephen suspected her of betraying the woman he loved.

He propped one arm next to her head against the wall. "Apologize for what?"

She leaned back to look into his eyes. "I'm so ashamed that you caught me with that foolish knight," she confessed. "Especially since . . . since . . ." Her voice trailed away and she averted her gaze.

Stephen expelled an irritated breath, but reeled in his anger lest he ruin her performance—and his chance to learn what the devil was going on.

"Since what?" he asked, encouraging her to continue by tilting up her head with his finger beneath her chin.

His touch ignited her words. "Since you're the man I wish to be with," she answered, boldly slipping her arms around his neck to draw him forward. It would have been simple to resist, but Stephen chose to pretend he was caught in her spell, her actions removing any doubt that she was involved with Hamlin Port. He kissed her passionately, grinding his lips against hers, plunging his hands into her hair as if she drove him wild with desire. She hesitated for a bare moment, seemingly surprised by his response, but then she returned his kiss with abandon, plundering his mouth with her tongue and wantonly rubbing her pelvis against his groin. Her hand snaked downward, attempting to cup his balls and stroke his manhood, but the effort was thwarted in seconds as Stephen's hand clamped around her wrist like iron manacles.

"Not here," he growled, looking around to maintain whether they were still alone. "Though you may have a penchant for coupling in the corridor, I do not. I prefer someplace more private without fear of getting caught."

"Please, my lord," Melina begged, "I'm on fire. I must have you."

"And so you shall. But not here; not now." He unwound the clinging girl from around his waist and quickly devised a plan. "Two nights from this, meet me outside the curtain wall at the north end of the castle. There's a large oak whose branches overhang the wall. Wait for me there. You'll be far from the men-at-arms guarding the area. Just make certain no one sees you."

"But where will we go from there?"

"Fear not, my lustful beauty," Stephen teased. "There's a falconer's shed a short ways beyond that, built on grounds that were once part of an old bailey. I'm told it was built well to keep the birds warm when the weather was fierce. I think it will serve our purpose quite nicely."

"I'll be there, my lord."

Before she could leave, Stephen gripped her arm and forced her chin up to stare into his eyes. "Remember, make certain no one sees you. We will be unguarded and alone. I wouldn't want anything to happen to you lest we cannot meet again."

His eyes were dark, piercing, and Stephen knew that Melina was a touch afraid. All the better. He watched her scamper away, aware of the danger he had intentionally placed himself in. If she were the one who had betrayed Victoria, two days was plenty of time to get word to Hamlin Port that Stephen would be outside Mistbury Arms and without escort, vulnerable to capture by Port's men. And if Port and his men showed up, it would prove beyond doubt that Melina were involved, for how else could they know of the planned tryst if not for her telling them?

Stephen walked back toward the great hall, no longer needing to speak with the laundress. Instead there were plans to be made, men to be organized, as they waited once again for the arrival of Hamlin Port.

Chapter Five

"Involved with someone else? But how could that be, my lady? The man wants to marry you."

Victoria shook her head, refuting Esmond's statement. "He promised me that he would find the one who's betraying us. So far he's done nothing. He's said nothing. Moreover..." She halted, a sudden hitch in her breath stopping the words.

"What, my lady? What else?"

They walked amid the kegs of beer in the storeroom, counting the inventory. Victoria stopped and leaned against a large oak barrel. Her voice was low and trimmed with sorrow. "Moreover, he has not come to my bed for two nights, and that, too, was part of our agreement." She resumed walking, holding her chin high and proud. "I asked him this morn if he would be joining me this evening. For a moment he acted as though he sorely wished it could be, yet he declined, saying only that he was engaged."

Esmond furrowed his brow. "What, pray tell, is so pressing?"

"I asked him that same question," Victoria replied, "but he would not answer. He said only that he's fulfilling his promise to me." She paused, then turned to face Esmond directly. "I want to trust him."

"Because you're in love with him."

She did not hesitate. "Yes."

"But you cannot?"

Victoria shook her head. "My heart wants to, but my mind is stubborn. I wonder if Stephen is really the man he says he is, and whether or not I can trust him."

"And that's why you feel he may be involved with someone else?" The steward did not bother to hide his skepticism.

"I don't know what to believe, Esmond, but I intend to find out."

"Find out? How?"

"Stephen said he cannot be with me this evening, and I would know the reason why. I shall follow him; see where he goes. Or who he meets."

It was risky, impulsive, and perhaps even foolish. But Victoria was determined, and Esmond knew there was nothing he could say to stop her.

"Stay out of danger, my lady," he told her instead, knowing her greatest danger would be to her own heart.

She crept along the wall, staying as far behind Stephen as possible while keeping him in sight. Her soft leather slippers were no more than whispers against the cold stone floor. They exited through the barbican and crossed the drawbridge, and though Victoria was astounded that the bridge was lowered at all, she scarcely had time to wonder about it for Stephen kept a fast pace, determined to get to where he was going. Had he arranged a meeting with Hamlin Port? Was that the reason behind Stephen's urgent pace?

They reached open ground, making it more difficult for Victoria to conceal herself. She hid behind some low-lying bushes and watched Stephen as he continued to walk toward a large oak tree. The darkness and distance away obstructed the clarity of her view, but as he reached the tree, Stephen appeared to look around, as if expecting someone. Victoria continued to watch, her heart pounding in her chest, gripping the branches of the bush til her knuckles went white. Several tense minutes ticked by, and then Victoria felt the hairs prickle and raise on the back of her neck as Hamlin Port walked into view.

It was evident by Stephen's body language—strong, confident, not surprised—that he expected Port. The two men spoke, and though Victoria could not hear their words, nausea twisted her stomach like the cold grip of death. Her pulse began to race as blood roared in her eardrums and chilling fingers of fear crept along her spine. *Stephen was the one betraying her!* She was sickened by the thought, yet irrefutable evidence stood before her eyes. He knew Port; had arranged a secret meeting to reveal what he'd learned at Mistbury Arms. Without doubt they were planning their next invasion, and this time Victoria knew whose side Stephen would take.

Suddenly she realized that she must get back to the castle immediately and organize her knights. She would fight for her home and her people until the last drop of blood was spilled from her veins, and she would never, *never* give up what her family had given her.

Crouching low, she ran along the bushes under the cover of darkness, crossed over the drawbridge, and reentered the castle. She raced, two at a time, up the stairs to where her guards were positioned along the wall walks. "Desmond! Thomas!" she called, expecting to be met at the top of the stairs by her senior men-at-arms. But when she reached the top, there were no knights to be found. Not an archer was in sight. No crossbowmen anywhere. She ran along the wall walk, utterly baffled. Her castle was deserted.

Blazing hot fury pumped through her veins. Where were her men? Had Stephen managed to recruit them away from her? Was he so hell-bent on destroying everything she lived for that he'd even decimated the loyalty of her servants?

She turned back toward the way she'd come, intending to return to where Stephen and Hamlin held their covert meeting. Perhaps she could get close enough to hear what they were planning. She reached the doorway, so focused on her mission ahead that she failed to see the hulking shape of Jonas Auber standing beneath the arched frame. Once she spotted him, it was too late, and a fraction of a second before the metal fireplace poker connected with the side of her head, she had time to wonder if she'd ever learn the truth.

Minutes passed. Or was it hours? *Days?* Victoria awoke, head pounding, sprawled upon the filthy dirt floor of an oubliette. But where was she? Was she still in Mistbury Arms? Never having been down in that particular dungeon of hers, she wasn't entirely certain. She tried to move, but her head screamed in protest. She opened her eyes, looking around. It was dark, and damp. The earth upon which she lay had an old, musty, discarded smell, as if it had been trapped for eternity in an airless void. Ignoring the fierce throbbing in her head, she forced herself to a sitting position, then crawled over to the curved stone wall to prop herself against it. Stagnant water seeped through her surcote and tunic.

"I've finally got you where you belong." The female voice from above sneered as she spoke. Victoria looked up. The speaker held a torch next to her face, and even at her distance from fifteen feet below ground, she could tell that the voice belonged to her head laundress's assistant, Melina Vesli. Standing beside her was Jonas.

"What are you talking about?" Victoria replied. "I've done naught but furnish you with a job and a home."

Melina snorted. "Home? More like a prison, you mean."

Victoria's head throbbed, distorting her vision so that she saw three Melinas instead of just one. Triple the agony. "I know not what you mean."

"I think you do, mistress. You prevented me from marrying Geoffrey Valon, the only man I ever loved. Think you that I should feel grateful for this *home* after that?"

Her voice was shrill and she punctuated her words in angry bursts. Victoria knew she would have to be careful.

"I meant only to protect you, Melina. Geoffrey had a vile temper. 'Twas said he beat women, including his own mother and sisters. I could not allow you to marry such a man."

"It's not true!" Melina shrieked. "Geoffrey beat no one. And besides, if you had such *concern* for me, why didn't you tell me at the time?"

Her high-pitched voice pierced Victoria's brain like a steel-edged dagger. "You don't believe me now. Would you have believed me then?"

"You're a fool, mistress. You act the pious protector, but I know you rut like a stag with that giant Viking of yours." She laughed, though the sound was without humor. "No more, though. Your stallion's been snared, caught by Hamlin Port. I set him up so you'll know how it feels to be torn from the man you love."

Victoria was horrified by what Melina had said, but part of her wondered whether there was a grain of truth to the girl's fantastic tale. From what she'd observed, Stephen planned on meeting Hamlin. Certainly he hadn't acted surprised to see him. And if it was a setup, what would have motivated Stephen to leave the castle, alone and unprotected?

As if reading her thoughts, Melina continued. "I seduced your lover two days ago. It was surprisingly easy. He lusted after me like a hound in heat. I even caressed his cock. 'Twas hard as a jousting pole." She licked her lips as if she were preparing to wrap them around Stephen's manhood. Thick, pungent nausea seized Victoria's stomach.

"He told me that tonight we'd finish what we started, and he arranged a meeting place for us by a big oak tree beyond the curtain wall at the north end. Won't he be surprised to see Hamlin and not me?" She giggled, relishing her power over Victoria.

Oh Stephen, Victoria whispered, feeling the tears shimmer in her eyes. Could any of this horrifying nightmare be true? Despite the superficial appearance that it was, uncertainty lingered in the back of her mind. Perhaps she didn't know Stephen as well as she liked, but she knew herself, and it was nearly impossible to accept that she could be so easily and thoroughly duped.

Voices, far away but growing strong, interrupted Melina's monodrama. Victoria turned her head in the direction from where they came, noticing Jonas and Melina doing the same. Suddenly she recognized one of the voices. It was strong, and low, and with a leap in her heart she realized that it belonged to Stephen. Melina and Jonas came to the same realization, but their reaction was far different. If Stephen was walking and talking within the castle, instead of lying dead upon the ground outdoors, then the plans they'd made with Hamlin had clearly gone awry.

"Get out of here!" Jonas hissed, shoving Melina in front of him as they raced off in opposite directions from the voices. For Victoria, their actions were as welcome as a gust of cooling wind on a humid summer day. They had not expected Stephen's arrival, which meant Melina must have been telling the truth about setting him up with Hamlin Port. But if Port meant to capture or kill him, what had gone wrong?

Victoria still didn't understand why Stephen wasn't surprised to see Hamlin, but she knew all would become clear once she was pulled from her own dungeon. Shouting with every ounce of strength she possessed, she began calling Stephen's name. No sound at first, then yelling, running feet, and Stephen's strong, sure voice calling Victoria's name.

In seconds he found her, and the horror on his face and frantic efforts to pull her out were the only proof of his love that she would ever need. Doubts about his feelings for her disappeared as easily as a dream upon waking. Stephen sent down the rope ladder so Victoria could climb out, but before doing so, she told him about Jonas and Melina and how they'd raced off when they heard his voice. Stephen commanded Hendrick to find and capture the traitors, but he himself remained to help Victoria.

The lump on the side of her head had swelled to the size and shape of a goose egg, blurring her vision and making the room spin. Her progress was slow but before her awaited Stephen, and despite the pain and the haze and the agony in her limbs, she knew she would make it, climbing toward his love that shone like a torch through the dungeon's murky darkness.

As she neared the top, he called for her to take hold of his outstretched hands. His steel grip pulled her from the oubliette as if she weighed no more than the wind. He set her upon the ground and she sank against his chest, relieved and exhausted. His arms encircled her, sheltering her in warmth. He turned her away from the oubliette, protecting her from its horrors, she thought, but not soon enough. Before he could hide her, she caught sight of the circle of knights behind him, standing guard over a shackled prisoner. As Victoria looked up at the captured man, she realized that she was staring face to face with the monster who had tried to destroy her castle: Hamlin Port.

Despite her pain and weakness, rage welled up inside her with the ferocity of a geyser. She broke free from Stephen's protective embrace and stalked over to her hated foe.

"You malicious, repugnant, pus-sucking worm!" she spat. "May you fester like a rotting carcass in the bowels of hell for what you've done to the people on my lands!" Fury blazed in her eyes, so trenchant and uncontrolled that she felt the sting of tears clouding her vision.

"Place Port in the dungeon," Stephen ordered, gently taking Victoria by the shoulders to lead her away. "Come, warrior princess," he whispered in her ear, "and let your knights put the prisoner where he belongs." She stepped out of Hamlin's path, somewhat mollified once she realized that the man who had caused so much strife to her villagers and to herself would be spending a good deal of time locked within her oubliette. Fortunately for him, he would not be alone. Jonas and Melina, easily captured by Hendrick and his knights, were already climbing down the rope ladder into the cold, sordid prison.

Without saying another word, Stephen led her up the stairway, through the great hall, and then up more stairs until they reached the comfort of her solar. Along the way he indicated to some of the servants to prepare a bath, and within no time a cylindrical oak tub was filled with steaming hot water and scented oils. Victoria insisted to Stephen that she was more interested in a talk than a bath, but Stephen assured her that there would be plenty of time for talking—later.

He pulled the door behind him, leaving Victoria to bathe with the profusion of her muddled thoughts as the only source of company. Her mind replayed the events of the evening so often and in such vivid detail that she feared she'd never again know a moment's peace. Yet after toweling herself off, she sat at the edge of her bed to dry her hair before the fire, and in minutes the lulling blur of sleep claimed her in its potent grip.

When she awoke, it was to the fragrant aroma of simmering stew, and the soft shuffling of Stephen's boots upon the floor as he moved about the room preparing their meal. At first she did not stir, but lay quietly in the bed so she could observe him unnoticed while he assumed she still slept. He moved in slow yet constant motion, a gentle warrior with hands the strength of granite arranging salt dishes and silver ewers. A surge of love for him washed over her, bathing her in its warmth. At the same time there remained an intangible distance between them, leaving her wary and unsure about what had happened and whether she could trust him.

He glanced over at the bed and noticed she was awake.

"There's food," he said simply, sensing her unease. She began to push away the covers, forgetting until that moment that she wore nothing beneath. Her hands went still as she cast furtive glances about the room, hoping she'd left her chemise close by. She saw nothing she could reach, but suddenly she was aware of her nipples hardening to rounded pebbles, and the flush of moisture between her legs. Stephen had become aware of her nakedness, and the atmosphere in the room became coated with thick, hot sensuality, palpable as humidity on a scorching summer day.

He stepped across the room toward her bed, his movements fluid, steady, like a panther on the prowl. He tore away items of clothing as he approached her, discarding them piece by piece until he was as naked as she. With one hand he gripped the silk and woolen covers and wrenched them away, exposing every inch of her to his lustful gaze as he climbed on the bed and lowered his body on top of her. She was excited by the sudden rush of his hunger, and she opened herself to him like the petals of a blooming flower, unfolding her legs, wrapping her arms around his corded back.

His mouth went immediately to the lush fullness of her breasts. His tongue swirled around one stiff nipple, teasing the pebblelike bud, nipping it with his teeth. She moaned, low and insistent, sinking her hands into his silken hair to press him harder against her breast, urging him to take more of it into his eager mouth. He complied with her desire, moving from one turgid nipple to the next while his left hand traveled down the smooth, soft plane of her stomach to the drenching moisture between her legs. He inserted one finger inside her, then two, three, plunging in and out, matching the urgent rhythm of her undulating hips. Suddenly he pulled his hand away, consumed by his savage need for her. He shifted his position so that he was directly atop her, his engorged penis hard as marble, and with one explosive thrust he buried himself inside her.

They mated with the untamed abandon of wild beasts, intent only on satisfying their raging lust. It was a primal, passionate fusion, stripping away all the uncertainty and distrust, bonding them as only the uninhibited essence of lovemaking will do.

His strokes became wild, frenzied, thrusting in and out as he lost himself in her unhampered sensuality. Wrapping her in his arms, he rolled over until he was on his back and she was positioned on top of him. Her lush, bountiful bosom was pillowed against his chest as she continued to ride him, her creamy thighs straddling his waist. His hands gripped her buttocks, guiding her up and down the length of his jutting cock. The pace of their feverish movements increased. Stephen could sense that she was approaching her peak, and as he continued thrusting, he slipped his first finger, then middle finger inside the heated orifice of her buttocks. The erotic invasion sent her over the edge as she shuddered and cried aloud from the intensity of her climax. His own release came seconds later, the hot seminal fluid seeming to explode from his body with the force of dynamite. He collapsed on top of her, bereft of all strength.

For several minutes they said nothing, catching their breath while drifting slowly back to earth. Stephen moved beside Victoria so she would not be crushed, but did not release her from his embrace. It was she who finally extricated herself, pulling on her chemise as she left the bed and took a seat at the would-be dinner table. It was time for some answers.

"I followed you this evening," she began, dispensing with small talk, "and I saw you talking to Hamlin Port."

"Undoubtedly much to your surprise," Stephen said, aware of how that must have looked to her. He fluffed the pillows and propped himself to a sitting position. "But why the secrets, Victoria? What compelled you to follow me?"

Victoria nibbled on a piece of dark bread. "You hadn't come to my bed for two days, although that was part of our original agreement. Furthermore, I'd heard almost nothing from you regarding the traitor you were supposed to uncover. I wanted to know why."

"And asking me outright wasn't an option?"

"Not if you were involved with Port," she snapped, her anger rising. "Which, based on your actions, I'd begun to suspect."

Her lack of faith wounded him, more than he cared to admit, though he could not fault her for it. She'd not succeeded as mistress of this castle by relying on unwarranted trust.

"And when you saw me speaking with him, you were sure 'twas I who'd betrayed you."

She met his gaze directly, her posture strong and proud. "I must look out for my people, Stephen. What would you have me think, based on what I saw?"

He turned and slid off the bed, throwing his tunic over his head without first bothering with braies. He took a seat opposite her at the table and began to explain.

"Hendrick and I suspected Melina and Jonas ever since I saw them coupling in that corridor. They lacked the pride for this castle that we saw in every single other member of your staff. But suspicions are one thing—proof is another. We needed to know for sure. We watched them for days, weeks, and there was nothing. Hendrick began to think we may be wrong, but I knew there was something there."

"The instincts of a skilled knight."

Stephen nodded his head, staring into her eyes. "I knew it had to be those two, but time was running out and still I had no proof. I decided to speak with Hilda to see whether she knew something about Melina that I did not. On my way to the laundress I encountered Melina. She tried to seduce me."

"And you allowed her."

Something about the catch in her voice when she made that statement revealed the jealousy that Victoria tried to keep hidden. And though he knew jealousy was often accompanied by pain, Stephen couldn't help but be flattered by knowing how much she cared for him.

He reached across the table to grasp her hand. "I needed *proof*, Victoria, and by pretending to fall under her spell, I knew she'd give me the proof I needed. We set a place and time to meet, two days' hence, allowing Melina enough time to get word to Port that I'd be alone and away from the castle. If Port and his troops showed up, I'd have the proof I needed that it was she who had betrayed you, for the only way Port would know where I'd be, and when I'd be there, was through Melina."

Cold tendrils of fear coiled in the pit of her stomach. "You placed yourself in tremendous danger," she whispered, gripping his hand.

Stephen smiled, the buoyancy of his grin melting away her apprehension. "Not with your trained soldiers to back me up," he said.

At once she understood the apparent absence of her knights. "That explains it," she said, nodding. "So they were positioned outside the castle?"

"Exactly," Stephen laughed. "It was surprisingly easy to capture Port, for he thought to catch me alone and unguarded. He'd brought along only a few of his own men, thinking more wouldn't be needed. Melina had told him I'd be outside expecting to meet her for our secret tryst. When Port showed up instead of Melina, as I'd suspected, your knights were ready, and he was captured."

There was still something in the story that didn't make sense.

"But on what grounds was he captured? All I saw was you and him talking, which certainly is no reason to throw a man in prison."

Stephen hesitated, then forged ahead to complete the tale. "We had to let him make the first move. But when he drew his sword and attempted to strike, he was ours for the taking."

He kept his tone light, as if it had all been a matter of little importance, but it was impossible to disguise the truth from her. He'd endangered himself solely for her. Her heart overflowed with love she held for him, rushing through every pore in her body. She rose from her chair and walked toward him, so consumed by the power of her emotions that it was difficult to speak. She held out her hands to him and he grasped her fingers and drew her by his side. She sat upon his lap, settling her head against his massive chest, a granite pillar of strength and comfort. Unable to help herself, tears streamed down her cheeks, wetting her eyelashes and spilling off her chin onto his thighs. She said nothing, yet he knew why she wept. Unbeknownst to her, his own eyes were moist.

He cradled her in his arms, comforting her with quiet strength until she recovered enough to speak. Lifting her head from his chest, she pulled slightly away to look into his eyes.

"You could have been killed, yet you took that chance for me."

"I'd do it again."

She held a wry grin. "Do you need a wife so badly, then?"

"Not just any wife. I need *you*, Victoria. I need the wife I've fallen in love with."

Tears anew shimmered in her eyes. "Just as I need and love you, my Herculean knight."

He brought his hands up to caress her face, then he drew her toward him and kissed her with such tenderness that she thought her heart would break. When the kiss ended he held her, and she longed to stay within his embrace forever. Until her eyes caught sight of the carved oak box.

It sat atop her nightstand in the place Esmond had put it after he'd first presented it to her. It was the box from her parents, as yet unopened.

She slid off Stephen's lap despite his protest and walked over to retrieve the box. She brought it back to the table and placed it next to him, then carried her chair over and set it down beside him. She explained to Stephen what it was.

"But you haven't opened it?"

"I'd forgotten to, until now."

He sensed there was more to the truth. "Don't fear the pain from remembering them, my love. I'm here for you."

It was as if he had read her mind. She'd loved her parents so deeply that she often pushed aside memories of them because she could not cope with the pain of remembrance. But the power of Stephen's love, potent and virile like the man himself, gave her the strength she needed. She unhooked the tiny metal clasp and opened the box.

Inside were three sheaves of paper laid neatly on top of one another. Her hands shook slightly as she opened the first document. It was dated late summer in the year 1232, when Victoria would have been nearly two years old. It appeared to be a contract of some sort. Her eyes flew over her father's tight, neat hand, and as she reached the end of the document, she recoiled in horror as if she were holding a snake. The paper was a formal contract, made between her parents and Lord and Lady Dominic Port, agreeing on the betrothal of Lady Victoria Woodville to their eldest son, Lord Hamlin Port. The wedding was to have taken place in August 1250, when Victoria turned twenty. Nausea, thick and oppressive, churned inside her stomach.

"This year," she whispered. "This year I was to have become his wife."

"Let's look at the other papers," Stephen said, his calm voice belying the jealous rage he barely held in check.

Victoria picked up the second piece of paper. This one was dated January 1244, one year before her parents' death. It was another agreement between them and Hamlin's parents, only this one nullified the marriage betrothal. With the astronomical sum of 10,000 pounds paid by Lord Harold Woodville to Lord Dominic Port, the betrothal between the two men's children was dissolved. There was no explanation given within the content of the text, only an agreement to end the betrothal and the signatures of both men.

The final document was a letter to Victoria dated only two

months before her parents' death, and signed at the bottom by both of them. She remembered that time very well, as both her father and her mother were sickened from the smallpox that would eventually kill them, yet kept a brave face for their lone-surviving child. Deep in their hearts they must have known they had precious little time left on this earth, so they penned the letter she now held.

To our Dearest Victoria,

If you are reading this letter then two things have happened. First, you have seen the passing of your 20th birthday, and for this we congratulate you. You've become a woman, and without doubt one whom we would be overwhelmingly proud of. Our only sorrow is that we are not there to celebrate with you, for the second thing that has happened if you are reading this letter is that you have seen our passing. Do not shed tears for us, dear daughter, for we are united in heaven with the rest of our beloved brood.

By now you have read the betrothal agreement for you and Lord Hamlin Port, along with the subsequent nullification of that agreement. Were we alive to speak with you, we would explain everything in person, but instead this letter must suffice.

We've always wanted only the best for you, and when you were but a babe we thought marriage to Lord Hamlin Port would fulfill that desire. But over the years we learned the sad truth about the young lord. He grew into a violent, malicious man, who mistreated anyone with whom he came in contact. As such we could not marry our beloved daughter to such a horrid man, and thus we broke the betrothal contract. Certainly Lord Dominic Port was furious, although enough coin in his hand whittled away his temper. We decided to wait before telling you the truth, for we did not want our decision to influence you in any way. Our one true hope is that you will find the man of your dreams, a man with whom you can laugh, and love, and share your life. Whoever that man, be sure that he is a man of your heart, for there is no love like that which unites two people body and soul, for all eternity.

Remember that we shall always love you, dear daughter, and await, albeit patiently, for the time when you will be with us once again.

Victoria replaced the letter in the sanctuary of the carved oak box, her manner light, reverent, knowing the voices of her dead parents were preserved on the translucent vellum. There was no sound in the room save for the occasional sparks and crackles from the fireplace.

"That explains why Port was so hell-bent on capturing Mistbury Arms," Stephen said at last. "He wanted to reclaim what was once going to be his."

"But which was taken away."

Victoria fell silent and Stephen was also quiet, respecting what he presumed to be Victoria's sorrow from the fresh opening of old wounds. Indeed he could see the tears streaming down her cheeks, and he was about to propose that he leave the room and resume their conversation tomorrow when Victoria's soft, low voice again filtered the silence.

"I've fulfilled my parents' wishes," she said, tears shining in her eyes.

"How so?" Stephen asked, holding his arms open as she slowly turned toward him.

"I've met the man of my heart," she whispered, breathless from the aura of love surrounding her as she slipped into his embrace.